IRISH
LOVE

IRISH LOVE

A Nuala Anne McGrail Novel

ANDREW M. GREELEY

A TOM DOHERTY ASSOCIATES BOOK
NEW YORK

IRISH LOVE

A Forge Book
Published by Tom Doherty Associates, LLC
175 Fifth Avenue
New York, NY 10010

www.tor.com

Forge® is a registered trademark of Tom Doherty Associates, LLC.

Library of Congress Cataloging-in-Publication Data

Greeley, Andrew M.
     Irish love / Andrew M. Greeley.—1st ed.
        p. cm.
     "A Tom Doherty Associates book."
     ISBN 0-312-87187-2 (acid-free paper)
     1. McGrail, Nuala Anne (Fictitious character)—Fiction. 2. Women detectives—
Ireland—Fiction. 3. Gold mines and mining—Fiction. 4. Americans—Ireland—
Fiction. 5. Irish Americans—Fiction. 6. Psychics—Fiction.
7. Ireland—Fiction. I. Title.

PS3557.R358 I825 2001
813'.54—dc21   00-048463

First Edition: March 2001

Printed in the United States of America

0 9 8 7 6 5 4 3 2 1

For the Lanes: Jack, Dani, and Jackie

The story of the Maamtrasna murders is a fictionalized account of actual events. All the persons and events in the contemporary Connemara story are creations of my imagination.

IRISH LOVE

— 1 —

"BLOOD!" MY wife announced. "There's blood every-where."

"This is a bad place, Da." The pretty redhead dug her fingers into my arm. "I wanna go home!"

Our beautiful Connemara day had suddenly turned somber. Dank fog had drifted in, Kilray Harbor and Galway Bay had disappeared; the ruined hovels my wife had been photographing had quickly changed from picturesque to desolate—and perhaps sinister. The ugly slabs of rock on which we were standing seemed somehow sinister, like the basement of a haunted house. With the fog had come a sudden blast of cold air. Despite my Aran Isle sweater, I shivered. We were in a horror film.

In my arms the Mick, big, blond, and lazy—like his father it was often said—continued to sleep contentedly, his usual mode of facing life.

I glanced around. The three females in our party were sniffing the air. I sniffed too. All I could smell was the acrid salt of seawater.

Nuala Anne was wearing the young matron's uniform: jeans, running shoes, and a sweatshirt, in this case a blue-and-gold sweatshirt from Marquette University.

"It smells!" The little redhead, my three-year-old daughter, Nellie-coyne, wrinkled her pert little nose. "I wanna go home now."

She was dressed as her mother was, though neither had ever seen Marquette, where I spent my last years of college (and failed to graduate). Like her mother, she wore a blue-and-gold ribbon around her hair.

There was patently not blood everywhere. However, my wife and daughter are fey. If they smelled blood, then there had been blood there once. Moreover, by the time we returned down the mountains to our bungalow in Renvyle it would be our family duty to find out why they smelled blood. I sighed, not as loudly or agonizingly as the locals sigh, but still vigorously for a friggin' Yank. This we did not need.

The third female in our party, Fiona, our snow white and presumably pregnant wolfhound, stuck her massive snout skyward and, falling back on her wolf ancestors, howled in protest.

I had not thought that Fiona was fey.

"I wonder who the last people who lived in this place were," Nuala Anne had said before the dark and icy pall had descended upon us. "And where they went."

"Probably to America," I said lightly, "where their descendants are now rich, complacent, overweight, and Republican."

I wondered how anyone could have possibly spent their whole life in a cave with a stone extension, or in a tiny hut not much bigger than a closet in our home on Southport Avenue across from St. Josephat's Church. Yet, at one time, the hut was home to three or four impoverished, illiterate families clinging to life on the hard rocks of County Galway. The roof and walls had collapsed, a few rotting timbers lay on the ground, a straggly blackthorn tree stood by, a dubious memorial. All that remained were a few piles of rubble. In another decade there would be nothing left. Yet, in Ma's time—my grandmother Nell Pat Malone that was—people would have remembered who had lived in this little cemetery and her father, Paddy Tom Malone, might have known them.

It was while I was pondering the melancholy scene—melancholy comes easy in the West of Ireland—that the pall of fog covered us. With the fog had come the stench. Had Nuala's question about the inhabitants of this harsh little place called both the fog and the smell?

It wouldn't have been the first time something like that happened.

My daughter deserted me and ran to cling to her mother's jean-covered leg. I walked bravely toward the largest hut. Fiona trailed after me, growling softly. Yet, she didn't try to stop me. Neither did my wife or daughter. As for my son, he continued to sleep, oblivious to the smell and to the wolfhound's howl.

Bravely, I walked into the shell of stone remnants. Fiona doggedly (you should excuse the expression) trailed behind me, growling at whatever was inside. I didn't expect to find anything. Nevertheless, every contact of my wife with the uncanny tempted me to believe that she saw more deeply into reality than I could ever hope to.

"There's nothing here!" I announced bravely.

Fiona barked happily and nudged me in approval.

The sun, perhaps reassured, promptly returned. The fog dissipated. The temperature climbed back into the seventies—perishing with the heat in this rocky, rainy island.

"Daddy made the bad smell go away," Nelliecoyne announced proudly.

"Isn't Daddy a brilliant exorcist?" my wife agreed. "Brilliant altogether?"

She was pale and tense, her Mavica camera hanging loosely on her arm.

DERMOT MICHAEL AN EXORCIST! said the Adversary, a voice hidden in the back of my head that frequently comments on my follies.

"Maybe we had better go home," I said gently.

"I think you have the right of it, Dermot Michael," Nuala agreed. "Enough of me picture-taking for this morning."

We were on the lip of a valley created by the Twelve Bens mountain chain. On the north was the Atlantic Ocean, and on the south stretched the valley, a picturesque, if barren and rocky, slice of land carved out by the Traheen River rushing among the mountains in a frantic search for the sea. Like most of the land in Connemara, the valley was brown even in late spring, save for the dark gash of the river, its grasslands stripped by generations of grazing sheep. Connemara had once been almost as green as Wicklow, over near Dublin. But the fierce struggle of the local people for life had denuded it of its trees and then its grasslands.

A few whitewashed stone houses dotted the sides of the valley, homes of the shepherds whose EU-funded sheep grazed the valley floor and hillsides, nibbling on the sparse meadows.

"Diamond Hill" Nuala had called it as we reached the top of the mountain. "See that manor house down there on the hill? Hasn't some fancy English lord restored it?"

It was a Big House in the sense of the English Protestant Ascendancy of the late eighteenth and early nineteenth centuries, but it was not particularly large compared to some of the great manors—a relatively small manifestation of Georgian culture, planted precariously in the midst of another, much older and more opaque, culture.

The latter might well have been called, up until the end of the last century, Neolithic.

"I imagine the locals don't like the fella very much?"

Nuala had shrugged indifferently. "Don't they say he's a nice man and really Irish? He's not oppressing anyone, is he?

Nuala had given up singing over a year ago and was now painting wild scenes from the Irish countryside. Since she didn't want anyone to see her watercolors, she would explore the countryside, photograph the sites, then return to the privacy of our home and paint with frantic haste.

Home was not our house on Southport Avenue in Chicago, right across the street from St. Josephat's Church. Nor was it our summer place in Grand Beach, Michigan. Rather it was a bungalow in Renvyle on the far coast of Connemara, a place the next parish to which is on Long Island, as the locals say. Renvyle, by the way, means "bare headland" in Irish, a grimly accurate description.

"Grand," I said, as I removed our son from my arms and put him in the sack around my wife's neck. Then I picked up his sister.

"Let me sit on your head, Daddy," Nelliecoyne pleaded.

"You're too heavy," I replied.

"I am NOT!"

We began to carefully pick our way down the mountain trail to the main road through Letterfrack National Park.

We had covered the first half of our ten-minute walk back to our Ford before Nuala Anne said a word.

"Wouldn't you think this psychic stuff is getting tiresome, Dermot Michael?

"It's not your fault," I said, repeating what had become my favorite mantra for the last year and a half.

"Still and all, I'm an educated, modern woman. I know that this psychic shite is all nonsense, isn't it now?"

I sighed as only someone from the West of Ireland—by adoption at least—can sigh.

"I'm not one of your superstitious Irish peasants, am I?"

My wife was indeed an educated, modern woman—Trinity College degree. She was also, if not exactly a superstitious peasant, a throwback to the Neolithic age.

"I thought it would all go away after I had this little gosson. Didn't me ma say that me Aunt Aggie, you know, the one in New Zealand, stopped seeing things after her second child was born?"

"Ah?"

I had never heard of Aunt Aggie before.

"And wasn't she the one who passed on the second sight to me? Isn't it always from aunt to niece, like me ma says?"

"That doesn't explain why Nelliecoyne is even more fey than you are."

She sighed, as if showing me how it should be done.

" 'Tis true."

"Daddy made the bad smell go away," that worthy little elf proclaimed from atop my head.

"Sure, darlin', there wasn't any bad smell. Wasn't it only the fog?"

Our daughter did not deign to debate that point.

Nuala began to hum the Connemara Cradle Song to her son, the first hint of music I had heard since his birth.

On the wings of the wind, o'er the dark, rolling deep,
Angels are coming to watch o'er your sleep.
Angels are coming to watch over you.
So list to the wind coming over the sea.

Hear the wind blow, hear the wind blow,
Lean your head over, hear the wind blow.

"Still, it was women's blood up there, wasn't it, Fiona darlin'?"

The wolfhound barked in approval as she always did when Nuala spoke her name.

"Women's blood?"

"Grandmother, mother, and daughter, all were murdered up there."

"They were?"

She nodded solemnly.

"And didn't the poor woman lose her husband over it?"

"One of those who died?"

"Och, Dermot Michael, don't be an eejit! They were already dead. It was the other woman."

"Oh."

When we reached our van, my son (whose real name is Micheal Dermod, pronounced MI-hall DIR-mud) emitted a small complaining sound, which usually meant that he wanted his diaper changed. Nuala promptly took over the task while Fiona, accompanied by Nelliecoyne clinging to her collar, sniffed round the parking area just to make sure that no other canines had invaded this sanctuary while we were up on the mountain.

When our daughter was in the diaper stage, I was frequently permitted to change her diaper. Nuala reserved changes for the Mick to herself.

"Poor dear little thing," she murmured, holding him close after she had reassembled his clothes.

On the lips of an Irish woman the word "poor" in that context ordinarily did not indicate either spiritual or material poverty. Rather it represented the superlative of the following adjective as in "dearest little thing." (Or "ting" since the Gaelic lacks an "h" sound.)

My wife was convinced that during her bout of postpartum depression she had neglected the Mick, and she was now trying to make up for it.

I was sure that behind my back she was calling me "poor dear Dermot and himself having to put up with a terrible wife like me."

"Your wife has always excelled, has she not, Mr. Coyne?" the psychiatrist, a handsome Jewish grandmother had said to me. "At everything?"

"Sports, singing, acting, lovemaking," I had agreed.

"Often by sheer willpower?"

"And raw talent."

"And she comes from a cultural background where there are no great demands for a woman to be good at everything all the time?"

"It's changing over there, but in her community that's still true."

"And now she believes that she's a bad wife and a bad mother and a worthless human being?"

"She cries all the time and loses her temper and then cries some more. She complains that I don't help her with the children and then shouts at me when I do help. She has to do it all herself because no one else knows how to do it right."

"But you did persuade her to see me?"

"Her own mother did, at my instigation. 'Me ma says I should see the doctor person.'"

The psychiatrist smiled thinly.

"She's overwhelmed, Mr. Coyne, by her own internalized demands and by the demands of our culture. Let me read you a quote from Dr. Thurer. 'The current standards for good mothering are so formidable, self-denying, elusive, changeable, and contradictory that they are unattainable. Our contemporary myth heaps upon the mother so many duties and expectations that to take it seriously would be hazardous to her mental health.' Your wife takes the myth very seriously indeed. Her saving grace is that in her better moments she laughs at it."

"She'll be all right?"

"Yes, of course, eventually. It may require several months, and she must take her medicine every day. . . . A woman's body undergoes hormonal changes constantly. There are enormous changes after she gives birth. When this is combined with a strong sense of personal responsibility, such as your wife possesses . . ."

"Is possessed by."

"Exactly . . . You understand the problem. Have her moods affected your son, do you think?"

"The Mick? A seven-forty-seven could crash outside our house and he would hardly notice. . . . Nuala Anne says that he's like his father."

"I doubt that she really means that," the doctor had said with another thin smile. "However, you must accept for the present her insistence that she is giving up her career. Eventually she may change her mind, but she must change it for herself."

"Naturally."

"When I told her that this kind of problem happens after ten percent of births, she seemed relieved."

"Oh?"

"Her exact words"—third thin smile—"were that she wasn't the only friggin' fruitcake in the world."

Later, as we were driving home from the "doctor woman's office," Nuala complained, "Dermot Michael, a woman is nothin' but a friggin' cesspool of friggin' hormones."

Despite myself I started to laugh. For a moment she pretended to be upset with me, then she laughed too.

There was another crisis over her medication. She didn't want to poison her "poor little tyke" and she didn't want to give up breast-feeding. Her mother, the good Annie McGrail, had persuaded her that it was more important for her son to have a happy mother than to drink her milk.

However, she often felt that since she was "better now" that it would be a sign of weakness to take her medication every day.

"Woman," I had thundered at her, "the doctor woman said you had to take it every day until she said you could stop. So you swallow the thing in me presence or I'll divorce you."

(The Gaelic lacks the possessive pronoun. Often, and despite heroic efforts, I slip into her idiom.)

"Och, sure, Dermot love, don't you have the right of it?" she had said, collapsing into my arms in tears. "I promise."

YOU'D NEVER DIVORCE HER.

So now she has indeed swallowed the medicine in my presence daily with a great show of phony obedience.

"She knows I'd never divorce her."

We arranged our offspring in their car seats. Fiona jumped into the rear seat of the van, rocking it with her hundred-and-forty-pound mass, and curled up for her nap. Nelliecoyne started telling stories to her gurgling and cooing little brother in Irish. Nuala began to drive down the narrow road that circles the Letterfrack National Park in the Ballynahinch mountains.

AT LEAST SHE'S SINGING AGAIN.

"Humming." I replied to the Adversary. Besides, she's fey again too.

NOTHING I CAN DO ABOUT THAT. YOU KNEW WHAT YOU WERE GETTING INTO WHEN YOU MARRIED HER. ISN'T SHE ONE OF THE DARK ONES?

"I'd be glad to have her fey, if it means that she's singing again."

Did me wife, oops, my wife really believe that the difficulties of her two pregnancies (on the flat of her back for the last three months before the Mick arrived) and two very arduous deliveries and then the depression were her fault? Were they proof that she was indeed a poor wife and mother?

You can live with a woman for five years, pleasurably enough, and realize that you know less about her than you did on your wedding day. My guess is that, in the opaque Irish idiom, she "half believed it." As best as I can understand the idiom, it does not mean half and half, but rather, totally some of the time and not at all, at all the rest of the time. Sometimes she thought she was a total failure, and other times she thought, correctly, that despite the depression she was a total success as a wife and mother.

The latter, of course, was the truth.

Letterfrack was swarming with Yank tourists shopping at the "Irish Crafts" store, which the Protestants had founded long ago in their totally unsuccessful efforts to win the locals away from their popish superstitions. At the edge of the town we heard a distant explosion and saw a puff of black smoke, a dirty hand that hung as if suspended against the pure blue sky.

"Is it a bomb now, Dermot Michael?" Nuala gasped.

"It looks like it is."

"In Renvyle, do you think?"

"Maybe."

"Och . . . I hope it's not our house!"

"There's no one in it, and it's insured."

Which was a characteristically stupid male response.

"Didn't the lads set off a bomb?" Nelliecoyne commented and then went back to her Irish babble.

"The lads" was an Irish euphemism—they are a people who love euphemisms—for the Irish Republican Army. After the Northern Ireland peace agreement, most of the lads had turned to more peaceful tasks.

"She did say that, didn't she?" I asked in a whisper, suppressing a shiver.

"It's probably something she heard us say when there was a loud noise," Nuala replied with little conviction.

When we reached the coast road, where the sapphire Atlantic brushed easily against the shoreline, leaving a thick white lace of foam, the cloud had faded to a smirch, a telltale hint of evil on the azure sky.

We were about a mile (Galwegians don't hold with kilometers) from our cottage in the shadow of Renvyle House Hotel, when a smartly dressed young Garda flagged us down.

"Papers, please," she said briskly. You didn't ask this brisk young woman about a bomb until you had identified yourself.

"Dermot?"

I searched my pockets as if I thought I really had them.

"Must have left the passports at home."

"Driver's license?" The constable frowned disapprovingly. I was patently a typically stupid Yank.

Nuala produced her license and spoke in Irish doubtless telling the pretty blond constable that her husband was an eejit altogether. I always assumed that when she went into her first language she was talking about me—and not paying me any compliments.

THE NAME OF THAT, BOYO, IS PARANOIA.

"You have the Irish," the Garda said, "but this is a Yank driver's license. . . . Oh my, who are you?"

A massive white snout had appeared between our two children and then a vast mouth with a wide grin.

"Isn't it Fiona?" I said. "And herself a retired member of the Gardaí. Whenever she encounters a colleague she wants to make friends!"

I got out of the van and opened the door. Delighted, Fiona bounded out, circled the van in an enthusiastic rush, and placed her two massive paws on the young woman's shoulders and licked her face. She was at least a foot taller than the constable.

"Oh, aren't you a great beauty now!" The officer hugged her new-found friend. "Sure, you'll smother me completely!"

She said a word in Irish. Our wolfhound sat down, her tail wagging furiously.

"Haven't we bred her with Sir Roy Harcourt de Bourk the fourth?" Nuala explained. "And don't we think she's pregnant?"

"I bet she gave him a hard time!"

Even when the female is in heat, wolfhounds would rather chase each other around and play than engage in sexual intercourse. Finally, the breeders had to constrain them to do so by a method that I will not describe.

"Isn't she an Irish female?" I said.

"Dermot Michael!" my wife shouted in protest.

"She's going to have three puppies," my daughter informed the Garda.

"Is she now? And what's your name?"

"Moire Ain Coyne," the redhead announced proudly.

"The problem, Ms. Coyne," the Garda said as she patted the head of the ecstatic Fiona, "is that there was an explosion down the road."

"Didn't the lads set off a bomb?" Moire Ain Coyne informed her.

The Garda was startled.

"Actually we don't know. . . ."

"She heard us say it," I tried to explain. "You know what mimics kids are at that age."

"I hope it wasn't our house," Nuala Anne interjected.

"No, it was Mr. MacManus's home. You know, the T.D."

T.D. is a member of the Dáil, the Irish parliament. God forbid that the Irish should call one of their parliamentarians an M.P.

"The next house down the road from us!" Nuala exclaimed, making an elaborately large sign of the cross.

"It was a big explosion . . . fortunately no one was home. . . . And your house was not damaged."

MacManus was off in Dublin at the Dáil session.

"Thanks be to God," Nuala said.

"Indeed, I'm sure you can go through to your house. However, there'll be a lot of us around for a day or two.

"Thanks be to God," I agreed.

"Fiona," the Garda said, "back into the van."

Reluctantly the wolfhound obeyed.

"Aren't you Nuala Anne?" The constable glanced at my wife's license before returning it.

" 'Tis me name," she said, bowing her head modestly.

"Aren't we all terrible proud of you here at home, Ms. McGrail? Not all our exported celebrities have your dignity and grace."

Me wife turned deep red.

"Thank you," she said quietly.

"Haven't I been telling her that all along?" I said as I closed the rear door on our faithless hound and retook my seat.

"Enjoy your time at home." The young woman saluted.

"Isn't she sweet, the poor dear thing?"

"Nice ass too," I added, just to make trouble.

"Dermot Michael Coyne! What a terrible thing to say!"

"Just an observation," I said. "Teats are cute too!"

"You're obsessed with sex," she said, trying to sound as though she disapproved.

"Not as cute as yours!"

"Will you be quiet now, and the small ones in the car with us!"

"I will. . . ."

"The woman is *not* from Galway," Nuala Anne observed.

"Ah?"

"She doesn't speak Irish like we do, not quite. There may be a touch of Kerry in her. . . ."

"God forbid . . ."

"Dermot Michael, give over! Isn't it important to you Yanks to know whether someone is from Texas?"

"If he is, he's probably carrying some kind of concealed weapon."

"Maybe East Mayo . . ." Nuala continued, ignoring me.

Our daughter was babbling again in Irish at her little brother, who continued to gurgle and smile.

The breeding of Fiona and Sir Roy, an attempt to combine presumably long-lived genes of the species, was the alleged reason for our trip to Ireland—that and the opportunity to see our new Irish bungalow and to expose Nelliecoyne to Irish culture. The real reason was to restore my fragile Irish lass to her Connemara milieu and to the common sense of her mother, Annie McGrail. ("The poor dear child has to learn to cope with all her talents, Dermot Michael. Don't worry about it; she will in time." But I *was* worried about it.) We were to have supper with Annie and her husband, Gerroid, that night at Ashford Castle.

We passed a blackened hole in the ground, which had been Colm MacManus's house. Guards swarmed around it. Two of their vans were already parked next to the rubble. They had come up quickly from their barracks at Clifden. One of them waved us through.

"The lads set off a bomb," Nelliecoyne repeated.

Nuala sighed loudly.

"Whatever are we to do with that one, Dermot Michael Coyne?"

I was saved from the need to respond by Nelliecoyne herself.

"Ma, sometimes this little brat drives me out of me friggin' mind. He's so dumb!"

"Shush, darlin', he's only a little boy and you're a big girl. You should be nice to him."

"Yes, Ma."

Two vans with satellite dishes rushed by us as we turned into our driveway.

"It's them friggin' media vultures," my wife protested. "They'll find out I'm here, Dermot. I don't want to talk to them!"

"I'll keep them at bay," I said bravely.

"They'll want to know why I'm not singing. 'Tis none of their business! The friggin' gobshites!"

" 'Tis not."

Why should anyone be interested in the fact that a young woman who had just earned a platinum disk for *Nuala Anne Sings American* announces that she's finished with her vocal career at twenty-five?

Why, indeed?

No reason given other than she was tired of singing—and on the flat of her back trying to save a baby.

"You can tell them I've taken up painting!"

"I can indeed."

We stopped in the bungalow's carport and stared down the road at the ugly black scar on the turf, a blot on the postcard-perfect azure sky, sapphire sea, and green vegetation. All right, our house had not been hit by the explosion. What if, however, we had happened to be driving by, or if Nellie—violating all our rules, had been too close to the house next door. I shuddered at the image of her thin little body limp and lifeless on the road. Nuala Anne was probably seeing a similar image. She snatched her son out of the car seat and carried him protectively to the door of the house.

"And tell them I won't have any exhibitions for twenty-five years!"

"Woman, I will."

—2—

"THAT ONE will do just fine, Dermot Michael," my wife said as she shrugged out of her sweatshirt.

After each of our photo-taking ventures, she would pick one shot off the screen of my Dell and require that I print out a color copy. As I feared, this time it was a picture of the hovel up in the hills where she had smelled the blood of the three women. It was the last picture she'd taken before the fog had closed in on us. Already the light looked sinister.

"Isn't it a brilliant picture altogether!" She removed the ribbon from her long black hair, letting it fall over her shoulders. "Print it out."

My pulse rate shot up. More love in the afternoon. Even if I had now passed my thirtieth birthday, I was not likely to refuse.

We had returned to our bungalow—given its size and comforts, "villa" would have been a better label. Ethne, our tiny and ebullient mother's helper (and herself a student at UCG—University College Galway), was waiting for us. She had poured out rumors about the destruction of "that gombeen man's house."

"Didn't it scare the shite out of me? And didn't I grab for my rosary? . . . Aren't the Gardai saying it was a professional job and if he was inside there'd be nothing but bits and pieces left and it could have been the lads or the Prots from up above and that there's no reason to waste good explosives on such a worthless gobshite . . ."

"Maybe it was the Russian Mafia," I suggested, a comment that stopped the loquacious young woman in her tracks.

Nelliecoyne, who had bonded with Ethne, rushed to embrace her leg. The two of them and me wife jabbered in Irish—about me I was sure. My son, placed on the floor, managed to pull himself in a crawl towards his adored minder.

Nelliecoyne had been walking at his age.

Overachiever.

Ethne swept him into her arms.

"How's me favorite little boy in all the world today!"

"Dermot Michael," Nuala asked, "would you ever unload me camera for me while we feed these hungry little demons?"

"I would, so long as you feed me too!"

More laughter and Irish chatter.

So after I had removed the diskette from her camera and loaded it into our Dell and flipped through her shots, Nelliecoyne arrived in the master bedroom, cautiously carrying a plate on which there was a salmon sandwich with the crusts cut off. She offered it to me as though it were a chalice with the consecrated wine.

"Ma says that you like peanut butter and jelly."

"If Ma says so, it must be true."

If my daughter should become a priest—which surely ought to be possible when she comes of age—they would have to ordain her a bishop.

"Ma says that if you eat every last bit of it maybe you can have some ice cream."

"I had better eat every last bit of it, huh?"

I often had the impression that I was the third kid in the house.

Nuala's shots were excellent. Naturally. She was good at everything she did. When I joined the rest of the ménage in the kitchen I found that there were roast beef, egg salad, and ham and cheese sandwiches, all on croissants, waiting for me.

Our cottage was often called a bungalow. However, it had nothing in common with the snug, sturdy brick houses by the same name on the west side of Chicago. Rather it was modeled on the style of British India, only far more elegant—four bedrooms, three baths, a family room with a large TV, a kitchen, a dining room, and a parlor, which

was usually left vacant for the "gentry"—the little people—should they
happen by. Nuala Anne did not exactly believe in the fairie, but she
did believe, as she explained to me, in traditions.

It was hardly your stone-and-thatch Connemara cottage of not so
long ago. Rather it had been designed for rich Yanks and, now that
Ireland was bursting with prosperity, for rich Micks.

After I had more or less cleaned the sandwich plate, Ethne and
the children withdrew to the nursery for the children's afternoon nap,
accompanied by Fiona, who had forsaken the master bedroom entirely
since we had come to Ireland. Nuala and I wandered down to the
master bedroom. Fortunately, given my wife's proclivity for afternoon
"naps," the nursery and the master bedroom were at opposite ends of
the house.

After she had chosen the shot she wanted me to print, she folded
her sweatshirt neatly. Her bra was the same navy blue as the sweatshirt.
In Nuala's world, it was proper that undergarments match outer garments because, as she said, "You never can tell when someone might
want to undress you."

"Aren't you going to print out me picture, Dermot Michael?" she
said as she deftly loosened the front hook of her bra.

"Momentarily distracted," I murmured as I clicked on the print icon.

"Are you now?"

She folded the bra neatly—in Nuala Anne's world everything
was neat.

She peaked out of the drapes.

"Them gobshites are everywhere!"

"Media?"

"Gardaí." She closed the drape. "I'm taking me pill now, Dermot
Michael," she said, popping a tablet into her mouth. "Just so you won't
call a divorce lawyer this afternoon."

"One day at a time!"

She sniggered and tugged off her jeans.

"Doesn't your daughter hound me about it every day. . . . Ma, have
you taken your pill yet?"

It had become difficult for me to sustain the banter. After five years of marriage the sight of my wife's breasts still intoxicated me.

Nuala Anne was conniving again, not that she ever stopped conniving. She knew what the afternoon seductions did to my body and my mind. She was scheming some convoluted and intricate Irish womanly plot. I didn't mind the conniving. In fact, I sort of enjoyed it. Hadn't Ma, my beloved Connemara-born grandmother, with whom my wife identified because they were both from Carraroe, been a conniver too?

"I may modify the threat from divorce to spanking you every day you don't take it."

"Now isn't that an interesting erotic possibility," she said as she folded her jeans.

Heaven help me if I ever tried it.

Was she perhaps trying to bind me closer to her against the fear that I might become impatient with her recent problems? Or was she attempting to make up for the long hiatus in our sexual games when she was pregnant and recovering? Or was she seeking to win my support for her decision to abandon her vocal career? Or was she consoling me because I was now past thirty?

All these obvious schemes were improbable and unnecessary, as I thought she well knew. The scheme had to be more complicated and devious.

WHY DON'T YOU JUST ENJOY IT AS LONG AS YOU CAN.

"I have to figure it out."

MAYBE SHE JUST ENJOYS BEING FUCKED.

"Don't be vulgar."

She kicked off her bikini bottoms and added them to the neatly folded pile. Then she leaned against the wall, head bowed, hands behind her back, a demure, fragile, almost virginal creature.

"You shouldn't stare at me like that, Dermot Michael Coyne."

"Woman,"—I gasped—"you're me wife. I'm supposed to stare at you that way."

Since our marriage I had made love with many different women, all of them my wife. Nuala might be a sophisticated woman of the world, a furiously hungry nymph, an urbane and experienced sensualist, or a shy, skittish bog creature from the wilds of the West of Ireland. The last was, I often thought, the ur-Nuala, the one on which all the others built. In this particular bit of conniving, she was the frightened Galway innocent.

"You'll destroy me modesty altogether."

"Impossible. Stark naked like you are now, there's always a veil of modesty around you."

She looked up, interested in this assertion.

"That's a load of shite, Dermot Michael Coyne."

" 'Tis not, woman. 'Tis the modesty behind the modesty."

"You're making fun of me Irish spirituality."

She argued that in the Irish way of things, there was always a reality behind the appearance—the mountain behind the mountain, the river behind the river. I had once suggested that this was Platonism. She had replied briskly that it was not so. Besides, the ancient Celts understood the truth long before them Greek fellas had come along.

"Woman, I am not. It is impossible for you to be lewd."

"Och, Dermot, stare at me as long as you want. Don't I love it something terrible when you eat me up with your eyes."

I had often told people that my wife reminded me of an ancient Celtic goddess, though I had not in fact ever met an ancient Celtic goddess.

Now she was a naked Celtic goddess, one of which I had never seen either.

Still, she'd do—long, firm legs, slender hips, trim waist, elegant breasts, the solid, graceful body of a woman athlete.

And dangerously strong too.

Her eyes were as blue as Galway Bay on a sunny day, her finely shaped face as mobile as Irish weather, and her voice hinted at echoes of church bells pealing over the bogs.

She had been grimly determined to recapture her figure after the Mick had appeared, and she set about the task with characteristic intensity as soon as she had begun to take the medication. The last five pounds didn't seem to want to go away.

"Dermot Michael Coyne, do you realize that if I have six more children, I'll have put on thirty-five pounds."

"I don't think you're going to have six more children."

"Regardless! And you just don't get it!"

I got it enough to fiddle with the scale in our bathroom at home on Southport Avenue so that the five pounds slipped away. Then she easily lost five more, which put her back at the weight at which she'd been aiming. She was quite proud of herself. I let it go at that. If it works don't fix it.

Then she had announced her fear that her waist would never return to its proper size. Wasn't it a quarter-inch larger than it should be? Would ten pregnancies make her two-and-a-half inches fatter?

I hadn't argued that she wasn't going to be pregnant ten more times. Rather, one day when we were playing, I had held her down amid much giggling, produced a tape measure, and informed her that her waist measurement was the same as that for her wedding dress and I wanted to hear no more complaints.

She had pondered the tape suspiciously. How did I know what her wedding dress measurements were? I recited them all. She complained that a woman had no privacy at all, at all, and then added that it was probably yesterday's exercise which had eliminated the offending quarter-inch.

I note that no one holds Nuala Anne down unless she wants to be held down.

I turned off the computer and walked across the room to where she was cowering against the wall. I rubbed the back of my hand down one breast and then up the other. I allowed the fingers of my other hand to play with her hard belly muscles. She arched her back and groaned.

No man should have that kind of power, I thought, over such a beautiful woman. Nonetheless, consumed by adoration and concern, I continued my gentle explorations.

"Dermot!" she sighed.

I took her into my arms. She was trembling.

"Aren't you my life itself?" she moaned.

SEE! SHE'S CLINGING TO YOU LIKE HER LIFE DEPENDS ON YOU FUCKING HER! YOU'RE LIKE THE PROZAC!

I was incapable of arguing with him.

As we ascended the heights of love everything else faded—the blood in the mountain hut, the explosion down the road, our fey daughter, our pregnant wolfhound, even her singing.

Much later, sweaty and exhausted, we lay side by side, holding hands.

"What did you mean, Nuala Anne, when you said I was your life?"

"I didn't say that at all, at all."

"Woman, you did."

"Hadn't you driven me out of me mind?"

"Still, you said it."

She sighed.

"Isn't it enough that you have me body? Leave me soul alone."

We began to dally with one another, as we often did when we were cooling off, a special bonus of pleasure.

"When I'm involved, I want to know."

She sighed as she kissed my chin.

"It isn't just the Prozac that keeps me on this side of the deep end, Dermot Michael, is it now?"

" 'Tis the Dermot behind the Dermot?"

"Sure, there's no Dermot behind the Dermot . . . only God."

Somehow I didn't want to be God for her.

YOU'RE STUCK WITH IT, BOYO.

"Now go to sleep, Dermot Michael. I don't want you nodding off with me parents at supper."

—3—

"WILL I be driving now?" me wife asked me, extending her hand.

The gesture was more important than the interrogative form of her remark. The Irish language loves the courtesy of the question. The Irish mother, however, loves to be in charge. So what Nuala meant was, "I'll be driving, so give me the friggin' key."

We were to join her parents, Gerroid and Annie, at Ashford Castle for supper. My wife didn't trust me on the narrow Connemara roads at night. Moreover, since she couldn't mix the "creature" with her medication, she alleged that her driving freed me up to drink "all that I wanted"—never more than a glass or two of wine and a sip of Baileys.

I had awakened, groggy and complacent, late in the afternoon. The springtime Irish sun was still high in the sky. In her terry cloth robe, Nuala Anne was huddled over her easel. I had noted from my comfortable spot in our bed that there was a lot of red on the watercolor.

"Dermot Michael," she had said, continuing to concentrate on her work, "why don't you take herself on her second run now and check on the kids?"

How did she know I was awake?

Don't ask.

So I had dressed in my jogging clothes, tied on my Nikes, and kissed her neck.

"Och, aren't you the brilliant lover, Dermot Michael Coyne?" she had observed, still concentrating on the painting, in which I thought I saw five bloody bodies.

"Brilliant" is the superlative degree of an adjective of which "super" is the comparative.

"Am I now?"

She had nodded her head slightly, in confirmation.

"Isn't the greatest pleasure for a woman in that moment when she gives herself totally to her man?"

"You'd know that better than I would."

I had kissed her neck again.

" 'Tis." She had sighed.

"When she's done that she knows she's captured her man completely," I had suggested.

She had paused, her brush poised over the painting.

"Sure, if she hasn't captured him completely, she has no business being in bed with him, has she now?"

I retreated with as much grace as I could muster under the circumstances.

Outside our bungalow, the tireless Ethne was frolicking with Nelliecoyne and a gaggle of three-year-old girls while the Mick relaxed in his car seat and watched the games with approval—and no apparent desire to join them.

He was indeed a big lug, just like his old man.

Fiona, who had also been watching the games, bounded up immediately, doubtless smelling my running clothes. In Ireland, unlike in Chicago, she was free from a leash when we ran.

We started down the road to the Renvyle House Hotel. Our bungalow was on the lee side of the bare headland, so the Atlantic Ocean was more tranquil. Connemara is a string of barren mountains on the north side and barren lowlands on the south side, both little more than a network of lace held together among inlets, harbors, coves, and loughs. It is dramatically beautiful for the first two sunny days, and then, as far as I was concerned, harsh and depressing after that. On the rainy days it was, again in my fallible judgment, an antechamber of purgatory.

No wonder, I thought to myself as we jogged along the narrow road, that my wife had some gloomy strains in her personality. No wonder she had thrown over her career as a singer.

"I won't do it anymore, Dermot Michael," she had said one night in our room on Southport Avenue, as she lay in bed protecting the "poor little lad inside me."

It was a given, a foregone conclusion that our second child would be a boy.

Fiona, inseparable from her mistress during these difficult weeks, stirred uneasily at the side of her bed.

"Everything's on hold till himself comes," I had replied.

"I don't want anything on hold," she had insisted. "I want everything canceled. No more recordings, no more concerts, no more Christmas specials, no more lessons with Madam. No more nothing, at all, at all."

"Oh."

"And it's not me hormones talking either, Dermot Michael Coyne. I've been thinking about this for a long time. I'm sick of singing."

"It's your call," had been all I could say.

"I hate it. I hate it altogether. I don't want to do it anymore."

We didn't need the money. I had been a total failure as a commodity broker, except for one very lucky day. I had given most of the gains from that luck to a brilliant stockbroker, who had turned each dollar into five during the great market run-up. Nuala had put her money into the market too—making her own investment decisions, naturally. My novels, which I worked on occasionally, brought in enough money to live more than comfortably. Our lifestyle was more or less frugal, save for buying a bungalow in Ireland, which could be rented to tourists when we weren't using it.

At twenty-five my wife had become a successful vocalist far beyond her wildest dreams. Her lovely, if limited, voice and her charm had won over both the United States and Ireland. Her most recent record, *Nuala Anne Sings American* had won her a platinum disk. She had worked hard at it, very hard, but seemed to revel in the work. Now she was quitting.

"I can't be a mother and a wife," she had continued, "and continue this singing. Tell everyone I'm retiring."

So I had done just that. No one had believed me. Hormones, they had said. However, they had not seen the cut of my wife's jaw when she made her decision.

In the back of my head, down in the deep subbasements of my brain, there lurked a faint hunch that she might change her mind. However, I would not have gone long, as the traders say, on that possibility.

As I had jogged along the road, yielding to the majesty of the ocean and the sky and the Twelve Bens mountains, I wondered whether I might be responsible for the problem. She had seemed so ambitious about singing before our marriage (despite her job at Arthur Andersen), that I had encouraged it and even arranged for voice lessons and her first recording. Perhaps I should have left well enough alone. Maybe it would have been better if she had limited herself to an occasional gig at the Abbey Pub in Chicago.

She had loved to sing. Music was in her bones, in her body, in her soul. Now she wouldn't even sing lullabies to our children.

Still, she had hummed the Connemara Cradle Song today, had she not?

A blue Garda car, coming up behind me, ended these ruminations. Our young friend from the morning got out of the car, much to Fiona's delight. A short, slender man in tweeds, looking like an English tourist, climbed out the other side.

"Mr. McGrail, uh, Mr. Coyne," said the young woman, who was busy responding to Fiona's enthusiasm, "this is Chief Superintendent McGinn from Galway City."

Fiona turned her attention to the detective.

"Good girl," he said as she embraced him. "Sure, you're still a Galway lass, aren't you?"

He said a couple of words in Irish. The wolfhound, her tail still wagging, settled back on her haunches.

" 'Tis a pleasure to meet you, sir," he said respectfully to me as we shook hands. "Deputy Commissioner Keenan from Dublin asked me to give you his warmest greetings."

"Give my equally warmest greetings back to him and to herself also."

"I believe you met Garda Sayers this morning."

"First name Peg?"

The young woman blushed and grinned.

"With an 'I,' sir."

"The famous woman from the Blaskets is an ancestor. Her Irish has a touch of the Blaskets in it."

"My wife noticed it."

"We're wondering, Mr. Coyne, if we might stop by tomorrow morning and have a chat with you about this little problem we seem to have."

"Dermot."

"Declan."

He had shrewd brown eyes, shrewd but warm.

So our friend Gene Keenan told the Galway Gardaí that me wife has certain skills as a detective. She had never said explicitly that she was giving that up too.

"My wife will be more help than I am, but I don't think either of us has noticed anything. However, we'll be happy to talk to you tomorrow."

"A Galway woman, is she?"

"Carraroe. Her parents still live there."

"One of the dark ones, is she now?"

"Sometimes," I conceded cautiously.

"Peig will excuse me for saying it, but there's a lot of that around Galway. Sure, the Iron Age has never quite ended here."

"And a good thing too," Peig said vigorously.

They returned to their car. Fiona hesitated briefly, torn between two loyalties, and decided on me.

Renvyle House was built by the Blakes, a Protestant family, in 1680. During the Land League wars two centuries later, the Blake widow who owned the house turned it into a hotel. Poet and author

Oliver St. John Gogarty ("plump, stately Buck Mulligan" in *Ulysses*) bought the hotel. Yeats and Synge hung around there. The "lads" wrecked it in the early twenties. The Irish government compensated for its destruction. It is a hotel again today and a nice place to hang your hat, especially if you're a fisherman and it's fishing season, which it was, or someone looking for a bit of peace and quiet, and itself having horses and a heated swimming pool and a great restaurant and a nine-hole golf course nearby.

Peace and quiet, in my judgment, did not include exploding homes and hovels that smelled of blood.

"Fishermen are friggin' eejits, chasing dumb fish when they don't need them to stay alive," me wife had told me once.

In front of the Renvyle House Hotel, we were stopped again, this time by a young man, probably just out of UCG, with a tape recorder and a mike. RTE radio.

"Mr. McGrail, is it now?" he had asked shyly.

Fiona had sniffed suspiciously and then approved him on a temporary basis.

"Coyne," I said curtly.

He blushed with embarrassment.

"Of course, Mr. Coyne. Sorry."

"No problem," I relented. "Everyone makes that mistake."

"And yourself a fine novelist too!"

The kid was all right!

"Could I ever ask you a question about Ms. McGrail?"

"Sure, but don't expect a straight answer. This is the West of Ireland after all."

He laughed and turned on his recorder.

"Will she ever sing again?"

"She has retired for family reasons. She considers the decision definitive."

"Do you think she will ever sing again?"

"What do I know?"

"Is it true that she's painting instead."

" 'Tis."

"Is her work good?"

"Very good indeed. However, I'm her husband."

"Will there be a gallery exhibition?"

"She said there will be . . . in twenty-five years."

He thanked me profusely and went into the hotel, doubtless to phone his interview to the station in Dublin.

"Come on, girl," I said to the dog, "back to Nuala."

She barked enthusiastically in agreement.

We turned around and raced back to herself—against the wind, which was stiffening, as they say around this part of Galway, a place where zephyrs don't exist. Fiona refused to run the last fifty yards, which was fine with me.

We entered the house and heard the noise of womanly voices in the kitchen—where else would Irish women be? In the kitchen and talking!

The weary wolfhound and I ambled out into the kitchen. My wife and my daughter and our mother's helper, cleaning up after supper, were jabbering in Irish with such enthusiasm that they did not notice our arrival. My son, his mouth covered with baby food, however, grinned happily at me and crawled over to hug my leg.

"Well, at least someone in the house welcomes me home!"

The chatter stopped instantly, proof, as I thought, that they had been chattering about me. I picked up the Mick and swung him over my head, an activity in which he reveled.

"Did you have a grand run, Dermot Michael?" my wife, still in the terry cloth robe, asked, trying to pretend that she was not flustered.

"Didn't your dog run out of steam?"

"Well, isn't the poor thing pregnant?"

Nelliecoyne tugged at my leg, demanding her turn for a skyride.

"Fiona is going to have three white puppies, two girl puppies and one boy puppy."

"Is she now?" I said, gently replacing her brother on the floor and lifting her up.

"Yes, she is, Daddy."

So that was that. What did I know?

"Dermot, would you ever take your shower and dress now? I'd like to have the room to meself to make me preparations."

"Doesn't Nuala have a super dress, Mr. Coyne? Sure, you'll be loving it?"

"Bought at a sale!" my wife assured me, as though I complained about her buying habits—which I never had. Nuala was a stylish dresser because she was lovely and had good taste. Since money couldn't buy either, she bought off-the-rack dresses that had been marked down and transformed them with her own personal elegance.

"Like every good Irish male, I do what I'm told."

The three women giggled. Because they knew it was true.

You will note that, to Ethne, my wife was Nuala Anne and I was Mr. Coyne. That's what comes of being over thirty.

In the master bedroom, I went immediately to the corner where herself played with her watercolors. I recoiled at the bloody horror on her easel—a charnel house with six torn and broken human bodies, three women, two boys, and an adult man, the remnants of their faces twisted in agony, their limbs broken, their skulls bashed in. They had died slow, agonizing, tortured deaths, at the end almost pleading that their suffering be ended.

I rushed into the bathroom and vomited.

Then I carefully cleaned up the mess and opened the window so that the Atlantic breezes would exorcise the smell of my sickness.

Was that what Nuala had seen up on the mountain? And Nellie-coyne too?

I sat on the edge of the bed trembling. Nuala's paintings were usually dramatic but peaceful. Yet the imagery of this one must be deeply buried in her soul.

Small wonder that she needed Prozac.

What was I supposed to do now?

Probably tomorrow morning I should pay a visit to Jack Lane, as everyone called the local priest, and ask some questions about the hovels on the mountain.

I was sweating, a cold, sinister sweat, as though a demon had temporarily invaded my soul. We should go home tomorrow and find a psychiatrist for my wife. The gynecologist had said that she didn't need therapy, that she was basically a healthy woman. No healthy woman could carry such a hell in her brain.

GET A HOLD OF YOURSELF, YOU FOCKING AMADON. YOU SAW HER DOWNSTAIRS WITH YOUR BRATS. DID SHE SEEM CRAZY?

She had not. She seemed fine, the Nuala of O'Neill's pub in the shadow of Trinity College. My chill faded. If she wanted to talk about it, I would. Otherwise . . . She must have realized that I would see the painting and didn't seem worried about it.

I should take a nice warm shower and get dressed for dinner.

"Well, you've spent enough time in there, haven't you?" my wife greeted me when I emerged from the shower. "Would you be thinking we have all night?"

"Sorry," I murmured.

"I need the room to meself, so I can look healthy and happy for me ma and da."

"I'll be out of here in a couple of minutes."

"Did you like me painting?"

"It's very powerful."

"That's what happened up there, Dermot Michael."

She tossed her robe at me, entered the shower, and closed the door.

I turned on the telly to see pictures of our bungalow, which the RTE was informing the world was right next to the destroyed home of T.D. Colm MacManus. Then MacManus himself appeared, a round, nervous man with darting eyes.

"I call upon the Garda to find the criminals immediately," he said in a voice quivering with not altogether convincing outrage. This is not Belfast. We cannot tolerate such violence in Ireland. Our invaluable tourist trade is bound to suffer in the wake of this wanton destruction."

Somehow his sputtering, self-righteous anger reminded me of the redneck Republicans in the American Congress.

Still, he had reason to be angry, didn't he?

Later, having assisted Ethne in putting the exhausted small ones to bed and telling her to study hard for her big test the next day, I sat

in the parlor and sipped a small jar (as they call it in Ireland) of
Jameson as I waited for Nuala to emerge for our trip over to Ashford.
She'd insist on driving, so the "jar" wouldn't hurt.

As my nerves and my queasy stomach settled down, my worries
increased. What the hell was I supposed to do with my wife?

MAYBE JUST LEAVE HER ALONE.

"Maybe."

Then the Adversary said nothing, most unusual for him. Or her.
Sometimes these days the Adversary sounds like my wife.

Too much talent . . . Those hints of crow's-feet around her eyes . . .
We're both getting older . . . Meself over thirty.

Maybe I should let her recover at her own pace . . . As long as
she continues to take the pills . . . She's fine with the kids . . . Maybe
she should be a painter instead of a singer . . . But the horror in that
painting!

"Well," she said, appearing in the room, "and yourself sipping on
a jar! Trying to recover from me painting, which shocks you more than
it does me, are you now?"

"Bracing for the shock of you in that super dress. Would I need a
couple of jars for that?"

She blushed, delighted as a kid on her first date that she had
pleased her man.

"Will I be able to fool me ma and me pa that I'm a healthy young
woman again?"

Her dress was red with a gold belt. It fell to just above her knees
and in that respect was modest by present standards. However a slit
reached at least to midthigh and the thin straps holding the dress in
place presided over a touch of cleavage that was tasteful indeed, but
left no question about the splendor of her breasts.

Gulp!

Hands on hips, she said, "You haven't answered me question."

"Well, Annie and Gerry will marvel at how beautiful you are,
though they won't be surprised. As for fooling the good Annie, you
haven't been able to do that since the day you were born."

I kissed her forehead and put my arm around her.

" 'Tis true enough," she sighed. "The problem is that I don't know whether I'm healthy again."

"Healthy enough to be a spectacular bedmate."

"Oh, THAT! Dermot Michael, I'd have to be dead and buried for ten years not to fock with you every time I get a chance. Don't you know all me secrets? . . . Come along, now, we don't want to be late."

In the car as she drove, I continued the discussion.

"I don't know any of your secrets, Nuala Anne. You're pure mystery to me. Wonderful, but always a surprise."

"Go along with you, Dermot Michael Coyne! When I'm with you, don't I feel naked even if I'm wearing all me clothes and me not knowing at all, at all, what's going on in that big, thick skull of yours?"

"Oh."

"Except that you love me something terrible, a lot more than I deserve."

"A lot less . . ."

"Och, give over, Dermot Michael!"

To change the subject I told her about the interview with the young man from RTE radio.

"Blatherskite!"

"Shy young man. I suspect that our Ethne knows him."

"Well, if she approves of him, that's different. Anyway, didn't you give all the right answers!"

"I'm glad to hear it . . . And how does our daughter know that the lads set the bomb down the road."

"She doesn't even know who the lads are, Dermot love. Doesn't she pick it up from me?"

"Pick it up?"

"Sure, when that terrible explosion happened, didn't I think that it might be the lads and didn't she hear what I thought?"

"She heard what you thought?"

"Just like me and me Aunt Aggie when I was a small one . . . Isn't that how she knows about Fiona's puppies?"

"You know how many pups and then tell her?"

"Dermot Michael Coyne! You simply don't understand! I don't tell her anything. Sometimes she hears my thoughts. 'Tis nothing to worry about."

The hell it isn't.

THIS SCARES ME TOO, BOYO.

"So we really don't, about the pups?"

She sighed in protest.

"Of course we do! Three white ones, two of them bitches. I know that and I always know those things. The poor sweet child hears it from me."

"When will the pups arrive?"

"Give over Dermot Michael! Did I know when me own small ones were to be born? Do I choose stocks by this shite? It's mostly useless when it isn't scary like up there in the Twelve Bens this morning."

"Oh . . . Still, you'd bet me about herself's offspring."

"I would . . . Dana, Deirdre, and Dano!"

"Do you still read Aunt Aggie's thoughts and herself far away in New Zealand?"

"On the odd day, mostly when she wants me ma to call her."

I had a horrible thought.

"Does she know what we were doing in bed this afternoon?"

"You're a friggin' amadon, Dermot Michael Coyne. She's only a little girl. She knows her ma and her da love one another and isn't that enough?"

I decided to shut up and watch the setting sun paint the Innishboffin and the other offshore islands rose and gold and silver and then ermine.

I touched my wife's thigh. She sighed complacently.

IF YOU WEREN'T SUCH A WORRIER, YOU'D BE CONTENT WITH THE PLEASURES OF THE DAY, WHICH ARE MORE THAN YOU DESERVE ALTOGETHER.

—4—

"DID SOMETHING terrible happen up there in the mountains behind Letterfrack?" I asked Gerroid McGrail over dessert—Baileys Irish Cream soufflé (a concession to the Yanks who, even in prosperous Ireland, were still an important part of the trade at Ashford Castle).

I had learned from Irish politicians in Chicago that one reserved serious matters for dessert.

Need I say that my wife created a sensation when she walked into the lounge of Ashford, a place of which it was said that it was the kind of castle God would have created if he had as much money as a Philadelphia millionaire. Every eye in the place turned in her direction. Most of them, of whichever gender, remained fixed on her in the lounge and the dining room. Though her only jewelry, in addition to her "sinfully large" engagement ring—which she had never tried to give back—were silver earrings and a silver pendant, she glittered as though she was awash in diamonds. "Isn't it remarkable, Dermot Michael, what a Prozac pill and a good afternoon ride will do for a woman?" The glitter, however, was in her archduchess smile, which she could turn on with professional ease when she was of a mind to do so.

"Will herself agree to sit at the table with Galway peasants like ourselves, Dermot Coyne?" Annie McGrail asked me as she hugged me.

"Peasants like ourselves," Gerroid agreed.

Technically, the elder McGrails were indeed peasants, as was their aristocratic daughter. When I first met them in what I thought were the preliminary stages of our courtship (and Nuala thought, correctly, were the definitive stages), they lived in a stone cottage only marginally better than the ruins we had visited that morning up in the mountain. Like their ancestors for a thousand years, they eked out a living from the harsh Connemara soil and had sent their children to the ends of the earth in search of a better life. Now, courtesy of the European Union and Ireland's incredible prosperity, they lived in a new home and enjoyed a middle-class lifestyle. They fit with ease into the affluence of Ashford Castle.

"It's the telly, isn't it now, Dermot Coyne? We know how to act like we belong in this place from watching posh people like me daughter on the telly."

"On the telly."

" 'Tis not, woman," I replied. "Class has nothing to do with income."

Nuala Anne was a clone of her mother, who was, at sixty or so, a lovely woman, though with a lot more wisdom and common sense than her daughter.

Nuala had begun a conversation with them in Irish as I ordered the drinks.

"Now, child," her mother had said gently, "talk English or your poor husband will think we're talking about him."

Me wife turned crimson.

"Who else would we be talking about, and himself not civilized enough to learn the language?"

"Whom else," I said, causing another surge of crimson.

"Good on you, Dermot Coyne!"

A couple of days every week, we would drive over to Carraroe or the McGrails would join us at Renvyle, allegedly so that the grandparents could spend time with the Mick and Nelliecoyne, but even more to provide time for Nuala to spend with her mother. Later that evening Annie would whisper to me, "The poor thing is a lot better, Dermot. She just needs more time."

This was an uncharacteristically direct statement for a West of Ireland woman. I relaxed. A little . . .

"Up on Diamond Hill," Nuala clarified my request for information.

"Aye, on Diamond Hill . . ."

Both her parents were quiet for a moment. I knew what was coming, a typically indirect, elusive, and opaque conversation. It was the way the Galway Irish normally talk when asked about something even mildly unpleasant.

"You were up there, were you?"

"We were."

"At the ruins, was it now?"

"It was."

"Maamtrasna."

"Is that what it was called?" Nuala asked.

No direct answers.

"Some say," Gerroid spoke slowly, "that there were terrible murders up there during the Land League wars."

"When the tenants weren't paying the rent," Annie added. "Back in the time of Michael Davitt and your man Parnell."

"Some say that maybe it was a secret society thing," her husband continued after a long pause. "Others think maybe it was about the stealing of sheep."

"No one talks about it anymore," Nuala said. "I've never heard a word."

"Heard a word."

Another long pause.

"They say the English hung the wrong man and sent some innocent men to jail."

"Perhaps betrayed by their neighbors."

More silence.

" 'Tis said that there was a big fight about it in the English parliament."

Yet more silence.

"It was all a long time ago."

That was more information than I had expected.

After another pause, Annie sighed the perfect West of Ireland sigh. "Those things should be forgotten, shouldn't they? Hasn't the world changed a lot since then?

"Since then."

I did not disagree. We all knew, however, that the Irish are not a people disposed to easy forgetfulness.

At the table next to us, a little man with silver hair and the angry face of an offended leprechaun was expostulating on the subject of Colm MacManus, member of the Dáil.

"It's about time someone did something about him. He's worse than a gombeen man. He's a crook. There isn't a shady deal in the Dáil that he doesn't have his fingers in. He runs Connemara like Daley runs Chicago. Too bad he wasn't in the house. He has too much power altogether!"

A gombeen man was a crooked businessman.

My fists clenched at the comparison.

"Sean O'Cuiv," Annie McGrail informed us, "is a bit of a gombeen man himself. He and your man have been fighting for years, and himself a land developer."

"Land developer."

"He ought not to be so public about it," I said. "Not today anyway."

"Won't the Gardaí suspect him anyway?"

"Anyway."

Then a handsome young couple approached us shyly and asked Nuala something in Irish as the man handed her an Ashford Castle menu.

She enveloped them in her smile and extended her hand to me for a pen.

"Me ma says I have to speak English when I'm with this lug. Is it your honeymoon now?"

She signed the menu with a big flourish, much unlike her usual accountant's script.

" 'Tis," they sighed, both of them blushing.

"Isn't it a grand place for a honeymoon and meself spending my own here with me first husband."

"And last," I added.

We all laughed.

"We love your songs."

"We hope you'll sing again."

"You never can tell. Right now I have two small ones to take care of."

They thanked her and bashfully bowed away.

She must have signed a dozen more menus with equal grace.

"You were very nice to those people, Nuala love," I said to her as she drove us back to Renvyle.

"They don't bother me, Dermot Michael," she sighed. "Besides, I didn't want to humiliate me parents."

"And themselves teaching you always to be polite to strangers."

"Doesn't the Lord himself come to us as a stranger?"

"And occasionally as a lover too?"

"Sure, doesn't that happen once or twice?"

"Your parents told us more than I thought they would about that place. . . ."

"Maamtrasna."

"I assume that they know even more."

"They won't tell us any more. Isn't it one of those things that the local people don't want to remember but will never forget? Sure, there's probably a few descendants around still, though most of the little villages on the mountains up there have disappeared. You'll have to talk to the parish priest."

I had thought of that myself. Now it was a command performance.

As we neared Renvyle, the touch of fog drifted off. On our left the Twelve Bens loomed over us and the ocean glowed placidly on our right, a nighttime postcard from the Country Galway.

"You can see him in the morning," Nuala commented. "Remember we're going water-skiing in the afternoon."

"In that ocean?"

"There are some perfectly calm coves and won't we be wearing wet suits?"

Later that night, after I had driven Ethne home and checked one last time on the two rugrats, both of whom were sleeping peacefully, I tiptoed into our bedroom.

" 'Tis yourself?"

" 'Tis."

"Come to bed quickly, Dermot Michael. Don't I want to sleep in your arms?"

So I took off my clothes and slipped into bed. We embraced each other happily—love tonight, deep love, no sex required.

"Falling asleep in one another's arms," I whispered, "is in its own way as sweet as making love."

"If you're over thirty," my wife said as she drifted off to sleep.

— 5 —

IN THE United States a perfect spring day is a pretty fair promise of one not too different the next day. Not so in Ireland. When I woke up the next morning, Nuala Anne had left our bed, the wind was rattling the windows, rain was beating down on the roof, and a thick fog blotted out everything more than ten yards from our house.

I dressed in a sweatshirt and pants and shuffled down to the nursery. Fiona had decamped, doubtless to run with her crazy mistress. The rugrats were playing contentedly on their respective pallets.

"Daddy," my daughter complained, "change Mick's diaper. He stinks."

"Right away, ma'am."

I changed the diaper and carried the two of them into the kitchen for breakfast. My daughter devoured hers with prim table manners. My son slobbered happily and covered his face with dire orange-colored stuff.

Then I turned to the preparation of breakfast for herself so it would be ready when she thundered in—Nuala Anne does not so much walk as bolt—muesli, bacon (Irish), orange juice, bagel, and toast.

Just as I was about to dig into my own raisin bran, the front door blew open and the wind rushed into the house, along with it my wife and faithful wolfhound, both soaking wet.

"Isn't it a grand day?" she shouted as she picked up our son and swung him through the air. "A fine soft day!"

"You went swimming!"

"Naturally! Didn't we, Fiona girl?"

The wolfhound barked in agreement and shook her wet fur, as always, so as to transfer the water from herself to me.

"You're both out of your friggin' minds!"

"T'was glorious." Nuala embraced me. She was almost blue with cold. "Not lukewarm like your friggin' Lake Michigan."

Ice cold or not, I was not about to break the embrace.

"Here's your morning tea!"

"I have to jump into the shower first. Keep it warm!"

A typical scene of matutinal bliss in the Coyne family.

An hour later, her long black hair still wet from her swim, dressed in gray slacks and blouse, Nuala received the Gardaí in full solemnity in our parlor, regardless of the fact that the gentry might be upset by our using their domain to receive mere cops.

"Commissioner Keenan sends his very best, Ms. McGrail," Declan McGinn began, "and hopes that you will visit him in Dublin before you return to America."

My wife nodded, now in her archduchess role despite her plastered hair.

"We surely will."

"We wanted to inquire, Nuala Anne," Constable Peig Sayers continued, "whether you have noticed anything while you've been here in Renvyle that might explain the explosion down the road."

If either of the two cops thought it was strange that they should be asking this hoydenish aristocrat for help, they did not show it. They knew that she was "one of them as *knows*." The Irish have no trouble accepting such people's insight, though they were also profoundly skeptical of such folks.

"Well." Nuala sighed. "When I first heard the explosion up above in Letterfrack, I thought it might be the lads, but sure, it wasn't them at all, at all, was it now?"

"We don't think so."

"This is Republican country and all and your man has always supported the lads as much as he can. Besides they wouldn't waste good plastic explosives on blowing up an empty bungalow."

"Precisely," the Chief Superintendent agreed.

"Maybe," Nuala Anne continued, "someone else is trying to send someone a message."

"The Russian Mafia," I suggested.

All three people looked at me as though I was out of my mind.

"There's a couple of fat Slavic types up at Renvyle House," I continued. "With all those Russian planes landing down below at Shannon—twenty-five hundred last year—some of them might have seen money to be made in Irish real estate."

The idea was crazy. Patently so, as the little bishop would say. I was playing games.

"We have looked into them, Mr. Coyne," Peig said, continuing the custom of addressing us as Nuala Anne and Mr. Coyne. "They seem to be honest businessmen."

"There are no honest Russian businessmen," I countered.

"Why would they blow up a T.D.'s house?" Declan McGinn asked.

"Beats me. If they're trying to send a message, they'll probably try again."

Nuala frowned.

"I think you may have the right of that, Dermot Michael."

The two Gardaí paid their respects to Fiona, who waited for them at the door. We promised them that we would stay in touch and report any further insights.

A few minutes after they left, the doorbell rang again. It was our angry little silver-haired leprechaun of the night before, Sean O'Cuiv, hat in hand with an attempt at a genial smile on his face. Nuala Anne politely asked him to come in out of the rain and even brewed a cup of tea for him.

"I hope you were not offended by my overloud comments last night, Mr. and Mrs. McGrail," he said anxiously. "Sure don't I always lose my temper when the subject is Colm MacManus?"

Before I could comment on Chicago, my wife took over.

"Ah well, 'tis a terrible thing altogether to have your house blown up even if you're not in it, isn't it now?"

"It is that, Mrs. McGrail," he said smoothly. "And I asked myself when I came home last night and began to say my prayers how I would feel if the same thing happened to me as happened to poor Colm."

"Did you now?"

"I did, and I realized what a frightening experience it would be and actually prayed to God to help him through the crisis. Even if he has another house in Dublin and rarely uses this one, it must have been terrible to lose all the things he had here."

"Did he have that much?" Nuala wondered.

Fiona wandered in, curious about the strange voice. She sniffed Sean O'Cuiv, who squirmed nervously and murmured, "Good doggie, nice doggie."

Fiona was not convinced. She curled up next to Nuala and watched O'Cuiv intently.

"Beautiful dog," he said nervously.

"Isn't she a grand lady altogether?" Nuala agreed. "Wasn't I after wondering about how much of his worldly goods poor Mr. MacManus had in his house?"

"Not all that much, I suppose. All the valuables, I'm told, are in Dublin. Still it's home, isn't it now?"

" 'Tis," she said with a loud and phony sigh.

Fiona continued to stare suspiciously at our visitor. Nuala patted her massive head.

"Well, I just wanted to tell you that I am as horrified as anyone else at this terrible outrage. I hope it doesn't cause you to leave Ireland. We don't want to frighten off any of our American friends."

"Ah no," my wife assured him. "We're not afraid at all, at all."

Speak for yourself, Nuala Anne.

YOU GUYS OUGHT TO PACK UP AND GO HOME RIGHT AWAY. WHY TAKE ANY CHANCES?

"She'd never agree."

YOU'RE THE BOSS, AREN'T YOU?

"You gotta be kidding."

"Well, I'm delighted to hear that," he said as if the purpose of his visit had been achieved. "I hope you have a grand time during the rest of your stay here at home."

"I'm sure I will, Mr. O'Cuiv, though my home is really in Chicago these days."

ZAP!

Fiona and my wife conducted Sean O'Cuiv to the door and bid him a courteous good day. Well, my wife was courteous. The wolfhound was silent and skeptical, as I was.

"Well," she said after she had closed the door, "sure I hope the wind doesn't sweep him into the ocean."

"Won't he find it warmer outside than he did inside the house!"

"We showed him, didn't we girl?" she said to Fiona, who had stood up and placed her forepaws on Nuala's shoulders.

Nuala hugged her.

"I love you too," she assured the delighted dog.

We returned to the parlor and sat on the couch. Me wife seemed deep in thought.

"It's bad, Dermot Michael, very bad. There are wicked people here in Renvyle. There is worse to come. . . . Now you better go see Father Lane and see what he knows about Maamtrasna."

"Jack Lane, Nuala Anne. Doesn't herself tell me that he's a brilliant priest, but he doesn't use the word 'father' or dress in clericals?"

"Isn't that because of all the sex-abuse scandals? The eejits probably deserve it for all the cover-ups. Still, most priests are good men, like his rivirence and the little bishop."

His reverence is my brother George, who thinks he knows everything, and the little bishop is his boss at the cathedral, who may well know everything.

Unlike some American priests who dress in T-shirts and jeans, Jack Lane looked like a respectable yuppie businessman—gray trousers, blue blazer, light blue shirt, red-and-blue tie, neatly trimmed black hair. Not a commodity broker, more likely a corporate mortgage manager.

He was a big guy, broad shoulders, not as tall as me, low forehead, quick grin.

"Hurling?" I asked.

"Rugby, actually, though I'm a bit long in the tooth for it . . . It's nice of you to stop by, Dermot. I've seen you and your family at Mass. I hope you'll let me take you to supper down in Clifden some night. . . . Should I turn off the disk?"

"I'm never tired of hearing her sing," I said. "Finish this song and then let's talk."

We were both silent for a minute, listening to the end of "Shenandoah."

"She's seen the river, I assume? She sings about it with so much love."

I decided that I liked this priest.

"Neither the Shenandoah nor the wide Missouri. Nor for that matter the Erie Canal or the Mississippi, save from the air. And she's never walked through the Streets of Laredo."

He sighed, shifted his position, and turned off the disk player.

"Let's sit around my coffee table. I don't like to hide behind a desk, though many of my parishioners would rather keep me at a distance."

"As for me wife," I finished my comment on her relationship with the places about which she used to sing, "she imagines all the places she sings about and makes them more real maybe than they really are."

"The river behind the river, I suppose."

"You have the right of it, Jack Lane."

"Let me put the kettle on. . . . You'll take a cup of tea?"

"I will."

"And a biscuit or two?"

"I've been known to have a weakness for a biscuit on the odd occasion."

"Good. Excuse me for a minute . . ."

"Jack Lane?"

"Yes, Dermot Coyne?"

"I don't pollute my tea with milk."

"Seriously?"

"Seriously."

"Well, I'm a multiculturalist, so I won't pass judgment."

He came back in a few moments and devoted himself to the ancient (and often, it seemed to me, timewasting) Irish ritual of steeping and pouring the tea. He did so with the grace of a bishop presiding over a solemn liturgy.

"How can I be of any help to you, Dermot?"

"First of all, you must extend your tolerance to my shanty Irish custom of dunking the biscuit in my milkless tea."

He laughed again. "You're a desperate man altogether, Dermot Michael Coyne. . . . Now, what is it you want to know?"

"You can tell me about Maamtrasna."

"Ah," he said, shifting uneasily. "In the five years I've been here, no one has asked. Yet it is a grand story, one that ought to be told. . . . Would you be after thinking about telling it yourself?"

"I might, if you don't mind. . . . You said it ought to be told. . . . Why?"

I dunked a cookie, as I still insist on calling it, into me tea. My tea.

"To show how corrupt and cruel and incompetent British rule was here. I'm not one of your revisionist historians who want to pretend that, all things considered, the British were pretty benign folk in nineteenth-century Ireland."

"You're a historian?"

"Every Irishman is a historian of a sort. Maybe I'm a little more systematic than some of the others. I try to distinguish between history and legend, though sometimes it's not easy. As a storyteller, of course, your intentions are a bit different, aren't they?"

He also dunked his biscuit, a man after me own heart.

"I have no objection to history so long as it makes a good story."

He laughed, a rich, generous, and happy laugh.

"Well, Maamtrasna would make a great story. Briefly, it was the early eighteen-eighties, and it was clear to everyone who had sense that English barbarism in this country had to come to an end. Unfortunately, most of the leaders in the English government had no sense. In the Land League, Michael Davitt and Charles Stewart Parnell hit on a brilliant strategy that the earlier nineteenth-century revolutionaries, filled as they were with wild rhetoric and romantic incompetence, could not have imagined. The Land League tapped into the agrarian discontent that had produced local violence for two centuries, the violence of men who cared less about a free Ireland and more about owning their own property."

"The twentieth-century leaders didn't quite get it."

"Collins, the bloody eejit, got it, but then he got himself killed. . . . Anyway, the various secret societies had been burning houses, stealing cattle and sheep, killing agents and even an occasional landlord, for at least a century and a half. Generally they are called 'Ribbonmen' because they wore various colored ribbons. They were clumsy, crude, and often brutal. But they did scare the hell out of the English. Davitt and Parnell had the idea of focusing this discontent in a massive refusal to pay rents. Their tactics were mostly nonviolent, anticipating Gandhi by sixty years, just as Collins anticipated urban guerrilla war by a couple of decades. Astonishingly enough, they managed to win much of what they wanted. However, out here in North Galway and Mayo, they had a hard time controlling the violent men, just as the Sinn Fein leaders have now up above. Like some of the IRA, the violent men mixed personal feuds with their political causes. At the time of our story, they had killed a couple of agents and even one English Lord. The Brits in this part of Ireland were scared stiff, as well they might be. Didn't the lads burn Gogarty's hotel down the road in 1922 and himself as Irish as I am? . . . More tea?"

"Yes, please . . . So the killings were the result of revolutionary activity?"

"Not exactly." He sighed as he refilled my teacup. "There were accusations that John Joyce had stolen money from the local secret society. More likely, however, his reputation as a sheep thief was the real motive. He was a big, hulking man, strong and determined. It was said that whenever he saw a sheep he stole it. Sheep were important property in those days. A man with a reputation like his could expect trouble. However, the violence of the killings was out of proportion to the crime of stealing sheep. Why kill three innocent women and a boy because the father of the family stole sheep?"

"Five killings?"

"And another boy barely survived injuries."

"For sheep?"

"My guess, formed perhaps by some evidence I'm going to give you, is that the men involved had discussed it for some time. August seventeenth, 1882, was a hot and humid day. A lot of the drink had been taken, and a plot that had been fantasy suddenly became real. Then, when the killers had disposed of John Joyce, in a mix of fear and fury, they felt they had to kill everyone else, including a lovely sixteen-year-old girl."

"It's hard to believe that anyone could have been so cruel."

I waved off another cup of tea. My thirst and appetite had dried up.

"Only if you don't understand the extreme poverty of the region. You were out here several years ago, weren't you, Dermot?" he asked, reaching into a drawer in his desk.

"Six years ago."

"We were poor people even then, before Ireland became, much to everyone's astonishment, richer than England. There's still some poverty out here, but not like the early nineties. Imagine, if you will, this part of Ireland a hundred years ago as the most densely populated section of Europe even after the famine. Most of the poor people were eking out an existence that was not much different from that of the Stone Age. They were destroying the environment too. The picturesque Connemara countryside, at which you Yanks marvel, is the result of overgrazing and deforestation. The English thought the people here were no better than savages in Africa, in fact probably worse. That they were reducing a people with a rich and ancient culture to savagery never occurred to them."

"It's the Ireland my father's parents left behind."

"A lot changed in the four decades before the Great War. However, at the time of the Maamtrasna killings, life was cheap here. Famine always threatened. Most people did not live very long. If it wasn't for their Catholic faith, there would have been a lot more killing. Moreover, the Church didn't have much influence up above in Maamtrasna. The five murder victims were buried in open ground without a funeral or a priest to bless their graves. In those days the Irish-speaking folk had only a frail connection to Catholicism. Most of the victims and the accused and their families were illiterate, except for the very young like Peggy Joyce, and herself with golden hair the records say, and could neither speak nor understand English. They could no more grasp the rules of English civil society, so-called, than the people Stanley and Livingston met in Africa."

He placed what looked like a manuscript on the coffee table between us.

"You know a lot about it, Jack Lane. Aren't you the one who should be writing the story?"

"I think not." He sighed. "No, not at all."

"And why not, if you don't mind my asking?"

He hesitated.

"No, not at all. It's not the kind of book that a priest could write, even today. A secular historian, should one be interested—that young woman who's your nanny—could do it. But a priest shouldn't. He'd be thought to be disloyal, perhaps rightly so."

"Really?"

"Back in 1982 didn't Father McGreil, you know the Jesuit sociologist who restored the shrine at MauMain, try to place a cross at the Joyce house with the inscription 'pray for the dead,' and didn't he give it up when the locals opposed the project?"

"And why did they oppose it?"

"They told him that the dead should be left alone. Even after a hundred years they were uneasy about what the valley had done."

I considered the manuscript cautiously. What secrets might it hold?

"Disloyal if it told about English cruelty?"

"No." He sighed, almost as loudly as my wife would. "Disloyal because it would have to tell about Irish brutality towards one another."

I said nothing. Jack Lane was determined to tell me the story, but in his own way and his own time.

"You've seen the film by your man about the informer?"

"Ryan's Daughter or Liam O'Flaherty's?"

"O'Flaherty's of course. The theme of the informer is important in Irish literature because so many of our ancestors were informers. In a cruel society, in which the foreign tyrant had reduced most of the population to penury, some men—and the occasional woman—saw informing on their fellows as the only way to survive. There is solid reason to believe that one innocent man was executed and others went to prison because some of their friends and neighbors saw a chance to pick up a few English pounds by falsely accusing them."

"And they survived?"

"They did and a few—a very few—of their descendants are members of my parish still."

"Wow!"

"Moreover, the people of the valley knew who the real killers were. They never denounced them to the English because they feared the wrath of English law if they told the unpleasant truth."

"My God!"

"Oh yes, Dermot Coyne. The real killers continued to live in the valley, even when innocent men were released after twenty years of prison."

"And survived?"

"There seemed to be no taste for vengeance after twenty years. Everyone seemed eager to forget about the murders. Some of the killers' descendants also live in my parish."

"They know you know about it?"

"No reason why they should . . . They know the story, however, in some mythological form. Alas, they don't comprehend the dangerous truth that lurks behind the myth—people who live in a cruel tyranny can easily be cruel to each other."

I nodded solemnly.

"I understand."

"Do you, Dermot Coyne? What do you understand?"

"That the story would reveal that the Irish lived up to the stereo-types the occupying power had created."

"Of course . . . The Irish-speaking culture is not warlike. It is gentle and quiet. It becomes violent only when pushed into the ground and violence is seen as necessary for survival. Even then it is not very good at killing, which is why we lost all the wars. The remnants of Maam-trasna living in this parish are quiet and gentle indeed and no longer are forced to be violent as were their ancestors. The story of Maam-trasna should be told, but not by the priest."

"I understand," I said again.

"Here is a strange manuscript." He pushed the stack of handwritten papers across the coffee table. "I found it when I arrived here, tucked away in the cellar. It's part of a longer manuscript. I haven't been able to find the rest of it, though to tell the truth, I haven't looked very hard."

" 'A Diary of a Galway Crime, by Edward Hannigan Fitzpatrick, 1882,' " I read, squinting at the old-fashioned handwriting.

"Your man was a young fellow, probably even younger than you. From your home city, in fact. Went on to become a journalist there. Lots of money. Came to Ireland in search of his family's history. Galway Town, not at all like our area out here."

"He is a reliable reporter?"

"Oh yes, he's all of that. Candid about himself. I don't know how the manuscript ended up in this parish house. He wrote about the story for one of your Chicago papers, accurately as far as I can tell from the quotes I've seen. For some reason he must not have wanted to take it home with him."

I glanced at my watch.

"Jack Lane, I am in deep trouble. Me wife, er, MY wife is waiting for me to go water-skiing. I'm already forty-five minutes late. Excuse me for running . . . May I read this?"

"Surely . . . I'll search for the rest of it. Ease my sense of responsi-bility. We can talk about what to do with it later."

I thanked him, shook his hand, and departed hastily, shielding the precious manuscript under my Chicago Bulls denim jacket (a memento of a happier time).

I was soaking wet when I stumbled into the bungalow. In the family room, my son had arrayed a fleet of trucks around himself, and my daughter was carefully constructing what might be a house with her building blocks.

"Dermot Michael Coyne! You've been lollygagging with the priesteen all morning."

"He's not little, Nuala Anne McGrail. He played rugby."

"For Ireland," Ethne interjected, proud that her local priesteen had represented the country in international play.

"Regardless, we have to leave now to go skiing and can't with yourself soaking wet. Go put on dry clothes, or you'll catch your death."

I had long since given up trying to persuade my wife that colds are caused by a virus and not by wet clothes.

"Did it ever occur to you, woman of the house, that the very fact that I'm soaking wet should dispense us from skiing?"

"If you're wet, you're wet," she said imperiously. "Hurry up now! Isn't poor Ethne dying to learn how to ski?"

Ethne's face suggested that this statement was something less than literal truth.

"Didn't he give me a manuscript?"

"Did he now?"

Manuscripts like that of Edward Hannigan Fitzpatrick had led to the solution of many of the mysteries on which we had stumbled.

I showed it to her.

"Och, isn't that wonderful, Dermot Michael, and meself a terrible witch?"

"I'll change my clothes," I said, enjoying the (temporary) moral superiority I had earned. "I don't want to keep Ethne waiting."

That young woman and perhaps future historian looked as though she wouldn't lament a delay. At all, at all.

In our bedroom, I debated donning swim trunks and chose discretion over valor. The Maamtrasna painting was back on its easel, more detailed and more terrifying than ever. The murdered young woman had golden hair. One of the two boys seemed to be alive. The dead man was, as Jack Lane had said, a hulk.

It was the first time I had seen proof of the detailed accuracy of my wife's, what shall I call it, psychic sensitivity.

Why *not* bet on the market on the basis of such evidence?

"Dermot Michael Coyne, are you wearing a swimsuit?"

"Woman, I'm not!"

"Sure, 'tis your call, isn't it now?"

My phrase turned against me.

Nuala and Ethne bundled our children, who were patently (as the little bishop would say) not eager to leave the warmth and the turf fire smell of the family room, into sweaters and rain slickers. They collected blankets and towels and clean jeans and sweatshirts for the return trip. The Mick would not leave his trucks, and Nelliecoyne refused to relinquish her toys.

Naturally, Fiona had to come.

"Sure we can't leave her here to be blown up with the house, can we now?"

Finally, we departed towards the small lake where, allegedly, there was a water-skiing facility. I wished that I had brought along the Fitzpatrick manuscript to read while the young women, as I had come to think of them, were frolicking in the lake.

It was not, to tell the truth, all that much of a lake, not in the same category as Lake Michigan or even Pine Lake, to which we retreated when Michigan was too angry to permit us to ski. This lake, which had an Irish name that I could not catch, was at the most two miles around, with a small tree-covered island on the far side. Island trees sometimes escaped deforestation because Irish culture had decided that islands were sacred, that is more sacred than other things in a land where the sacred loomed everywhere.

The perverse Irish winds had chosen the moment we arrived at the lake, having bumped down a muddy dirt road, to sweep the sky clean of clouds and leave the little mud puddle of a lake an inviting turquoise.

"See, Dermot Michael Coyne, aren't you disappointed now that you didn't wear your swimsuit?"

"No."

"Go 'long with you!"

"That boat is older than the Republic of Ireland and the motor produced fifty horsepower only when it was brand-new, and that was a long time ago."

"Well, I suppose it wouldn't be able to lift a big, old man out of the water."

That was unfair.

The "water-skiing facility" was a rundown frame house, an equally rundown little pier, and a wooden boat that might be useful for fishing, but little else. An elderly couple were in charge and welcomed us with characteristic Irish hospitality, offering us a small drop of something to keep us warm on the water. The young women declined, but Mr. Coyne, who was neither driving nor skiing, said he wouldn't mind a wee jar at all, at all. Our host and hostess reacted as though my request had made their day a complete success.

"The boats at Grand Beach have four times as much power," I whispered to my bride.

"Isn't that because they have to pull old men out of the water?"

After she had picked over a range of decrepit wet suits, she and Ethne retreated to the bedroom of the house and emerged after considerable delay in wet suits, which included wet boots. I arranged the children near the single window of the house so that they could watch Ma and play with their blocks and trucks.

I thanked the angels for inspiring my decision to avoid the challenge.

Rory, the man of the house, went out to the boat and, using a funnel, poured maybe half a gallon of gas into the tank of the old outboard. Nuala gave Ethne detailed instructions on how to bounce out of the water. The skis, I noted, as my wife carefully fit them on the young woman, may well have existed before the founding of the Republic.

Fiona, who had showed little interest in joining us in the house, was poking around the environment, sniffing for other dogs who might be present.

"Come on, kids," I said, lifting the Mick into my arms, "let's watch Ma hotdog."

"Hotdog, is it?" my wife said, a dangerous edge in her voice.

Neither child seemed interested in my suggestion. However, Nelliecoyne, with a sigh, abandoned her blocks, captured her current favorite dolly, and walked out with me.

After several minutes of tugging at the starter cord, Rory was able to persuade the ancient motor to come reluctantly to life. Still carrying their purses, Nuala and Ethne climbed into the boat, which seemed to me to sink dangerously close to the waterline. They putt-putted out into the lake. The winds died. The water was as smooth as glass or—as I thought—a sheet of ice.

Rory stopped the boat twenty yards offshore. Fiona snuggled up to me, uneasy about the whole process. My son, who had never seen his mother ski, began to make noises like the beginning of a howl.

"Hush, Mick," his sister ordered. "Ma's going to ski!"

With that Nuala Anne, having tossed out the tattered rope and the aging ski, dove into the lake with supple grace. She shouted briefly with the shock of the cold and then yelled, "Och, Dermot Michael, 'tis brilliant!"

The Mick wailed. Fiona barked. Nelliecoyne, having seen it all before, was bored.

Rory started the boat and pulled the line taut. I wondered whether there was power enough to pull my wife out of the water.

She popped up immediately. I feared she would tilt the craft over its stern. However, it struggled manfully—you should excuse the expression—and chugged around the lake as best it could. My wife shouted triumphantly.

She was a picture of pure grace as she cut back and forth across the wake, a sketch of beauty against the blue lake and the sun-drenched sky. Fiona barked approval, and the Mick stopped his howl.

Then it was Ethne's turn, on two skis, naturally.

"Won't she get up right away? She's a canogie player, isn't she now?"

Canogie is the women's version of hurling, one of the Irish national sports. It equips a couple score of Irish women with clubs and a puck and sets them loose on a field. To compare it to hockey is unfair to the civilized gentleness of hockey.

Poor, sweet Ethne, as my wife called her (in her absence), made it up on her third try and circled the lake once, screaming hysterically. She tried to cross the wake and flew into the air with a wondrous somersault.

Nelliecoyne clapped her hands in approval.

"I'll take another turn," Nuala informed her, "and then you can do it again."

She dived in again, rose triumphantly from the lake, now rough from the wakes the ski boat had created, and shouted joyously as she rose and skimmed the waters.

This was the Nuala Anne I had married, a young hoyden innocent of depression.

Then a crackling sound cut the air. Rifle shots, I thought. Nuala fell into the water.

I heard a scream.

It was mine.

—6—

THE WORLD went into slow motion. Nuala was swimming towards the boat, too slowly I thought. Bullets were slashing all around her.

Marie, Rory's wife, was keening, an Irish cry for the dead, a wail that began with three low notes and then two soul-wrenching high notes. Fiona was howling; the Mick was screaming.

Nelliecoyne clutched my hand.

"Ma's all right, Da. She's all right."

Ethne hauled my wife into the boat. Rory huddled on the thwarts, a man paralyzed. Ethne climbed over him and grabbed the lazily spinning wheel. She aimed the boat towards shore as the rifle bullets pinged in the water behind them.

I was numb, frozen, dead. I could not move, speak, even feel. Marie was still keening, Fiona was still barking, the Mick was still wailing. It was a nightmare. It wasn't really happening. Soon I would wake up.

And the little girl next to me was still clutching my hand, still muttering, "Don't worry, Da. Ma is all right. The bad man wasn't trying to hit her."

The boat nudged against the dock. Ethne put the motor into reverse. The engine died. The boat started to slip away from the dock.

YOU FOCKING EEJIT! DO SOMETHING!

"What!"

GO HOLD THE BOAT!

"Right!"

GIVE THE KID TO HIS SISTER!

"Right!"

In a trance, I put the Mick on the ground.

"Take care of him, Nelliecoyne."

"Yes, Da!"

Fiona stopped barking and thundered over to take charge of both children.

With my lead feet slogging through a bog, I stumbled onto the pier and grabbed the bow of the boat. I pulled it to the pier.

And fell into the water.

"Dermot Michael Coyne!" a familiar voice shouted, "Whatever are you doing to yourself! You'll catch your death!"

God designed me to be a comic hero.

Nuala Anne tied the bow of the boat to the dock and pulled me out of the water. As I lay on the dock, shivering uncontrollably, she and Ethne lifted poor Rory out of the boat. I struggled to my feet. Ethne was talking to someone on her cellular phone—everyone in Ireland has one! Marie had stopped keening and was now singing a lullaby to the Mick. Nelliecoyne had her arms around Fiona's neck. The world was slipping back to its proper form.

YOU FOCKING AMADON. MADE A RIGHT PROPER GOBSHITE OUT OF YOURSELF, DIDN'T YOU!

Then my wife clung to me, shuddering but alive.

"Och, Dermot love, I'm so sorry!"

"You didn't push me in the water," I said through quivering lips.

"I was terrible mean to you, and meself thinking I would die without telling you I was sorry and I love you with all my heart!"

"I'm not processing things very well, I'm afraid."

BECAUSE YOU'RE THE GREATEST ASSHOLE IN THE WESTERN WORLD. YOU LET THAT SHITEHAWK SHOOT AT YOUR POOR WIFE.

"Dermot Michael, don't you need a good strong shot of the creature and meself a hot cup of tea!"

Then she seized her daughter and swept her into the air.

"I told me da that the man wasn't trying to kill you," the little redhead informed her mother. "But I was scared too."

"So was I, me love, so was I. But we're all fine now, aren't we?"

"Yes, Ma."

A few moments later I was in the cabin, wrapped in towels and drinking my second "small jar."

"The focker was on the island," Rory said for the fourth time. "He must have rowed over in a dory and hidden the boat."

"His car was on the far shore," Nuala added grimly. "I'll know him when I see him. I may break his friggin' neck."

How would she know him when she saw him?

Better not ask.

"He wasn't trying to hit you," Ethne said. "Just to scare you?"

"If he was trying to hit me, wouldn't I be dead?" She shivered, slighted. "Still, what if he had killed me by mistake, the friggin' gobshite!"

"You're planning on catching him?"

"Of COURSE!"

The children were back with their toys. Fiona was curled up protectively at her mistress's feet.

Everyone was treating me gently, as though I had been the intended victim.

"Aren't you grand at the water-skiing, Ethne?" Nuala asked. "The next time you'll be after doing it on one ski!"

Next time, indeed.

Then, with considerable noise, a large delegation of the Galway Garda arrived on the scene—cars, vans, and swarming blue-clad officers. Peig Sayers and Declan McGinn in the lead. At the sight of all the constables, Fiona went mad with delight.

"We'll get the focker," Nuala Anne informed them. "Don't I know what he looks like?"

"He was on the island?"

Chief Superintendent McGinn wondered how she could have seen him.

"He was . . . hiding in the bushes . . . and look what I found in the boat!"

She opened her hand.

A spent rifle slug.

I ALMOST FEEL SORRY FOR THE FOCKER.

"It's a miracle he missed you."

"He wasn't trying to hit me. The only danger was that he'd hit me by mistake."

Declan McGinn tried to take that in.

"How do you know he wasn't trying to hit you?"

"Because he didn't. . . . These people, whoever they are, don't want to murder anyone. Why blow up an empty house? Don't they want to scare us?"

"Why shoot at a world-famous singer?"

"Retired singer at that. But did they know it was me?"

Later in bed, during our afternoon nap, and after a frantic bout of love in which we both grasped desperately for life, my wife was busily kissing me. All over.

"Och, Dermot, aren't you still practically frozen to death?"

"Woman, I am not. Didn't you set me on fire?"

"I mean inside. It was a terrible thing that happened to you."

"They weren't shooting at me, Nuala Anne."

"But I knew they weren't trying to hit me."

"So did I. Our daughter kept telling me."

The kissing paused for a moment.

"Did she ever? Ah, that child is really one of the dark ones, isn't she? Still, she's a good little girl and she'll be all right."

I offered no comment.

She began to kiss me again. Frantically, as though she were afraid of losing me.

Outside the rain and the winds had returned. Gardaí swarmed around our house. Better late than never. We had invited them inside, but they declined. Fiona wanted to join them, but we kept her in the house "because of her condition, Dermot Michael."

"I thought to myself when the first bullet went by me ear, poor Dermot! If he only knew that night at O'Neill's pub on College Green when I decided that I wanted him, he would have run away in the fog."

This was revisionism, pure and simple. Long ago, however, I learned not to disagree.

"I said to meself as I fell into the water, the poor dear man, he didn't know he would end up with a bitchy wife with a nasty mouth and like as not to be depressed and too fey altogether, and meself never loving him properly."

"Bossy too . . ."

"Be quiet, Dermot Michael. I'm talking."

"Yes, ma'am. If you continue to kiss me that way, you're likely to get assaulted again."

"Isn't that the general idea? . . . Now be quiet so I can finish what I'm saying. Wasn't I saying to God as I swam towards the boat, if you let me live, won't I try to be a perfect wife all the time? Won't I keep me bitchy, bossy mouth shut? Won't poor, dear Dermot be happy he married me?"

"And what did God say?"

"I'm not sure, Dermot Michael. I think he laughed at me."

When I woke up later, the sun was shining through the blinds and I was alone in our drenched and savaged bedsheets. I tried to figure out where I was and what had happened. Then I remembered the shots out on the lake. I sat up with a start. . . . No, my wife had survived. So, come to think of it, had I, though with little of my dignity left.

Then I remembered what had happened to our sheets and my troubled mind caught up with my complaisant body.

God had laughed at her, had he?

Well, good enough for God, but what did God expect me to do with her?

LAUGH TOO, YA FRIGGIN' EEJIT!

"Then what?"

I struggled out of bed as the memories of our amusement flooded back. Well, I couldn't complain to God about her as a bed partner, could I now?

YOU'D BETTER NOT!

What would it take to persuade her that I didn't regret my choice at all? Or maybe she knew it already but thought I should.

I picked up the Fitzpatrick manuscript.

I looked up and saw a drawing of a man's face on her easel.

The man with the rifle?

Who else?

— 7 —

I SAT down, opened the Fitzpatrick manuscript, and began to read it.

Galway, August 14, 1882

I have decided to keep a diary of this trip. I'm not sure why. Perhaps to remind myself as the years go on how I felt in the depths of my soul, as distinct from the dispatches I'll send to the Daily News.

I have come here in search of adventure and romance and perhaps an Irish wife. I didn't tell this to my family, though they might have guessed it. As my mother says, I am the romantic in the family.

"Thank the good lord that we have at least one in the family," my mother adds.

I wish to test and to prove my manhood. I desire to develop the pure and upright character the Jesuits at St. Ignatius advocated for a man who wants to be a Catholic gentleman. I want to be the kind of steady, stalwart man my father is. I want to be reliable and dependable in time of crisis, a credit to myself and my family and my religion and my country. I want to be gentle and protective with women. Is that romantic? I don't know. I do know that cowardice and concupiscence tear at my soul, putting my salvation in jeopardy. I will never be a brave and gentle man unless I can master these two demons.

Now I feel very lonely for my family and my friends in Chicago. I've never been away from them for more than a weekend or two. I miss them

terribly. I did not think I would. Add loneliness to cowardice and concupiscence.

I also desire to have my way with a woman, in a fashion I never did
when I was at home. I suppose that's because I'm lonely.

I am terribly depressed by the poverty, the misery, and the dirt here.
Galway is a gloomy, depressing place—gray and ugly and foreboding. The
people walk around with their eyes down. Most of them live on the edge of
destitution. They are thin, emaciated, pale. I want to help them all.

It is worse, I am told, out in the countryside.

The help here at the Great Southern Hotel are better off, so polite and
quiet and eager to please. They speak English, as do the shopkeepers and the
publicans and the businessmen in town. Many of the ordinary people, especially those who come in from the country for market, speak only Irish, a
fact of which they seem to be ashamed. The hotel manager told me that the
country people will continue to be poor until they learn to speak English like
civilized human beings. He, of course, is English. He also says that the
country folk are the last of the white savages and that in another generation
English rule will have ended the savagery.

I don't like him very much.

The people seem to me to be very friendly. They avoid me because my
clothes mark me as a gentleman. Yet when I ask for directions they smile
shyly and give me elaborate directions that I can't understand. They blush
when I offer them a shilling for a tip and pretend they can't take it. When
I insist, however, they do, with much gratitude.

In the pubs at night they guess quickly that I'm American and not
English. Then, when they learn that my grandparents came from this city,
though before the famine, I am made to feel most welcome.

Were the people in Galway this poor when my grandfather and grandmother ran away? They never talk much about their lives here. They have
no desire to return for a visit, though they certainly can afford it. I think I
understand that now.

In the pubs at night, there is laughter and song and not too much drinking. I buy a round each night because I'm a visitor from America. How can
people who live such sad lives be so happy?

Maybe that's what it means to be Irish.

Still, we're not poor at home and we sing and tell stories. Maybe the Irish don't have to be poor to be happy.

This morning a ferryman rowed me across the Corrib River—which runs through the city like the canals run through Venice—to a fishing village they call Claddagh, which means quay. It's a most unusual place. The ferryman said that they consider themselves an independent kingdom with their own king and speak a very different kind of Irish. The tiny houses are made of piles of stone and thatch, and the streets of the village twist and turn. The people seem very different from those on the other side of the river, more confident and proud. They stared at me in my American clothes, more curious than unfriendly.

The women wear red petticoats, which are quite striking. Some of them are very handsome, unlike the poor women in the city, who seem worn and old even when they are surely the age of my sisters. They sit at the doors of their huts, waiting for their husbands to return and either smoking clay pipes or singing haunting lullabies to their attractive children.

I stood and listened to one woman singing to a newborn babe. She looked up and smiled at me, as if she thought I adored the child as much as she did. At that moment I think I did.

An Irish Madonna.

"Strange people," said the ferryman as he rowed me back. "There's them that say it's the way we all were before the English came. Fishermen make good money sometimes."

"Is it a dangerous life?"

"They fish mostly on the bay, which isn't too bad except when the big storms come in. Still, a lot of them die young."

It was a melancholy comment for a melancholy day. I would leave for home tomorrow, if I did not seem a coward.

Galway, August 15, 1882

Yesterday was another hot and humid day, with a haze over the city. Even with the windows open in my hotel room, it was stifling. I'm sure it is worse in Chicago this time of year, but somehow the heat in Chicago always seemed tolerable.

There is a small college here for the children of the "better class," the hotel manager told me. I found the college pub last night, on the banks of one of the streams which are the delta of the river. The young people— students and young women—were much better dressed than those in the pub on the square, where I was the night before. They were, however, just as relaxed and friendly and happy to meet an American. Some of them were Protestants, sons and daughters of agents and managers, and some were Catholics, children of doctors and lawyers and accountants, the first sign of prosperous Catholics I have encountered here.

I was surprised that seemingly well-to-do young women were in the pub, as relaxed and confident as the young men. I found myself talking to a girl named Regina, a young Protestant woman (something which never happened in Chicago). Her father is an agent for one of the great landowners up in County Mayo. He has sent her to live with an aunt in Galway town because there is so much danger in the countryside. The Land League has organized the people into a campaign of refusing to pay their rents. The secret societies are active again, she says, murdering agents like her father and even one major landlord. There is fear in her eyes as she says this.

"We're Irish too," she tells me, "even though we're Protestants. We're entitled to rents from our land and to a life without terror. The rebels are brutal killers. They kill their own and they kill us. I wish we could go home to England, but England isn't really home."

"Can't the government stop the killings?"

"Mr. Gladstone is afraid of Mr. Parnell and the Irish Nationalist members of Parliament. I'm afraid he'll send in the army only after there are more killings. Then it might be too late for us. . . . My father is loved by the tenants, but that doesn't mean he's safe."

"What do the tenants want?"

"They want to take our land away from us."

I did not argue with her. I was afraid to hurt her. Yet it seems to me that the land is not theirs but belongs to the starving people.

She was an attractive young woman and pleasant to talk to. As we talked I imagined kissing her and taking off her clothes. She too was lonely. However, I could not fall in love with a Protestant, especially one who was caught up in the horror that apparently rules this poor land. We parted as friends. I promised her that I would come back to the pub, but I doubted very much that I would.

I dreamed about her all night. I tried to protect her from masked men who were attacking her. I failed. They beat her to death with clubs.

I wish I were home.

August 18, 1882

There's been a brutal murder up in the mountains of the Connemara region. A family of five sheep farmers murdered in their beds at night. Roderick Doyle, the Chief Superintendent of the Royal Ulster Constabulary in Galway, to whom the manager of the hotel had introduced me, knowing that I was a reporter, invited me to accompany him and his men on the ride up the mountains where the crime occurred.

I don't want to go. Five bloody bodies in this hot weather! I fear I am not much of a reporter. Nor, despite my mother, a romantic in search of adventure. I have the heart of a romantic perhaps, but the stomach of a stay-at-home.

However, I must go.

August 20, 1882

The last two days have been terrible. The ride on horseback along the coast and then up into the mountains in the unbearably hot weather was exhausting. Connemara is an exceedingly sterile place. There are almost no trees, only bogs and rocks and sterile mountains in the distance. The ocean seemed sullen and menacing. Though I am an experienced rider, I was exhausted when we finally arrived at the "hut"—an iron building—just beyond the town of Letterfrack, a pretty little place where the Quaker influence is strong, I am told. Then we had to go into the hut for the coroner's autopsy.

Outside the hut a mass of people—several hundred at least—were gathered. The women, in their red petticoats and tattered shawls, were moaning a strange, unearthly dirge that cut at my heart with its despair and sadness and stayed there. The men, in old and rough brown clothes, stood, caps in hand, silent, passive, and grim. They reminded me of the sharecroppers along the Illinois Central tracks when my father took us to New Orleans. These folks were indeed sharecroppers too. That would be the lead of the story I would file in the telegraph office in Letterfrack before the day was over.

Then we entered the hut. If hell is like that hut, I certainly do not want to go there.

The heat inside was worse than outside, but I hardly noticed the heat because of the stench of the five bodies stretched out on tables. Mr. Bolton, the Crown Prosecutor from Tipperary, a lean, haggard man with a white beard and a derby hat, was presiding over the autopsy. He was accompanied by ten tall men who, I would learn, always traveled with him.

"Pretty little picture, isn't it, Chief Superintendent? Shows how creative our Irish savages can be. The doctor is finishing his report for us. Then I have some interesting information for you. . . . You were saying, Doctor?"

I hope never to see anything like those five bodies ever again. Three woman beaten brutally to death, heads cracked open, faces purple and blood-soaked, bodies a mass of vicious wounds. One seemed young. She had golden hair that must have been beautiful. Grandmother, mother, and daughter, the doctor said. The fourth was a boy whose face had been bashed in beyond recognition. The man's head had been torn by gaping bullet wounds.

I rushed for the door to vomit.

A sergeant, not one who had come over the barren mountains with us, stood next to me as I retched up everything that was inside me and then kept on retching.

"Let it come, Eddie boy. There's not a man among us who hasn't done the same thing."

"What kind of monsters would do that to three women and a child?"

"Monsters who were probably drunk. Don't worry, we'll get them and they'll swing for it."

Regina had told me the night before that many killers were still on the loose in Galway and Mayo. Somehow, it did not make me feel any better that the men who had committed such a terrible crime would suffer a horrible death themselves.

"Will they really hang?"

"Please, God," he said, making the sign of the cross. Perhaps, I thought, he is not so certain.

"Thanks for standing by, Sergeant . . ."

"Finnucane, lad. Tommy Finnucane."

I shook his hand. We grinned at each other, despite the horror. Two Irishmen who understood one another.

"You think this was a drunken brawl?"

"The lads out here may kill one another in a brawl, but not women. There's something deep going on."

"Will they catch the killers?"

"Mr. Bolton always finds killers, lad. Not necessarily the real ones."

So he wasn't so sure.

"Everyone seems to be named Joyce," I said.

" 'Tis confusing to an outsider, I'm sure. This is Joyce country up here, lad. There are three Joyce families in the Maamtrasna valley: the Johnny Joyce family that was wiped out, though they have relatives and allies around here still, the Myles Joyce family, at the other end of the valley, and the Anthony Joyce family, which has informed on the Myles Joyce family, though your man George Bolton isn't telling anyone that yet. To make matters more obscure, they are all intermarried, so it's hard to tell which of the three clans someone named Joyce might belong to. None of the three get along with each other.

"Myles and the late John are big, strong men. They've fought in public for a long time. No one around here, however, thinks that they would kill one another, even though Myles has said often enough that John was the worse sheep thief in the whole West of Ireland. Tony Joyce, on the other hand, is a weakling, but with a loud mouth. His branch of the clan and the Myles Joyce branch have been at war with one another for generations, bitter war at that."

"He is the one who is informing on the Myles Joyce bunch, accusing them of murder? Does Mr. Bolton know that?"

"He doesn't know and doesn't care. Anthony and his two brothers are already called, 'independent and unreproachable witnesses.' "

"Men who might be settling a grudge?"

"You got it, lad."

"I'll try to keep it straight."

"To complicate things even more, there are two Casey families—Big

John Casey, who is the most prosperous man around here, and Little Tom Casey who is also well enough off. They get along with one another well enough, though their relatives have complicated relations with the various Joyce clans. That bothers Little Tom, whose son Young Tom is one of the accused, but Big John doesn't give a damn."

"Three Joyce families—John is dead along with his own immediate family, Myles and his allies stand accused by Anthony and two of his friends. Two Casey families involved to some extent with one or the other factions—Big John and Little Tom and Little Tom's son Young Tom is accused."

"You have the right of it, lad."

I went back into the hut, fought down my gorge this time, and tried to listen.

"So what will you report to the coroner's jury, Doctor?" Mr. Bolton asked in a supercilious tone.

I now had the presence of mind to start scribbling in my notebook.

"Premeditated murder by person or persons unknown."

"You think one person could have committed this abominable crime, Doctor?"

"That is up to the police to discover, sir. I will report my opinion to the jury the day after tomorrow."

"Very good, Doctor . . . Chief Superintendent Doyle, I believe you are in charge now that you have finally arrived. Would you please tell that rabble outside that they can have their corpses tomorrow morning to dispose of them as they see fit."

"Yes, Mr. Bolton . . . Sergeant Finnucane, would you please translate for me into the natives' language?"

"Don't any of them speak any English?" I asked my new friend.

"Some of the younger people who have been to the National School have a bit of it. An occasional older person understands it, lad. This is a foreign country out here."

Another line for the story I would file.

I trailed them out of the hut. The wailing stopped.

"The doctor has finished his work. His opinion is that Margaret, Breige, and Peggy Joyce were murdered, as were John Joyce and Michael Joyce. You

may collect the bodies tomorrow morning to dispose of as you see fit. The police investigation will continue."

There was a slight stir in the silent mass of natives.

Tommy Finnucane translated it all into Irish—a savage language, perhaps, but a singularly melodic one.

As soon as he was finished, the keening, which is what they call the wailing, began anew. It sounded like a cry from the depths of hell. Men were passing bottles of a clear white liquid to one another.

I wished that I were home on North Park Avenue in Chicago, safe within the confines of family warmth. All my dreams of manliness in time of crisis had been dashed the first day of my adventure.

"Some will go home," Tommy told me. "Others will stay all night. There'll be a lot more for the burial tomorrow."

"Will there be a requiem Mass tomorrow?"

"Not very likely. Way out here is no priest country."

I didn't know what to make of that.

"They're Catholic, aren't they?"

"Oh, they are that all right. Look at the women with their rosaries. Catholics in their own way. Masses cost money, and they don't have any money."

Then I saw the most beautiful woman I had ever observed in my life. She was tall and graceful, with black hair and a glorious young body. She stood erect and proud as if in this rabble of near slaves she was a free woman, come what may. She was tolling her rosary beads, her lips moving in prayer. Tears were slipping down her sad and lovely face. She was not keening, however. Somehow, she held herself aloof from this old custom. One hand rested on the arm of a stocky man next to her, doubtless her husband.

My romantic dreams, I told myself, were folly. Still, she was so elegant as to linger in my imagination, a countess perhaps, lost in a world that was not really hers. Now both cowardice and concupiscence possessed me.

We walked back towards Letterfrack as the sun began to slip towards the distant ocean. Blessedly the temperature fell rapidly, and a sea breeze stirred the air.

"You had information for me, Mr. Bolton?" Roderick Doyle asked the prosecutor.

"I do indeed, sir. Your local men have been very effective, for which I congratulate you. They have information received," he winked at the superintendent "from eyewitnesses to the crime. These eyewitnesses heard the criminals abroad last night and followed them to the scene of the crime. They heard the cries and the shouts from inside John Joyce's house. They are willing to testify in exchange for British coin."

Next to me, Tommy Finnucane sighed and whispered a single word: "Informers."

"How many killers?"

"Ten men, sir. Three of whom went into the house and did the actual killing. I suggest that you interview the witnesses in the morning and have your forces arrest the criminals before the day is over. Would that we could resolve all the murders out here so easily."

"Indeed, Mr. Bolton."

Somehow I thought that Doyle was less enthusiastic than he should have been. Perhaps he shared Sergeant Finnucane's skepticism about informers.

In my small room, in an inn in Letterfrack, I wrote my story, then brought it over to the telegraph office. The operator was preparing to shut down for the night when I appeared. He glanced over my message, nodded thoughtfully, and began to dispatch it to the Chicago Daily News.

What a remarkable world we live in, I thought, when you can send a message from this foreign and savage land to Chicago almost instantly. Then I came back here and scrawled out my feelings. I will not even try to reread them tonight. Or ever.

Much later.

As the sun was setting at the end of the long August day and I was preparing for bed, there was a respectful knock at my door.

"Sergeant Finnucane, sir."

I opened the door.

"Yes, Tommy?"

"I wonder, lad, and yourself being a journalist, whether you'd like to come to the wake. I expect they're different out here from anything you might see in the States."

All I wanted to do was to go to bed and blot out the miseries of the day with a few hours of sleep. I was a journalist, however, and must live up to the solemn and serious obligations of my profession.

"Thank you very much, Tommy. I'd like very much to see the wake."

"You better take your coat, Eddie. It'll be cool with the sun going down."

We hiked up the mountain in the moonlight. The air was still. From a long way off I heard the keening.

"Have the bodies been released?"

"Not till tomorrow."

"How can they have a wake without a body?"

"They'll be outside around the corpse house. It's not the usual way, but there must be a wake."

"Strange."

"It's all of that. . . . There's been a new development, lad. Young Patrick Joyce has been laying in one of the outhouses since yesterday morning. He's in terrible pain. One of our lads has been begging people to help him. They refuse to do so. The resident magistrates knew there was a doctor staying at the inn over in Outhergard. He brought him here just a few hours ago. He said that the lad could live if he was given attention. Some of our lads carried him away."

"Why would they not help him?"

"They're afraid of something, perhaps that if Patsy lives maybe he'll identify the killers, though he told our lads that he did not recognize the three men that came into the house because their faces were covered with dirt."

"It seems heartless."

"They're frightened. Still, they'll all say thanks be to God if Patsy lives."

We came upon the wake scene. At least two hundred people were gathered outside the house in the eerie light of the full moon. The women, sitting for the most part in a semicircle, were either keening or smoking clay pipes. The men milled closer to the house, grim and silent as they passed around bottles of a clear liquid, which I gathered was something called poteen.

"They aren't talking much, Tommy."

"Not with police all around."

We walked into the crowd of men. They nodded at Tommy, but did not speak to him. He said a word or two in Irish to one of the men, who passed the bottle of poteen to Tommy, who in his turn gave it to me.

"Take a sip, lad, so you'll know what it's like."

I took a sip and felt that someone might have blown off the top of my head. The man who had given us the bottle smiled slightly and said something to Tommy in Irish. I returned the bottle and thanked him.

"He said you're a game one, lad. In a few weeks you'd be drinking as well as the rest of them."

"I don't think so."

Liquor leads to both cowardice and concupiscence.

"See that stocky man over there with the young wife?"

"The woman who's saying the rosary?"

"The very one. . . . The man is Myles Joyce."

"Does he know he's accused?"

"I'm sure he does not. Yet, he's certainly a dead man."

I shivered.

— 8 —

August 21, 1882

Today began even warmer than yesterday. I ate a slice of toast and drank a pot of weak tea for breakfast and then set out for the Royal Irish Constabulary hut. Even in the center of the town we heard the keening.

"Pagan savages," Mr. Bolton murmured. "Like an African tribe."

Superintendent Doyle did not reply.

"If you ask me, it's too bad that all of them didn't die in the famine or migrate to America."

In my mind, I agreed that it was too bad that they all hadn't migrated to America like my grandparents. Good journalist that I was—or hoped to be—I kept my mouth shut. I would, however, remember Mr. Bolton's remark for possible later use.

A huge crowd of people waited patiently outside the hut, the women keening, the men drinking. The young woman who had captured my heart was still saying her rosary. She seemed so very sad. Did she know that her husband was a dead man? The constables carried out the five bodies, now in shrouds, on boards. Men emerged from the crowd as if by prearrangement and shouldered the boards. Then they began to walk up the mountains slowly and solemnly.

There was no priest to bless the bodies or to pray at the graves. Yet, somehow there was a touch of Catholicism in the solemnity of the march.

I removed my rosary from my pocket and, despite Mr. Bolton, prayed. The police lurked on the edges of the procession, watching carefully.

"What are they doing, Tommy?"

"They are getting ready if there's a riot, which these poor folks are too hungry to do, and keeping an eye on the suspects."

Finally, we came to a level place. The ruins of an old church loomed over a scattered collection of stones. There were five empty graves, four in one place and another at some distance. This was a cemetery for poor people! Carefully, the pallbearers, if one could call them that, lowered the corpses into the ground.

" 'Tis called the Church on the Hill. They've been burying people up here for centuries. See that manor house at the edge of the cemetery? Lord Ballynahinch lived there for a while, till the local Ribbonmen and the Fenians made it too hot for him. He was before my time, but they all say he was a bit of a monster."

"The house is empty?"

"Has been for twenty years. Occasionally someone comes over from England, looks at it, stays a couple of weeks in Letterfrack, and then decides to go home."

"Why the separate grave?"

"It's for Breige. They're lying her next to her first husband, Tom O'Brien. Her marriage to John Joyce was a second for both of them. They both lost their spouses at about the same time. She was a fine looking woman. Peggy and the two boys were John's children by his first marriage."

A big, handsome man with long black hair walked up to the first grave, picked up a shovel, and cast a first pile of dirt on the corpse. The pitch of the wail rose higher. He passed the shovel to another man, who did the same thing. One by one the men marched in procession from grave to grave until the last one had been covered. Some of the mourners placed rough stones at the head of each grave. There was a last prolonged wail of keening, and then the crowd dispersed, some down the mountain, some up the mountain.

"Do they keen because they're sad?" I asked Tommy Finnucane.

"More like the opposite," he said. "They keen, and that makes them sad. Most of the women will have recovered by teatime. Then they'll take out their clay pipes and begin to smoke again."

"Have you been to the crime site, Mr. Bolton?"

"I hardly think that is necessary, sir. We have our criminals. I believe one or two of your men are up there, however."

"I want to see it myself."

We walked up the mountain—Rod Doyle, Tom Finnucane, and myself. I felt miserable. Heavy heart and heavier stomach. Lonely, weary, sick. And very sorry for myself. I despised all of those emotions. I was in truth a coward, not an adventurer. I'd never be anything else.

Romantic indeed.

Clouds raced in rapidly from the Atlantic. Heat yielded to damp. Drizzle started when we reached the house of the murder. Gloom hovered over us like an impending plague.

"House" is too strong a word. The blood-splattered hovel was little more than a cave, with stone walls extending from the walls of the cave and wood beams supporting a thatched roof. A few pathetic outhouses clustered around it.

"It wouldn't seem that stealing sheep is a very profitable occupation in this part of Ireland," I exclaimed.

Doyle glanced at me quickly and then looked away.

"Nothing is very profitable around here, Eddie. Nothing. They manage to stay alive and produce children. Only just barely . . . Yet why so much violence?"

I felt rebuked, a fool once again.

"The drink," Tommy Finnucane muttered.

"Aye, the drink."

"Hatred," I plunged in again. "Hatred so great that it was necessary to kill John Joyce and his whole family with as much brutality as possible."

"And themselves all relatives up here too, eh, Tommy?"

"Still, Chief, this one is unusual."

The Superintendent sighed heavily.

"A lot more unusual than Mr. Bolton seems to think . . . Well, we've seen enough. Let's go back to the police hut."

I was soaking wet when we finally stumbled into the hut, buffeted by rain and fierce winds. I sat by a peat fire trying to dry out. I should go back to my room in the inn, I thought, write a dispatch, and sleep the rest of the day.

"Here's the story, Eddie." Tom Finnucane sat on the floor next to me with a diagram. "If the story the 'independent' witnesses tell is the truth, seven of the killers, who lived east of the John Joyce house, went out of the houses here, walked down to the other end of the valley to collect Myles Joyce and his cousins down there at the west end, and came back here to the John Joyce house in between to do the killing. They did this making enough noise on the road to wake Tony and his other witnesses, but not to disturb anyone else. Moreover, the witnesses claim to have followed them along that wandering path for several hours, hiding behind bushes and out-houses and never once were spotted by the killers."

"That seems impossible, Tom. Do you think the informers are lying?" He hesitated.

"Not to say lying, lad, just adding to the truth a little more than is required. They probably heard the crowd carousing through the valley and made up the story. They don't know who went into the house and did the killing. So they're not really accusing anyone. . . . The lad that survived, Patsy Joyce, says that the three men who did the killing had dirt on their faces, so he can't identify them. The informers figure they'll earn a few English pounds and do no real harm to anyone. Moreover, they'll even the score with Myles Joyce. They may even have had a pretty good idea who the real killers might be and put them on their list of ten. They don't know how Mr. Bolton works."

"Does anyone know who really killed John Joyce and his family?"

"Everyone in the valley knows except us."

"What!"

"The women know which husbands were in their beds that night and which weren't. They talk to one another. The men know what plans were whispered around the last two weeks. They talk. The valley has already solved the crime."

"And they won't come forward?"

"No one ever comes forward to English law."

"Not even to save the lives of those they love?"

"They don't believe that it would do any good. Most of the older ones speak only Irish. They're afraid even to talk to English law. They're in terror of the real killers, if any of them are not on the list the informers turned in.

Moreover, they have to live with each other for the years ahead. They'll tell themselves there is enough hatred already. They really can't believe that the English will hang men who are not really guilty. Like I say, they don't know the way Mr. George Bolton works. By the time they find out it will be too late."

"You mean that he really doesn't care whether he arrests the innocent or the guilty?"

"He cares about making arrests and getting convictions."

"Innocent men might hang for this crime?"

Tommy sighed.

"Probably not, lad. Probably not."

"What happens next?"

"We arrest the suspects and transport them to the jail in Galway Town. I'm supposed to take four men and arrest Myles Joyce, the dead man's cousin."

"Four men?"

"Aye. He's another big fella, not likely to come quietly."

"Was he at odds with his cousin?"

"Myles Joyce is a fierce man, but peaceful enough until he is pushed too hard. He had no serious quarrel with John Joyce that we know of. Still, these people up here are quiet about their grudges. You discover their hatreds only after the explosion. . . . Do you want to come along?"

I didn't. I was too much a coward, however, to refuse. Yet I told myself it was time to prove that I had still a remnant of manliness. So I told him that of course I did.

In the mists, the mountain we climbed and the little valley into which we descended were foreboding places, permeated, I thought, with hatred, revenge, and death. Myles Joyce's house was as small as the others, but it had been whitewashed and flowers had been planted in front of it. A child of eleven or twelve, a girl to judge by her red petticoat, saw us coming. She stared at us and then darted into the house.

"That's the wife's niece. She doesn't live here but spends most of her time with the wife. Myles Joyce has no English, but Nora, his wife, can speak both languages well enough. This will be difficult. They say the woman is pregnant."

An icy shaft stabbed at my soul.

A moment later Myles Joyce and his wife emerged from the hut. He was a short, burly man with iron gray hair and a dark, handsome face, probably in his middle forties. His eyes were deep black pools of hatred. She was wearing a thin red cloak, which set off her beauty, but no shoes.

"What do you want?" she demanded, glaring at us.

"Myles Joseph Joyce," Tommy intoned solemnly, "it is my duty to arrest you on suspicion of the murder of John Patrick Joyce."

Nora translated for her husband, though there was little doubt that he knew what had been said. He responded in a fierce flow of Irish.

"My husband says that he had nothing to do with the murder of his cousin and his family. He was here in our bed all that night. He will not come with you."

"He must come with us, Nora," Tommy insisted. "If he is innocent, he has nothing to fear."

Nora translated again. She was, I thought, containing her fury by sheer willpower. I was ashamed of the attraction I felt for her, a pregnant, barefoot woman whose husband was about to be dragged off by the police of a foreign nation.

Myles Joyce's dark and handsome face twisted in rage. He shouted his defiant reply in words that needed no translation.

Nora, her arm around her husband now, hesitated and then translated.

"My husband says that he has no faith in English justice and that he will not permit himself to be arrested."

"Nora," Tommy Finnucane pleaded, "he must come with us or we will have to take him by force."

"You'll have to take me too," she raged.

"Take him and chain him," the Sergeant ordered.

The four men approached Myles Joyce warily. Then they lunged at him. He threw two of them off his body with a shrug of his powerful shoulders. Nora and her niece beat at the constables' backs with their fists. Myles gave a gruff command. Rebuked, Nora backed off.

"Josie," she said to the girl, "go home now!"

He must have ordered his wife to think of their unborn child.

Josie hesitated, still eager for a fight.

"You heard me, Josie. Go home!"

The child turned and ran off sobbing.

After a long struggle, the constables finally subdued Myles Joyce. He was a gallant warrior, I thought, overcome by his enemies. They dragged him down the path into the valley. Nora ran screaming after them.

Again Myles Joyce gave a brief command. Nora, head bent, shoulders slumped, returned to the house, where Tommy and I were standing.

"You can visit him in the Galway prison in a couple of days, Nora," Tommy said, trying to be kind.

"I've lost him forever," she moaned. "He'll never hold me in his arms again."

It sounded almost like a death sentence. Was she one of these Irish women, one of the dark ones, who knew the future? I shuddered at the thought.

I strove desperately for something to say to this woman in her terrible grief. No words came to my mind, no thoughts to my lips. I was helpless.

Josie appeared again, hesitant and wary. Sobbing, Nora lurched back into the house. Josie followed her on the run, pausing only to spit on me.

"Josie! Shame on you!" Tom yelled after her.

"I feel like I deserved it," I said.

"Aye, lad. I understand."

"I believe her."

"What woman, Eddie, would not lie for her husband?"

"She might well lie, Tom, but this time she's telling the truth."

"Mayhap she is. They all say she's a fine young woman. She would not have had to marry Myles, and herself so young, if her parents had not died and her brother off in America, no one knows where."

"She obviously loves him."

"No doubt about that."

"What happens to her if he does not come back?"

"The way times are now, she and her baby will be lucky if they don't starve to death."

Great sheets of rain beat against us as we returned to the police hut. Already six men in chains sat sullenly on the floor. Only Myles Joyce glowered defiantly at the constables.

Worn and dejected, I walked back to the inn here in Letterfrack and drafted a dispatch for the Daily News. I described the funeral service without a priest and the arrest of Myles Joyce with as much detachment as I could achieve. The passionate cry of Nora Joyce did not need any elaboration from me.

There was a wire from the paper congratulating me on my previous dispatches. I crumpled it up and threw it away.

I write this entry in my journal with the sense that I am a callow, worthless young man, caught up in tragedy beyond my experience or my comprehension. I stood by, silent and powerless, while a family's future was destroyed and while perhaps a death sentence was passed on all its members. I am an interloper, a voyeur, a shameful participant in what increasingly seemed to be a vicious game being played by the English authorities.

I am quite incapable of any more lustful thoughts about Nora Joyce, but the pain of loss in her wondrous blue eyes will haunt me for the rest of my life.

— 9 —

"ARE YOU all right, Dermot love?"

My wife, in a Mayo 5000 sweatshirt and the inevitable jeans, had thundered into our bedroom with the same serenity as that of a herd of cattle en route from Texas to Dodge City.

I had been sitting on the bed reading Eddie Fitzpatrick's book and identifying with his feelings of being a callow youth. I looked up at Nuala Anne and grinned.

"As best as can be expected after the attack on me in my own bed."

"Och, Dermot Michael Coyne, aren't you a desperate man altogether!"

She threw herself on the bed and embraced me.

"Didn't I say to meself that night at O'Neill's pub that it would be grand to slip into bed with that big blond Yank and tumble with him? Didn't I know then that he would be the greatest lover in all the world?"

The history of our encounter that foggy evening was subject to constant revision. I very much doubted this new essay in revisionism. Moreover, I had hardly been the aggressor in our earlier romp.

"As I remember this afternoon," I said, putting aside the manuscript, which was a good deal less compelling at the moment than my wife, "I was hardly the active partner."

"Go 'long with you, Dermot Michael Coyne." She slapped my arm.

"Wasn't I just the defenseless woman overwhelmed by your violent desires?"

Total lie. I had, however, enough sense not to argue.

"Well," she continued exuberantly, "haven't I forgotten to take me pill? So, lest I be divorced and lose the custody of me children, I'm going to take it right now, in your presence."

She produced a pill from the pocket of her jeans and gulped it down.

"See, am I not a good and obedient little wife?"

"Good, anyway."

She laughed as though I had said something wildly funny.

I wondered if her new-found exuberance was an indication of a manic phase. How would one be able to tell the difference between a manic Nuala Anne and the ordinary garden-variety Nuala Anne?

"Well, now, aren't we going off to O'Donnell's pub tonight for a bowl of soup and a bit of a sandwich and a drink for you and a glass of Evian water for me?"

"Are we?"

"Haven't I just said so?" She hugged me more tightly. "And not to worry about them shiteheads with guns? Won't we have ourselves a bodyguard like we're really important people?"

"Will we?"

"Haven't I just said so? Now will we have our shower and yourself sitting here on the bed without any clothes on?"

The woman was conniving again. However, as exhausted as I was from the terrors and the pleasures of the day, hadn't she made me an offer I couldn't refuse?

Our fun and games in the shower were limited to gentle kisses and caresses—which, all things considered, was just as well.

"How did you know that the young murdered woman was blond?" I asked.

"Well, she was blond, wasn't she? Very pretty, poor little thing."

"Her terror is long since over, Nuala Anne."

"Indeed, and her tears wiped away. Still, you hear a noise in your house, you come running into the room, and a man has just shot your father and then they beat you to death."

"Why would they do such terrible things?"

"Hate, Dermot. And the drink!"

"I suppose so."

"What about Ethne?" I asked as I covered my wife's breasts with suds.

"What about her?"

"Does she come home with us to get her Ph.D. in history?"

"Och, Dermot Michael, what do you know about that?"

"I'm fey on occasion, though only when fondling a woman in the shower."

"Any woman?"

"Any woman, so long as she's my wife."

"Well," Nuala adopted her fishmonger's tone, "don't the kids simply love her? And doesn't she want to study in America? And won't it be nice for me to talk to someone who has the Irish?"

"About me."

"Sure, we could do that in English when you're not around, couldn't we now? . . . So, what would you be thinking about it?"

Actually, I didn't get a vote. However, I did earn some points for guessing one of the schemes that were going on. Not many, however.

"I think it's a brilliant idea!"

My wife hugged me.

"You're a wonderful man, Dermot, always so kind and generous."

I was no such thing, but I let it pass.

"I'll read some of your man's manuscript," Nuala continued, "when we come back from O'Donnell's. What's it like?"

"Painfully candid."

"Och, I don't need that at all, at all! . . . You know, Dermot Michael Coyne, wouldn't I like to stay in this warm shower with you for the rest of me life!"

However, we eventually left the shower, dressed, kissed the children (whom Nuala had already fed), and left them in Ethne's charge.

"Aren't there enough Gardaí outside, Ethne Moire, to put down a revolution? There's nothing to worry about."

"Who's worried?" the young woman asked. "Except about passing me comprehensives?"

Fiona bestirred herself from her close watch on our children.

"No, girl," Nuala admonished her, "stay here and take care of the wee ones."

The wolfhound settled down, happy perhaps to have a peaceful evening after an exciting day. And herself expecting, as my wife would have said.

Two Garda cars waited in our driveway. Peig Sayers, in jeans and a sweater like my wife's, was in one, and two uniformed constables were in the other. We entered Peig's car.

Both sweaters represented the current women's fashion of leaving uncovered the navel and varying amounts of associated flesh. As I had remarked to my wife, navels aren't as erotic as asses or teats, but in a pinch—you should excuse the expression, Nuala Anne—it will do.

"Don't be vulgar, Dermot Michael. Besides, would women be doing it these days if it weren't difficult to get men's eyes off the shameless hussies on the telly?"

There was a lapse in logic there to which I wisely did not point.

"No, don't you dare ogle her tonight, Dermot Michael Coyne," my wife whispered to me, "and yourself exhausted from almost raping me this afternoon."

"Love one woman," I whispered back, "love them all."

Inside the car, I congratulated Officer Peig on her promotion to the rank of detective.

"Sure, isn't it only for the night, Mr. Coyne? . . . We have the house surrounded, Nuala Anne. Nothing to worry about at all, at all."

"Unless the Russians land commandos from one of their subs."

"Their subs don't work anymore, Mr. Coyne. And, if they did, wouldn't your American navy pick them up long before they got to shore?"

"Right," I said, slipping into silence.

Mr. Coyne, indeed.

O'Donnell's was filled with people that night, noisy, contentious, difficult people. Which is to say, mostly fishermen. I quite agreed with my wife's judgment that they were eejits. Peig came in with us while the two uniformed officers waited outside. A table was reserved for us in a corner, as far from the door as possible, so that if any Mafia types entered, they would have to walk across a crowded room.

I collected two pints and one Evian water at the bar. "You an alcoholic or something?" a redneck American fisherman asked me.

It would have been very easy to get into a fight with him. People look at me and think I'm a pushover, probably because I have a boyish face and a sweet smile and curly blond hair. They learn the hard way that such appearances can be deceiving. However, an elderly man now with two children, I tended to act mature. So I ignored the guy. I carried the drinks to our table. My wife never complained about her forced abstinence from the "creature." She hardly seemed to notice the glass. She was busy scanning the room, as though looking for a face.

My heart did a flip-flop. She was looking for the man who had shot at her on the lake. What would happen if she found him?

It didn't seem that he was in the room. Nuala abandoned her search, temporarily at least, and joined the conversation.

Then a tall, rather striking woman in her early forties ambled over to our table. Her body had been poured into tight jeans and tight sweater, her long black hair hung defiantly around a face that displayed more makeup than it needed. She carried a half-empty pint of Guinness in her ring-bedecked hand. All in all, she was worth a second look. Maybe even a third.

"Mind if I sit down?" she asked as she sat down.

We didn't say no, but we were less than enthusiastic about her joining us, even Nuala Anne, who normally personified West of Ireland courtesy towards strangers.

"My name is Margot Quinn. I'm an estate agent down in Clifden. I understand you've bought the bungalow next to the one that was blown up yesterday?"

" 'Tis true," Nuala Anne said, "and a brilliant bungalow it is."

"Well, its lost a lot of its value since yesterday, hasn't it now?"

She sipped from her pint.

"Maybe not," I said. "Curiosity value."

"You put it on the market tomorrow and you'll find out how much curiosity value it has!" Margot Quinn sneered.

Not a word about our experience on the lake earlier in the afternoon. Perhaps she didn't know about it.

"We're not about to put it on the market tomorrow," I said firmly. "We've just bought it, and we like it. A couple of years from now, people will have forgotten about the explosion."

"If there are not any more." She smiled knowingly. "Once these things start out here they tend to continue."

Peig Sayers was listening attentively. No one would imagine that this pretty young woman was a police constable in mufti.

"You expect there'll be more explosions?"

"Someone is up to something, aren't they now? That prick MacManus has a lot of enemies. If you ask me, they've only begun to work him over."

"Och, sure, our bungalow isn't for sale at all, at all," Nuala said firmly.

Margot Quinn looked at Nuala as though she were out of her mind.

"Well, it's up to you, but, if I were in your situation, I'd think about a quick sale. It happens that at the moment I have some clients who are interested in constructing condos along this stretch of the coast, and they'd be willing to pay pretty much what you've put into it."

"Ah, no," Nuala said gently.

"Well, here's my card," Margot Quinn said, rising from her chair. "Call me when you change your mind as I'm sure you will."

My two companions stared after her as she walked away.

"Aren't those jeans a size too small?" Peig observed.

Me good wife, who is catty only when the situation absolutely demands it, disagreed: "Two sizes."

The sweater was apparently beneath their notice.

"Feminism has apparently created gombeen women in Ireland," I offered.

"Sure, she didn't know you were a constable, did she now?"

"Och, that one wouldn't care at all, at all!"

They exchanged a couple of sentences in Irish that I thought might be a more clinical comment on Ms. Quinn.

"It's almost like she wants to be a suspect."

"Wouldn't it give her more publicity?" Peig said, sniffing disdainfully.

"So what DO the Gardaí think is happening out here on Long Island East?" I asked.

"Officially, we're continuing our investigations. Unofficially, we think someone is trying to scare people away from Renvyle, depress property values around here, and then buy up a lot of land for development. However, there is no evidence that anyone has made any offers for the hotel or the land. The bomb at the T.D.'s house was planted several days before the explosion and then detonated by remote control."

"Them things cost a lot of money, don't they?" my wife asked, frowning. "And I suppose there's some expense in hiring a man to take wild shots at harmless water-skiers. . . ."

"Was it the kind of bomb the lads would use?" I asked.

"It was," Peig agreed, "but a lot of people know how to make them bombs. We're inclined to think that the man who made the bomb has some experience with the paramilitaries up above. It doesn't follow that he is working for the paramilitaries now."

"He could have planted the bomb," Nuala reflected, "given the remote control to someone else, and be far away when the bomb went off. 'Tis dark enough out here at night that someone could have done it very quickly and not been noticed."

"We're afraid that we'll never find him." Peig sighed. "We hope we find the man with the rifle."

"We'll find him all right," my wife said softly.

"Even if we do," I cautioned, "the people behind these events probably covered themselves."

"If they are as clever as they seem to be," Peig agreed, "that is undoubtedly true. Still, no one is perfectly clever. They'll make a mistake, and we'll get them."

I did not find that hope terribly reassuring.

Nuala stiffened next to me. She seemed to be watching three men who had just entered the pub as they picked their way through the crowd and found a table at the far side of the room.

"Peig, would you ever check the car of that little fella who just came in with them big fellas? I wouldn't be surprised altogether if you found a thirty-caliber rifle with a telescopic lens in the boot."

Peig glanced towards the three men.

"Just a quick look, mind you. We don't want them to know that I'm suspicious."

Peig slipped away.

"Are you sure, Nuala?"

"Of course I'm sure, Dermot Michael. Would I send herself out to search the shitehawk's car if I wasn't sure?"

Good enough for you, Dermot Coyne.

I waited anxiously and fervently hoped that my wife would not engage in any mayhem. The little fella was little all right, but the other two fellas were big enough.

Peig entered the door of the pub and nodded briefly. There were two Gardaí behind her.

Nuala bounded out of her chair and thundered across the room like an NFL tight end. I tried to follow.

"You know," I heard her say to the little fella as she picked up his pint of Guinness, "I'm not going to try to throw this in your face. I hope to miss it. Still, I make mistakes occasionally, don't you know!"

Thereupon she splashed the contents of his glass right in the middle of his face.

"Oh, shite! Didn't I miss now! What a shame! Here I'll try again with this man's pint! Och, didn't I miss again!"

"What the fock!" the man cried as he rose to his feet.

The two other fellas bounded up. One of them tried to grab Nuala's arm. For his pains, she hit him in the throat with the edge of her hand. He gasped sickly and fell back against the wall. Somewhere in her career, long before she met me, my wife had learned how to be an alley fighter, though only when someone she loved was at risk.

The other fella found himself on the floor, nursing a very sore jaw, before he knew what hit him. In this case it was my fist. I only look sweet.

Nuala shook the little fella, who, his spectacles askew, was cowering in terror.

"You focking little gobshite! Endanger my husband and children's lives will you! And too much of a focking eejit to take your focking gun out of your focking car!"

"Alfonse Ryan"—Peig took charge—"I arrest you on the charge of attempted murder. I must warn you that anything you say will be taken down and may be used against you in a court of law. . . . Nuala Anne, please put the focker down!"

The pub exploded in applause. They all knew what had happened earlier in the day. They did not quite understand how the Gardaí, with my wife's assistance, had apprehended the gunman. If we explained it to them, they probably wouldn't believe it—or would make the sign of the cross and run home for their holy water.

"Good on you, Nuala Anne!" someone shouted.

"Serves the focker right!"

"Hooray for Nuala Anne!"

My wife waved her hand in appreciation.

"A round of drinks," she announced, "on meself for the whole house!"

Then she whispered to me, "I hope you have one of your credit cards, Dermot Michael."

—10—

August 23, 1882

     A sorry procession wound its way out of Letterfrack in the rain this morning, carriages carrying Mr. Bolton and the other government officials and armed constables on horses, a lumbering covered wagon filled with the still-chained prisoners, and a pitiable little band of wives, parents, and children of the ten accused men.

I had rented a carriage and driver for myself. Or rather for Nora Joyce and Josie.

"Excuse me, madam," I said to Nora. "I wondered if I could offer you a ride in my carriage. It might be easier for one in your condition. . . . You too, Josie."

"You're an American, are you?" she stared at me without any hint of emotion.

"Yes, ma'am. Well, Irish American."

"That's evident. . . . Josie, apologize to the nice man for spitting at him. He wants to help us."

"I'm sorry, sir," Josie said morosely. Then she added with a bewitching grin, "Sure if I knew you were an American I wouldn't have spit on you. Didn't I think you were English!"

"Josie!"

"I'm sorry," the child said again, still grinning.

"I am grateful, Mr. . . ."

"Fitzpatrick."

"Mr. Fitzpatrick, for your kind offer; but I am young and strong. I think I would rather walk as the others must."

"I understand." I tipped my hat politely and returned to my carriage. Then I realized what an awkward fool I was. I walked back to her.

"Perhaps I could offer a carriage ride to some of the older folk. . . ."

She smiled briefly. I melted at the radiance of her smile.

"You are a gentleman, Mr. Fitzpatrick."

"Would you invite some of them for me? I'm afraid I don't have the Irish."

"No reason why you should."

She spoke in Irish and three elderly folk, two women and a man, hesitantly approached me. Nora Joyce insisted, and they came to the side of the carriage. I helped them in. They murmured sounds of gratitude.

"Are you a religious man, Mr. Fitzpatrick?" Nora asked me.

"I try to be a good Catholic."

"Then pray for us, please." She was holding her rosary again. "For the dying and the dead."

"Good-bye, Mr. Fitzpatrick," the ineffable Josie said with a raffish grin.

I thought that someday it would be good to have a daughter like Josie—a piquant imp, not unlike my own younger sisters.

The long ride to Galway was dreary and mournful. Wind and rain lashed us as we bumped over the muddy roads. My passengers talked to one another occasionally in Irish, the only language they knew. I did not know what they were saying, but I was sure that their exchanges were melancholy and uncomplaining. Indeed, the people of Maamtrasna did not seem capable of complaint. Myles Joyce had denounced British justice but did not complain about it. His wife had fought furiously to protect him, but she did not bemoan her lot. The straggling mass of relatives slogging through the mud to Galway Town were mostly silent and patient. Perhaps they had learned from their earliest years that complaints accomplished nothing. They knew that they were doomed to tragedy and that their only defense against the fates was patience.

The black wagon was a hearse and we were a funeral cortege.

Nora Joyce, in her familiar red cloak, seemed somehow to be in charge of the relatives. Head high, back straight, she moved among them, assisting,

encouraging, consoling, while Josie bounced along after her. Though her husband was at least two decades older than she was, she clearly loved him.
She knew he was going to his death and that she and her child might well
follow them soon. She had resolved that she would suffer bravely.

I had no right to my admiring and tender thoughts, not unmixed, as I
am ashamed to admit, with lustful emotions towards her. At most she would
remain a poignant memory that would haunt me for the rest of my life.
So I prayed for her, as best I could, and for all of them on the intermin-
able ride.

The prison in Galway is surely one of the bleakest buildings in all the
world—a heavy mass of foreboding rock across from the salmon weir. As I
peered at it through the icy fog that shrouded Galway Town, I thought that
the walls of hell could not be more threatening.

My guests whispered words of thanks as I helped them out of the carriage.
They stumbled over to where Nora was talking to a tall, white-haired man
in a frock coat.

" 'Tis his lordship, the Bishop of Galway," my driver told me. "He'll
find them places to stay while they're here. They say he's a very good man."

At some point I would want words with him about the funeral service.
Where was the priest for these people when they needed a priest?

I was admitted to the prison yard because the constables knew me to be
a reporter. There were at least a dozen from the Irish and English papers. I
was the only American. We watched as the accused were unloaded from the
wagon. Their muscles stiff and cramped from the ride and their chains, they
hobbled into the prison building, shoved by harsh guards who seemed to delight
in their work.

Several of my colleagues gasped at the sight of the ten. At first I thought
they sympathized with the poor wretches. Then the man next to me, speaking
in what I suspected was a lower-class English accent, said, "What a dis-
gusting lot of animals. Typical of people out here. The whole lot of them
should swing."

"Will they?" I asked.

"Not the way Bolton works. He has already heard the cries from Dublin
and London for swift justice. Some of the brutes will turn on the others and
testify against them. A few will hang, the others will plead guilty and spend

twenty years in prison. All neat and quick and easy. The script is already written."

"Apparently, the actual crimes were committed by three of them. Will those be the ones who hang?"

"Bolton couldn't care less as long as he gets three executions."

"Is that English justice?"

He looked at me in surprise.

"We're not talking about justice out here, son. We're talking about controlling an uncivilized people and placating Dublin Castle and Westminster. Bolton is not a nice fellow, but London needs someone like him out here."

The lead for my dispatch was forming in my head. The English treated the Irish the same way we treated the Indians in the American West. Most of us, like most of the English, thought it was a superior people driving off an inferior people. Or so my father said, much to the dismay of most of his friends.

Outside the prison in the fog, the Bishop of Galway stood glaring at the prison. I walked up to him boldly and introduced myself.

"I'm Edward Hannigan Fitzpatrick, Your Excellency."

He was a broad, solid man with a broad, solid face and gray hair. The expressions on his face changed rapidly. When he heard my name, his angry frown turned into a warm smile.

"John Kane, Bishop of Galway and Kilmacduff. I am told that you are the kind gentleman who brought some of the older folk over in a carriage. That was good of you, sir."

"I wish I could have brought them all."

"You did what you could. . . . My wish is that they would all go back tomorrow with their men. That, of course, will not happen."

"I gather not."

"They'll leave the next day after the first hearing. There are cows to be milked, gardens to be tended, even if someone they love is in mortal danger."

I tried to understand the poverty that would drive wives and parents and children to that necessity. Nora Joyce, so deeply in love with her Myles, would leave him in the Galway jail to go back to Maamtrasna?

We said nothing for a moment, both of us depressed by the fate of the accused.

"Mrs. Myles Joyce told me that you are a reporter."

"From Chicago. My grandparents were born in this city."

"Welcome home, then." He shook my hand vigorously. "What will you tell your readers in Chicago?"

"I will indicate, subtly perhaps, but not too subtly, that English justice is a farce here in the West of Ireland."

He nodded grimly.

"That is only the truth. . . . Nora Joyce assures me that her husband never left their marriage bed that night. She is the kind of woman who would never lie to a priest, much less a bishop. Yet her husband will surely hang."

"Why is that, Your Excellency?"

"Because he is a strong man who will never admit guilt to save his life, much less perjure himself against others. Those are the kind the English like to hang."

"What will happen to her and their child?"

He shook his head sadly.

"She will not marry again, I think. Without marriage there is no future for her."

"She reminds me of my own sisters."

"If her grandparents had migrated her life would be very different, would it not, Mr. Fitzpatrick? You doubtless wonder whence came her grace?"

"I think, Bishop Kane, that's the precise word."

"Consider how difficult it would be for your sisters to maintain such grace if they lived out there. Poverty and suffering destroy it in most people. Nora Joyce is simply stronger than other women."

"It's more than that, Bishop Kane."

He sighed again.

"You're right, Edward. God has touched her with a special grace. Yet I fear she will be destroyed too, as so many others have."

In my head were the foolish words that I would not permit her destruction. I knew, however, that I ought not to make that promise, both because it was inappropriate and because I could never fulfill it. So I changed the subject and asked the Bishop about the absence of a priest at the funeral.

He grimaced and sighed.

"I'm afraid that's my fault. There is no curate in the Maamtrasna valley because I have been unable to persuade a priest to go up there. However, one young man, Father Corbett, has just volunteered. I will fill that vacancy immediately. You must understand that such funerals were typical in penal times when it was a crime to be a priest. The people are used to such burials. Unfortunately, the tradition of their saying prayers over the bodies of the dead has died."

"And no requiem Mass?

"A requiem Mass is very rare out in the country, and then it is only in the house of the corpse. We're trying to revive the custom. It takes time. The penal years are still with us."

He offered me supper. I pleaded that I had to write my dispatch. We agreed that I would accept his invitation on another day.

I returned to my room at the Great Southern. The fog was so thick that the square across the road was invisible from my windows. I had been away from the room for only two nights, and yet it seemed like a lifetime. I wrote a strong dispatch, then modified it so that it was more restrained, but, I thought, still effective. I went over to the telegraph office and sent it off to Chicago, marveling again at the efficiency of the modern world.

As I write this account of another terrible day, I finish the last bit of whiskey in the bottle that I had kept in my room. I have drunk more whiskey tonight than I have in all the rest of my life. I must be careful. The ugliness and the horror of what I have witnessed could make me a drunk.

I have also seen grace, as Bishop Kane said. I wonder why God creates grace only to permit it to wither. One does not, as my father has often said, litigate with God. One does pray, however. So I now I will pray for all of them, for the living and the dead.

Especially for Nora.

— 11 —

TEARS STREAMED down my wife's cheeks. Nuala Anne wept easily and often. There were different kinds of tears, however, and they meant different things. My task, indeed my obligation, was to interpret them all correctly

"What a sweet young man." She sighed her most pathetic sigh as she put down a chapter of Eddie Fitzpatrick's journal.

"Meself?" I asked, though I knew who she meant.

"Certainly not, Dermot Michael Coyne! You're sweet in your own way. But this poor lad doesn't even realize he's sweet, and you do some of the time. He won't unless he finds a woman who persuades him that he is, like I've persuaded you."

That settled that.

"It doesn't look all that good for him and herself, however."

"Have you peeked at the end, like you usually do?"

That was pure defamation. She was the one who always read the last page of a novel before she read the first page.

"It breaks off. Jack Lane thinks there may be other segments around the parish house. He promised he'd search for them."

"The poor dear little priest probably doesn't want his heart broken when he reads an unhappy ending. . . . Don't give up hope, Dermot Michael. This is a very special young man. Nora may die before her time, but he'll do his best to save her."

The century and a quarter that separated us from them had somehow slipped away. The two lovers were alive as we were.

"Does she know he loves her?"

"Don't be silly, Dermot. Certainly she does. Women know those things, even if they won't admit it to themselves. There's too much grief in her now to pay any attention. Still she likes him, as any woman would."

"I kind of identify with him," I said, "callow lad that I was and maybe still am."

"Aren't you a terrible amadon altogether, Dermot Michael Coyne! I would never have fallen in love with a callow lad, would I now?"

"I felt callow."

" 'Tis different. Didn't you want to take me to bed with you when you saw me boobs that night in O'Neill's and didn't I know it and didn't I want the same thing? Your man wanted the same thing, of course"—she lifted the manuscript—"but wouldn't he have been more afraid to show it?"

I decided not to argue. As Nuala often said, a man should listen to what his woman means and not what she says. I knew what she meant all right.

We were sitting in the parlor, with some disrespect for the "little people," drinking our last cup of tea. The kids were sound asleep, under Fiona's guardianship, in the nursery. My wife had settled down from her exuberance in the pub, where she had captured the gunman by methods that the Gardaí wouldn't believe if they knew and didn't want to know anyway. Her moods had always changed rapidly. Since she had begun to take the medication, I had not noticed any unusual mood swings. Yet, I was afraid of the possibility. On the other hand, I half suspected (as they say in Ireland) that she had recovered from her depression, just as the doctor had predicted.

"Somehow," she began, putting aside the Fitzpatrick manuscript, "I'm more worried about the problem out here now than about the one back in 1882."

"That's not unreasonable," I said cautiously.

She mounted her chin on the pyramid of her long and graceful fingers—strong from playing the harp—and frowned. I remained silent.

When my wife is communing—I can think of no better word—that was the only sensible thing for me to do.

"The evil in those days was clear enough. The English government and its oppression and injustice. There's evil out there in the fog tonight. I can feel it, smell it, taste it, almost hear it. But I don't know what it is."

"Surely not as bad as, say, Mr. Bolton?"

"He's been dead a long time, Dermot love. Isn't this one out there and alive?"

I shivered.

My wife's mood changed again.

"I don't supposed you'd fancy one more fock before the day is over, Dermot Michael Coyne? I wouldn't want to be wearing out an old man, would I now?"

I was exhausted from the excitement and the pleasures of the day. Three romps in one day was too much altogether, wasn't it? Still, I figured, one might as well enjoy the possibilities as long as one can, especially if one is an old man. My body, weary as it was, had no doubts about the possibility.

"I might not mind," I said casually.

"Mind you, something really sweet and gentle."

"Sort of what I had in mind," I said, sneaking my fingers under her sweater and sweetly and gently caressing her belly.

"Hmm," she cooed, "haven't you got the right of it, Dermot Michael Coyne?"

We did not make it to our bedroom. Afterwards, she insisted that I carry her to bed and then go back and collect our clothes and hang them up in good order.

When I finally slipped in beside her, she was weeping again.

"Did I hurt you, Nuala?"

"Och, Dermot, you know you didn't. I'm weeping for all those poor people in Maamtrasna, especially poor, sweet Nora, and for that poor gobshite we arrested tonight, and for you and me and for everyone."

I let her weep herself to sleep.

She had, I told myself, survived the day with flying colors, flying tricolors to be exact. The intense lovemaking of the day was not part of any conniving. It was pure—one perhaps should excuse the expression—unbridled desire for her husband.

Good on me.

Yet I had, without altogether realizing it, an implicit condition for her complete recovery. When Nuala beat the depression, she would sing again.

WHAT AN EEJIT YOU ARE, ASSHOLE! HOW MANY MEN YOUR AGE GET THREE GOOD FOCKS FROM THEIR WIFE IN ONE DAY? WHY ISN'T THAT ENOUGH FOR YOU? IS SINGING BETTER THAN FOCKING?

I thought about that as I slipped off into sleep and gave the Adversary a blunt answer.

"I want both."

The next morning, with sun streaming through the drapes, my wife stormed into the bedroom

"Wake up, Dermot Michael," she ordered. "Something terrible has happened!

I rolled over. How could the woman possibly be so vigorous? She had been shot at, captured the gunman, and made love three times. Ought not she be in bed beside me, as drained as I was?

"What's happened?" I said, desperately searching for full consciousness.

"Weren't the three Russians at the hotel killed last night! Someone slit their throats while they were asleep."

That woke me up. While Nuala was smelling and tasting evil, it was doing its deadly work.

"Get your clothes on. Peig and Declan are here already."

"Woman, I need me tea."

"Isn't it on the night table right next to you?"

I dressed and, bleary-eyed, teacup in hand, joined the group in the kitchen, most of them sitting around the table, drinking tea and eating

Nuala Anne's fresh scones. The exception being the rugrats and Fiona playing on the floor. Don't the Gardaí come calling every morning in this house?

Had Nuala already done her morning run and swim? How late was it?

"Sorry to trouble you, Dermot," the Chief Superintendent said, glancing at his watch. "I know you and your wife had a difficult day yesterday. Still, we did want to tell you about last night's horror."

No reason to send out the troops to tell me about it, except the Gardaí were at a loss and were asking me wife for help. They were not exactly consulting a soothsayer or a clairvoyant or a "wise woman." They were merely talking to a young woman who seemed to know a lot. Sure, weren't there others like that out here in the "real" Ireland?

I had been dragged out of my well-earned sleep by the need to pretend that they didn't. The clock over the sink said it was 10:15. Impossible!

"Apparently, the killer slipped into their rooms sometime after midnight," Peig continued. "He had a carving knife from the hotel's kitchen, which he left in the room of his final victim. He locked the doors after he left. We have no idea where he left the key. When the housekeeper, a child from Letterfrack by the way, knocked at eight-thirty and no one answered, she opened the door of one of the rooms with her passkey to see if she might start on making up the room. She saw a terrible bloody mess, screamed loudly enough to wake up anyone still asleep below in Clifden, and ran for help."

Peig was in uniform this morning, her long blond hair up in a knot and her belly, alas, covered again.

STILL HORNY? DON'T YOU EVER HAVE ENOUGH?

"Were there keys missing?" Nuala Anne asked, putting to rest the polite fiction that I was required for the conversation.

Ethne refilled our teacups and put a plate of warm scones in front of me. Knowing my tastes, my wife always loaded her scones with raisins.

"Not that the hotel administration is aware of. However, it would not have been very difficult for someone to make a copy of one of the skeleton keys," Declan McGinn replied. "As you may imagine, Renvyle House is not troubled by frequent crime."

"He must have acted very quickly," Nuala said thoughtfully.

"We don't know that there was only one killer," McGinn observed.

"If the person was a professional, he would have wanted to do it alone, wouldn't he now? 'Course he could have been an amateur like your man yesterday."

"We don't know for certain that the crimes are connected," Peig sighed. "Though, there aren't many crime waves here in this part of Ireland."

"What about the man you arrested last night?" I asked, figuring I ought to say something intelligent.

"He's still, ah, helping us with our inquires," the Chief Superintendent said wryly. "Not much help. Some chap in Galway City gave him a hundred pounds to take a few shots at someone out here and miss. Doesn't quite remember who the chap is. Insists he had no notion at whom he was shooting."

"He's a petty criminal," Peig went on. "Eventually he'll remember the name of the chap that gave him the money. Most likely at some point the trail to the man behind him will dry up. That's the way it usually is. Or so I've been told."

"IRA connection?"

"We don't think so," McGinn replied. "Not their type at all."

Silence.

I had finished my last scone. I glanced up at Ethne, who grinned and shook her head negatively.

"Mr. Coyne," Peig began hesitantly, "you once suggested that these unfortunate men might be members of the Russian Mafia? Did you have any reason to think that?"

"I'd seen them drinking over in Renvyle House last week. They looked like the Russian Mafia people on the telly."

Damn it! I was going native! The word is television!

"Actually, it turns out that they were officers in the Russian Army, according to the Russian Embassy in Dublin. As you may imagine, the Embassy is very upset about their deaths."

"They don't say what their officers were doing here, I suppose?" my wife asked.

Declan McGinn smiled his tiny, wry smile. "On a well-earned vacation . . . We are checking with Interpol to find out if they have known criminal connections. We assume that they do."

"Factional fighting among them?" I asked.

"Perhaps."

No one said a word. We were at a dead end. The Gardaí had decided that it would be wise to brief Nuala Anne about the situation and hint that they would welcome her help. As well they might.

"We'd thought we'd keep you informed. Naturally, we'll maintain the security around you and your house in light of yesterday's incident."

We thanked him. They departed quietly.

"I don't like it, Dermot Michael," my wife informed me, unnecessarily, I thought. "Not at all, at all."

"Nor do I."

"It's something worse than the Russian Mafia, something profoundly evil."

"Yes, ma'am."

"Anyway, you'd better put on your running suit and take herself out for another run if she wants. We might have a busy day. We have lunch with the manager of Renvyle House Hotel at half one."

"So we are an auxiliary of the Garda now, are we?"

"In a manner of speaking."

I donned my running suit and shoes, kissed my children and wife, and collected my wolfhound, who, "expecting" or not, seemed eager for more exercise. It was a glorious day for running, ruined only somewhat by the blue Garda car that trailed behind me at a respectful distance.

— 12 —

Galway Town, August 23, 1882

The "Magisterial Hearing" here today in the prison was ludicrous. The large room in the depths of the Galway jail was also used for hangings, a fact that could not escape the accused in their loose frieze prison garb. The immediate families were admitted and all the reporters who were interested. The hearings were in English, with Irish translations—occasionally.

In the United States the case against the alleged criminals would have been dismissed out of hand. Here George Bolton permitted a shameful display and then adjourned the hearing to a later date.

Henry Concannon, a Protestant who appeared for the accused (later I would learn, at the insistence of the Bishop of Galway), tore the so-called independent and irreproachable witnesses apart.

"Mr. Anthony Joyce, how is it that you followed the accused for more than four hours on the night of August seventeenth without them once seeing you, even though the moon was full?"

Anthony Joyce, a thin, spiteful little man in a suit and linens that the Crown had provided to make him look respectable, squirmed uncomfortably.

"They had the drink taken and didn't notice anything."

"Not so much that they couldn't commit a murder?"

"No, not that much."

"Now, how far away from the house were you? Let's see, in the blackthorn bush was it?"

"It was."

"And that was ten yards away?"

The faces of the prisoners were expressionless during this exchange as they had been through the whole hearing, perhaps because, like Sioux being tried by an American military court, they did not know enough English to understand what was happening.

"More than that."

"Twenty?"

"More than that."

"More like a hundred?"

"No, not that far."

"Maybe seventy-five?"

"Probably fifty."

"Ah, and by that time, if my memory serves me properly, the moon had already set."

"I guess so."

"Yet you were able to see the faces of Myles Joyce, Pat Joyce, and Pat Casey when they went into the house?"

"It wasn't that dark."

"Wasn't it now? Isn't it odd that the surviving member of the family, Patsy Joyce, could not recognize the killers because their faces were covered with dirt?"

"I wouldn't know what Patsy said."

Periodically I would glance at the families of the prisoners. Like the accused, their faces were blank, resigned. Many of them could not understand English, I knew. Nora Joyce, however, who could understand English, was equally without expression. Perhaps they all took tragedy for granted.

"I see. . . . . Now you reported that you heard cries of terror and anguish in the house."

"Yes, sir. Terrible cries."

"Yes, indeed, I suppose they would sound terrible even at a hundred yards. But let's see here now . . . Yes, in your deposition to the police, you do not report hearing a gun shot. Yet in fact John Joyce died of a gunshot wound to the head. How is it that you did not hear a gun?"

"We didn't hear it," he said, the sweat pouring down his face. "Maybe *the cries of the victims drowned out the sound of the gun. Perhaps that's what happened."*

"I see . . . Now let me ask you another important question. Why did not you and your associates go immediately to the police hut and report the crime? Perhaps some of the victims might have been saved, like young Patsy Joyce was later saved."

"We were frightened for our lives. There were ten of them, and they were mad with drink. Only when morning came did we realize that we should report it."

"When it was too late for the police to see if the accused might still be in their own homes?"

"We did not think of that. We were frightened."

"Frightened? Yet not so frightened that you couldn't follow these men for several hours on an improbably circuitous route while they talked of murder?"

"We didn't think they meant it."

"Ah, I see. . . . Now isn't it true that your family has been at odds with the family of your distant cousin, Myles Joyce, since your grandparents' time?"

"We are not close friends. . . . We don't associate with habitual sheep thieves."

"A very proper attitude . . . Is it not true that you attacked Myles Joyce with a club in your boreen only three months ago?"

"He was trying to steal one of my sheep. He couldn't see a sheep without wanting to steal it."

"I understand. . . . You don't think very much of him then?"

"I think he is the worst man in the whole County Galway."

"Do you now? Enough to want to see him hang?"

"I don't have to answer that question."

"No, Mr. Anthony Joyce, you don't."

"Old Joe certainly destroyed him," an Irish reporter sitting next to me whispered. "Bolton is in trouble."

"Is he?"

"Indeed he is, but he'll wiggle out. The bastard always finds someone to hang."

Mr. Bolton announced a continuance of the hearing till September 4. The families sighed. They would have to walk back to the valley and return another day. I sought out Josie.

"Could I have a word with you, Josephine?"

"Call me Josie, Mr. Fitzpatrick," she said with her mischievous smile.

"I'm giving you this envelope with twenty pounds in it. . . ."

She pushed the envelope away with a comment in Irish that meant, I thought, that she wanted Jesus and Mary and Patrick to defend her. I pushed it into her hand.

"You know what I want you to do with it?"

"Bring food to me cousin and take care of her."

"You'll do that for me, Josie?"

"I will," she said bravely. "I promise you I won't take a pence for myself."

"I never thought you would."

She shoved the envelope into a pocket of her skirt. "God bless you and keep you, Mr. Fitzpatrick. You're a wonderful gentleman."

Then I sought out her aunt, who was staring at the river, lost in thought. Or perhaps despair.

"Mrs. Joyce," I said cautiously.

"What!" she exclaimed "Oh, I'm sorry, Mr. Fitzpatrick. . . . There is no hope for us in that prison, is there, sir?"

"We must never give up hope, Mrs. Joyce," I said, realizing how hollow my words were.

"That's true. . . . They say the English don't care about the truth."

"Some of them do, I'm sure."

"Perhaps," she sighed.

"I've taken the liberty of ordering the carriage again for the return trip."

"Will you come back to Maamtrasna?"

"Not immediately. . . . The carriage is for my previous guests."

"You are very kind, Mr. Fitzpatrick."

"This time I insist that you ride in it, taking my place, as it were."

How stilted I sounded.

"I cannot, sir." The tears spilled out of her eyes.

"You can and you will, madam, and that's settled."

Her eyes pondered me, trying perhaps to understand why I was being so kind. I did not know myself.

"In Ireland," she smiled ever so slightly, "it's the women who give the orders."

"As it is in Irish America. Nonetheless, you will obey me in this matter."

She lowered her head and looked at the ground.

"That's what my husband would say. . . . You must take care of the little one."

"He would be right."

"Thank you very much, sir," she said meekly. "I will obey you this time."

"We'll see what the next time brings, madam."

Head still averted, she slipped away.

I was still a shallow child. However, I had proven to myself that I could be authoritative with a woman when the situation demanded. My mother would have been very pleased with me.

"You have to learn to stand up to women, Eddie, including myself. Sometimes you're just too nice."

Sergeant Finnucane joined me at the riverside. The fog was rolling in from Galway Bay.

"Insisting that she ride back in the carriage with you?"

"You're an excellent detective, Tommy. However you're wrong on one point. I'm staying here."

"And yourself giving money to that little imp that's with her all the time."

"Josie . . . Am I that obvious, Tommy?"

"Wouldn't I be inclined to say that your goodness is obvious? . . . We don't see that in many reporters."

I felt myself blushing.

"Well," he went on, "there's a couple of new developments."

"Ah?"

I dared not think what I was indeed thinking. If Nora would be a widow in a few months, she would need someone to take care of her.

"They're saying that Johnny Joyce was the treasurer of the local secret society and that he held back ten pounds, a lot of money out there."

"Who's saying this, Tommy?"

"Some of the locals. It's all very indirect, mind you. That's the only way they can talk. They're also saying that they thought Peg was an informer because she used to chat with our lads, as if talking to a policeman means you have something important to say to him."

"Do they believe these are the motives for the murders?"

"They could just as well mean that I shouldn't pay any attention to these stories or that I should pay attention to them. My hunch is that they're telling me these are excuses, which is just about as far as they'll go with the Royal Irish Constabulary."

I raised the question with Bishop Kane later that night as we were eating supper in his house by the bay.

"Do you think, my lord, that the people in the valley know who the killers are?"

"Absolutely, Edward, and why they were murdered. They probably can't account for the violence of the murders, so they'll ignore that. By now, however, they have an explanation with which they'll live and which they will pass on to their children."

"And they will not tell the police?"

"They don't trust the police, though they like some of them. They think that if they try to tell anyone the truth, they won't be believed and worse things might happen. And they're probably right."

"Someone like Nora Joyce will let her husband die for a crime he didn't commit, as you yourself say, and not try to tell the truth?"

"She's more intelligent than most of them, Edward," he said, filling up my wineglass. "Still, she's a fatalist. The rules against talking to the police are as natural for her as breathing air. Myles probably told her not to tell the Royal Irish Constabulary who killed his cousin. It would do no good, and she has no one to defend her against revenge."

"Didn't Tony Joyce break the rules?"

"On a spur of the moment opportunity for money and revenge without thought of what might result. People in the valley might shun him when he returns from his comfortable quarters in the inn in Outhergard. They'll also have explanations for what he did that they may not approve but that will stand. Nor is there anyone likely to want revenge against him, especially with Royal Irish Constabulary lads protecting him for the rest of his life."

"He'd be safe and Nora wouldn't?"

"Not unless she married again, which I don't think she will in any event."

"Not even to protect her child?"

"We don't know yet that the child will be born or live or whether Nora will survive."

How, I wondered, could everyone be indifferent to her fate? Perhaps because they saw its inevitability. I didn't, however, though I wasn't sure what that meant, much less what I could do.

"When will Bolton reconvene the hearing?"

Bishop Kane lifted the last of his small piece of apple pie to his lips. I had long before finished my very large piece.

"Those who say he never will wouldn't be far from wrong. Next month he'll announce that the hearing has been adjourned to Dublin, the day after he's loaded the accused on a special train and carried them off to Dublin."

"Why would he do that?"

"It will be easier to get indictments and convictions there. The judges and juries will have little time for savages from the West of Ireland. Bolton would not trust jurors, even Protestants, out here with the weak case he has."

"Then there's no hope?"

"None, as far as I can see. A few of them may end up with twenty years in Dartmoor. If Bolton is desperate enough he may even set someone free if they provide evidence for the Crown."

"Does it not matter whether a defense lawyer could tear apart the case as Mr. Concannon did today?"

"You don't understand, Edward. The defense doesn't matter, especially not before a jury that is mostly Dublin Protestants and a few Catholics who want to prove how responsible they are, especially after the murders of the new Lord Lieutenant and his secretary in Phoenix Park last year."

"I told Nora Joyce today that she should never give up hope."

The bishop sighed and put down his wineglass, which he had just picked up.

"That is true in so far as God is concerned. She should hope in God's eventual goodness. She is far too intelligent to hope that good will triumph over evil in this world, especially for Irish-speaking peasants from Connemara."

Back here in my hotel room with Galway Bay glowing in the moonlight outside my window, I feel the same despair. As an American I believe that good will always triumph over evil. That obviously isn't true.

Yet the fatalism here in the West of Ireland is pervasive and insidious. These people believe that, when faced with the power of Dublin Castle and Westminster, they will always lose, no matter how unjust the English behavior may be. I try to remember my Galway-born grandparents. They were not so pessimistic, but perhaps that was because they left this terrible place when they were still young.

I make two resolutions tonight. I will continue to follow this case to its conclusion, and I will go up to Maamtrasna again to try to interview some of the people. Maybe while I'm up there I can slip a few more pounds into Josie's grubby little hand.

— 13 —

"HERSELF WOULDN'T run all the way with you?" Nuala was sitting at the table with a late morning cup of tea, reading the Fitzpatrick manuscript. She did not look up at me.

"She did not. She sat down halfway and waited patiently for me to return."

"Stubborn wench . . . We'll be having puppies making a mess in a couple of days. You'll have to clean up after them and myself with such a delicate stomach."

"You're having me on, woman, and yourself with the least delicate stomach in the world."

She giggled and turned a page.

"Aren't the children watching *Barney*? Herself will be along soon. She did well in her exams."

Had Ethne phoned from Galway or had Nuala merely picked up a signal? Better not to ask.

The exuberant, passionate woman of yesterday had disappeared. My wife was now a cool and disciplined professional woman in a severe blue suit, with her hair tied into a bun: Nuala Anne the accountant and the detective.

"Well," she said, closing the manuscript and returning it to the folder from which it came, " 'tis clear, isn't it, who the chief killer was and probably why?"

"You've figured it out?"

"Haven't you?"

"What's the motive for the violence?"

"What it usually is: sex."

"Won't you tell me?"

"No, you'll have to figure it out yourself."

Ethne bounced in, overjoyed that she had done well on her examination.

"Now I'll be able to go to postgraduate school, like the priest says I should."

"And in the United States!" Nuala chimed in, hugging our mother's helper.

It was all settled. Naturally.

The small ones dashed into the room, the Mick crawling furiously. Fiona ambled in after, wagging her tail. Family celebration.

"I'm so grateful for all your help, Mr. Coyne!" Ethne said to me, her eyes shining.

I had not done anything at all.

Our celebration was interrupted by the Mick's grabbing the leg of a chair and tottering forward a step. He promptly fell on his rear end and gurgled with pleasure.

Nuala picked him up and hugged him.

"Aren't you getting to be the great big grown-up boy?"

He gurgled again.

My feeling was that he would milk the one-step phenomenon for a long time before he tried the second step. It is alleged, probably untruly, that his father had done the same thing.

"Well, Dermot Michael, isn't it time that you got dressed? Don't we have lunch at the Renvyle House at half one?"

"We do indeed."

Later, as we strolled up the road to the hotel with ocean pounding on either side and Inishboffin glowing in the sunlight, my wife gave me an envelope.

"Isn't the solution to the Maamtrasna mystery in there, Dermot love?"

"If you say so. . . . Does it ruin the story for you to know how it's going to end?"

"Sure, we don't know. I only know who was behind the murders. I don't know what happens to Nora. I don't think she's as strong as your man thinks she is and himself such a fine young man."

"He probably wants to bring her to America with him."

"Och, nothing good will come of that, will it? Yanks shouldn't marry immigrant Irish women."

"Especially if they're from Galway."

"More especially if the girls are from Connemara."

"No good will come of that at all, at all."

"Just so," Nuala said, concluding the banter.

Then she added, "Your man is a lovely, sweet boy, but he isn't as tough as you are, and she's a brave lady, but not as tough as I am."

"Who is?"

She slapped my arm in protest, gently however.

Renvyle House is a charming old place, though there's probably not much left of the seventeenth century home of the Blakes. Still, the various restorations had paid proper attention to the past while adding the conveniences of the present—heated swimming pool, nine-hole golf course, and tennis courts.

Nuala and I had bought rights to use the sports facilities. We had engaged in fierce tennis matches in which she had won more than she lost and in sullen golf matches that I always won and herself having a handicap. We tried to swim in the pool a couple of times a week. Nuala—in a one-piece suit because she wasn't sure that she wasn't still too fat—had, needless to say, created a sensation.

Oliver St. John Gogarty's paragraph about the hotel hung in the lobby and at every table in the dining room. As "stately, plump Buck Mulligan" had put it, "My house stands on a lake, but it stands also on the sea, water lilies meet the golden seaweed. It is as if, in the fairy land of Connemara at the extreme end of Europe, the incongruous flowed together at last, and the sweet and bitter blended. Behind me islands and mountainous mainland share in a final reconciliation at this, the world's end."

He was a good poet who lived long enough to be tarred with the Buck Mulligan label. How he must have hated Jimmy Joyce.

The comfortable dining room, casual and restrained but charming and homey, provides striking views of the lake and the ocean and the islands beyond. The food, river trout today, was superb, and the smell of smoldering peat reminded one that one was indeed in Ireland.

"We'll have themselves here for supper over the weekend," my wife informed me. "Sure, shouldn't we eat here more often?"

"We'll have to bring the kids."

"They'll be perfectly well-behaved."

Sure.

"After our golf match."

The sensible thing for Nuala Anne would have been to give up on golf. However, she never gives up on anything, except singing. She'll never be able to beat me on the golf course because there's no way she can hit a drive as far as I do. Even on our small course here at the hotel, where drives are not so important, she doesn't have the calm required to one-putt a green.

"I'll beat you this time," she promised. The dining room was practically empty at half one because the fishermen from all over Europe were out taking advantage of the May fly season.

Seamus Redmond, the manager, joined us. He was a trim, handsome man in his early forties, with a red face and a touch of white at the sideburns of his black hair. Immaculately dressed and unflappable, he was a product of the best hotel management school in the world— not that he needed to learn about charm.

"I'm sorry to be late," he said smoothly as he joined us. "Things have been a bit dicey all morning, as you may imagine. I think, Nuala Anne, you'll find the trout to be to your taste."

"Wouldn't I be astonished altogether if I didn't?"

Her brogue became thicker when she was talking to someone from this part of the world she had not met before.

"I would imagine you don't have mornings like this very often."

"No." He sighed. "Thank God."

"Will the killings hurt business?"

"If there's no more of them they won't. On the contrary, they'll probably attract the curiosity seekers. . . . Isn't that the place where they did for the three Russians? . . ."

"Have you had them before?"

"Not this particular group. They come, surprisingly enough, for the May fly season. Russians, same as everyone else, love to fish."

"Did you know they were military officers?"

He shrugged.

"I did not. If you ask me did I think they were into some kind of crooked business, I would have said that probably they were. Most Russians with money are. They didn't bring women along, as they do in other places, and generally the kind of women you don't think are their wives. I assumed they liked to fish. I still do as a matter of fact."

"The Gardaí have no clues?"

"Not that they're telling me. The murders, they say, were 'professional.' We don't have anyone staying here who looks like a professional killer, whatever they look like."

The trout was served. My wife tasted a delicate bit of it with a fork and rolled her eyes.

"I'm glad you like it, Nuala Anne. . . . We have Russian cops coming out here tomorrow with their ambassador and people from our foreign office. We don't exactly need that. The Russians characteristically assume that if someone dies in a hotel, the hotel is responsible. I'll be diffident and polite since it's all for show anyway."

"Do you see any connection between their deaths and the other incidents around here?"

"Like that gobshite shooting at you? I honestly don't know. I suppose there must be a connection, but no more than the Gardaí do I know what to make of it."

"No one has been trying to buy the hotel?"

"Scores of people have been trying to buy it for the last several years. It's a gold mine, as you might imagine. The Station House down in Clifden isn't really competition. Indeed, I think we actually help one another. The company that owns Renvyle House will never sell it because it will simply become a richer and richer gold mine. There are not"—he swept his hand—"many views like this."

Nuala cautiously raised the wineglass to her lips. She rolled her eyes again. The doctor said that an occasional half glass or even a small full glass would do her no harm. This was, however, the first time she had experimented with it.

"And with a heated swimming pool," my wife said innocently.

"Yes." Seamus Redmond grinned. "The rugged West of Ireland coast and a heated swimming pool. I'm told, Nuala Anne, that you swim in the ocean."

"Sure," she said, "I'm a Galway woman. Where else would I swim? I don't mind the heat in the pool at all, at all, because haven't I become half Yank? No one grimly determined to buy it, come what may?"

"Not really. There's so many places around the world, the big companies don't waste their time on someone who is reluctant to sell. There's also gombeen men in Dublin and even in Galway City, who would like to develop this stretch of the world. However, we're not about to sell any of our land and none of the major landowners are either. Bungalows like yours are fine, and we could even stand a few more. We don't want a Bull Island beach out here."

My wife winked at me. Bull Island had marked a kind of turning point in our relationship.

"I imagine that the environmentalists," Nuala remarked gently, "would have a grand time altogether if anyone seriously tried to ruin Renvyle."

"They would indeed and, the way things are now, they'd probably win."

"You bought up the land before Ireland's burst of prosperity?" I asked.

He smiled and said, "One that no one of my generation believes can possibly last, even though it seems evident that we have crossed a critical turning point."

"Higher standard of living than the bloody Brits," my wife, who didn't used to be a Nationalist, added.

"Indeed yes. Besides our holdings, the T.D. has some good stretch of land. If he tried to develop it, he'd be voted out of office the next time around, and that would be the end of his political career. That's

why he's as astonished as everyone else at the destruction of his bungalow."

"He wants to be the Taoiseach?"

The word is pronounced something like "tay-shock" and is what they call the Prime Minister of Ireland.

"Well, a minister first. He's an able man, concerned about both the economy and the environment of the West of Ireland, which isn't an easy course to steer. . . . Incidentally, he came up here this morning and would very much like to have coffee with you after dinner. . . . Or lunch as you would call it, Dermot."

" 'Tis the only thing himself and I fight about," Nuala said in a blatant lie.

" 'Tis the only thing I've won so far," I added truthfully enough.

"We'd be delighted to have lunch with the T.D.," Nuala said. "Dermot and I have a tennis match sometime this afternoon, but there'll be plenty of time for that."

"Golf," I said.

"Tennis," she said, and that was that.

"Lord and Lady Ballynahinch own most of the rest of the land along the coast," Seamus Redmond said, returning to the question of land ownership. They are even more committed environmentalists than our own Greens. Heaven knows they don't need the money."

"Lord and Lady!" I exclaimed. "I thought most of the Brits were out of here."

"Most of them are, thanks be to God. Lord Ballynahinch, or Matt Howard, to use his real name, is the head of a large group of insurance companies in London. Labor, friend of Tony Blair, in favor of th Northern Ireland peace agreement, technically a hereditary Lor though the family lost its lands here over a century ago, mostly becau of incompetence. Attends the Lords these days because he's keep an eye on things for Tony until he can shut it down completely. N has made a lot of money. He decided that he would put some into acquiring some of the old family holdings. Rebuilt the ruin manor house out in Maamtrasna. Not his family house, but enough place. Kind of hobby of his. His wife is more intere

being Lady Ballynahinch than he is in being Lord Ballynahinch. Only reason he'd want to sell his lands around here would be if he needs money, which he doesn't. Moreover he hired an expensive architect named Tomas O'Regan to design the house. O'Regan is a bit of a gombeen man, if you ask me. You can count on him to lecture Matt on the importance of the house."

"Down in Carraroe where I come from," Nuala Anne commented, "they think Lord Ballynahinch is a bit of a gombeen man."

"Well, Nuala Anne, they wouldn't be completely wrong, but he's a charming one and basically honest."

We chatted amiably for a few minutes more and then he asked to be excused because he had to make preparations for the arrival of the Russian military tomorrow.

"Will they put ashore in a rubber boat from a nuclear-powered sub?" I asked innocently.

"I don't think . . ."

"Pay no attention to the man, Seamus Redmond. Hasn't he seen too many films on television!"

"Film" is pronounced in Ireland with a *u* as in "filum." The Irish not unreasonably assume that there should be a vowel between the two consonants.

"Well," she said, as the manager of the Renvyle House Hotel drifted away, "that was all a crock of shite, wasn't it, Dermot Michael Coyne?"

It had not seemed so to me. However, I agreed with her. Her detective modality did not take kindly to disagreement.

"It was all of that."

"As though even the May fly fishermen would keep coming if Renvyle had a ritual of sacrificing guests every week or so, especially if they were foreigners."

"Right!"

"And as though any big hotel company in the world would not sell this place or any other property if the price was high enough."

"Right!"

"And as though they give a good shite about your environmentalists."

"Right!"

"And as though a T.D. from out here would not trade a minister's
post for an opportunity to find a big pot of gold."

"Right!"

"And as though you and I are dumb enough to be taken in by all
that shite!"

"Right!"

"The Gardaí know better too, but like us they can't figure out
what's the point of the local terrorism."

"Russian money laundering!"

"I told you before that you had the right of it. They're involved
somehow and offended someone, someone very powerful and very
wicked."

"Like your gombeen man from down below on the road?"

"Wasn't I thinking the same thing meself?" she agreed. "Why would
Seamus Redmond bother to lie to us?"

"Maybe because he was told to?"

"Och, Dermot, you're the quick one!"

In the early days of our romance I had resented the fact that she
was Holmes to my Doctor Watson (or Poirot to my Captain Hastings,
or Flambeau to my Father Brown). I broke up with her, well, tried to
break up with her, because Dermot Michael Coyne was no spear-carrier,
right?

Wrong.

Now I didn't mind anymore. Well, not much.

Colm S. MacManus, who waited for us in the lounge for tea, would
have perhaps made Ward Committeeman in the Cook County Dem-
ocratic Organization, but only if there was no real talent in the ward.
The media, however, would certainly not describe him as a "key Daley
adviser."

In white sport coat and light blue trousers, Colm S. was a round man,
with a round body, a round bald head, a round face, and a round mouth
that was never shut.

"Ah, Ms. McGrail . . . So happy to know you and yourself, I believe, a constituent . . . We're so proud of you out here. . . . You prove that the great Irish cultural traditions of the West can speak loudly to the modern world. . . .

" 'Tis a grand time for Ireland with young women and young men like yourself. . . . And, Mr. Coyne, your family was from out here too I believe. . . . An important part of the Irish Diaspora. . . . I was delighted when my estate agent told me that you had bought one of my bungalows. . . .

"We built only three you know. . . . Yours and Mr. Redmond's, just up the road . . . And, of course, mine, which was tragically destroyed the other day . . . I'm sorry if the explosion caused you any inconvenience. . . . And terribly troubled by the dastardly attempt on your life . . . And the Gardaí swarming all around . . . I hope your vacation will not be ruined. . . ."

Would he ever run down, I wondered. Well, it was Ms. Holmes's job to intervene.

"Wasn't it a terrible shame to have your new house blown up by them shitehawks? I hope nothing valuable was destroyed."

She sighed loudly, and so did the T.D. In that blessed interval of silence, I sat down and signaled to the expectant waitress to bring over the tea and scones. There was no reason to let the tea turn cold. Nuala Anne thanked the waitress, not in Irish but in Spanish, much to that young woman's delight.

"Ah, no, not at all . . . Just the usual summer cottage furniture . . . Everything covered by insurance, of course . . . Terrible inconvenience to have to rebuild, don't you know . . . And then this horrid murder right here in the hotel last night. . . . I must say I am not happy at the prospect of having a lot of rich Russians around. . . . Still, everyone is welcome in Ireland, aren't they? . . ."

"Even your Romanians?"

"Well, no, they're not part of the EU, you know. . . . That young Italian woman you spoke to, on the other hand, her kind is always most welcome. . . ."

"Spanish."

The man was patently a fool. It did not follow, however, that he was not using his folly to cover something up or that he was not a dangerous fool. Whatever he was hiding, however, was not something that could be completely unknown to the Gardaí.

"This woman from down below, Margot Quinn, seems very interested in the land around here, doesn't she now? Wanted to buy our house for a condominium development, didn't she?"

"That woman is not to be trusted, Ms. McGrail," he said, his jowls trembling with outrage. "She does not know the meaning of truth. Worse still, she is in league with thoroughly corrupt speculators. I would not want to deal with her if I were you. . . . And I trust you are not considering selling your bungalow."

"Not at the moment . . . A lot of money to be made out here, isn't there now?" Nuala interrupted his free-association flow.

"Oh, yes indeed. West Galway and South Mayo are potentially great resources for Ireland and indeed the whole European Union. Tourism, minerals, skilled workers. It has become increasingly clear that the government should direct more funds out here to balance the enormous riches of the East."

That was a campaign speech. It meant everything and nothing. Come to think of it, he would never rise beyond the precinct captain role in Chicago.

"Minerals?" my wife asked innocently.

"Recent studies . . . Offshore oil . . . deep but still there . . . recoverable at costs not far above present-day prices . . . Zinc in the mountains . . . Maybe gold . . ."

"Like that under Cro Patrick?"

"Improbable . . . Environmentalists wouldn't let us explore . . . Good people . . . Sometimes a bit unreasonable . . . Still and all . . . Can't dig up a holy mountain, can you? . . ."

"I suppose not. However, I would think, sir, that the greatest source of income here in Connemara would be from tourists. Expand the Galway airport so that flights from New York or Frankfort could land, a score more places like Renvyle House or Ashford Castle. Lakes, inlets, harbors, marinas, concert halls, casinos and theater, local talent which, as we all know, is quite good, better roads, vast possibilities with little damage to the authentic countryside . . ."

I doubted that she believed a word of it. Yet it was a very good show. The woman was dangerous. I had known that, however, for a long, long time.

The T.D. bubbled ever more rhapsodically as he perceived in my innocent wife a kindred visionary spirit.

"Obviously someone is trying to frighten the rest of you off," she said softly as she interrupted a particularly big bubble, "why else the bombing and the murder?"

It was like she had pricked a child's balloon.

"I really cannot understand it," he said, suddenly dejected. "Clearly we've had offers from respectable companies. We are determined not to sell this land to anyone. It is part of Ireland's natural treasure. The sheep herders up in the mountains are unlike anyone else in Europe. The songs they sing . . . the stories they tell . . ."

"Like the Maamtrasna story?"

The conversation came to a dead halt.

"I think that's more legend than story," he said fretfully. "It was so long ago."

"I have often wondered," Nuala mused, "whether the ghosts of Johnny Joyce and his wife and mother and children don't haunt that old cemetery up above beyond."

If you did it right you had to combine three such prepositional adverbs in an Irish sentence.

She had stopped the T.D. dead in his tracks.

"Oh, that cemetery is gone. Matt Howard built his house on top of it."

"He moved the graves?" my wife asked in horror, whether mock or real I didn't know.

"No, that would have been impossible. His wife loved the spot. They simply built over it."

"And tore down the little church?"

"There wasn't much left of it. Actually, the cemetery was an untidy place. Eyesore. Scattered gravestones and such like. No one to keep it up. Local people didn't protest."

The T.D. seemed so surprised by the question that it never occurred to him to wonder how Nuala knew about the cemetery if it had been covered over. Perhaps he thought she had seen it as a child.

"Well, there was certainly a miscarriage of justice up there. . . ." Nuala said soothingly. "I would be inclined to guess that your three Russians represented a group that was attempting to outbid another group, perhaps also laundered Russian money lifted from the International Monetary Fund."

"Oh, I certainly hope not. It's all too complicated and evil for our lovely bit of ground here on the far end of Europe."

"Or," I said, "the near end of Long Island."

"While we're thinking of development projects," my wife continued, "isn't it time we thought of doing something for them poor folk out on the Aran Island?"

"Aran!" The T.D. almost choked on his scone.

"Wouldn't it be brilliant altogether to have three luxury hotels, one on each island. Each one would have its own heated swimming pool, its own eighteen-hole championship golf course, its own convention center, and its own condominium development for Yanks or Germans or even Russians who wanted to own a piece of Irish history. Wouldn't such a scheme mean hundreds of jobs for the poor natives, maybe thousands of jobs? Isn't it time to end the poverty out there once and for all?

Colm S. MacManus hesitated.

"Clearly the idea is brilliant, Nuala Anne. . . . I don't think the time is quite right for it now. I quite agree, however, that we need ingenuity and imagination to create parity between the West and Dublin."

"Couldn't we have artists' colonies and theater companies which would create permanently an enclave of Irish-language culture for the whole world, kind of a Gaelic culture museum?"

The T.D. remembered an appointment he had with a constituent and pleaded to be excused. He rolled out of the lounge as if he were a pastel, multicolored balloon pursued by a Russian clown with a knife.

"You scared the shite out of him, Nuala Anne," I said.

"I thought I was very persuasive. . . . Give the poor man a couple of days and he'll be whispering me scheme into the ear of any gombeen man who wants to listen."

Absently she buttered a scone, drenched it in strawberry preserves, and plunked it into my mouth—with the same reverence a priest might have put the host on the mouth of an elderly person who did not want to receive the Eucharist in the hand. It was an old ritual between us with a deeply erotic overtone.

"I don't know why I mentioned Maamtrasna, Dermot Michael. I really don't. It scares me now."

"The dead can't hurt us, Nuala Anne."

"I know that, Dermot. They can only help us if they want. 'Tis the living that scare me."

She lightly buttered a piece of scone for herself.

"What are they all so worried about, Dermot?" she said, resting her chin—a determined chin, I might remark—on the pyramid of her fingers. "Both he and Seamus Redmond are worried about something. Maybe there's a deal about to go down, as you Yanks would say, that would make them all a lot of money. Now someone else, more powerful perhaps and certainly more dangerous, is trying to edge into it. And those poor Russian fellas got in the way."

"We must talk to Lord and Lady Ballynahinch."

"Won't I ring them up and tell them we're coming up because of our interest in the Maamtrasna affair? That will scare the living shite out of them, won't it?"

"It will that."

"Well, Dermot Michael Coyne, let's go home and change into our golf togs. This time I'm going to beat you."

—14—

"WELL," SHE said as we walked back to our bungalow, "neither one of them fellas is a master criminal are they now? Sure, wouldn't they have a hard time organizing a crooked football pool?"

The sun was still shining brightly, but the wind was picking up and the breakers were growing louder. There might be a "blow" coming in from Long Island or some such place. Then the rain would be "hard" instead of "soft." We would consider an Irish "soft" rain, by the way, a torrential downpour in Yank Land.

"You have the right of it," I agreed.

"Och, they're a dead end, I'm afraid. The Gardaí will be sniffing around the financial world. They'll be finding out that, while there's a lot of talk about developing the harbors and inlets and lakes out here, there's no real money for it yet, and not likely to be. . . . The weather is daunting, if you take me meaning, and picturesque will take you just so far."

"Actually, I thought you missed an obvious benefit of your Aran scheme. . . . You would have to build a marina on each island. . . ."

"And a friggin' tunnel into Galway . . . and, faith, why not a factory to mass-produce Aran Island sweaters."

"You ought to write it up and send it to the *Irish Times*."

"You're the author in the family, Dermot Michael Coyne. . . . And wouldn't there be amadons who would take it seriously like that poor round gobshite of a man!

Then she turned thoughtful. I thought it best not to disturb her. She was on an emotional roller coaster, steeper and wilder than her usual mercurial romp through life.

On the way back to Renvyle House, I asked, "How come we switched from tennis to golf?"

"I'm sick of being the domineering bitch who always gets her way. You really shouldn't put up with me, Dermot Michael Coyne. I'm a friggin' spoiled brat."

OK, WISE GUY, YOU DON'T RESPOND TO WHAT SHE SAYS BUT TO WHAT SHE MEANS. LET'S SEE YOU FIELD THAT HOT GROUND BALL.

I tried, "Annie McGrail didn't raise any spoiled brats."

"Hmm," she snorted. "Doesn't yourself say all the time that I'm bossy?"

"Wasn't Ma bossy and didn't I love her?"

My grandmother, also from Carraoe, was both bossy and conniving and I adored her. Nuala, who had translated her diary for me, identified with her. She even sometimes seems to be claiming that she heard from her, even though Ma, as we called her, had been dead for seven years. I chose to believe that she was merely asserting, sometimes with re- markable accuracy, what Ma would have said under the circumstances.

"You never win any of the arguments. You wanted to play golf, I wanted to play tennis, so you were willing to play tennis just to keep me happy."

"No," I said. "I knew if I agreed too easily, you'd switch to golf!"

"Go 'long with you, Dermot Michael Coyne. I'm serious. You never win any of the arguments."

"Only the serious ones."

"For instance?"

"Coming over for these two months, buying a bungalow, taking your medicine."

She pondered that.

" 'Tis true," she said reluctantly. "I guess I'm confused. Maybe I should take two of them pills every day!"

"Don't you dare!"

"Och, I'm just funning you, Dermot! . . . Would you look at that . . .

the Gardaí are checking golfers! . . . Me name is Nuala Coyne and I'm not a guest at the hotel and this is me husband, Dermot Coyne, and we have playing privileges here."

"May we see your identification?" The young man, red hair with freckles, was immune to the smile of a beautiful woman.

"Dermot, do you have our passports?"

"Woman, I do not."

"No identification at all?"

"Not at all, at all . . . Except me husband usually carries a wallet with a crock full of credit cards."

"I'm afraid that won't do. You certainly cannot play golf here. Moreover, failure to produce a valid identification document is in itself a violation of Irish law."

The other guard, a tall black Irishman, seemed a little more lenient.

"Sure, Brendan, we could ring up the hotel, couldn't we now?"

"Or Chief Superintendent McGinn."

The man waiting on the tee, perhaps for golfing partners, turned around and grinned. "Oh, Shenandoah," he crooned, "I love you so. . . . Officer, you might also check with those two plainclothes Gardaí who are Ms. McGrail's bodyguards and are standing over there by the pool and wondering whether you're out of your mind."

Brendan looked skeptically at the priest, "You ought not interfere in matters of Garda business, Father Lane."

"Would you ever look at our lads over there, Brendan? Aren't they waving them through?"

"Well, I guess it will be all right. . . ."

Jack Lane considered the cop carefully.

"Clergymen, officer, are citizens of Ireland just like anyone else. They have the right to make representations to Gardaí who are acting inappropriately."

"Och, sure An t'Athair, Sean O'Laighne," me wife said with the infinite respect she reserved for the clergy, "wasn't the poor lad just trying to do his duty? And don't I look like the kind of woman who would have a carving knife with me golf sticks?"

"Jack, Nuala Anne," he said as we approached the tee. "I hope you wouldn't mind my playing with you?"

"With a holy priest, sure I'll have to watch me language now, won't I? And anyway, Father, won't I be beating the both of you?"

"We'll see about that!"

The course had nine holes all right, five par four and four par three, not the kind of course I liked to play. The first one was a hundred and fifty yard par three. We let herself shoot first, not that the matter came up for discussion. In long red-checked shorts and a red sweater she was a fearsome sight as she swung her eight iron and hit the ball into a sand trap short of the green.

"Shite," she protested.

" 'Tis only a vulgarity," Jack commented as he teed up. His nine-iron shot sailed over the green and into the rough beyond.

As is well known, the greens in Ireland are like our fairways, and the fairways are like our rough.

I put my drive some three feet from the pin.

"Looks like this is going to be easy," I announced.

"A friggin' birdie," me wife protested. " 'Tis not fair, at all, at all, and the wind helping you too!"

"She really has no respect for the clergy, Jack. She beats my brother, George, all the time."

"I didn't know you had a brother who's a priest, Dermot."

"Yeah, and he's a smart-ass," I said. "Thinks he knows everything."

"Isn't his reverence a good and holy priest and himself now the parish priest of his own parish after working for all them years for the little bishop at the Cathedral?"

"*The* little bishop?"

"The very same . . . By the way, Father, have you found the second part of your man's manuscript yet?"

"I've been searching for it, but no luck yet."

"Sure, you've been looking in the wrong place, haven't you now?"

We had reached Nuala's sand trap.

"Where should I be looking, Nuala?"

"Well," she said, approaching the ball with a sand wedge,

"shouldn't you be looking in that old closet down in the little basement behind the water pipe?"

She chipped the ball over to the far side of the green.

"Shite!" she protested again.

"There's no little closet there," Jack Lane, his golf bag hanging limply in his hand, said as he stared at me wife. My wife.

"Ah, there is now. You'll just have to remove the old furniture that's in front of the door, won't you now?"

She put the sand wedge in her bag and began to amble to the other side of the green. As if in the presence of the uncanny, Jack Lane followed her gingerly.

"There's a third segment of the manuscript somewhere in your house, or maybe in the church, but I haven't figured out where yet."

"You are indeed one of the dark ones, Nuala Anne?"

"Och, sure, only charcoal gray! . . . You're away, Father."

Jack got the ball on the green, on the opposite side of the lie of his first shot.

"Would you guys please concentrate," I demanded. "I want to putt for my bird."

"Gobshite," me wife muttered darkly.

On their fourth shots they managed to get their balls closer to the cup than mine. Naturally, I drilled in the putt. A bird for me, a double bogey for each of them. Jack Lane was obviously a very good golfer, a valid competitor for meself. Myself. Nuala Anne, however, had disconcerted him altogether.

"My wife claims, Jack Lane," I said as we went to the next tee, a two hundred and forty yard par four, "that she knows who the killer up on Maamtrasna was and why the killing occurred and herself not even finishing the first manuscript yet."

"Sure 'tis clear as the nose on your face," Nuala said, tilting her pert nose skyward as though everyone knew who the killer was. "And wasn't the motive for the violence sex, like it usually is? And haven't I given my husband the answer in a sealed envelope?"

"I see."

He was down in five on the hole and Nuala actually produced a par. With an easy swing I put my ball once again within a few yards of the pin. Dermot Michael Coyne was on a roll. A bird and an eagle.

"We should be playing for money," I commented to my disgruntled companions.

"Did you know, Father Jack Lane," Nuala Anne, all innocence, asked, "that Matt Howard built his manor house on the Maamtrasna cemetery?"

Jack considered his five iron as though he were wondering whether it would serve as an exorcist's cross.

"No, Nuala Anne, I didn't know that," he said cautiously.

"The Irish name means 'Church on the Hill,' doesn't it now? And didn't your man walk up there in the funeral procession and didn't Lord Ballynahinch build his manor house on top of it?"

"Did he?" The priest was thunderstruck.

"And isn't it a lucky thing that we're not superstitious about such things or we'd be thinking that he'd have terrible bad luck for such a thing?"

"Dermot," the priest said, "why don't we hit our drives and then discuss this new message from the charcoal gray world?"

"A brilliant idea!"

I used a four wood, which dropped my ball maybe twenty yards short of the green. Nuala dubbed her four wood and was at least a hundred yards short. Jack Lane's five iron didn't serve him much better. I figured that with a good chip I would earn myself a bird.

"You were saying, Nuala Anne?"

"I was asking what you think of this Matt Howard person and his wife."

That was not what she had said, but it was indeed what she was asking.

"Lady Daphne."

"And his wife Lady Daphne."

"Would you be thinking that Matt Howard might ask someone to creep into this historic house and slit the throats of three Russian army officers?"

"Would he?"

"Not very likely. He has oceans of money, all of it earned more or less honestly. No reason to engage in risky violence to make a few dollars more."

Nuala merely sighed.

"As to what I think of him, he's a nice enough fellow, generous to the Church, supports the peace process up beyond above, and is a friend of Tony Blair. He rubs me the wrong way, I guess, because there's enough Republican blood in me not to like English landlords, even of the modern New Labor variety."

Nuala's nine iron dumped her ball on the green, two putts away from the cup. Jack Lane's shot fell in the rough beyond the green.

"Do you deal in controlling golf balls?" he asked her suspiciously.

"That would be telling, wouldn't it?"

I had never thought of that possibility. I started to think about it when she sunk her thirty-foot putt and I missed my six footer. A bird for me wife and a par for me.

"Shite!" I exclaimed.

"And Lady Daphne?" I asked as we hiked to the next tee.

"She's a little odd, Dermot. No, I take that back. She's more than a little odd, she's . . ."

"Round the bend altogether?" Nuala asked helpfully.

"You have the right of it. Vague and unfocused."

"She'd worry about living over a cemetery?"

"More likely she'd love it. . . . There's lots of strange people that hang around the Howard family."

"That's what we're interested in, Jack Lane," I said. "The more strange people the better."

So the match continued. Dark clouds rushed in from the Atlantic, the wind picked up even more. I pulled a Chicago Bulls windbreaker out of my golf bag and wrapped it around my wife's shivering shoulders. I won the match, naturally, with a miserable three under par, herself came in one over par, and the poor little priest finished at five over par.

"Worst game I've ever had at this course." He sighed. "I'm no matched for preternatural powers."

"Sure, wasn't it just the wind? . . . Would the Howards ever mind, do you think, if I called them and said I wanted to talk to them about the Church on the Hill, which isn't on the hill anymore?"

"If you identified yourself as Nuala Anne McGrail, they'd be willing to talk to you about almost anything."

"Wouldn't that be grand!"

A trip to a manor house over an ancient graveyard with my wife in her current woman-leprechaun mood would be like an episode from the *Addams Family*.

"Could I save my reputation as a good loser, if not as a good golfer, by offering to take you to supper down at the Station House in Clifden?"

"Would your reputation last till Monday night, Father Lane? Aren't me poor ma and da coming up from down below in Carraroe for the weekend?"

"Monday night it is. . . . Now, I think I'll go home and drench myself in holy water."

"Go 'long with you, An t'Athair!"

Just after we had parted, Nuala shouted after him, "Och, Father Lane?"

He turned, a man badly beaten. "Yes, Nuala Anne?"

"Don't forget to look in the closet behind the old furniture back at the parish house."

His agreement was lost in the wind.

Nuala huddled in the lee of my arm as we fought our way back to the bungalow.

"Was I awful, Dermot Michael?"

"Terrible, woman, and that poor priest so badly confused that he couldn't concentrate on his game."

"Sure, I didn't want him to beat you, did I?"

"You spooked him and charmed him at the same time, and, what's more, young woman, you did it for the pure hell of it."

"Purgatory of it . . . Besides, we need that manuscript, don't we now, if we're going to find out who the killers really were?"

"We do indeed. . . . And you knew where it was only when he joined us on the links, of course."

"No, while we were walking down the road and meself knowing he would be on the links . . . Hold me tight, Dermot Michael, I'm perishing with the cold, and me poor ma and da coming up from Carraroe tomorrow."

"Where it will be warm and sunny, it being so far away."

In the bungalow, the whole ménage was in the toy-littered family room, where my son, face smeared with baby food, diaper hanging loose, silly grin on his face, was experimenting, to general amusement, with his first steps.

"Ma, he's wonderful!" Nelliecoyne enthused. "Look at the way he laughs when he falls on his ass!"

Whereupon Michael Dermod did just that. He pulled himself up on a chair leg and then tottered two steps towards his mother, down whose cheeks tears of joy streamed as she grabbed him in her arms.

Like I say, the woman wears many different faces.

As we sat down to supper, the phone rang.

"Dermot Coyne," I informed the caller.

"Jack Lane . . . Do you keep holy water in the house?"

"With what else would we sprinkle everyone when the thunder and lightning dash in from Boston?"

"I thought so!"

"You found the manuscript."

"I did. It's not in good shape, but you should be able to read it. There's no ending yet. Whenever herself figures out where it is, I'll hunt it down."

"Good!"

"I also found a picture of the cemetery up there. It was actually in front of the old manor house. It's pretty clearly a cemetery."

"Thank you," I said briskly.

At the table, Nelliecoyne was throwing baby food back at her brother.

"Jack Lane," I said. "He found what he was looking for."

"Brilliant!" my charcoal gray wife chortled. "Didn't I tell him he would!

— 15 —

Letterfrack, County Galway, October 15, 1882

I have not had the moral courage to set words on paper other than for my dispatches to Chicago. As to them, my family reports that they are prominently displayed in the Daily News and well received. They congratulate me on my success as a journalist. How could I tell them that my journalistic career does not matter to me anymore. I am too deeply involved in the tragedy and the injustice of Maamtrasna to care about my career. I feel compelled to turn the tide of doom rolling towards those men in Kilmainham Jail in Dublin. Yet I am not wise enough to know what to do nor strong enough to take action.

I am back in Connemara interviewing men and women in the valley for my dispatches to the Daily News. I hope to find some clue, some hint of the truth. The people are quite willing to talk to me but not at all willing to tell me what really happened. Bishop Kane and Nora Joyce both had warned me that the truth would never be told. Now I fear that they were right. Yet I must try.

At the end of last month, late in the night, the accused were hustled out of the Galway jail, loaded on a special train under the railway hotel—where I was sleeping in oblivion—and taken to Dublin. They are locked in Kilmainham Jail, isolated from one another and usually even from counsel. The sudden and secret change of venue was particularly cruel, because the families had been promised visits the following day. I traveled to Dublin immediately. Before I left, I found my carriage driver and told him to take the

same passengers back to the valley when they learned that their men had been shipped to Dublin.

There was little to be learned, except that Bolton was trying to turn some of the accused against the rest of them. The fiasco in Galway had convinced him that the "irreproachable" witnesses were quite reproachable. For the valley folk, Dublin was another world, a mysterious, terrifying place from which men rarely returned. The horror deepened.

The indictment would come at the end of October, the trials in November, and the hangings right after Christmas. No time wasted. George Bolton knew that all "right-thinking" people in England and in Ireland were calling for the blood of the murderers.

So I have come back here to search for more evidence. I have picked up a few hints.

An old woman, a Mary Joyce (of the Tony Joyce clan) whispered to me, "Didn't they have a meeting, about a hundred of them, about what to do with your man?"

And a shifty-eyed young woman said boldly, "Didn't Breige O'Brien marry your man too soon after her husband died?"

Most of the local people couldn't answer my questions because they didn't speak English—or at least pretended they didn't speak English.

Martin Joyce, a younger brother of Anthony Joyce the informer, a sullen, resentful young man with thick black hair and a hard face, seemed ready to fight me when I met him on the road.

"Why can't you people leave us alone?" he demanded. "Everyone knows that Johnny Joyce got what he deserved."

"And the women and children in his family?"

"They weren't innocents either. . . ."

"Even Peggy?"

"She was a whore for the Royal Irish Constabulary. No honest woman in the valley mourns her."

"Don't people resent Anthony because he informed?"

"They know he had his reasons. . . . All my brother did was reveal the names of the killers before they killed more people. Mind you, they deserved killing. No one blames Anthony for telling the truth. When the police release him he will be welcome back in the valley."

Anthony Joyce and his fellow "irreproachables" were being protected by the police over in Outhergard by Loch Corrib.

"And Myles Joyce?"

"Them that knows will tell you that he's not the saint some people pretend he is. And that wife of his is a slut as them with eyes can plainly see."

I wanted to hit him. The only reason that he had not fought with me at the beginning of our conversation was that my size intimidated him. Someone ought to teach him to keep a civil tongue in his head, especially about women.

However, I was a professional journalist. I would not permit myself the luxury of an easy fight.

I then visited Little Tom Casey, one of whose cousins was an accused (also called Tom). With his fourteen-year-old son, Tim Casey, acting as translator, he assured me that his cousin Tom had been in bed with his wife all night. Then he added, "They have some that did and some that didn't."

He wouldn't say any more.

I hiked up the valley to the house of Big John Casey, the most prosperous of the farmers. His large house was whitewashed, the yard in front clean, the outhouses neat and well maintained. The furniture inside was new and comfortable. Big John himself was also neat and clean—dressed in trousers and vest and a white shirt, open at the neck, his hair neatly cut and his chin shaved. He was a charming, genial man, only ready to talk, but not ready to say anything. Yet his strong, square face, his quick smile, and his laughing eyes suggested that he knew he was a cut above the other people in the family and that intelligence and hard work entitled him to respect and admiration.

"There's been too many murders around here, Ed my lad, too many altogether. Lord Mountmorris up in Mayo, the Hudleys who were agents for the Lord, the Walshes and the Lydons down in Letterfrack only last year. It's violent country. Until now our valley has been spared, thanks be to God. Now"—he sighed—"don't we have the worst murders of them all? . . . And forgive me for not wetting the tea for you as soon as you came. . . . Since my wife died, God rest her soul, I haven't been so quick at greeting guests."

He talked on as we sipped our tea.

"It will take a long time to calm the valley down again. Everyone is in fear. No one knows when the constables will come and take one of us away. The hatred is so thick you could feed the sheep with it."

"It still seems very quiet and peaceful."

"Ay, lad, most of the people are good, hardworking men and women. Still there are some violent folk in the valley. . . . And some with long memories."

"One less than there was?"

"Well, the Joyces have always been a fighting family."

"Even Myles Joyce?"

"Och, poor Myles and himself with a young wife. . . . He's a quiet man until you stir him up."

"And themselves members of the secret societies?"

"That's mostly talk, lad. The Ribbonmen are a grand story, but your men Davitt and Parnell have the right of it, if you ask me."

"And Anthony Joyce?"

"Well," he sighed, " 'twas a fine story he had to tell wasn't it? Yet there are those who say you wouldn't be all that far from wrong if you thought that maybe Anthony had his reasons."

That comment was typical—elusive, indirect, mysterious. It said nothing but hinted at many things. The implication was that if I knew what everyone in the valley knew, I would understand all that had happened.

Also, he seemed to be saying that the sooner the dead buried their dead, the sooner there would be peace in the valley.

I have a dispatch in my head about the strange attitude of the Maamtrasna people, but it won't take shape yet.

I now permit myself but one jar a night. I do not want to go home to America a drunk.

Tomorrow I will see Nora and Josie. I dread the meeting. I know she will be suffering terribly and that I will be able to do nothing to help her.

Letterfrack, County Galway, October 16, 1982

This morning I road up the side of the mountain to Myles Joyce's home. My heart beat eagerly at the prospect of seeing Nora again, yet I was afraid that I would have nothing to say to her that would give her hope.

Josie met me at the side of the path about a quarter mile from the house.

"Good morning, Mr. Fitzpatrick," she said, curtsying respectfully. "And a grand morning it is, isn't it?"

I had not noticed, but it was a grand morning, a cool, pleasant, sunny day.

"Good morning, Josephine Philbin," I said bowing back. "Jesus and Mary be with you."

"Jesus, Mary, and Patrick be with you," she responded, still respectful. I dismounted.

"Would you think someone might spit on me today?"

"Ah, sure you never can tell, can you now?" she said with her wicked grin. "The young women around here are terrible hot tempered."

In a few years Josie would be a blooming, beautiful young woman like my sister Marie. What hope for her was there in this grim, hate-filled valley?

"How is Nora?"

"Very brave, Mr. Fitzpatrick, sir, and herself sick almost every day."

"Does she have any hope, Josie?"

"No, sir. She knows that Myles is a dead man. He'll never come back from Dublin. She lives now for the little one."

"Oh."

"Mr. Fitzpatrick, sir, I have nine pounds, eight shillings, and six pence left." She said, offering me money with her grubby little hand.

"Not at all, Josie. Keep it to take care of Nora . . . Does she know that you have money to take care of her?"

"I don't know, Mr. Fitzpatrick, sir. She never asks. . . . Are you sure you don't want the money back?"

"Absolutely certain, Josie. In fact, I brought some more for you."

I reached in my pocket and removed four five-pound notes, which I had folded in preparation for my encounter with Josie on the road. I assumed that she would be waiting for me.

" 'Tis too much, Mr. Fitzpatrick, sir." She hesitated to take the money.

"Josie, you're the only one up here who will take care of Nora. If you need more money, tell Sergeant Finnucane. He'll pass the word to me."

She nodded solemnly. "Yes, sir, Mr. Fitzpatrick, sir. I won't waste a single pence."

"If you see a hair ribbon you would like to buy for yourself, you are to do so, understand?"

Tears streamed out of her vast brown eyes and streaked her dirty face.

"I couldn't do that, sir."

"You can and you'd better or you will disobey me."

"Oh, I'd never do that, Mr. Fitzpatrick," she said, her wicked grin replacing the tears. "I'd never disobey you, sir."

Inside this filthy little urchin there was a mighty soul, loyal, brave, resourceful. God protect her, I prayed silently.

Nora was sitting outside the house on an old chair, peeling a small pile of potatoes—food for a week perhaps. She was obviously pregnant, though gloriously so. Her face was pale and drawn, but she still greeted me with a radiant smile. Her spinning wheel stood besides her.

"Jesus and Mary be with you, Mr. Fitzpatrick."

"Jesus and Mary and Patrick be with you, Nora Joyce."

"This little imp has been pestering you, no doubt. . . . Do sit down. . . . Josie, would you run and wet the tea for Mr. Fitzpatrick, please? . . . Here, I'll take the book, Mr. Fitzpatrick."

The book was a tattered and very old collection of the plays of Shakespeare.

"Josie is a wonderful girl," I said as the urchin disappeared into the dark interior of the stone house. "She will flower into a wonderful young woman."

"At least one with a mind of her own . . . You seem surprised that I am reading the playwright?"

"Not at all . . ."

"Of course you are." She smiled. "We are not all illiterates out here. My father was a great reader, especially this book and the Bible. I still have some of his books. They and my rosary are my treasures these days."

I could think of nothing to say.

"I hope you are right about Josie," she continued with a sigh. "There are too many children down at her house. So she adopted me, without asking my leave. I don't know what would happen to me if she were not here."

"She is both fearless," I said, "and fearsome."

Nora smiled ruefully, "Both traits that I lack. I am told that you have been wandering around the valley trying to discover the truth of what happened the night of the killings."

"What do they say of me?"

"The people in the valley? Why should you care what they say?"

"Curiosity, I suppose."

"They say that you're a nice young Irish American gentleman who does not and cannot possibly understand us. . . . They all like you, however."

"They're right about not understanding them. . . . Everyone knows what happened that night and yet no one will speak about it."

She shook her head in disagreement. "Everyone thinks they know the events the night of the murder, but no one does. We all have bits and pieces of the story and we've all heard rumors and perhaps passed them on. Yet, if you could compile all the tales in the valley about that terrible night, you would find many contradictions and you'd be no closer to the truth than you are now."

"Do you know who killed the Joyce family, Nora?"

"Perhaps."

"Are the killers in jail in Dublin?"

"Perhaps . . . some of them."

"And there are others free?"

Her rosary appeared in her hand. Her fingers clenched it. *I should take pity on the poor woman.*

"Possibly so . . . Many people think they are."

"Could you not go to the police and tell them?"

She sighed.

Josie appeared with the "wet" tea and a few slices of warm brown bread.

"Thank you, Josie. I'll pour for us."

"You want me to leave you two alone for a while?"

"That's not necessary, Josie."

Nonetheless, the waif slipped away.

"You are an educated man, Mr. Fitzpatrick, are you not?" Nora said continuing our discussion.

"I went to St. Ignatius College and read law in my father's office."

"Ah, that helps me to understand you. You believe in the rule of law."

"Well, yes . . ."

"Out here there are two kinds of law . . . theirs and ours. Theirs is written down and enforced by police and the courts. Ours, which is much older, is not written and is enforced by the community."

"Anthony Joyce broke that law."

"He meant no harm, except to my husband. He will be punished, not violently, but punished just the same."

She refilled my teacup.

"Would they blame you if you went to the authorities to save your husband's life?"

"No . . . All the women would support me. Most of them. Myles is a good man. Everyone knows that, even some of the Anthony Joyces. He never sought a fight and only fought in self-defense. I would do anything to save Myles."

"Then why don't you go to the authorities and name the killer?"

"Even in your American law, would they believe a wife who accused someone else without proof?"

"No," I admitted reluctantly.

"You see, there's nothing I can do."

"Are you afraid of the real killer?"

She was silent for a moment.

"Of the men who I think are the killers?"

"Yes."

"I don't care what they do to me. My life is over anyway. I want my baby to live. I want Josie to live."

"They wouldn't kill Josie!"

"They killed Peggy Joyce, didn't they?"

It dawned on me at last that fear permeated the valley, more fear of the killers than of the English. Having killed once, they might easily come back and do it again.

"If I could find proof . . . ?"

"You won't find proof, Edward. If you keep searching, your life will be at risk. I don't want to have that on my soul."

"Was there a meeting in which a hundred people voted to kill John Joyce?"

"Some people had a meeting. I don't think there were that many people at it, maybe only twenty."

"Myles wasn't there?"

"Certainly not. He knew of it, however. Naturally."

"Anthony Joyce could have guessed the names of some of the killers, if he was at the meeting."

She absorbed me in her clear blue eyes, hesitated, and then said, "Probably."

"Was John Joyce active in the secret society?"

"Some of the time. Like most such groups, it is not well organized."

"Did he steal some of its funds?"

"He may have. He liked to steal, I think."

"Were Margaret and Peg informers?"

"Only a few fools think so."

"Other men besides John Joyce wanted Breige O'Brien when her husband died?"

Nora bowed her head and said nothing for a moment.

"It is wicked to discuss such matters. . . . She was a fine-looking woman. Many men, not all of them without wives of their own, wanted her. Everyone was surprised that she married John Joyce. I have no doubt that she loved him, God have mercy on them all."

Three motives for murder—personal hatred, politics, and jealousy.

"What will you say about us, Edward Hannigan Fitzpatrick, when you write your story?"

"I will write that there were three possible motives for the murder: personal hatred, politics, and jealousy. I will say that many people in the valley know who the killers are, that they believe some of the accused men are guilty and some are not, that virtually all agree that Myles Joyce has been unfairly accused, and that they have no hope that English justice will be fair."

She nodded her head. "You may certainly say those things without risking yourself here. But say no more."

"All right."

"Promise?"

"Yes."

She sighed in relief.

"You might add," she said, "that no one in this valley doubts that English justice will hang innocent men."

She began to cry, not hysterically, but inconsolably. I was tempted to put my arm around her, which would have been a very bad thing to do. Josie saved me from that temptation by appearing out of nowhere to embrace her aunt.

Nora gradually calmed down, apologized for her grief, and thanked me for my visit.

"You promise me solemnly, Mr. Fitzpatrick, that you will not return to talk to anyone in this valley?"

"Not even you?"

She hesitated.

"You can come to tell me about Myles. . . . Josie, will you show Mr. Fitzpatrick the way back to the road?"

"Yes, Auntie Nora."

"What will happen to her, Josie?"

"You mean when Uncle Myles swings?"

I winced.

"Yes."

"Well, she may die in childbirth. She and the baby may starve during the winter. If she lives, some men will want to marry her. The land is good here and she is beautiful. She will have none of that. Others may kill her."

The child recited her litany of horror with perfect calm.

"Kill her! Why?"

"Because she knows too much, because she may be the only one in the valley who wants the truth to be told, because they found out that they enjoy killing beautiful women."

I swore as I road back here to Letterfrack that I would not let that happen. It is a vain oath. What can I, a callow lad, do against a whole valley? Nonetheless, I will try.

I have written my dispatch and brought it to the telegraph office. I assumed that the telegraph operator would relay its contents up to the valley.

I reformulated my oath: I would do everything I could to protect her. Then I prayed for her to God, and Mary and Jesus and to all the saints in heaven, especially the Irish ones.

—16—

Dublin, November 1, 1882

The trials began today in the grim, ramshackle Green Street Courthouse. It has rained in Dublin every day since I've been here. It fits the mood of the trial. I would call the trial a comedy if the outcome would not be tragic for the innocent as well as the possibly guilty. Most of the defendants speak little or no English. A policeman translates when necessary to obtain an answer from them, such as guilty or not guilty.

Otherwise they are being tried in a foreign country by men who speak a foreign language. They are mute and passive participants in a process that would determine whether they would live or die. Judges, lawyers, and most of the juries will be Protestant. Even their lawyers, John Stritch and George Malley are Protestant and do not speak Irish. They are reputed to be decent if not brilliant men. Neither their solicitor nor their counsel seems to have much taste for his work. One of the Queen's Counsels is a man named Peter O'Brien, whom everyone calls Peter the Packer because he is so expert at packing juries with Protestants, especially Protestants with Catholic names. The other is one James Murphy, who is said to be one of the best counsels in Dublin.

According to the rumors from Kilmainham, Crown Solicitor George Bolton, wary of a repeat of the debacle at the Galway jail, is trying to break two of the accused so that they will become "approvers"—witnesses for the Crown. According to some of my Irish colleagues, Bolton wants the names of the three men who did the actual killings while the others lurked outside the house—or at least of the three men who were most likely to appeal to the jury as murderers—Pat Casey (of the Little Tom Caseys), Pat Joyce (a distant relative of Anthony Joyce), and Myles Joyce.

"There's not much doubt that the first two were involved," my best Irish colleague informed me, "though Bolton doesn't have enough to convict them, maybe not even in this Protestant courtroom. Myles is another matter. Even the police from Galway have their doubts. He is some kind of Gaelic chieftain out there. He looks like a criminal, however, and hence Bolton can't afford to let him get away."

I cannot get over the cynicism that surrounds this trial. The difference between the lawyers and judges and the journalists is that the latter do not even pretend to believe in the process. I will say that in my dispatch.

It seems to be well known in Dublin that Anthony Philbin (a cousin of poor Josie) and Tom Casey (a relative of Little Tom Casey) were the two men on whom Bolton concentrated his efforts to find an "approver." The former was a weak, seedy man just back from England and was almost certainly not in the party that raided the Joyce House. The latter may well have been there, as he is said to claim to have been on the outside, watching.

"He'll have them testify against the three he wants to hang. Then the others will plead guilty and get long terms in prison," my Irish friend, Martin Dempsey, told me in the pub after the first day in court. "That's the plan, don't you see? And there's nothing anyone can do about it."

"Except report it in your stories."

He sighed. "Imply it in our stories, lest we face libel charges. It really doesn't matter, you see. The Protestants and some of the middle-class Catholics already know that all ten men are guilty because they are Irish savages who can't speak English. Most of the Catholics know they're innocent and that they'll be convicted anyway. It's a game they're all playing to satisfy Dublin Castle and Westminster."

I quoted that paragraph verbatim in my dispatch tonight. Let them try to sue us in a court in Chicago! My parents tell me that my stories are being used by papers all over the country. In my own weak and ineffective way perhaps, I am bearing witness against the tyranny and hypocrisy of English imperialism, not that many Irish Americans would have any doubt about it.

None of this will save Nora's husband or Nora herself. I try to force

myself to be as serene in my resignation as she is in hers. Irish American
that I am, I find that very difficult.

I still limit myself to one drink of whiskey, except on a rare occasion like
tonight I will have two. In the pubs I have only one glass of stout.

Dublin, November 13, 1882

Today is the first day of the trials. Bolton has succeeded in putting them
off until he had his turncoats well in hand. The problem was not that Philbin
or Tom Casey were reluctant to testify. The problem was to manipulate their
testimony so that they would say the same thing and confirm each other's
perjury. I gather from the talk around the courtroom that the principle problem for poor Tom Casey was that he had testified that Philbin was not at
the crime scene, which cut the ground out from under the first witness that
Bolton had turned. Bolton, they say, yelled at Tom Casey that he would
come to trial after Myles Joyce and would hang unless he got his story right.
Finally, Tom figured out what was wanted and did bring his story into line.

Thus Philbin lied when he admitted to being at the crime scene, and
Tom Casey lied when he said Philbin was there.

The announcement of the fact that two of the accused had become
witnesses for the Crown electrified the courtroom the day the trial of Patrick
Joyce began. Even counsels for the Crown were surprised. We journalists
were not surprised at all.

"Bolton usually gets his perjury earlier than this," Dempsey whispered
to me.

Defense counsel immediately asked for a transfer of the venue to Galway
where the jury could actually view the crime scene. Motion denied. Then he
asked for a delay to consider the new evidence that had been brought forth—
an elementary right in the common law tradition. The judge, a wizened little
man with wild tufts of white hair jutting out from the edge of his otherwise
bald head denied that motion too. The Defense Counsel demanded access to
the new evidence so that it might be considered overnight. "How else can
we defend our clients?" Final motion denied.

Then the jury was selected, a couple of shopkeepers, a stockbroker, a
band manager, a jeweler, a major, a landowner, a "gentleman" from Merrion

Square—probably not a Catholic among them. Peter the Packer had done his work well.

The witnesses were excused and the attorney general himself, lead Counsel for the Crown when he bothered to show up, laid out the case against Pat Joyce. It was the same old stuff. The three witnesses' story of their night-long trek following the murder party and the two approvers describing who among their group actually went into the house and did the killing. My colleagues stirred restlessly.

"They heard there was a crowd out that night," my friend Dempsey told me, "and since they knew who was likely to be in it they ran off to the Royal Irish Constabulary as soon as they heard about the killings. They were no-where near the scene of the crimes. They thought they'd get money from the police and revenge against Myles."

"Even the police out in Maamtrasna have figured that out," I replied.

The performance of the five perjurers was pathetic. Their stories counteracted one another, the attempts of the Crown counsels to lead them through their torturous tales of lies so that they would sound plausible were ridiculous. Perhaps the most telling assault on the Anthony Joyce band was asked in cross-examination by counsel for the defense, John Stritch.

"Now, Mr. Anthony Joyce, you were perhaps a hundred yards away from the house while the killings were taking place?"

The same question as in Galway.

And approximately the same answer. "A little less than that I would think."

"Are you aware that before he died, young Patsy Joyce testified that he could not recognize the three men who actually came into the house and did the killing because their faces were covered with dirt?"

"I have been told that he said that, yes."

"Yet you were a hundred yards away from the house, the moon had set, and you were able to recognize Patrick Joyce when he went into the house."

"I'd know him anywhere!"

"You have remarkable eyesight, sir."

My father has won cases on interchanges like that. In English Dublin, no one was the least fazed by it.

"From that distance you were able to hear the shouts of pain and horror from the victims?"

"Horrible they were, sir. I will hear them for the rest of my life."

"I'm sure you will, sir. And now, sir, we know from the testimony of the medical examiner that John Joyce was shot in the head. Yet, in your initial testimony to Sergeant, ah, Finnucane, you make no mention of hearing a gunshot. Is that not strange?"

"The sounds were so terrible, I could not make out what was happening."

Pretty lame.

"On reflection, however, and after learning of the medical report, you seem to have been able to recall that gunshot heard from a hundred yards away."

"I recalled hearing a sound which might have been a gunshot, yes, sir."

"How convenient."

Tom Casey, the approver, was an even worse witness, perhaps because Bolton had little time to prepare him. He listed the names of the men who were with him the night of the crime and added two more of whom no one had ever heard before. Patrick Kelly and Michael Nee, who joined them as they were approaching the house. Michael Nee had given him a gun. Though he had not gone into the house with Myles Joyce, Pat Joyce, and Pat Casey, he thought they were armed with guns. He had heard many shots.

Counselors for the Crown were clearly disconcerted.

"What did you do when you heard the shots?"

"I turned and ran."

"Why?"

"I wanted to have no part of murder."

"And the gun this Mr. Nee had given you?"

"He came around the next day, before we were arrested, and I gave it back."

More damning contradictions—Anthony Joyce had heard no gunfire, at least one gun was fired, the one that had killed Johnny Joyce, and now Tom Casey had heard several gunshots.

Philbin had previously testified that he had seen no guns at all.

"Philbin wasn't there," I muttered to Dempsey, "so he couldn't see any

guns. Casey was there and he heard many gunshots. My father could get a case thrown out in Chicago on such testimony."

Dempsey chuckled. "This isn't Chicago, laddy-boy. This is Dublin in the reign of Queen Victoria."

"And my father would start a search for Patrick Kelly and Michael Nee."

"Defense Counsel doesn't have the money or the time for such a search. They'll try to get their clients off, but their hearts aren't really in it."

Sure enough, neither Defense Counsel pursued the question of Kelly and Nee. They disappeared as soon as they had appeared.

However, George Malley, the lead Defense Counsel, made a spirited presentation of his case in the afternoon. I scribbled down his words as he spoke:

"Gentlemen, this is one of the most extraordinary cases that has ever been brought under the notice of twelve men in a jury, a case that makes no sense at all. To inquire into and probe the reasons for this betrayal of some of the men by others is essential. It is a false betrayal, a betrayal that contradicts in many important details the case made by the original witnesses, a case that suggests that the Crown had constructed, in its haste for a guilty verdict, a veritable house of cards. Patently, the new accusers have acted purely for their own selfish purposes to throw the guilt upon innocent men."

It seemed to me that his argument was masterful, one that should have been obvious, one of which my father would have been proud. It was clear, however, that it had made no impression on those in the jury box.

He then turned to his underlying argument:

"The Crown has not presented the slightest hint of a motive for this slaying. Mr. Patrick Joyce, the defendant, is a close relative of the slain family. What possible motive could he have for such vile behavior? Why would he want to murder a cousin and innocent women and children?

"The Crown has produced these dubious and contradictory witnesses, whom you are far too intelligent to trust. But no one has explained the motives for the killing. Unless the crown can find a motive, the case must be dismissed."

Not a juror stirred.

As he went on he laid out all the weaknesses in the Crown's case:

"In murder cases, the defendant, in addition to being charged of a murder, is also implicitly, at least, charged of having a motive. In the case before you and I, gentlemen, is there a particle of foundation for suggesting a motive on the part of the prisoner? There was never the faintest whisper of a disagreement between Pat Joyce and the murdered man. For a Joyce to murder another Joyce and his family would be foul and unnatural. . . . It strikes as most peculiar that Anthony 'individually' recognizing them on the road, was incapable of giving any description of how they went along that road. He could not say who was the first or who was last, or in what order they went, but he gave a general answer that they were dressed in dark clothes. Yet the approvers will have us believe that the murderers wore bainins that were bright in color. In no way could they be described as 'dark clothes.'

"Anthony Joyce tells you that he was influenced to take this course of watching and pursuing those men out of pure curiosity. Is it not likely they would have been seen by the parties whom they were watching and pursuing? You are told that these three men, through pure curiosity, followed ten men in the dead of night, crossing rivers, going through an almost impassable swamp and up a steep mountain, a distance altogether of between two and three miles to the house of the victims, one of them shoeless!

"Gentlemen of the jury, is it not strange—is it not exceedingly strange—that these three men went straight to that house? How did they know these other men were going there, for they sometimes lost sight of them? It is plain they arrived by a different route, but it is not plain that they arrived simultaneously at the house, or what length of time elapsed between the arrival of the two parties. There is an incoherence between the account given by these three Joyces, and it is inconsistent in any event with the account given by the two approvers. You are told they are sometimes parallel with and sometimes behind them. Gentlemen, if you were there and had an opportunity to see the place, you could form an opinion of the nature of these obstacles—boulders, swamps, stone upon the walls, streams, bogs, and so on. These mountain districts are celebrated for their almost impassability. Is it not possible that they must, at some time, have looked round?

"Gentlemen, when men are going to perpetrate a crime of this character, they are always on the lookout for fear of detection. Gentlemen, it appears

to me that in part of the story there is an inconsistency, an incoherency in the account that must necessarily lead to a disbelief in the story as concocted.

"If these men, the ten assassins, came into the yard from the stile and came round and went into the door there, that corner of the gable of the cow house which is in front of the door would just shut out, not the door itself, but the entire part of the house, and, therefore, they would be seen disappearing only. Their story, I submit, does not hang together. If they were panic-struck, why did they not go to the police barracks, which was nearer? Instead they go to their own homes, indifferent as to the horrors of the night.

"Patrick Joyce is married to a young wife, with no family as yet. His only companion on this night was his wife and she cannot give evidence for him. . . . I ask you to scorn the case made by these conspirators and to release that unfortunate man.

"Consider that they wait until the afternoon of that day, Friday, before they gave the slightest intimation that this frightful murder had been committed. Their story was not concocted until they had gone over it together. . . . After they had ample time to make up their minds and find a coherent story between themselves, they then, at last, go and give information upon the subject.

"As for the so-called approvers, such a pair as was never seen, they are the originators of this transaction, they are the persons who first seem to have the intention of doing something that night. It is impossible for me to show that my client had nothing to do with any organized lot except what follows from the deductions that you can reasonably make from the facts that have been proven before you.

"Gentlemen, it unfortunately happens that Patrick Joyce is the first that has been arraigned, but being the first it throws the greatest responsibility upon you. In your hands are not alone the life of that unfortunate man himself, but following upon it, perhaps, the lives of seven others. Though the weapons that were used must have been wielded with the most fiendish malignity, which scarcely any cause for revenge can palliate or even suggest, let alone justify, yet be slow in this case to come to the conclusion, if ever you do, that the hand of Patrick Joyce ever wielded the weapons that inflicted these terrible wounds.

"Gentlemen, I am obliged to throw myself principally upon the weakness of the case for the Crown. However, I shall be able to prove to you that feelings existed on the part of the Joyces that clearly showed that they were determined, if they possibly could, to fasten criminality for this offense and the imputation upon the head of the prisoner at the bar."

My hand was numb from scribbling his address. He had a powerful case. He made it reasonably well, though he wandered and hesitated. How could defense counsel put his heart in the argument when only a couple of jurors were listening, some were patently asleep, others nodding—as was the judge.

His witnesses were not very persuasive. Most of them were Irish speakers—shy, hesitant men whose honesty was lost in translation from a language that the jurors thought was both comic and barbaric. Moreover, James Murphy, the razor-sharp Queen's counsel, was able to twist the testimony of the defense witnesses to mean exactly the opposite of what they were trying to say. Murphy was riding high. He too had seen the bored and sleeping jury. He had no doubt, Protestant that he was despite his name, that his Protestant jury was in his pocket. All they needed was a little more ridicule.

At supper that night in the Royal Hibernian Hotel where I was staying, Martin Dempsey asked me, "What's your lead tonight, boyo?"

"Judge, jury sleeps through defense."

He raised his eyebrows.

"Great lead! Wish we were brave enough to do it here!"

"What will happen tomorrow?"

"Tomorrow? Summations in the morning; judge's instructions to the jury, mostly saying that it is not unreasonable for them to ignore the seeming contradictions in the stories and the absence of motives; jury verdict in less than ten minutes, sentence to hang by his neck until he's dead. Next case in the afternoon."

"I can't believe they can send a man to death without a motive for the crime."

"There are plenty of motives. The police and the Crown solicitor were too dumb to get them."

"And they were?"

"If I tell you, and you print them, we'll be playing into the hands of George Bolton."

"We wouldn't dare print them anyway. It's between you and me."

"Theft, politics, and jealousy."

"You can document that?"

"I've already put something in a dispatch, obscure enough so the Crown can't use it. Later, I will tell the whole story or let someone else tell it."

"Good on you . . . What do you think happened?"

"It would be clear even to James Murphy if he'd try to consider the obvious. A group of men went to the John Joyce house on the night of the murder, probably acting under the excuse of a secret society vote, to kill John and Breige Joyce and Margaret and Peggy too, on the grounds that they were informers."

"Were they?"

"Certainly not Peggy. Probably not Margaret either. When news of the deaths swept the valley the next morning, people were shocked, not at the murder, which many knew was coming, but at the violence of it. Anthony Joyce and his friends saw a chance to make some money and get revenge on Myles Joyce. So they put together a list of the men they assumed were involved and turned it over to the police. The people in the valley knew that most of the men on the list had actually been there, either inside or outside. They knew Myles Joyce was not."

"They didn't come forward?"

"Who would have believed them?"

"Was Anthony Philbin involved?"

"I'm sure not. . . . Would you want him in your band if you were planning a rural murder?"

"Tom Casey?"

"I think he was one of the actual killers."

"And you're going to tell the story?"

"One way or another."

"Won't your life be in danger?"

"Out there, maybe . . . I'll know better when I finally find out who the killers were. Anyway, I'm not planning on spending time out there."

"Was Pat Joyce really inside the house?"

"Probably . . . But he shouldn't hang for the crime without proof that he was. The Crown has no proof."

"Pat Casey who will be up for trial tomorrow?"

"Most likely, but they won't have any more evidence against him than they did against Pat Joyce. He'll hang too."

"I know you think Myles Joyce is innocent. . . . Home in bed with his wife."

"Yes, indeed."

"Yet he will hang?"

"Unless there is a pardon."

"I wouldn't wager on that."

"I promise you this, Martin Dempsey: If Myles Joyce hangs he will become one of the great Irish folk heroes of this century. George Bolton, the Crown Prosecutors, Dublin Castle, and the whole system of English justice in this country will pay a heavy, heavy price."

"You will see to that?"

"One way or another," I said grimly.

I was astonished at myself back in my room. I realized that the commitment I had made to Martin Dempsey had been building up within me for a long time.

Nora?

In the absence of an unlikely pardon, her husband would die. Would her life end soon?

Perhaps. Yet somehow I would try to take care of her.

— 17 —

November 15, 1882

Each day I think that the corruption cannot become worse and yet it does. Murphy in his summation this morning gratuitously introduced the motive for the murders into the trial. The Crown had never addressed the question previously. The absence of motive was a glaring hole in their case. So Q. C. Murphy plugged the hole by attributing the violence to the secret societies in the West of Ireland. He was clever about it. He talked about the evil of such societies, of their ruthlessness, of their brutality. He insisted that a guilty verdict would be a rebuke to them and a warning that they could not escape punishment for their violation of civilized law. Not once did he say that members of a secret society had killed the Joyce family. He knew he couldn't prove that. All he had to do was to suggest it indirectly and he would have won over whatever hesitant jurors might, improbably, remain.

I knew that Ribbonmen were the killers. So did most everyone in the valley of Maamtrasna, including the police. But the Crown had no proof of this, had not tried to obtain proof, and doubtless felt that no proof was necessary. Now Murphy was simply stating the motive as a known and proven fact.

Malley and Stritch, the defense counselors, simply repeated their argument that the testimony of the Crown's witnesses was both dubious and contradictory. I wished that they had been more spectacular in their attack, but they knew they were beaten.

Mr. Justice Barry's instruction to the jury was equally corrupt. He virtually insisted they bring in a guilty verdict.

"Whatever horror you may entertain, however you may desire that the guilty perpetrators should be brought to justice, recollect that the law requires no victim. The question you have to consider is, has the guilt of the prisoner been established by testimony that satisfies your conscience and judgment of his guilt? A true verdict finds according to the evidence. If you have a doubt, it must be the doubt of a rational reasonable man—no crotchet, no chimera, no cowardice. I cannot believe you would be capable of such a state of mind as I have now suggested. I have no doubt you will do your duty as becomes high-minded citizens of this great city, that you will discharge your duty between the prisoner and the country, faithfully, calmly, impartially, and regardless of consequences and may God direct you to a right conclusion."

After an absence of eight minutes the jury returned.

The verdict, however, could not be announced because Mr. Justice Barry was taking his lunch. Pat Joyce, handsome, calm, by far, as one of the papers said, the most likeable of the accused, waited patiently for the better part of an hour. There was no doubt in anyone's mind, least of all Patrick Joyce's, about the verdict.

"They could have given the impression that they debated a little," I said to Dempsey.

"Why? After the charge of the Judge what was there to debate about? Their friends and neighbors would have been angry at them if they had shown any signs of hesitation."

When the Judge returned, he expressed some surprise in his fidgety movements that the jury had already reappeared and arranged himself at the bench with a fussy sorting of papers. The Clerk of the Court began the hollow litany:

"Gentlemen, have you agreed to your verdict?" There was a deep hush of expectation.

The Foreman: "Yes, we have."

The Clerk of the Court: "You say that Patrick Joyce is guilty of murder?"

The Foreman: "That is our verdict."

The Clerk of the Court addressed the prisoner: "You, Patrick Joyce, heretofore stood indicted for that, on the eighteenth of August, 1882, you feloniously and willfully and of your malice aforethought did kill and murder one John Joyce. To that indictment you pleaded Not Guilty, and for trial put yourself upon God and your country, which country has found you guilty. What have you now to say why judgment of death and execution should not be awarded against you, according to law?"

With haunting calm, Pat Joyce replied, "I am not guilty." This he said in a voice firm and without tremor.

Then the Crown formally dropped the case against the two approvers, Anthony Philbin and Thomas Casey. Debt paid.

Pat Joyce's expression did not change. I wondered if perhaps he wasn't one of the killers after all. Or maybe he thought of himself as a soldier in a war and would be brave until death. A nice young man with a new wife. How could he have become involved in such a brutal crime?

The Judge put on the black cap and said:

"Now, Patrick Joyce, after the most patient trial, a jury of your countrymen has convicted you of the crime of murder—a crime committed by you and your confederates under circumstances so horrible that I cannot endure to recapitulate them. In form, you have been convicted of the murder of John Joyce, in fact, you murdered him, his wife, his mother, his son, his daughter, and it was the accidental interposition of Providence that prevented you adding another victim to that scene of slaughter. It is not for me now— possibly it would be useless, indeed, to attempt to awaken you to a sense of the position in which your enormous criminality has placed you. Mercy in this world you have none to expect. Mercy at the hands of man you have none to expect. But you shall have what you did not permit to your poor victims—time to endeavor to seek the forgiveness of the God whom you have so grievously offended. And, we are told that even sinners whose crimes equaled yours will not turn to Him in vain.

"It only remains for me now to pronounce the sentence—the dreadful sentence of the law. And dreadful as your crime has been, I am not ashamed to say that I feel the position of a man who is sentencing his fellowman to death."

The old faker began to cry.

"The sentence of this court is, and I do judge and order that you; Patrick Joyce, be taken from the bar of this court where you now stand, to the place from whence you came, and that you be removed to Her Majesty's prison at Galway, and that on Friday, the fifteenth day of December next of this year of our Lord, 1882, you be taken to the common place of execution, within the walls of the prison in which you shall be then confined, and that you shall be there and then hanged by the neck until you be dead, and that your body be buried within the precincts of the prison in which you shall be last confined after your conviction.

"And may God have mercy on your soul."

I pushed my way by Martin Dempsey and ran from the courtroom, out into the street and into the dreadful alley behind the courthouse, where I vomited my breakfast and last night's dinner. I leaned against the rickety wall, gasping and sobbing.

I admit that I'm not much of a man. Such behavior is deplorable in a professional journalist. I wonder whether I will ever be able to sit through such a trial again. I had formed my lead for my dispatch that night. "Judge invites verdict; Jury agrees in eight minutes."

Such words restored a little of my manhood.

I walked a quarter mile or so in the rain and then, thoroughly soaked, returned to the courtroom. The Crown had already begun the trial of Patrick Casey.

He is a middle-aged man, rough and tough looking, the kind of man who might possibly commit a brutal murder. If his young predecessor in the dock had not aroused any sympathy in the jury or in the mostly Protestant courtroom, this man surely would not. To emphasize his dangerous appearance, two guards stood at either side of the dock. Since he could not understand or speak English, a policeman deputed to translate for him, a policeman who was Welsh, not Irish!

I knew it would be more of the same. So I did my best not to listen.

Mr. Justice Barry told us at the end of the day, after the jurors had been selected, that he hoped to finish the trial in a single day.

Outside the court, the reporters gathered in two groups to discuss the trials. In one group there were the representatives of the English papers and the Irish Protestant papers; in the other the men from the Catholic and the American press. In the latter group the consensus seemed to be that the

Crown wanted to get to Myles Joyce and then force guilty pleas out of the other five men still accused.

"Was Myles there?" asked a man from Brooklyn.

There was some debate among us. I remained silent.

Finally Marty turned to me, "What do you think, Eddie? You've been out there in the valley. Myles Joyce looks like he may be a killer. Is he?"

"He looks more like an Irish chieftain to me," I said. "There is not a man or a woman in the valley that thinks he was with the killers. They believe that the accusation against him is based on Anthony Joyce's malice."

They were silent for a moment. Though I was the youngest of the crowd, somehow I had earned their respect for my work out in Galway.

"He'll swing anyway," someone said.

"Perhaps he will," I said. "If he does, it will not only be a grave miscarriage of justice, but a grave mistake by the English. He will become one of the great folk heroes of Ireland, like Wolf Tone and Robert Emmet. He will never be forgotten."

Again they were quiet. I turned and walked away and then back here to the Royal Hibernian.

I had said the same thing last night to Dempsey. The words had sprung to my lips without reflection both times. Yet, I was sure that they were true.

That truth, however, would not save Myles Joyce, Nora Joyce, nor their unborn child.

Who was this Myles Joyce to whom I had never spoken, whom I had seen for the first time only at his arrest, and for whose wife I hopelessly lusted despite my best efforts not to? Why was I so certain about him?

Because the people in Maamtrasna were certain about him? More likely because Nora Joyce loved him. About that love there could be do doubt. A mere child, she had no choice but to marry this gruff man twenty years her elder if she wished to avoid starvation. Could there have been any love at the beginning of such a strange marriage?

Perhaps not. There was certainly love now, however. Therefore Myles Joyce must be a remarkable man. If he was hung, if the English Crown murdered him, Nora would be free. I wanted her, but I did not want her at such a cost of suffering. Even if she lived—and I was not sure she would—she could never possibly love anyone else.

Now I feel ashamed of that calculation. How much I wish I were not so weak.

Dublin, November 16, 1882

Today was a replay of the Pat Joyce trial. If anything, the Defense Counsels were weaker and the Crown stronger, as well they might be given the quick verdict in the previous case. They knew that they could not possibly lose. I wondered if they knew how weak their cases really were. Or if they cared how later history would evaluate their work. O'Brien and Murphy would surely be rewarded with judgeships for their zeal. Perhaps they care only about winning.

After Murphy's summation the courtroom rose in a standing ovation, everyone except most of the reporters.

Last night I dreamed of Nora on the scaffold with her husband.

Perhaps, I tell myself, I will take the early train to Galway on Sunday morning, ride over to Maamtrasna to visit her, and then return early Monday morning.

For what purpose? To look on her again? That would be sinful. To offer her hope? That would be a lie.

No, I will not do that. I hope I have some small trace of honor left.

Dublin, November 17, 1882

I had assumed that Pat Casey was one of the killers; but now I am not so sure. He was found guilty, of course. It took the jury three minutes longer than the jury who had convicted Pat Joyce, although the Judge's charge to them was even more blatantly biased.

When the Clerk of the Court asked him if he had anything to say in response to the verdict, Pat replied briefly but with considerable dignity in Irish. The Welsh police officer translated, "I have to say that I had nothing to do with it."

Almost eagerly, Mr. Justice Barry donned his black handkerchief and repeated the sentence. Pat Casey asked the interpreter the date. The man told him December 15.

Pat nodded and said, "I have still my experience of heaven."

The translation was almost lost in the hubbub of the courtroom. Would a guilty man say something like that? Perhaps not. In any event, he had given me the theme for my dispatch tonight.

Immediately, Mr. Justice Barry proceeded to the case of the Crown versus Myles Joyce. There was a stir of excitement in the courtroom. Somehow everyone knew that this was the big case.

Myles sat in the dock as would a king who knew he was under the judgment of a mock court. His eyes surveyed everyone in the courtroom with an even, intense scrutiny. He knew in his heart that they were all guilty and he was not. Some people turned away from his gaze in fear, perhaps in guilt. I thought he favored me with a brief, friendly smile, but I am sure I deceived myself. He paid little attention to the proceedings, often resting his head on his arms folded on the dock. Such contempt could hardly win a jury's sympathy, but it might haunt them, just a little bit for the rest of their lives. Though Myles did not know a word of English, the court did not see fit to provide him with an interpreter. He was in much the same position as a Sioux or an Apache who did not know a word of English in an American courtroom without an interpreter. I would make that comparison in my dispatch.

Defense Counsel again asked for a postponement so they could study the allegations of the two approvers. Crown Counsel did not seem greatly opposed. Perhaps they wanted a Saturday and Sunday with their families. I knew that if the Judge granted the delay, I would catch a late evening train to Galway. However, Mr. Justice Barry, in his squeaky voice said that he could not allow such a delay and the trial must continue.

The formal charge that Myles Joyce had butchered his pretty blond cousin, Peggy, was read. Jurors were selected, the insane dance of death began.

I sit here in my room at the Hibernian and wonder. Why is this the most important of the trials? Because everyone assumes it will be the last? Or because the Crown wanted two convictions before it battled with this dangerous-appearing foe? Or because everyone who looks at this man knows that he is a man of substance and character, even if, in the English view, little more than a savage?

I wonder if I should leave for Galway tonight. There is still a train that would put me in the Great Southern by two o'clock Sunday morning. Maybe I could find some new evidence out in the valley. I dismiss such temptations. Who would believe a callow young American reporter? I was deceiving myself.

The fate of Myles Joyce was sealed.

Dublin, November 18, 1882

I slept not at all last night. I searched in my pockets for my rosary and said all fifteen decades of it for Myles and Nora. I tried to explain to God that, although I wanted her, I wanted her husband to live even more. I could never make her happy and he had and would. I begged for a miracle. I insisted to God that I meant it.

The trial proceeds on its eerie way. Everyone in the courtroom is awed by Myles's contempt for a process that he not only cannot understand but does not want to understand. There is a look of a curse in his eye as he periodically lifts his head from his arms and glares around the courtroom, as if he is remembering our faces so that he can deal with us on a later day.

Once again, I had the impression that I was favored with a faint smile. Had Nora told him about me? Did he approve of me? How could he possibly approve if he knew what I felt about her?

"Didn't he smile at you, Eddie?" Martin Dempsey asked.

"Hardly," I said, dismissing the possibility with a wave of my hand.

So I had not imagined it. Had he entrusted Nora to me? That was an absurd and dangerous thought. Nonetheless, I reveled in it.

At the lunch break, someone among the journalists lamented that Myles's pregnant wife was not in the courtroom.

"If Eddie here is right that he's a kind of Irish king, she certainly would appear to be an Irish queen, and herself pregnant at that."

"Does she speak English?" someone else remarked.

"Eddie?"

"I believe she speaks it and reads it."

"Would she look like a trollop to the Brits?"

"I know nothing about English sensibility," I replied. "She certainly would not to an American sensibility."

"Are you going to write about her? It might help his cause."

"I had not thought about it," I said. "It would certainly win sympathy for him in the States. However, nothing will help him in this courthouse."

"What happens to her and the baby?"

"I suspect they both will die."

That was the end of the conversation.

Now, at the end of this appalling day, I work on my dispatch about her. It is respectful and restrained. I doubt that she will ever see it. If she does, I hope she is not offended. My thesis will be that if Myles is an Irish prince, Nora is an Irish princess, a literate and intelligent woman who, if the English did not oppress this sorry country, would radiate intelligence and goodness and beauty for the whole world.

I will be more restrained than that. I find that I can skillfully hint and let the readers draw their own conclusions.

During the trial today, I wondered about the effect on the court of trying a prisoner who did not know the language of the trial process. If he were a Sioux in Minnesota, the fact that he could not speak our language would mean that he was a savage and therefore suspect. If you do not speak English, you are an inferior being. Similarly here. The English wish to stamp out the Irish language because it is inferior. If the Irish could be forced to speak English, they would become more civilized. It is Myles Joyce's own fault that he is a savage because he has not learned English.

That will be another dispatch. Many in Chicago will not like it because they would agree that English is the only civilized language. Still they'll have to read it.

Anthony Joyce testified that he knew Myles's voice very well. They were cousins after all, were they not? He had heard him talk to the other members of the crowd. Myles was, Anthony thought, in charge of the killers. He heard him distinctly giving the orders.

" 'We have to do it,' " he said. " 'We have to get rid of all of them. They are thieves and traitors.' "

"In those very words?" Crown Counsel asked.

"In those very words."

"Was Myles Joyce a leader in the valley?"

"The most powerful and feared leader," Anthony said with a scarcely contained shudder.

Defense Counsel did not think to ask how Myles could have used those very words in English when he did not speak English.

When Anthony walked up to the witness stand, Myles lifted his head from his arms and stared at him, not malevolently, but rather with steady contempt. Anthony saw the stare and did not look at his cousin again. When Anthony's testimony was over, Myles once more rested his head on his arms.

Anthony Philbin, the slimy little traitor, testified today that he clearly saw Myles Joyce enter the room by the light of the full moon. He knew it was Myles because he recognized his face. The demoralized Defense Counsels did not rise to point out that the full moon had long since set and that Patrick, in his testimony, had said that he could not recognize the killers' faces because they were covered with dirt.

Court was finally adjourned at five o'clock in the evening till Monday morning. The Crown will present Tom Casey as its last witness. The Defense will offer its same pathetic arguments. Both sides will present their summations. Mr. Justice Murphy will, in effect, instruct the jury to find Myles Joyce guilty of the murder of Peggy Joyce. They will do so promptly. Mr. Justice Barry will put his black cloth on his head and condemn Myles Joyce to hang by his neck until he's dead.

I hope I am able to sleep tonight.

Dublin, November 19, 1882

I must have consumed half a bottle of Irish whiskey last night before I collapsed into my bed. At least I slept, though when I finally awoke this morning, I was not refreshed and suffered from a terrible headache, which has persisted all day. I was fortunate enough to find a church before the last Mass this morning. As best I could, I tried to pray for everyone involved in the crime, especially for the repose of the soul of Peggy Joyce, for Myles Joyce, and for Nora Joyce and their unborn child.

I wondered whether God heard the prayers of those who drank too much the night before. My mother has always insisted that God hears everyone's prayers. I hope she's right. She usually is.

Then I wandered aimlessly around the wet and dreary city. I tried to order my thoughts without much success. Finally, I came back here to write my dispatch about Nora. The words flowed freely. I was pleased with the result. The readers would understand that this journalist respected the woman, as did everyone in the valley. They would, I was confident, not realize that he was in love with her.

I have thought all day about Myles's smile at me. Did that smile mean he was entrusting his wife to me? Did it mean he knew that I loved her and did not mind? Did he expect, indeed demand, that I take care of her?

How could any of those messages possibly be accurate? What right did I have to read them into his smile? Were they the products of my besotted imagination?

To my surprise, I find that I do not want to take responsibility for Nora and her child. Assuming that Myles is offering both of them to me, do I want them? My answer is that I do not. Or rather that I am afraid of that responsibility. What would I do with Nora Joyce? She would be too much for a young and inexperienced man like me. I am not ready for a wife and a family.

I would much rather have her as a sad memory than a living woman!

— 18 —

On this last, tumultuous day of the trial of Myles Joyce, the defendant sought out my face as he entered the courtroom. When he found it, he smiled more broadly than he had before. He had given me my commission. He had said, in effect, I can face the end of this foolishness so long as you take care of my wife and child.

On what grounds, I wondered? Had he seen me watching her at the eerie wake by the Church on the Hill? Had my mouth fallen open with awe when she tried to resist his arrest? Or had he merely decided that I was a nice, honest-seeming young American who could be counted on to accept his gift and demand.

I shivered at the challenge he had given me.

Tom Casey was a slippery witness. He said everything in response to the questions of both Crown and Defense that the Crown wanted. Yet, he gave the Defense certain openings on which they might have seized. Again, he raised the names of the mysterious eleventh and twelfth men, Nee and Kelly. He claimed that it was a fine, clear night, but quite dark by the time of the murder.

A juror interjected a question. Who were the three men who forced the door and entered the house? He had apparently missed the point that the Crown has subtly changed the number of murderers from three to five.

Casey replied, "There were five in the house, the two men already convicted, Kelly and Nee, and the present defendant."

"Whom you could see despite the darkness?" Defense Counsel Malley demanded.

"Yes."

"Five will get you ten," Martin Dempsey whispered to me, "that he was one of those inside himself."

I had not thought of that. Perhaps that suspicion would be useful later.

"He has said as much repeatedly," Mr. Justice Barry snapped.

"Yes, m'lord."

"Did you count the number of shots that were fired, Mr. Casey?"

"I believe I counted nine, sir."

"Nine!"

"Yes, sir."

"I believe that Anthony Joyce testified he didn't hear any shots."

"I can't help that, sir. There were at least nine shots fired. All of the men who went into the house had guns."

A constable had previously testified that the Royal Irish Constabulary had found nine bullets, three of them in the bodies of victims.

"He said nine," Mr. Justice Barry intervened. "Stop badgering him."

There was no point in pursuing the contradictions in the testimony against Myles Joyce. He was doomed.

Murphy received another standing ovation for his summation. Several of the jurors slept through Malley's.

The key hint in the Judge's charge to the jury were words I scribbled down: "Gentlemen of the jury, notwithstanding the difficulties suggested by the able and eloquent counsel who addressed you on behalf of the prisoner at the bar, I feel confident that you will discharge the duty imposed upon you at once with firmness and accuracy."

"Ignore the defense's arguments and find them guilty," I said to Martin Dempsey.

"He hardly had to tell them that, boyo."

The jury was out six minutes. Thus did English law mete justice to Irish-speaking chieftains. Not for the first time.

The clerk asked Myles whether he wished to reply to the verdict. Not having understood the words (though he must have known its meaning) he continued to stare at the Judge.

The interpreter was asked to explain the sentence.

Suddenly the bored, resigned man was transformed. His face began to glow, his eyes to shine. He spoke in fluid, musical Irish, slowly, confidently, and with enormous power. He gestured easily and smoothly, a druid or a priest or maybe both. Or maybe a king bidding farewell to his loyal people. Could Moses coming down from Sinai, I wondered, have made more of an impression in the courtroom? No one stirred, few had the courage to look at him, everyone knew that, even if they did not understand the words, this was the plea of violated innocence.

The translator strove to capture his meaning:

"He says that by the God and the Blessed Virgin above him that he had no dealings with it any more than the person who was never born, that against anyone for the past twenty years he never did any harm, and if he did, that he may never go to heaven, that he is as clear of it as the child not yet born, that on the night of the murder, he slept in his bed with his wife, and that he has no knowledge about it whatever. He says he is quite content with whatever the gentlemen may do with him, and that whether he is hanged or crucified, he is as free and as clear as can be!"

Later, an Irish-speaking reporter told us that the interpreter had not come even close to capturing the fervor and the beauty of Myles Joyce's last words in the court. Won't they be reciting them in poems and songs for a thousand years, he promised.

I understood for the first time why Nora loved him.

If the passion, the musical beauty, the grandeur of what Myles said had an impact on Mr. Justice Barry he did not show it. He shuffled among his papers, found his prepared sentencing speech and recited it as though Myles Joyce had not suddenly transformed himself, the courtroom, and the trial.

"Myles Joyce, after a most careful trial, you have been convicted of a crime committed under circumstances of aggravation so dreadful that I do not care again to recapitulate them. Although an opportunity has been afforded you of addressing the court in that language which is more familiar to you than any other, (clearly Barry thought that Myles, at least, understood English), yet, you have informed us that you understand what I am saying, and if I refrain from making observations to you on the enormity of your

guilt and the fearful position into which that guilt has now brought you, it is because I cannot but feel that to address such subjects to a man who went out at the bidding of some unknown, unseen authority, to slaughter his own cousin and that cousin's family—to address, I say, upon topics such as I referred to a man guilty of that crime, it would be indeed a waste of language and an assumption of a possibility of weight and authority, that I do not pretend on such subjects to possess.

"I believe no piece of evidence ever given in a court of justice produced a greater impression than that statement of the witness, Anthony Joyce, yesterday elicited by one of the jury, when he announced the fact that the witness against you, this respectable, honest, truth-telling man, you, the convicted murderer and the man the head of the house whom and whose family you slaughtered, were all united by ties of blood of the closest kind. It has communicated a peculiar significance, I may say, a peculiar horror to this case, that such a state of society should exist in that apparently primitive and remote part of the country—that, at the bidding of this unknown authority, as I have said, you should go out without remonstrance or hesitation to do that work of slaughter upon the young woman, who, perhaps, above all others in the community you should have stood up to protect.

"It only remains for me now to perform, for the third time during this commission, the dreadful duty of condemning my fellow man to doom. It is a dreadful duty, and I am not ashamed or afraid to own that I feel it to be so. But, if there were a case in which feelings of distress or pain or hesitation at the performance of that duty should sink into abeyance, it is in a case like yours, where the guilt has been so enormous, without a particle, even a shadow of any mitigating or even reasoning circumstances connected with it, to justify, I cannot, of course, say to justify it, but even to palliate or excuse your dreadful act."

Mr. Justice Barry then put on his black cap.

"The sentence of this court is, and I do adjudge and order, that you, Myles Joyce, be taken from this court, the place where you now stand, and that you be removed to Her Majesty's jail in Galway, and that on Friday, the fifteenth day of December next, you be taken to the common place of execution, within the walls of the said prison, and that you there and then be hanged by the neck until you be dead, and that your body be buried within the precincts of the prison in which you were confined after your conviction, and may the Lord have mercy on your soul."

Myles remained standing rock-stiff in the dock in total incomprehension of those lofty sentiments of the learned Judge. He deliberately reached over for his hat and then turned slowly away, and with a step, lingering and sorrowful, and a heavy sigh with which there was an indistinct exclamation in Irish, audible only to a portion of the courthouse, he left the courtroom.

Quite by chance I encountered Mr. Justice Barry as he was leaving the courthouse.

"Mr. Justice Barry," I said briskly.

"Er, yes, son?"

"Myles Joyce will have no need of God's mercy. Someday you will. May God have mercy on your vile soul."

He gasped and ran away from me.

How childish can I be!

Dublin, November 21, 1882

It is finished now, save for possible appeals. The five remaining prisoners appeared in court this morning and pleaded guilty. They were sentenced to death, but their case was submitted to the executive committee of the court with the understanding that the sentence would be commuted to twenty years in prison. While Myles Joyce was declaring his innocence before God, Jesus, and the Blessed Mother, George Bolton was in jail in the basement of the courthouse browbeating—with the help of a priest and the Solicitor for the Defense—the men who had yet to be tried to make a guilty plea. The journalists here have learned that only one of the five, a sixty-year-old man named Michael Casey, was in fact in the raiding party. The others were victims of either the malice or the ignorance of Anthony Joyce. It had taken only eight days for the Maamtrasna trial. George Bolton, Crown Solicitor for Limerick, had wrapped it all up in a neat little package.

What was the score? Only three (perhaps only two, if one grants Pat Casey the benefit of the doubt) of the accused had actually participated in the crime. One innocent man (and perhaps two) had been condemned to death. Four innocent men would spend twenty years in prison. Two men, one of them—Tom Casey—perhaps guilty, had won their freedom by lying to save their skins.

If one counts Pat Joyce and Pat Casey (both sentenced to death) and probably Tom Casey as actual killers, then three of the five murderers were still at large, perhaps including the mysterious and sinister Nee and Kelly.

The Crown had convicted seven completely innocent men and one guilty outside observer. Three killers were still free to wander the lanes of Connemara.

That will be the theme of my dispatch tonight.

—19—

"THE POOR sweet boy." Nuala, reading glasses perched on her nose and wrapped in an all-encompassing robe, was sitting upright in our bed, finishing the last pages of the first segment of Ed Fitzpatrick's journal. She was weeping. Naturally.

After coming back from our golf match, we had set about cleaning the bungalow to prepare for the advent of her parents the next day. It was inconceivable to my wife that the house should be anything but uninhabitably neat for a parental visit, an obsession she had not inherited from the good Annie McGrail, who was relaxed about neatness—not slovenly, just not as obsessed as her daughter. Ethne had been banished for the weekend (with pay) because she ought to celebrate her successful exam, but also because Nuala feared that the presence of even an apparent servant would embarrass her ma and da.

As if the outspoken Ethne gave the slightest hint of servility.

Finally, she judged that the bungalow was as clean as it could possibly be, "under the circumstances." The kids were long since sound asleep (with the monitor next to her on the nightstand to report the slightest extra breath). So, to relax a little, my wife had turned to Ed's journal.

"Thank goodness," she said wiping her eyes, "that kind of trial can't happen in the United States."

"What do you mean, can't happen?" I replied, turning away from the computer screen on which I was recording a description of a *real* storm like the one which was threatening just now to wipe out the whole of the County Galway—and maybe Clare and Mayo too for good measure. "Haven't you and I experienced ambitious and unscrupulous prosecutors like George Bolton? Don't African Americans feel about the white criminal justice system exactly what folks like Nora Joyce felt about the English system, a century and a quarter ago?"

"Och, Dermot." She sighed. "Don't you have the right of it like you always do!"

A fearsome gust of wind threatened to drive our house all the way back to Loch Corrib. The gentle breathing on the monitor continued unperturbed.

"You did sprinkle them with holy water, Dermot Michael, when you sprinkled the rest of the house?"

"Yes, ma'am."

"Isn't water the source of life and isn't it supposed to keep us alive?"

"And counteract the effects of the rain?"

She mumbled something, apparently unconcerned that the rain, to say nothing of the hysterical ocean, was composed of water. The doorbell rang.

"That isn't the doorbell, is it Dermot Michael?"

"Sounds like it?"

"Whoever would be out on a night like this?"

"Maybe some evil spirits?"

"They have sense enough to come in out of the rain. . . . You aren't going to answer it, are you?"

"I think I'd better. It might be important."

"Take a golf club with you!"

Yank shillelagh.

"Which iron?"

"Five iron of course!"

So equipped with my trusty five iron, I ambled out to the door. Huddled outside in rain slickers were the two members of our faithful Gardaí and someone else also in a rain slicker.

I opened the door. It was Jack Lane, covered with a massive oilskin.

"I had to bring it over, Dermot. I've blessed it with holy water and exorcised all bad spirits. It takes him up to the executions. Herself will have to figure out where the final section is. Here's the picture of the cemetery too."

"On a night like this?"

He seemed genuinely puzzled.

"Sure, you haven't lived through our November storms, have you? This is just a mild breath of wind, isn't it lads?"

The two Gardaí laughed in agreement.

"Would you all ever come in for a cup of tea?"

Heaven help me if they did. But also heaven help me if I returned to our bedroom and confessed that I hadn't asked.

" 'Tis too late. We'll see you at church tomorrow evening?"

"With the in-laws."

"Our orders are to stay outside in the car, sir."

I went back to the bedroom. My wife was sound asleep, the manuscript on the spread next to her. She looked so young, so frail, so desperately in need of protection. Gently I lifted the folder and placed it on the dresser. Then I turned off the light and as quietly as possible slipped into bed next to her.

She did not stir. I settled back into my pillow and ventured in the land of Nod myself.

Almost immediately, or so it seemed, my daughter, in the green Connemara T-shirt that had become her nightie was shaking me vigorously.

"Wake up, Daddy, wake up! Something terrible has happened!"

I had visions of the Atlantic Ocean claiming the nursery.

"What?" I said, struggling to sit up.

"Fiona has had her three puppies and they're all fine, two girls, Dana and Deirdre, and a boy puppy, Dano, but they've made a terrible mess and Ma will be very upset!"

I tried to adjust to that news.

"They're all snow white like she is!"

Ma isn't snow white. . . . Oh, but Fiona is!

I struggled into my robe and permitted my daughter to lead me to the nursery. There, on the blanket that served as her bed, was Fiona, looking inordinately pleased with herself. She thumped her tail in greeting as the three small snowballs sucked nourishment greedily from her body.

Nelliecoyne had not exaggerated. There was a terrible mess and a smell to match.

None of this seemed to bother my son, who was jumping up and down in his crib and shouting something like "Dawgies!"

I leaned over and petted the new mother.

"Congratulations, Fiona!" I said.

What else does one say to a wolfhound who has just produced three splendid and apparently healthy pups?

She replied by licking my hand.

Nuala would collapse. A terrible mess in the house and her ma and da coming at noon.

"Aren't they pretty, Daddy!"

"Yes, Nelliecoyne, they are very pretty!"

"Can we keep them all?"

"Wouldn't that be selfish?"

"Yes, Daddy." She sighed.

Another blast of wind shook our bungalow to its foundations.

Then the foundations were shook again as my wife charged into the nursery.

"Dermot Michael! What's wrong? . . . Oh, how wonderful!"

She knelt on the floor next to Fiona and cradled the dog's massive head in her lap and spoke to her in Irish. Fiona responded by licking her face. Nuala hummed something that might have been the Connemara Cradle Song.

"They're all right, dear," Nuala assured the dog, "just let me have a look at them!"

Gently she removed the pups one by one from their feeding frenzy and inspected them.

"Och, Dermot Michael, aren't you thinking that the bitch population of the house has doubled!"

"Certainly not!" I lied.

The pups went back to work.

"They'll be grand, love," she informed Fiona. "Three healthy puppies."

Each worth several thousand Irish pounds, I reflected.

"Nelliecoyne," Nuala instructed our daughter, "go back to bed, young woman, and your grandma and grandpa coming in the morning!"

"Yes, Ma . . . Make Mick go to bed too."

"Isn't he already asleep, dear?"

Our son; easily bored with the show, had curled up in his crib.

"Dermot Michael, back to bed with you too. I'll clean up here."

"I'm sorry there will be a mess for your parents, Nuala."

"Aren't we all three of us peasants and aren't we used to animals giving birth? Go to bed now, I don't want you to be irritable in the morning."

Me, irritable? Good old, calm, cool, even tempered Dermot Michael Coyne?

YES!

"Shut up!"

I went back into the bedroom. Before I turned off the light, I glanced at Nuala's easel. She was working on the beginnings of a sketch of a woman in the fashions of the late nineteenth century. Nora? Who else?

I shivered at the thought that Nuala actually knew what Nora Joyce looked like. Only much later did it occur to me that perhaps she was only guessing.

In the morning the pups were cuddled up in their mother's protecting body, sleeping peacefully despite the wind and the rain still assaulting the house.

"Aren't they lovely, Dermot Michael?"

"They are."

"Eat your oatmeal now. We have to go over to Renvyle House to see the Russians."

"It's yucky," Nelliecoyne protested.

How had that obligation entered our schedule?

"In this weather?"

"Sure, we'll go over in the van, won't we?"

I ate my oatmeal, which Nuala always prepares for my breakfast when she's in charge.

She called the veterinarian down in Cork, who had presided over the breeding, and gave him a detailed description of the pups and their condition.

"Won't he come up on Monday to check on them?"

"Grand."

"Finish your oatmeal, Dermot Michael."

"It's yucky."

She ignored me and turned her attention to dressing the small fry in several layers of sweaters and raincoats.

The van rattled and shook in protest as we inched our way down the slippery road. The Gardaí didn't want to let us in until Peig appeared and waved us through.

Nuala opened the window.

"Three white puppies, Peig. Come over and see them when you're off duty."

"Brilliant!"

A fleet of eight black limousines, four of them with small tricolor flags on the hood, blocked the driveway of the hotel.

"Gobshites!" Nuala exclaimed, breaking her own rule about language around her children.

"Shitehawks!" Nelliecoyne agreed.

Nuala was too busy buttoning up our children and getting them out of the car to comment.

What was I supposed to say—Nelliecoyne, don't imitate your mother's language? Especially today with her ma and da around.

I kept my mouth shut.

I carried Nelliecoyne and Nuala carried the Mick into the hotel lobby. A crowd milled around, Irish diplomats, Gardaí in plain clothes, Russian diplomats and the Russian brass—six big, overweight men, three of them in military uniforms with big hats and chests laden with medals. Everyone was sipping clear liquid from water glasses. The Russians were complaining loudly in Russian while a woman translator strove to render their complaints in English.

They were either very angry or feigning anger. Well, just let them try to invade Ireland! The English had tried that and it hadn't worked. Besides, the friggin' Yanks would protect us wouldn't they?

"Ours are drinking water, theirs are drinking vodka," Declan McGinn, the Garda superintendent from Galway, whispered behind us.

I had asked no questions about our visit to the hotel. I knew that Nuala was supposed to be a kind of psychic police dog, a human Fiona. Again the Gardaí were not exactly consulting a clairvoyant. Merely asking the opinion of one of the dark ones.

"You'd be thinking that you wouldn't be so far from wrong if you believed that those poor men were killed by their own?"

"It might not be altogether a mistake to conclude that this solemn high visit is a bit of a show," Declan agreed.

Nuala built the pyramid of her fingers under her chin and stared intently at the crowd. The Mick squirmed in my arms. Nelliecoyne, for all I knew part of the psychic screening process that was going on, held her mother's hand.

"The thin little fella over there on the fringes with big black mustache, who would he be?"

"Second Secretary of the Embassy."

"He knows a lot more about what happened than he's letting on."

"That wouldn't be a great surprise to us, Nuala Anne. He's certainly secret police, or a member of one of the factions of the secret police."

"Funny looking men," Nelliecoyne observed. "Bad men."

"Not all of them, dear," I said.

She nodded solemnly. "Some are Irish."

"You can't question him, I would imagine?"

"Not himself. We can ask around and see who he might hire for a thing like this."

Nuala Anne removed her fingers from her chin. "Dermot Michael Coyne, we should bring these ruffians home."

Her assignment was complete. The Gardaí had wanted reassurance that their hunches were valid. If you have a local witch around, why not consult her, especially in the West of Ireland, and most especially on the ocean edge of Connemara? Mind you, nothing would go into the reports about this consultation.

I was tempted to make the sign of the cross, but restrained myself.

"Your man over there," Nuala murmured to Declan McGinn, "could also be involved in the other stuff too."

He grimaced.

"We know that, Nuala."

Was a war under way between two Russian factions way out here on the western end of the West of Ireland? Perhaps. I wondered if the Russians, a people far more superstitious than the Irish, could not realize what they were getting into.

As if to confirm that insight, the Russian Embassy Second Secretary began to cough and then, unnoticed by his colleagues, rushed off in the direction of the washrooms.

"Time for us to leave," Nuala announced.

"Did you do that to him?" I asked her.

"His own conscience did."

That was that.

YOU DIDN'T ASK HER WHETHER SHE STIRRED UP HIS CONSCIENCE.

"I don't want to know."

At the bungalow, Fiona greeted us at the door, tail wagging happily.

"You didn't think we'd walk out on you and your family, did you dear?" Nuala said as she hugged the great beast. "They're all right now, aren't they?"

They were indeed. We moved them to the laundry room, where they would be safe from potential rugrat depredation.

Then the elder McGrails arrived. They stoutly maintained that the storm was nothing at all, at all. I should have been here for the one on Paddy's Day.

It was a good weekend for us. Nuala always relaxed when her parents were present. The kids adored them. Fiona and her pups had a new audience. Father Jack Lane, as Nuala had introduced him at the Saturday afternoon Mass, greeted her ma and da in Irish.

"Any hints yet, Nuala?" he asked her.

"Sure, don't stop looking for it yourself, Father," she admonished him.

That night she had informed me, "Och, Dermot, you can't expect me to relax with lovemaking with me ma and da in the house."

I had not suggested that we should. Much less did I suggest that they might very well be doing just that in their room down the corridor.

However, in the middle of the night, the wind still screeching, she woke me with gentle fingers.

"I love you, Dermot Michael."

"Do you now?"

"I do."

"What do you intend to do about it?"

She demonstrated her intentions by rolling over on top of me. Under the circumstances, how could I resist?

When we were falling back asleep, she whispered, "Please never stop loving me, Dermot love?"

"Not a chance." I sighed.

"I'd die if you ever got tired of me."

"The day after the sun rises in the west."

Judging by the contentment around the breakfast table the next morning as we ate our oatmeal, everyone had enjoyed a good night's sleep. The winds had died. The sun was breaking through the clouds. "Won't it be a brilliant day altogether?" Annie McGrail demanded.

"Yes, Ma," Nuala, always the diffident and obedient daughter in the presence of her ma, agreed meekly.

Fiona's offspring were already beginning to play with one another. The poor fella was outnumbered by his sisters.

Later, it was decided that the weather had cleared sufficiently that we could take a nice walk along the strand, the children in their stroller. Nelliecoyne enjoyed such expeditions, especially because she

could give orders to everyone from her position as captain of the stroller.

While we were dressing in warm clothes for the venture, I trapped herself in bra and panty and put my arms around her.

"Wife, I love you in all your versions, but I especially delight in Nuala the meek and respectful daughter."

She rested her head on my shoulder, "Och, Dermot Michael, isn't that who I really am?"

"You won't be wearing one of them sinful sweaters when your ma is around?"

"I wouldn't dare, Dermot."

I kissed her gently and let her put her clothes on. Naturally, she found a black sweater which revealed a bit of her belly.

"Och, Nuala Anne," her ma said when she saw the sweater while Nuala was putting on a thick jacket, "doesn't that look cute on you. Zip that jacket up tight, or won't you catch your death of cold?"

"Death of cold." her father added helpfully.

"Yes, Ma," she said docilely, and flashed a smile of triumph at me.

Along the road by the strand, with our Gardi protects trailing us in an unmarked car, Nuala and her da drifted behind me and herself.

"The child is much better now, isn't she, Dermot Michael?"

"She is," I said with more confidence than I felt.

"In a few weeks time, won't she be singing again?"

"Is that important?"

"It is to her, don't you see?"

"I think you have the right of it."

Long pause.

"I ask myself often why she worries so much. I don't think she caught it from us."

I laughed.

"I'm sure she didn't."

"Even as a tiny one, didn't she have to be perfect altogether at everything?"

"And," I added, "isn't she pretty good at almost everything?"

"Ah, you'd be knowing about that, wouldn't you Dermot Michael?"

That was a sexual allusion if I ever heard one. I ignored it.

"So she had to be perfect at pregnancy and giving birth, even though that's not under her control, is it?"

"God did not consult with her."

"And she didn't understand that a good mother need not hover over her children every minute?"

"A better mother if she doesn't," I agreed.

"Sure, don't you have the right of it, Dermot Michael? . . . Doesn't she know all them things now in her head anyway?"

I wasn't so sure about that.

"I hope she does, Annie."

"You wait and see, lad. She'll be herself again soon, if only you're patient with her."

"I'll be patient with her, Annie McGrail, till the end of the world if I have to."

"I wouldn't think it would take that long."

After a big lunch of sandwiches and chocolate ice cream and a pint for all of us but Nuala and the kids, we drove down to Cleggan for a ferry ride out of Innishboffin six miles off the coast, half of it in the relatively sheltered Cleggan Bay. The Atlantic had recovered from its snit rather quickly and, according to Nuala, was as smooth as a meadow that's just beginning to bloom.

The accuracy of the metaphor escaped me. I was happy that I had swallowed a couple of Marazine tablets before we left the bungalow.

Innishboffin is a pretty little place of well-scrubbed and white-washed homes, swarming at this time of the year with artists and musicians and actors who had come across for the May Festival.

"Aren't your professional performers a strange-looking bunch?" Nuala Anne marveled. "Sure I'm glad I was never a singer or an actress or a storyteller."

"Or a liar?" her ma added.

"A liar," her da filled in his line.

Nuala snorted and ignored them.

"Don't fall asleep on us, Dermot Michael Coyne," she ordered.

"And yourself taking them pills because you're afraid of a little bit of ocean."

"Can I rest in Nelliecoyne's place in the stroller?"

They all thought that was very funny.

Nuala lectured me about the island—St. Colman, defeated by the English at the Synod of Whitby, which outlawed the Irish celebration of Easter, had retreated here with Irish monks to keep the correct (i.e. the Irish) rites alive. St. Flannan, one of his successors, had discovered a famous holy well, the O'Flahertys had taken over, and Grace O'Malley built a castle. Cromwell had used the island as his head-quarters. Now at last it was peaceful and free.

We visited Cromwell's fort, the Doon Grania, the colchans (bee-hive huts) of Colman's monastery, and the holy well. Nuala knelt by the well and prayed fervently. Then she blessed her whole family with the water and filled a bottle to bring home for Fiona and the small ones. The bottle was large enough so that some of Flannan's water could be brought home to America against tornadoes and similar threats.

Nelliecoyne had the time of her life, running around on her de-termined little legs to take in everything, even ducking into one of the beehive huts.

"Can we bring one of these home to America with us, Daddy?"

"I don't think that the Irish government would like that, dear. They want to keep all these houses here in Ireland."

"That's selfish," she informed me.

Nuala decreed that we would have to stop at Day's Hotel for a cup of tea, "To wake poor Dermot up."

The tea tasted good, as did the buttered scones with jelly. They could not wake me up, however. I'd be sleepy till the morning.

I was tempted to take another couple of pills for the ride back to Cleggan, especially since the sea seemed rougher. Bravely, or so it seemed to me, I decided against it. I felt queasy until we arrived in the sheltered waters of Cleggan Bay. My children, ensconced in the laps of their grandparents, loved every second of the ride.

"Poor Dermot," my wife consoled me, "sure aren't I a terrible eejit for taking you out on the ocean and yourself prone to *mal de mer*."

"A rose is a rose," I replied, "even if it is called '*une rose.*'"

Back in the bungalow the McGrails had a bite to eat—American-style hamburgers—and departed for Carraroe before it turned dark. Fiona was allowed a brief stroll outside while her pups whined for her. The kids were put to bed. Dermot Michael was already under the covers, not sure that he would ever wake up.

Nuala turned to her easel and with sure strokes continued on her portrait.

"Nora Joyce?"

"Poor brave thing," she agreed.

"Did she really look like that?"

"Certainly! Why else would I paint her this way!"

"Poor Edward Fitzpatrick can't even admit to himself that he wants to save her husband but he also wants her and he can't have both."

"Och, Dermot, doesn't he know it. So does she. I don't know what will happen. I promised her out beyond at St. Flannan's holy well that we'd get back to work on the mystery tomorrow."

"Which mystery?"

"Sure, Dermot, aren't they both connected?"

— 20 —

Galway, December 10, 1882

I have come here for the hangings, five days hence. For some reason I am one of the reporters chosen to witness the actual event. I dread it. At the last minute I may flee. I have never seen a living man turned into a dead man.

It is bitter cold here in the West of Ireland. Ice has closed the docks and the wharves. Snow covers the frozen river and lake. People shiver when they leave their homes to walk down the street. Some children have frozen to death over in the Claddagh. I have been giving money to beggars and to hungry children who don't beg.

Lord Spencer, the stupid fool who is Lord Lieutenant here for the Queen and despite some pressure from her, has agreed to commute the sentence of the five men who pleaded guilty to life in prison. It is widely believed that they will be released after twenty years. No mercy, of course, for Pat Joyce, Pat Casey, or Myles Joyce.

Nora wrote the Earl Spencer in a letter in the Freeman's Journal, *a simple plea for her husband's life. It will have no effect on that terrible man who blames all of Ireland for the brutal murder last year of his Chief Secretary and Assistant Chief Secretary in Phoenix Park:*

Dear Sir,
    I beg to state through the column of your influential journal that my husband, Myles Joyce, now a convict in Galway jail, is not guilty

of the crime. I publicly confess before high heaven that he never committed that crime nor left his house on that night. The five prisoners that pleaded guilty will declare he is innocent, they will swear now and at their dying moment that he never was implicated in that fearful murder. Does not everyone easily imagine a man going before his Almighty will tell the truth? In telling the truth they must confess that he never shared in it. Will the evidence of two informers, the perpetrators of the deed, hang an innocent man whilst the whole party on the scaffold will declare his innocence?

I earnestly beg and implore His Excellence the Lord Lieutenant to examine and consider this hard case of an innocent man who leaves a widow and an unborn child. I crave for mercy.

I am, sir, Yours truly, Nora Joyce, the wife of Myles Joyce that is to be executed on the 15th.

As her letter hints, there was a last desperate attempt to save Myles's life, even as William Marwood, the public executioner, was supervising the construction of the scaffold in the jail yard.

Galway Town was rife with rumors about what actually happened. It was well known that the people up in the valley believed that most of the accused were innocent. Anger had somehow swept the valley—though not enough anger to be effective—and from the valley it had crept down to the town. The Bishop of Galway, Father Graven, the prison chaplain, the Mercy Nuns who visited the prisoners every day and provided housing for some of their relatives, even the governor of the prison—all working against time are trying to prepare a final memorial to the Lord Lieutenant. They have statements from two of the condemned men, Pat Joyce and Pat Casey:

I, Patrick Joyce, now a prisoner in this prison make the following statement of my own free will: Myles Joyce is as innocent as the child unborn of the crime of the murder of the Joyce family. Seven persons were present at the time of the murder in the house. Namely myself, Michael Casey (prisoner); Pat Casey (prisoner); Thomas Casey (approver); and three now at liberty and I don't like to mention their names. Thomas Casey used three revolvers and it was he who did all *the shooting. Two of the three men, now outside, had a hammer and used it to kill those of the Joyces not dead after receiving the pistol shots.*

Anthony Philbin was not present, and I have never seen him in the neighborhood for the last three years. The Anthony Joyces, who swore against us, did not, nor could not, have seen us the night of the murder. There was no meeting whatever at Michael Casey's house. The meeting took place in the house of one of the men who is out and is a farmer. The murder was not the work of a secret society, but was caused by this man, the farmer who is outside, for spite. I asked Thomas Casey (approver) when he shot at John Joyce, the man of the house, what was the cause for it? He said if I did not hold my mouth, he would soon let me know as I was not doing anything to help him. Myles Joyce and all the other prisoners are innocent of the crime and were not there at all.

Pat Joyce

Made before us at H.M. Prison, Galway, this 13th December, 1882.

Geo. Mason, Governor
Richard Evans, Chief Warden

Pat Casey's statement was shorter and blunter:

H. M. Prison, Galway, 13th December, 1882. Statement of Patrick Casey.

Patrick Casey, now a prisoner under sentence of death, makes the following statement at his own request and of his own free will:

I say that prisoner Myles Joyce is innocent in that case, namely the murder of the Joyces. There were present at the murder and in the house: myself, Thomas Casey (approver), Pat Joyce, and Michael Casey; the other three are outside. I will not name them. Anthony Philbin was not there. Thomas Casey fired the first shot. John Joyce was the first man that was shot and that by Thomas Casey. All I did in the matter was to put my hand upon John Joyce's shoulder.

Neither Anthony Joyce nor his family saw a sight of any of the men that committed the murder that night.

Pat Casey.

Made and signed in our presence at H.M. Prison, Galway, this 13th December, 1882.

Geo. Mason, Governor

Richard Evans, Chief Warden

These two documents are powerful proof of the innocence of most of the accused, especially Myles Joyce. They enjoy a certain credibility because the prison officials took them down and put them in a memorial to the Earl Spencer. The journalists here know about them, though they don't have the text as I do. I have promised not to use the copies I have and I will honor that promise. However, I can and will write the substance of them in my dispatch tonight.

There's great hope here in Galway Town that the memorial will be a success. Even the English journalists here concede that Myles Joyce is an innocent man. I wish I could share the hope.

I have not seen Nora. I sent my carriage up to Maamtrasna, but Josie tells me that, though Nora is almost eight months pregnant, she walked all the way herself. She is staying with the Mercy Sisters. I do not want to see her. I would feel obliged to try to ease her pain. That would merely make it worse. I am powerless to prevent her husband's death and powerless to help her bear the agony of waiting and the even greater agony of the event itself. I pray that the memorial is successful.

"How is she?" I asked Josie as I slipped another twenty pounds into her hand.

"Sick." The little ragamuffin was grinning no longer. "She doesn't care whether she lives or dies. She'll probably die."

Tears streaked her dirty face.

"And the child?"

"Babies are already dying up in the valley, Mr. Fitzpatrick. People are afraid there'll be another famine."

"Is there anything I can do, Josie?"

"You've done all you can, Mr. Fitzpatrick. . . . Do you think Lord Spencer will spare Myles at the last moment?"

"No, Josie, I do not."

"Neither do I."

Galway Town, December 14, 1882

Still bitter cold. More snow. It's almost like Chicago this time of the year. No word from Earl Spencer, except that he has authorized payment of $1,200 pounds to the Anthony Joyces, blood money if there ever was any.

Should I walk over to the Mercy Convent to see Nora? Josie says there's nothing I can do. Am I being prudent or cowardly? I don't know.

A long letter from my father today. Proud of me . . . Which is normal. No matter what I do he is proud of me. Would that I had his courage and wisdom—and his ability to love without hesitation. Everyone in Chicago, which means all his friends, are greatly impressed by my dispatches and horrified by the mockery of justice in Ireland. He adds, characteristically, that it is probably no worse than in the American South, despite the civil war in which he fought.

He adds that my mother and sisters all wept at my description of Nora. "They instruct me to tell you to bring her home with you when you return. I would not take such an instruction seriously. You know how women are always trying to make matches. On the other hand, if Mrs. Joyce and her child need a place of refuge, our home on North Park Avenue has plenty of rooms."

My father is a shrewd man in the ways of the human heart. He also knows me very well. Has he sensed behind my dispassionate description of Nora Joyce other, and perhaps baser, feelings?

I cannot permit myself to think of such matters.

I saw Josie again today in front of the Great Southern Hotel, which by the way is almost empty save for reporters. She was waiting in the cold, her thin little body protected only by a shawl, shuddering in the wind.

"Are you waiting for me, Josephine Philbin?"

"I am, Mr. Fitzpatrick, sir," she said.

"If you wait again, come into the lobby."

"Oh, no, Mr. Fitzpatrick, that's too grand a place for the likes of me."

"What is it you want?"

"I want to tell you that Nora is having pains. The nuns say that her time hasn't come yet, but I think they're worried too."

"Is there something I can do?"

"No, sir. I just wanted to tell you."

"Come, Josie, we're going shopping."

"For what, Mr. Fitzpatrick, sir?"

"For a warm cloak."

"For me?"

"I have a coat as you can see."

"Oh, no, Mr. Fitzpatrick, sir! I couldn't . . ."

"You can and you will. Is that clear?"

"Yes, sir," she said meekly.

"Does Nora have a warm cloak?"

"No, sir. Only that thin red one she prizes so much.

"Then we will buy her one too."

"She might not wear it."

"Tell her it's an order from me that she wear it."

"Yes, sir."

So we bought two heavy winter cloaks.

Thus did I soothe my conscience.

I wrote back to my father. I told him that if Myles Joyce died tomorrow, as I think very likely, the fire will go out of his wife's life.

Galway Town, December 15, 1882

Earl Spencer turned down the memorial. He sent a sixteen-word telegram to the governor of the prison: "Having considered statements, I am unable to alter my decision. The law must take its course."

He probably felt that he had been too generous even in remitting the death sentences of the five men who had pled guilty.

I will leave now for the prison.

Later in the day.

It is all over now. Myles Joyce is dead. His body has been consumed by quicklime. The black flag hangs over the prison. I hear the mournful keening of the women of Maamtrasna. I imagine Nora's brave, young voice among them. I cannot think. I cannot write. I can only sob with grief and rage. I will try to write tomorrow.

Galway Town, December 16, 1882

Martin Dempsey, fresh from Dublin, stood next to me in the bitter cold prison yard.

"Spencer will never live this down," he said. "Even the Protestants in Dublin say that this is too much."

The door of the jailhouse opened and the governor of the prison appeared, followed by the three prisoners, Myles Joyce, his arms tied behind his back, in the lead. Seeing us, Myles began to shout in Irish. One of the Irish reporters translated.

"I will see Jesus Christ soon. He was hanged in the wrong too."

"Myles knows what he's doing," Martin said. "He's creating a heritage."

Most men, I thought, would not do that when they were about to die. Myles Joyce, however, was not most men.

At the foot of the scaffold, he slipped out of the hands of his guards and bounded up the steps.

"As God is my witness," he shouted, according to the translators, "I never did it. It is a poor case to die on a platform when you're innocent. May God help my poor wife and her unborn child. I had no hand or part in it. But now I have my priest with me."

Eight iron hooks hung over the scaffold. On three of them were ropes. Hangman Marwood had prepared for the execution of all the prisoners.

The hangman put leg straps around his victims and then adjusted the nooses around their necks. Pat Joyce and Pat Casey did not resist. Still shouting in Irish, Myles Joyce continued to fight the hangman. Marwood pushed him about roughly. Somehow Myles managed to twist his head out of position. Marwood pushed him back into place.

"The man's a butcher," Martin said to me. "He's going to mess this one up."

Marwood reached for the lever that would spring the three trapdoors. The noose slipped loose from Myles's neck. The traps were sprung. The ropes around Pat Casey and Pat Joyce's necks snapped taut. Both died instantly of broken necks. Myles Joyce's rope spun back and forth. Myles screamed in terrible agony as he slowly strangled. Marwood, cursing Myles loudly, had to climb down the ladder, duck under the scaffold platform and, as Martin said to me, "kicked poor Myles into eternity."

"Was the suffering worth it?" I later asked him.

"Come look down the trapdoors."

I didn't want to. I knew the image would lurk in my mind for the rest of my life. Somehow I owed it to Myles. The heads of the other two men were twisted to one side, broken necks. Myles's head was erect. He had defied them to the end.

I had the lead for my dispatch.

Marwood told the reporters that Myles had died instantly. We laughed at him, even the English reporters.

Strangely, I did not vomit till I reached my hotel room. I did not look at the women keening outside for fear I might see Nora's face.

Martin walked back with me, perhaps to keep an eye on me. "As long as Irishmen are alive anywhere in the world, the memory of Myles Joyce and his horrible death will never be forgotten."

It is the darkest time of the year and still fiercely cold here in Galway. Many people claim to have seen the ghost of Myles Joyce and heard him running through the streets of the city. In this place, at this time of the year, and after what happened, I am prepared to believe almost anything.

Galway Town, December 17, 1882

As would be expected, they are already singing ballads to him in the pubs. I hope someday Ireland will have something more to sing about than dead heroes.

Apparitions continue in the town. I don't believe them. Well, I think I don't.

I am tempted to ride up to Maamtrasna and spend Christmas protecting

Nora. Would Myles want me to? What else could those smiles have meant? Yet, I am afraid to do so. Maybe this is not the time. Maybe later. Am I a coward? Probably.

There was another inquest today. The Catholic minority on the jury wanted to question Marwood, to accuse him of deliberate sloppiness in the execution. The coroner, a Protestant of course, forbade it. I'm not sure what difference it makes anymore.

An Irish M.P. came to my room this afternoon. He carried a pile of my dispatches from the Daily News. Would I come to London and help them bring a motion before Parliament to investigate the Crown's handling of the whole Maamtrasna affair?

"Will you win on the motion?" I asked.

"Not very likely. Yet we'll tell the story so it will be heard again, both in Ireland and England."

"All right," I said. "I owe it to Myles."

There was nothing else to do.

Martin Dempsey invited me to celebrate Christmas with his family in Dublin. I accepted.

I will leave tomorrow morning. In my heart, I promise Nora that I will return. In my head, I know that I won't.

London, February 3, 1883

A brief letter from the Bishop of Galway today.

Nora Joyce, widow of Myles Joyce, delivered a baby girl three days ago after returning from her weekly keening outside Galway jail. Mother and child both survived. Their prospects, however, are poor. The child was baptized by her aunt, Josephine Philbin. She is called Mary Elizabeth.

I put the note away with a sigh. I hope that Josie still had some of the money I had given her. When spring returns I will go back to Galway to visit them. If they are still alive.

London, May 9, 1883

Tim Harrington, the M.P. whom I'm assisting, said to me this morning, "There is something big happening out in Galway."

"What?"

"It's not clear. Apparently someone is going to make a major statement at Mass next Sunday when the Archbishop comes to Maamtrasna. The new priest up there, Father Corbett, is behind it. We'll have people there, of course. Yet, you know the valley better than anyone. Would you go out and observe what happens?"

I hesitated. I did not want to know whether Nora and Mary Elizabeth Joyce were alive or dead.

"It might provide great material for one of your dispatches."

I had not sent a dispatch to the Daily News for several weeks. It was time I went back to being a serious reporter.

"All right," I said reluctantly. "I'll leave tomorrow morning."

"Tonight," Tim insisted. "I want you to be out there for the show."

My heart is pounding.

—21—

 I FELT lips brush my forehead. A gentle scent touched my nostrils. The aroma of tea and fresh scones and oatmeal lurked in the background.

"Are you awake, Dermot Michael?"

"Woman, I am not."

"Yes, you are, Daddy."

Half the bitch population of the household.

"Would you ever like a bit of breakfast?"

"I might just." I rolled over.

My wife, in a green and white Galway sweatshirt and jeans leaned over me. A matching ribbon bound her long hair in place. She was carrying a breakfast tray. Behind her, similarly attired, was my daughter, holding, very cautiously, a plate of scones.

"Are you feeling all right?" my wife asked me.

"I wasn't till you came into the room, woman of the house."

She blushed as she lifted the tray over me. If Nelliecoyne had not been with her, I would have fondled her breasts, neatly outlined under the sweatshirt.

"You had a good night's sleep, did you now?"

"I did. No distractions."

She continued to blush.

Nelliecoyne put the plate of scones on the tray.

I was feeling in the mood for love and Nuala Anne was well into her busy day.

"Wasn't the vet from Cork here already? And didn't he say that the three puppies are in wonderful health? And isn't our Fiona a proud doggie mother if there ever was one? . . .

"Should we feed Daddy his breakfast, Nelliecoyne?"

"Just like we feed the Mick?"

"Yes, dear. Just like we feed your brother."

"What time is it?" I asked as she fed me my first spoonful of oatmeal."

"Ten-thirty on this grand spring morning."

"You've done your run already?"

"And wasn't the ocean water terribly refreshing?

"You smell refreshing."

"Do I now?"

"And to what do I owe the honor of this special service?"

"Didn't your daughter and I think it would be nice and ourselves laughing at you yesterday because of your seasickness and your medicine?"

I couldn't quite remember that they had actually laughed at me. However, I would not reject the attention.

"Nelliecoyne, dear, why don't you go play with the puppies. I think I can handle Daddy by meself."

My daughter said something in Irish that I think might have hinted that the puppies were more interesting than Daddy anyway.

Some may suggest that being fed breakfast in bed by your wife is hardly an erotic experience. I assure them that if the wife is Nuala Anne McGrail, it can be a very erotic experience.

"I didn't mean to hurt your feelings yesterday," she said contritely. "I'm a terrible, thoughtless bitch altogether."

"I was so dopey that I can't remember my feelings being hurt."

Nuala Anne is so magical that my feelings are almost never hurt. However, there is no point in arguing with her that she hasn't hurt my feelings when she thinks she has. So I don't try.

"You were a terrible good sport about it, like you always are, except when I beat you at tennis."

"I'm delighted to hear it."

She eased back the sheet that covered me and caressed my chest and belly.

"Woman, I thought you were feeding me breakfast."

"Can't I do both at the same time? . . . Drink your tea while I butter some scones for you."

I sipped the tea and teased one of her breasts. She sighed and smiled.

"How is it, Dermot Michael Coyne, that you know exactly what I want exactly when I want it?

"I'm fey."

"Are you now? . . . Ah . . ."

"Where's me scone?"

"Beast," she slipped a scone dense in cream and raspberry jam between my lips. I didn't take my hand off her breast.

"I should warn you"—she sighed—"that we'll have to wait till later. Don't we have to go to Lord Ballynahinch's for luncheon?"

"For a woman like you, Nuala Anne, I can wait a lot longer than that."

"Go 'long with you, Dermot Michael Coyne."

So we proceeded with a mixture of foreplay and scones. If the kids were not awake and Ethne not in the house, Nuala might not have got off so easily. Still her tease was a promise of wonders yet to come. It would be delightful to wait to find out what she had in mind.

"Enough lollygagging," she informed me, rearranging her sweatshirt, which I had disordered. "Time to get to work."

"What did you think of himself deserting Nora at Christmastime?" I asked her as she lifted the breakfast tray off the bed.

"Isn't your man too hard on himself altogether?"

"You think he should have left her alone?"

"If he didn't, wouldn't he have made matters worse for the poor woman?"

"She and the baby might have died."

"Wasn't that a chance he had to take?"

My wife is almost always more fiercely realistic than I am.

"Well, we'll have to see what happens next."

"Won't we now?" She bent over and planted a lingering kiss on my lips. "Am I forgiven?"

I had learned through the years that instead of arguing that there was nothing to forgive, I would be much wiser to say something. "You bet. I can't stay angry at you for long, Nuala Anne."

"Now get your lazybones out of bed and take a nice shower."

"Alone?"

"Certainly! . . . Get a move on now. . . . And that picture of the cemetery the priesteen gave us is interesting, isn't it now?"

" 'Tis."

"I'd like to know why they covered it over with their park in front of the house."

"You can't expect a Lord to look out of his front room on graves of Irish peasants."

She swayed out of the room and I forced myself out of bed and threw on a robe. Then I stopped dead in my tracks. A new painting of Nora Joyce was almost finished. She was dressed in Irish peasant clothes this time, including the famous red petticoats.

She was my wife.

I couldn't believe my eyes. I grabbed our wedding picture off the mantle and held it next to the easel—same tall, slim body, same long black hair, same elegant breasts, same slender face, same dazzling blue eyes, same mysterious smile.

I gasped. What the hell was going on?

"Nuala!" I screamed.

She came running.

"Whatever happened, Dermot? Are you hurt?"

"No, no! It's that picture!"

" 'Tis only Nora Joyce."

" 'Tis you."

" 'Tis not, not at all, at all!"

"Compare her with this bride."

She took the wedding picture from my hands and held it next to her painting.

" 'Tis definitely not me at all, at all."

"How's she different?"

"Well, for example, I'm not wearing a red petticoat. . . . Ohmigod! Dermot Michael, it is me!"

She recoiled, holding our wedding picture against her breasts. Now she was genuinely spooked. She quickly made the sign of the cross.

"Should I get the Holy Water?"

"Don't be blasphemous, Dermot Michael," she reprimanded me. "Nora won't hurt us."

"I'm sure she won't."

"After all . . ." She rubbed her determined chin in serious thought. "Isn't there Philbin blood in me too?"

"What?!"

"Me ma's grandma was a Philbin from this part of the County Galway. Hadn't I forgot that altogether!"

"And Nora Joyce was a Philbin?"

"And her little niece Josie was a Philbin too, and the poor man who was arrested."

"So you're their descendant?"

"I don't think so, Dermot Michael. More likely a distant cousin, but with enough of the genes in me so that I look like herself." She gestured towards the painting, still a little uncertain.

"So there's a perfectly natural explanation for the similarity," I said with a rationalist's sigh of relief.

"Och, isn't it all natural? There's just different kinds of nature. . . . Some things are linked in ways we don't understand, aren't they now?"

"They are," I said, knowing that this was true, even if I didn't understand it. At all, at all.

"Still"—she shivered again—"'tis passing strange, isn't it?"

" 'Tis," I agreed.

"Well, don't stand there all day without any clothes on. Don't we have to go out to lunch with the nobility?"

"Tony Blair nobility," I said.

"Better than some of the other kind."

A half hour later, herself in a light gray spring suit that suggested a competent business person and meself in a dark blue business suit that suggested a commodity trader taking his leisure, we were preparing to depart the bungalow.

The doorbell rang.

I opened the door to discover Margot Quinn and Sean O'Cuiv outlined against the gray sky, a leprechaun and a banshee come to call.

"Would you ever mind having a word with us?" O'Cuiv began.

"We have an engagement for lunch," I pleaded.

"We will take only a minute," Ms. Quinn said confidently. "It's about your house."

They elbowed their way in. I showed them to the parlor. My wife was not pleased. She believed in punctuality as strongly as she believed in neatness. She offered them no tea. They reclined in parlor chairs as though they were in for a long talk. Margot Quinn's V-neck dress, I noted, showed a good deal more décolletage than was necessary.

"We thought you should know," Sean O'Cuiv began with his usual attempt at genial charm, "that there have been some important developments on the matter of development in this region. . . ."

"We must leave almost at once for lunch," Nuala said flatly.

"MacManus's silly plots have fallen through," La Quinn waved aside my wife's objections as though she had not made them. "You have a marvelous opportunity, but you must move quickly."

"Our house is not for sale," Nuala said firmly, as though she were the head of the family, which, of course, she was.

"Because of your influence in the world beyond Connemara," O'Cuiv continued the argument, "we could offer you today—tomorrow might be too late—half again as much as you paid for your house."

"Not for sale, even if it's twice as much."

I relaxed. There was no need for my sales resistance.

"Some important people worldwide have a deal virtually in place"—Margot Quinn plunged ahead—"for a massive development in this region. It will reach all the way down the Traheen River to Matt Howard's place. It's not generally known that he's in over his head back in London and has to sell out his Irish holdings."

"Everything from here to Letterfrack"—O'Cuiv grinned happily with his offer of his pot of gold—"is on the table. We'd like to include you in the deal while there's still time."

"No." Nuala's face was clouded over, a big blow was coming in from the Atlantic of her soul.

"It's your loss if you don't come on board," Quinn warned us. "By tomorrow night you may well be kicking yourselves."

Nuala stood up. The Archduchess was not amused.

"Me family and I are very grateful for your consideration and generosity. However, we must leave at once for our engagement at Lord Ballynahinch's. Our decision is final, irrevocable, and not subject for further discussion. Our bungalow here is not for sale at any price. Thank you very much for your offer. Dermot Michael, would you show our guests to the door?"

I would and did. They left most ungraciously, not that I was particularly gracious as I virtually shoved Quinn out the door.

"What was that all about?" I asked.

"Trying to outmaneuver the T.D., I suppose. We can worry about them later, Dermot Michael. We must not keep the gentry waiting. Come along."

"Yes, ma'am."

In the family room, Ethne was presiding over a scene of relative domestic bliss. Nelliecoyne was teaching her brother how to play with blocks, making clear to all observers that she was the soul of long-suffering patience. Fiona was nursing her pups complacently. Ethne herself was busy with her books. An unattended cartoon program played on the "telly."

Nuala bent over to kiss the kids good-bye. Suddenly and without warning our daughter went into a tantrum. She kicked over the blocks and ran screaming to me.

"Daddy, Daddy, Daddy! Don't go away!"

Not quite sure what was wrong, the Mick joined in the chorus of wailing.

Her mother turned deathly pale.

"Dermot Michael, shouldn't we stay at home? I'll be after calling his lordship and telling him that our children are sick."

"No, you won't," I said, as if, strong male of the house that I was, I was in complete charge of the situation.

"But she's so upset!"

"She's manipulating us, Nuala, like all kids do. . . . Now listen here, young woman, your ma and I are going out for lunch. Ethne will take care of you until we come back. Stop crying like a baby."

The comparison with a baby was perhaps not a good idea. She released me, ran across the room, and began to pound the wall hysterically.

It was, I had to admit, a good act. For a terrible moment I was ready to give in. I glanced at Ethne. She nodded her encouragement.

"Come on, Nuala, this show will stop the minute we're out the door."

It had better or I would be in the deepest of deep trouble.

Despite her guilt and her worry, Nuala extended her hand to me for the keys to our van. She did not trust me to drive on an Irish country road—even though I had taught her to drive on just such roads meself. Myself.

A couple of hundred meters behind us a blue Garda car pulled out and joined our procession.

"You told them where we're going?"

"Of course!" she snapped.

I picked up our cell phone and called the bungalow.

"Hi, Ethne, Dermot here."

"Och, sure, Mr. Coyne, aren't they fine altogether? Playing with their blocks and having a grand old time! Didn't she calm down as soon as you walked out the door! Tell Nuala everything is fine."

"Everything is fine," I repeated. "Having a grand old time with their blocks. Calmed down as soon as we walked out the door."

"That's the way kids are, Mr. Coyne."

"Tell me about it."

Nuala drove the car onto the shoulder of the road, and turned off the engine.

"Bitch!" she said between clenched teeth.

"Just a little girl learning painfully that she can't always have her way."

My wife sighed loudly and pounded the steering wheel.

"Och, Dermot, why can't I be as sensible and sane as you are? Why do I act like a terrible amadon and meself already taking me Prozac thing?"

How do I answer a question like that?

"Because you make too many demands on yourself."

"That's what the woman doctor was after saying."

She wasn't crying. It would have been easier if she was.

"How old are you, Nuala love?"

"Twenty-five, almost twenty-five and a half."

"Consider all the things that have happened to you since you were nineteen."

"Fer instance?"

"You graduated from college, migrated to America, worked at an accounting firm, began a singing career that has been successful beyond all expectation. . . ."

"I hate it."

"I know that, but let me finish me list."

"My list," she corrected me with a giggle.

"You fell in love, married, adjusted to marriage, discovered that you could give and receive powerful sexual love, solved mysteries, and produced two rugrats after difficult pregnancies and complicated birthing. Isn't that a busy agenda?"

" 'Tis," she said with a soft sigh.

"Maybe you had too much to do too soon in your life and yourself only a few years away from Canogi Field and the lanes of Connemara. Still you did them all well, some times incredibly well and never any less than reasonably well. Right?"

"I suppose so," she admitted.

"Yet, you still have to be perfect and make no mistakes at all, at all."

She snorted, both a protest and a concession.

"And take me pill every day."

"Thank the good Lord that there are such pills to help people get through difficult times."

She turned over the ignition of the van.

"And God thinking what a terrible eejit I am for making such a fuss when I should be grateful for all his blessings!"

"You said it, woman, I didn't."

"Well," she steered the car back onto the road, "at least we showed the little bitch who the bosses were, didn't you?"

We both laughed. Another crisis survived. The Garda car followed us onto the road.

We had recited that scene in one form or another at least two dozen times since we had come to Ireland. In her head, my wife knew I was right. In her gut, she wasn't altogether sure. We were, I thought, making progress. The conversations were more likely to end in laughter than they had been earlier in her recovery from the birth of the Mick.

YOU'LL BE HAVING THAT CONVERSATION WITH HER FOR THE REST OF YOUR LIFE, YOU FRIGGIN AMADON.

"I suppose you're right."

YOU'LL GET TIRED OF IT.

"I love her too much ever to get tired of it."

"There's really not much of the old manor left," Matt Howard said to us as he met us at the door. "Still, it's a pretty good restoration with the addition of plumbing, electricity, and central heating. We have peat fires in the fireplaces just to preserve some of the atmosphere. You live more comfortable lives in your bungalow down the road than any of the lords and ladies lived in their Big Houses a century ago, more comfortable than they could have imagined as a possibility."

"And themselves not having motor cars," Nuala Anne noted, a touch of irony in her voice.

We had pulled up on the paved driveway of the house amid the two Rolls, a Bentley, and a Mercedes. No BMW, however. Maybe around in the back. We parked at the end of the line, behind a Rolls. Someone had polished it so brightly that it was immune to the thin mist that hung in the air, a mist perhaps rising out of the cemetery beneath the ground.

"And myself a member of the Labor Party," Matt Howard laughed genially.

"New Labor," Nuala said.

We had driven through the valley, along the Traheen River bank on a dirt road. The sky was gray and ominous. Or it would have been if it were in America. As it was, it might have been a typical Irish sky. There were sheep on the hills and still a few homes in which the last of the descendants of the men and women of 1882 still lived and still tended sheep. There were television antennae on all the roofs. I could barely pick out the ruins of John Joyce's house, halfway up the mountain. The manor house was on a hill all right. The hill of the church, as Nuala said it was?

How dare I doubt?

"Come on in! Come on in! It's a pleasure to have you visit us!" Matt Howard enthused. "I don't know much about the history of these parts, though my wife does. She's a Philbin and a Casey, names with long local histories, I gather. I'm astonished that you think our house is built on top of a cemetery. The original house was here for a long, long time."

"Not to say under the house," Nuala remarked as we entered the parlor of the rehabilitated manor. "But in front of the house, underneath the park land you've created."

"Hmm . . . Interesting!"

The parlor—or perhaps I should call it the drawing room—was a perfect recreation of a small Georgian manor house that in other parts of the country would now be a gourmet restaurant. The furnishings, the paintings, and the carpet were all authentic antiques. The room had electric lights and the peat in the fireplace was mostly symbolic. There was running water nearby. The inhabitants of the room wore modern clothes. Yet for a moment I felt that we had crossed the barrier of two centuries.

My wife seemed to sniff the air, as if she were looking for something.

We were introduced to the other luncheon guests: Daphne How-ard, Matt's blond and perfectly groomed wife, pretty but with a rather vacant look in her eyes; Ona, a teenager in the required jeans and UCD sweatshirt, whose short stature, red face, and smile were dupli-cations of her father; and a tall, bald man with hooded eyes in a dark suit, Tomas O'Regan, the builder who had restored the house. I remem-bered that Seamus Redmond had told us that he was a bit of a crook. Having earned a nice fee for his design of the house, he might well want another fee for adding to it or rebuilding it from another owner.

Preluncheon drinks were served. Nuala asked for some Tipperary Water and I for a drop of Bushmill's, straight up, of course.

" 'Tis the Green Label you're drinking, is it now?" Matt asked.

"Is there any other kind?" I asked, confident that the house would have it.

"That's what me da says all the time," Ona exploded. " 'Tis grand altogether and it clears the sinuses, he says."

"Dear . . ." her mother protested weakly.

"I'm sure you don't touch the stuff, my dear," her da said as with a very heavy hand he filled a Waterford goblet for me. Powerscourt, of course.

"Sure, isn't Guinness the best?"

" 'Tis," my wife said with a sigh.

"You don't drink, my dear?" Daphne asked. Her accent was very much upper-middle-class British. Her husband talked a bit like a Lon-don cockney who didn't care what people thought.

"Didn't me son drive me into a fit of depression he made such trouble in coming, so I'm taking them little pill things for a year and doesn't me doctor say if I so much as ride in a car with a man who has knocked off a jar of Bushmill's, I'll go over the top and round the bend and across the edge altogether?"

She offered this perfectly honest explanation with such good hu-mor that everyone laughed with her. This was a new twist, a new persona—Nuala Anne laughing at her infirmities and luring everyone into laughing with her.

She donned a new personality with the same ease with which she drew on a new bikini thong.

"I don't know much about the history of this area," Matt continued the conversation. "My cousins who lived here deserted it long ago, driven out by the Land Leaguers, I believe."

"It was a ruined house before 1882 when the Joyces were buried out where your park is," Nuala explained, "and the old church was over there where that Rolls thing is parked in front of our van."

"Really? How interesting! Was Myles Joyce buried there?"

"Och, wasn't the poor man buried in quicklime under the jail where that terrible Cathedral thing is now? 'Twas the John Joyces, all five of them, who were buried there, them as who were murdered."

"How dreadful!" Daphne exclaimed with little affect, a kind of for-the-record protest.

"In their house up on the side of the mountain," Nuala gestured, "the one with the blackthorn bush."

"And Myles was innocent, was he not?" Matt asked, interested in getting the facts and getting down to business.

"He was," Nuala replied, "and himself leaving a young pregnant wife."

"And the Brits knew he was innocent, didn't they?" Ona insisted vigorously.

"They did," I said, "as did everyone in the valley. But Dublin Castle wanted men at the end of the rope and the valley knew that no one would listen to them."

"What happened to the poor woman?" Ona asked.

"We don't know yet."

"I think Jimmy Joyce had a word to say on the subject." Matt Howard frowned as if trying to remember a quote from that most quotable if least intelligible of men.

He picked up a phone, "Simon, would you bring down that passage from Joyce I found last night?"

To us he said, "Simon Tailor is my confidential secretary. He will join us for lunch. Now, however, he is putting the finishing touches on some remarks I must make in the House the day after tomorrow for the P.M."

Simon Tailor was a tall, lank, young man with thick glasses and long black hair. He behaved with the shy courtesy of the very upper class Oxford graduate, which some people confuse with diffidence.

"I have the quote, m'lord," he murmured. "It's from Joyce's article 'Ireland at the Bar.' "

Matt Howard took the old book, produced glasses from his jacket pocket, put them on, and then took them off to provide a preface.

"Joyce wrote this twenty-five years after the event, I'm told. He may have some of the details wrong. It's strong stuff. I must tell you, for the sake of candor, that the P.M.'s wife called it to my attention."

Who else?

Matt put his glasses back on and began to read.

" 'Public opinion at the time thought him innocent and today considers him a martyr. The court had to resort to the services of an interpreter. The questioning conducted through the interpreter was, at times comic, at times tragic. On one side was the excessively ceremonious interpreter, on the other, the patriarch of a miserable tribe, unused to civilized customs, who seemed stupefied by all the judicial ceremony.

" 'The figure of this dumbfounded old man, a remnant of a civilization not ours, deaf and dumb before his judge, is a symbol of the Irish nation at the bar of public opinion. Like him, she is unable to appeal to the modem conscience of England and other countries. The English journalists act as interpreters between Ireland and the English electorate, which gives them ear from time to time and ends up being vexed by the endless complaints of the Nationalist representatives who have entered her House, as she believes, to disrupt its order and extort money.' "

He closed the book, returned it to Simon, who slipped quietly out of the room.

After a moment's pause for emphasis, he took off his glasses again.

"Is that accurate enough, Ms. McGrail?"

"Doesn't everyone call me Nuala Anne?"

"Fair enough," he agreed.

"Well," she said, "the tribe wasn't all that miserable and he wasn't all that old, but your man has the right of it about what happened."

"What a mess England has made of Ireland," Matt said, with a sad shake of his head.

"And ourselves with a higher standard of living these days," she murmured as if that were a terrible thing altogether.

Ah, the woman knew how to make points.

"Well,"—Matt Howard rubbed his hands together briskly—"let's go in for lunch."

The dining room was also a replica of the era when the judicial murder of Myles Joyce was possible, though the crystal and the china were, I thought, considerably more modern than anything that would have been available in the West of Ireland, say, in 1850. The "lunch" was French—sea bass and then veal with mysterious sauces. The portions were small, indeed too small for me. My wife ate cautiously and carefully, as if she were afraid that too much food would dull her investigative sensitivities. The wine, incidentally, was a white burgundy and exquisite. I went easy on it because I did not know what amusements might await me back at our bungalow.

YOU'RE A HORNY BASTARD. STOP STARING AT HER.

"She's mine. I have a right to stare at her. Whenever she dons one of her new personae, I fall in love with that character."

YOU'RE FULL OF SHIT.

"I'm a polygamist. I love all the different women she is."

I GIVE UP ON YOU.

"Now, Tom," Matt Howard turned our luncheon chatter about children and fashions to more serious concerns, "were you aware that there was a cemetery in front of our house?"

"Hardly," Tomas O'Regan said, in a very tony English voice, despite his Irish name. "If there were one, we certainly would have respected it, both because of the stern Irish laws on such matters and out of reverence and respect. In fact, all we found was an overgrown meadow with stones scattered about. We could always unearth it, m'lord, if you wish."

"And the old church?" Nuala asked.

O'Regan looked at her as if she were an impudent and disrespectful young woman.

"My dear, I am in the restoration business. I have, if I may say so, an international reputation for preserving monuments from the past. There may have been a church there in centuries past, but there was none such five years ago."

"Isn't it odd," I asked, "that the Lord of Ballynahinch, who built the house, would have put it up opposite a cemetery?"

"If there were indeed one there, it might have been odd. However, it might have looked to him like an unkempt meadow, just as it did to us."

"In fact," Matt Howard interjected, "the man who built it lived here for only a few years and, after his death, his son abandoned it and returned to London. The house was sacked many times from 1850 on by Ribbonmen and Fenians and such like. When my ancestors came over here they stayed in a townhouse in Galway."

"Is there a tradition that the house was haunted?"

"My dear young man,"—Tomas O'Regan turned his patronizing eye on me—"if one believes the legends, every manor house in Ireland is haunted."

"And they may be," Nuala murmured softly.

"Wouldn't it be fun," Ona said, "if our house were haunted?"

"Dear . . ." her mother protested ineffectually.

"I think, Dermot . . . more wine? Good . . . I think I can assure you that there are no psychic manifestations here. It is a pleasant place to visit occasionally, but otherwise dreadfully dull."

"No Ribbonmen or suchlike around?" Nuala said gently.

No one laughed.

"Except for that explosion and the murders up at Renvyle House, which we could quite do without," Matt said grimly. "We could, of course, dig up the cemetery and have the bishop come over and bless it, if you think that best."

"Darling, wouldn't that be quite vulgar?"

"Sure, aren't they at peace," Nuala agreed. "Still maybe just a little digging to be sure and then we could put up a nice memorial marker to the John Joyce family and to all the others buried on this hill through the ages."

That didn't sound exactly like something Nuala would say. She was up to something.

"Well, we might just do that. What do you think, Tom?"

"I would not recommend it, m'lord. It might attract tourists, which I don't think is quite what you have in mind. Perhaps a plaque in the house that the Bishop might bless . . . ."

"Isn't it strange,"—Simon Tailor spoke for the first time—"that the locals didn't protest when the Big House was first built here in the last century? Surely they could have made representations to your ancestors that this was, uh, hallowed ground?"

"I don't think my ancestors took too kindly to representations in those days, Simon. The local people were savages who were best kept at bay with a stout club and a gun or two when necessary."

"Of course, m'lord . . . Still that wouldn't be true today. If the Caseys or the Joyces that still live in the valley thought this land was sacred ground, would not they have complained, perhaps not quite so respectfully as their predecessors?"

"A point well taken, Simon. Naula Anne, what would you say to that?"

"We're quiet folk out here, Matt," my wife said gently, "even as were the folk who lived in the valley in the 1880s. We're not like your Dublin or even your Galway folk who will announce a protest at the drop of a brick wall. Maybe they'd just as soon see the past covered up and forgotten and who could blame them? So maybe me idea about a monument wouldn't be so wise after all."

My wife never, I repeat, never changed her mind that quickly.

The meal turned to sherry trifle with heavy (very heavy) cream and the conversation to politics.

Then me wife played another card.

"None of your mining folks have been exploring around here, have they now?"

"Hunting for mountains of gold is it?" Matt Howard beamed. "No,

I'm afraid not. Your hordes of protesters from Galway and Dublin would be swarming all over the place if there were any hints of gold or even zinc in these mountains. You remember the fuss they made several years ago when there were stories about Cro Patrick being a mountain of gold. Of course, worse luck for Ireland, there wasn't a word of truth in it."

"And, sure, we didn't need the gold anyway, did we?" Nuala said briskly.

"You certainly did not, but it would have helped," Matt said with a shrug of his big shoulders.

"All the precious metals are gone?" I asked.

"I wouldn't go so far as to say that, Dermot. You never know for sure about such things. Still, the hills of the West of Ireland have been pretty well assayed, and no one has found much of anything. There might be a few strains of gold or silver or copper or zinc here and there and they might mean a tidy sum for a poor farmer, but hardly enough to affect world markets—any more than that petroleum which is supposed to be deep beneath the ocean off Cork but just now would cost too much to bring to the surface."

"As Nuala suggested, Ireland no longer needs fantasies to have a decent standard of living, more decent, I quickly add, my dear, than that across the Irish Sea, despite our current prosperity."

"Touché," Nuala admitted with a smile.

There was something sinister about that smile, I thought. She's playing a deep game, relying partly on her shrewd native intelligence and partly on whatever that other thing is that hides inside her.

We returned to the parlor for coffee and drinks. I opted for a cognac, which turned out to be the best I had ever tasted in my life.

"You must tell us, Nuala Anne,"—Matt turned us to serious conversation after he had poured the drinks—"what you think of the strange crimes over at the hotel—poor Colm MacManus losing his house in that explosion, which, to be candid, rocked our windows way out here, the dastardly attempt on your life, those unfortunate Russians . . ."

"I think the Russians are a separate matter," Nuala said calmly,

"though perhaps not completely unrelated. The others were attempts to frighten people. I assume that they will continue until the proper people are frightened."

"My goodness," Daphne whimpered.

"Do you think they're trying to frighten me?" Matt Howard demanded. "If they are, they're wasting their time."

"M'lord, I think we should be careful," Simon Tailor said meekly.

"Careful be damned!"

"Do you consider yourself Irish or English, Matt?" I asked, hoping he didn't mind the question.

He didn't seem to mind.

"Well, how would you describe yourself, Dermot?"

"We have a category for it—Irish American."

"And you Nuala Anne?"

"Irish and American."

"So, despite my London accent, I choose a definition that fits between the two islands, both English and Irish."

"Och, are we Irish ready to define as Irish anyone who wants to be! Doesn't me man even have an Irish passport so he doesn't have to wait in line at immigration and his grandparents being from right here in Galway!"

We chatted a bit more. Nuala seemed satisfied. I stood up.

"We should be taking our leave," I said, rising. "We have two little ones we must check on."

Suddenly Nuala looked grim, frightened, maybe unearthly. What was wrong?

We went through the usual round of handshaking. Then Matt Howard glanced out the window.

"Damnation! The plumbers have locked your van in, Dermot. . . . Ona, would you run out and move the Rolls for them?"

"Da permits me to drive it about ten yards," the young woman said to us as she bounded up and grabbed the key, "and I'm insured for that too."

She left the room. I watched her out the window running down the driveway and realized that in ten years I would have a teenager.

There was a shattering sound behind me, a herd of zebra stampeding in one of those films about the Serengeti. Or Nuala on the run.

Out of the corner of my eye I saw her bolt out the front door, kick off her shoes, and run after Ona. Their race seemed in slow motion. Frozen at the window and dreading I knew not what, I thought Nuala would never catch up with the girl, who herself was running towards the Rolls.

Ona was short and not a practiced runner. Nuala was tall and a long-distance runner with incredibly solid legs. Yet she was too far behind. She gained on the child as I watched, but she'd never make it in time.

Whatever in time meant.

Key in hand, Ona was at the door of the car. Nuala at least ten feet away. Ona moved the key towards the door. Nuala leaped through space, pulled the girl way from the car, and wrestled her to the ground.

In the distance the blue Garda car began to move.

—22—

PEIG SAYERS knelt on the driveway and peered gingerly under the Rolls.

"Holy Mother of God!" she screamed. "There is a bomb there! Seamus call the Super and tell him to get the bomb squad out here! Now! . . . Stand back everyone! This car has a bomb!"

I held Nuala in my arms and she held Ona in her arms.

"I ruined me tights," Nuala murmured, "and me knees."

Her nylons were indeed a torn and bloody mess.

"And saved a wonderful young life!"

"Nuala," Ona sobbed, "you were so brave!"

"Everyone move back," Peig was taking charge. "Over to that mound of oak trees, at least a hundred and fifty yards from the house. Evacuate everyone in it immediately!"

"I'll take care of it immediately, ma'am," Simon Tailor responded. "Don't any of you go back for anything! You have your lives, and for the moment that's enough!

The droopy Oxford scholar had become a young commando second lieutenant in one of the old war movies.

"He didn't salute you," I said to Peig, who was staring after the young Brit in astonishment.

She glanced at me and grinned.

"Me orders include you and your wife, Dermot Michael Coyne. Over to those trees now. You too, Seamus. We don't want to start our car lest it ignite something. . . . You rang up the Super?"

"He's on his way, ma'am."

I noticed that it was raining, not hard yet, but steadily, a fine soft day as the Irish would have it.

Ona stumbled into her mother's arms. They clung to each other, sobbing.

"How did she know, Dermot?" Matt asked me as we hiked rapidly towards the protecting line of trees, my wife still hanging on my arms.

"She's one of the dark ones," I said. "She sensed danger. She herself probably couldn't tell you why."

"The Rolls was evil," my wife moaned. "It wanted Ona and I wasn't going to let it have her."

"Thank God," Matt said.

"And the Blessed Mother."

"And"—I concluded the litany—"Patrick, Brigid, and Colm!"

I glanced over my shoulder. Peig and Simon were hustling four servants and two plumbers out of the manor house. The latter tried to go to their own van. Peig pushed them towards safety. They looked like they wanted to argue. Simon snapped at them and they ran towards us.

"I've never quite seen Simon act like that," Matt said to me.

"Commando officer," I replied.

"And a competent one."

"The car is going to blow up," Nuala whispered to me. "It really is, Dermot Michael. We'll have to rent a new van. All four of them will blow up."

"Four?"

"The Garda car too."

"You saved us all, Nuala."

"God did. And the blessed mother. And Brigid, Patrick, and Colm."

She giggled.

"And, Dermot, you have to learn to put Brigid first."

The servants and the plumbers arrived at our little circle.

"Now, then," Simon Tailor announced, "Constable Sayers has assured me that we will be perfectly safe out here, though it would be better if all moved behind the mound. . . . That's all right. . . . The Garda are already on their way with the bomb squad and they'll fix things in a jiffy."

"No they won't," Nuala said sadly. The rain turned from soft to hard, very hard. We were all soaked to the skin. No one dared to complain.

"We're right on top of the cemetery," Nuala told me. "Isn't Johnny Joyce buried right over there?"

DON'T YOU WISH SOMETIMES THAT YOU WERE MARRIED TO A NORMAL WOMAN.

"No!"

It seemed like hours. The rain continued to pour. Daphne held her husband in one arm and her daughter in the other. They were weeping and she was not.

"We still have each other," she said. "That's all that matters. We can rebuild the house, can't we, Thomas?"

"We can indeed. However, it's still there, isn't it now? The Garda will disarm the bomb, if there really is one, and everything will be all right."

"No it won't," Naula told me.

"Ma'am," Simon Tailor said to Peig, next to whom he had been standing, "do you think I might go back to the house and bring some rain garments for the women?"

"Simon Tailor, you're a fockin' amadon," Peig said affectionately. "Better that they stay wet than we have a casualty."

"Yes, ma'am," he said obediently.

"Well?" I said to Nuala.

"Haven't they both seen their destiny and liked it?"

Finally, when I was expecting Noah and family to float across the park in front of the manor, I heard the sirens of the Garda in the distance.

"Peig,"—Nuala grabbed the constable—"we have to go down to the road and stop them or won't they all be blown up. . . . Dermot Michael, you stay here."

The blond constable had more sense than to argue with one of the dark ones. She rushed towards the road, perhaps fifty yards away. Like Ona she was on the short side. So me wife made it to the road first and held out her arms.

The Garda caravan ground to a halt. Declan McGinn tried to argue with Nuala and Peig and, as all Irishmen are fated to do, lost the argument.

The Gardaí poured out of their cars and vans and huddled behind a big van, which was perhaps the bomb squad's.

The bedraggled band behind the oak cover mound grew silent and tense. They knew something was about to happen. We waited anxious seconds.

Than a great dirty orange ball emerged from the Rolls. It quickly spread to our van, the plumbers' van and the Garda car. Three more orange globes ballooned into the air, then the sound and the blast waves hit us. People were screaming all around me. I felt like a furnace door had hit me, followed by the acrid stench of burning gasoline.

The Howard family rocked into me. I steadied them.

"Good God!" Matt screamed.

"She saved our lives," his wife said, quite calmly. "Fuck the house."

"Right," Ona agreed, "fock the house!"

At that point some caring material spirit, Brigid the Blessed Mother, or a motherly God opened the floodgates of heaven. The torrent of water didn't put out the fireball, but it damped it down and prevented its spread.

"Matthew Howard, Lord Ballynahinch," I said, "can I tell you that you have two wonderful women in your life."

"He knows it," Daphne said, "but it's good for him to hear it from someone else."

Speaking of wonderful women, where was mine?

Wasn't she already holding me in her arms, her face blackened, her clothes torn, soaking wet and incredibly beautiful.

"Are you still alive, Dermot Michael?

"Woman, I am!"

"Thanks be to God!

"Wasn't it terrible beautiful altogether?"

Come to think of it, I guess it was.

We waited around till the fire brigade arrived and pumped water from the river all over the park and the driveway. The second Rolls and the Bentley were badly scarred but had not ignited. The Mercedes was untouched. The windows had been blown out of the front of the house and the side wall and part of the front singed by fire. But it stood.

"Well, Tom," Matt Howard said to Tomas O'Regan, "I think we'll be moving over to the Station House in Clifden. You can begin reconstruction as soon as the Garda permit. I will not be driven out of Ireland like my ancestors were."

"I imagine Mr. Blair will want to send some security people over, sir," Declan McGinn said respectfully. "I'm sure they'll be most welcome."

"Good, good! . . . Nuala Anne, we all owe our lives to you! I promise you that we'll never forget it."

"Thank God and the Blessed Mother and Patrick and Brigid and Colm."

"Brigid, Patrick, and Colm," I corrected her.

"And all the poor souls buried beneath our feet," Nuala went on, "who were praying for us too."

"Constable Sayers," Simon Tailor began nervously, "would I be wrong to assume that you are a descendant of the famed Blasket Island woman?"

"You'd not be wrong," she said, a mischievous grin on her pretty face, "though I'm not as immoral a woman as she pretended to be."

He blushed and stammered.

"I'm sure not . . . I was, uh, wondering if I might buy you a drink at O'Donnell's tomorrow night?"

"You want to chat me up, do you now?"

"Er, well, not exactly. I'd rather like, however, to chat with you."

"Well, what do you think, Nuala Anne?" Peig said, still mischievous.

"To use your own words, Peig Sayers, if you don't accept the man's invitation, you're a fockin' amadon."

We lingered around the ridge of oak trees as our fellow survivors departed. Nuala sunk to her knees in the mud, made a fearsome sign of the cross, and began to pray fervently, if silently. What could I do but join her?

To whom was she praying? The souls of the departed for many centuries who were buried beneath the ground of Ballynahinch Manor?

The Gardaí drove us back to our bungalow. The two young constables, both male, promised that they would keep close watch on us.

"You wouldn't want to be too close to us, would you now?" my wife told them. "We seem to collect explosions."

Ethne, her face stained with tears, was waiting for us at the open door.

"Glory be to God! 'Tis yourselves and still alive. When I heard that awful explosion, I thought it would mean the destruction of you altogether. . . . Come on in out of the rain! I'll make a pot of tea for you!"

"Very strong tea," Nuala requested as we entered the warmth of our home. "Did the explosion wake up the small ones?"

"Didn't they sleep right through it, the little lambs! And aren't they still sound asleep!"

We crept into the nursery. Sure enough, our little redhead and our even smaller blond were both sound asleep. So too were Fiona's puppies. Their mother flapped her tail against the floor when we entered and then went back to sleep.

"Before we take our shower, Dermot Michael," my wife instructed me in our bedroom, "you have one thing to do."

"And that is?"

"Call your good friend Eugene Keenan in Dublin and tell him he should get himself out here first thing in the morning."

"Now?"

"Yes, now!"

"You figured it all out?"

"Sure, isn't it as plain as the nose on your face? I just need some details . . . and to put some ointment on me poor knees. . . ."

She disappeared into the bathroom. I heard the shower and longed for it's healing waters.

After considerable bureaucratic resistance in Dublin, I was finally put through, as they say, to the Deputy Commissioner.

"Gene Keenan," he said with his usual brisk courtesy.

"Dermot Michael Coyne!"

"Good heavens, man! What are you and that wild wife of yours doing to this poor island! Blowing up our manor houses, threatening the lives of our gentry, driving me poor colleagues mad with worry! . . . The two of you are all right, aren't you?"

"Herself banged up her knees tackling Ona Howard and saving the lives of all of us. Otherwise we're enjoying the weather."

"Are you now? Well, I'm glad to hear it. . . . I suppose she just knew there was a bomb in the car?"

"To quote her very words, the car was evil and it wanted Ona and she wasn't going to let it have her."

"You can imagine me shivering Dermot."

"I have no problem with that."

"Has she solved the mystery yet?" he asked, somewhat more casually than I thought was appropriate.

"She's being very mysterious about it. . . . However, she wants me to give you a message. She expects to see you out here tomorrow morning."

"Does she now?"

"Doesn't she now?"

"Well, you can tell her that I've already made me plans and I'll be taking me midmorning tea with you."

"I'll do that."

"Oh, one more thing, Dermot. We arrested a Russian cabin attendant at Shannon, one of their professional goons, and charged him with the murder of the three men at Renvyle House. They'll want him back over there and, between you and me, I don't think we'll let them have him."

I headed for the shower.

"Make it all go away, Dermot Michael Coyne," my wife begged me as I joined her under the hot water.

"I'll do my best."

Later, after watching the news on the telly—news that fascinated

Nelliecoyne because she recognized her friend Peig at the scene of the explosion but not her parents lurking in the background—eating supper, and putting the kids to bed, Nuala and I sat in the parlor—rather in violation of her strict rules about "them"—and prepared to finish reading the second section of Edward Fitzpatrick's memoir of Ireland in 1883.

"What do you think about them two this afternoon?" I asked.

"Yanks say those two. . . . Which two?"

"O'Cuiv and Quinn?"

"Oh, them two . . . Probably trying to beat MacManus at one of his shady games by being even shadier. All of them are perpetual conspirators, though MacManus has the edge because he's in the government. Now give over, Dermot Michael, while we read the rest of the story."

— 23 —

Letterfrack, County Galway, May 11, 1883

Marty Dempsey was waiting for me in the pub of the Letterfrack Inn.

"The woman sends her best," he began, nodding in the direction of his home in Dublin. "Doesn't she say she's after hoping you're happier now than you were at Christmas?"

"My best back to her, Martin. . . . She's a wonderful woman."

"Aye"—he sighed—"aren't some of us luckier than we deserve?"

"So what's happening out here?"

"The valley is bestirring itself, something unusual for this part of Ireland. Secret societies, yes. Silent pressure, yes. Demands for public penance, that's a different matter altogether."

"Who's stirring the pot?"

"The new priest out here, Father Corbett. He's a fierce and admirable young man. He preaches every Sunday about informers and perjurers. Tom Casey and Anthony Philbin don't come to Mass anymore. Everyone knows, of course, whom he means."

"There're four innocent men still in jail."

"Right you are . . . And one innocent man in the quicklime beneath the Galway jail."

"Another martyr for poor old Ireland."

He looked at me to see if I was being ironic. He saw that I was and smiled thinly.

"And isn't that man's widow stirring up the trouble too."

"Nora Joyce!"

"Aye, your Irish princess is acting like one. She goes up and down the valley with that poor little babe in her arms and that fey urchin who trails after her demanding justice. As you know, that's a dangerous thing to do. The peasants have their own way of punishing informers. They don't like such direct campaigns."

"And most of the brutes who murdered the Joyces are still at large?"

"They are, boyo. In theory, mind you, they could still be indicted for those murders, though the Crown isn't likely to admit they made a mistake. If they killed Nora Joyce the authorities might be open to a new murder charge, but that isn't probable, if you take me meaning."

"And Nora?"

"They say she doesn't care whether she lives or dies. It's amazing to me that she survived the winter. That pretty child who follows her around, her niece they say, is supposed to be one of the dark ones. They say she warns Nora when there's danger. They're all afraid of the poor dirty little thing."

"Fey or not and dirty face or not, she's a grand spirit."

"Aye," Marty said with a sigh.

"So what happens tomorrow?"

"So doesn't his gracious lordship John Joseph Kane, Bishop of Galway and Kilmacduff and apostolic administrator of Kilfenora, come up here to say the Mass at half eleven."

"Is that usual?"

"It is and it isn't. Your bishops like to get around their diocese when they can. However, when the priest is new like Father Corbett, they usually leave them alone for a few years so that they can settle in. There's them that say that himself is involved in this scheme."

"And what does the valley think about it?"

"Sure, aren't they Irish? So typically they are of two minds. One mind says that the Bishop and the priest and Nora Joyce should leave things as they are. Don't we have enough troubles as it is? The other mind says there are still four innocent men in jail."

"What is supposed to happen?"

"After the confirmation and the reading of the Gospel, Tom Casey is supposed to come up to the altar and confess to the bishop that he lied at the trials to save his own life."

"Tom Casey!"

"The valley has been punishing him in its own way. His wife, who it is said is not exactly a paragon of virtue, refuses to sleep with him till he tells the truth."

"It should be an interesting Mass."

"Oh, it will be all of that, boyo, all of that. Another jar?"

"No thanks, Marty. It was a long ride over here. I'd better get some sleep."

Letterfrack, County Galway, May 12, 1883

The weather this morning was in sharp contrast to the grim business ahead of us. It is a glorious spring day; gentle breezes caress your face, big puffy white clouds drift lazily across the sky, and the smell of spring flowers has overcome the usual stench of manure and peat fire. Men, women, and children are dressed in their best clothes and wearing shoes to greet the bishop, and there is an ambience of agitation and expectation in the crowd, as if something exciting and important is about to occur. They whisper to one another, speculating, no doubt, about what might happen.

I am struck by how handsome the women look when they wear their Sunday best. Just like my mother and my sister, though the latter don't wash their feet in a stream and don socks and shoes a hundred yards away from the church.

I see my old friend, Sergeant Tommy Finnucane.

We shake hands briskly.

"I thought you might be around, lad," he says. "It promises to be a grand morning for you fellas."

"And what do you think about it, Tommy?"

"Well, Mr. Bolton never asked us what we thought. He was convinced that his unimpeachable witnesses were all he needed. We never believed the bastards from the beginning."

"Why are you lads here? They're not concerned in Dublin Castle about what Tom Casey might say, are they?"

"Not a bit of it. They're concerned that there might be some disorder here, especially with a bishop around."

"Will there?"

"Not a chance of it. The people respect the Bishop too much."

I didn't have the courage to ask him what he thought about the execution of Myles Joyce, the man he had arrested last August.

"Jesus and Mary be with you, Mr. Fitzpatrick, sir."

"And Jesus and Mary and Patrick be with you, Josie Philbin."

The little ragamuffin had made an attempt, mostly unsuccessful, to wash her face. A decrepit bonnet sat askew on her head. Her bright eyes shone with excitement.

"How's herself?" I asked.

"She'll be here shortly, sir. With the baby. Neither are keeping very well."

"How are your finances, Josie?"

"I ought not to answer that, sir."

"Why not?"

"Aunt Nora is uneasy about where I get the money."

"Does she know?"

"I think she suspects, sir. . . . When our cow died during the winter I had to sell our warm cloaks to buy a new cow."

"She told you not to take any money from me?"

"No, Mr. Fitzpatrick, sir, she did not. We'd all of us be dead save for your money. She doesn't care for herself, but she does worry about me and Mary Elizabeth."

"Good," I said, slipping another twenty pounds into her grubby paw.

She looked dubious but took the money.

"Thank you, sir," she said with a wink.

What would happen when I returned to Chicago as I would in the fall, after the debate in Parliament? Perhaps I could send money for them to Father Corbett.

Then Nora appeared, her child clutched in her arm.

"Mr. Fitzpatrick, may I present my daughter, Miss Mary Elizabeth Joyce."

The child, perhaps five months old, was pretty despite her wasted face and thin body. I wondered how many more days she might live. Her mother

*was also wasted and thin, almost ghostlike. Yet oddly she was radiantly
beautiful in her prized red cloak; her eyes glowed and a touch of unearthly
color illumined her sunken cheeks.*

My heart wrenched in sadness.

*"Good morning, Miss Joyce," I said respectfully, touching the child's
face. "You are very beautiful, just like your mother."*

The little girl opened her eyes and smiled slightly, then went back to sleep.

Dear God in heaven, I must help them!

"She is a very good little baby," her mother said proudly.

*"I am told that you are in part responsible for this morning's visit, Mrs.
Joyce?"*

*"We all hope for truth and justice, Mr. Fitzpatrick. We will have to wait
and see what happens. Tom Casey may not even appear."*

*"We have places reserved for your lot in the church, Mr. Fitzpatrick,
sir," Josie informed me.*

*She led Marty Dempsey and me into the already crowded church. A
buzz of whispers filled the church. I was so shocked and so moved by Nora
and her child that I could hardly concentrate on the dramatic revelation that
was about to occur.*

*At a quarter to twelve, led by a young cross bearer and two equally
young acolytes and preceded by a half dozen young people—a few years
older than Josie—in their finest clothes, Bishop Kane in full regalia, with a
priest on either side, came up the aisle in solemn procession. A small choir
sang vigorously in off-key Latin. The Bishop preached briefly and effectively
in Irish. The congregation listened intently. Then he administered the sac-
rament of Confirmation. It was a solemn moment. The congregation seemed
aware that the Holy Spirit was somehow among them. Then, as the young
people returned with their sponsors to the front pew of the church, the Bishop
began the Mass.*

*The church had now become stuffy and uncomfortable, the congregation
restless and uneasy, wondering what would happen after the Gospel. One
of the priests, perhaps Father Corbett, watched the congregation intently.*

*The Bishop returned to the pulpit and read the Gospel in Irish. He closed
the book and waited, looking around the church. I felt the tension increase
as the members of the congregation turned to each other expectantly. Then,*

just as one waited for something to snap, the door opened and a man walked hesitantly down the aisle, a lighted candle in his hand. Sweat pouring down his white face, he swayed as he approached the Bishop.

He mumbled something.

"Louder, my son!" the Bishop demanded.

The conversation was to be in English. Doubtless for the journalists. Presumably the Irish-speakers knew what was to be said, had perhaps known it for a long time.

For all the drama, my mind was on Nora. What was I to do about her!

"I'm Thomas Casey, m'lord. I'm the son of Little Tom Casey. I'm called Young Tom Casey."

His voice was little more than a croak, like perhaps that of a dying bird.

"What do you wish of me, Thomas Casey?"

"I wish to confess my terrible sin."

"What is that sin?"

He hesitated. The congregation scarcely breathed.

"To save my life I obeyed the Crown Solicitor and accused innocent men of the murder of John Joyce and family. Mr. Bolton said that if I did not perjure myself, I would be convicted and hung. He gave me a half hour to make up my mind to say what he wanted me to say."

"Who were the innocent men?"

"All those in prison now, milord, except Michael Casey and he, like me, was outside when the murders occurred."

"I see. . . . Anyone else?"

Casey whispered a name.

"Speak up, my good man!"

"Myles Joyce, m'lord. He had nothing to do with the crime!"

His candle went out. The wax began to drip on the floor in front of the bishop.

A wave of inarticulate sound swept across the church.

"The man hung in the Galway jail before Christmas?"

"Yes, m'lord." He gulped. "He was completely innocent."

"And those who reported these men to the police?"

"Everyone knows they were lying! They were not there that night. It was too dark for them to see anything."

"I see. . . . Now, who were the killers?"

"M'lord . . ." He hesitated, frightened.

"Yes?" Bishop Kane demanded

"It was all Big John Casey's idea! We had met before at his house, and he said that John Joyce had to die or he would steal all the sheep in the valley!"

"And then?"

"The night of the killing we met again at his house. There was much drink taken. We were all drunk. He said they were all informers and had to die. Michael Joyce and I begged that the women be spared. John Casey said that we couldn't take the chance that they would recognize any of us. He was very angry at Breige O'Brien for marrying John Joyce. He appointed three men to go into the house—his son Young John Casey, Pat Joyce, and Pat Lydon. He told me to go into the house, but I said that I would not."

The congregation snorted with skepticism.

"These three men did the actual killings?"

"Yes, m'lord."

"And Young John Casey and Pat Lydon are still free?"

"Yes, m'lord. They were called Kelly and Nee but those were false names. Pat Joyce that was hung was one of the killers. Pat Casey that was hung was inside, too, but I don't think he killed anyone. I don't think that Big John Casey ordered him to go in, but he might have."

"So you are telling us here in this church that Big John Casey planned this brutal killing and that his son and at least two more men carried it out?"

"I am, m'lord."

"Because John Joyce was accused of stealing sheep, because the family was suspected of informing to the police, and because he was angry at John Joyce's wife?"

"Yes, m'lord."

"And Big John Casey, Young John Casey, and Pat Lydon are still at large, perhaps to kill again?"

"They are."

"And four totally innocent men are in jail and one totally innocent man is dead?"

Casey choked for brief moment, as if he were sobbing. " 'Tis true."

"You admit your responsibility for these crimes?"

Thomas Casey waited, sighed, and began again.

"I admit my guilt, yes. However, the Anthony Joyces lied about who was there. The English would have hung Myles Joyce anyway, no matter what I said. They would have sent the others to jail anyway."

"That is a poor excuse, Thomas Casey. I charge you that for the good of your immortal soul you will tell this story to anyone who asks so that the innocent may be set free. Will you do that?"

"Yes, m'lord. Gladly."

"Very well, you may go in peace now and work out your sorrow for the rest of your life."

"Thank you, m'lord!"

His candle dropped from his hand. He turned and staggered towards the door of the church. A couple of men helped him out.

Exhausted and drained, the congregation could not so much as stir. It seemed that no one was breathing.

The Bishop waited till the door of the church was closed. Then he spoke again in Irish. I suspected that he was denouncing the killers, violence, the silence of the valley about the crime, and the English. I glanced around the church. Almost every head was hung. Not Nora Joyce's however. She sat in her pew, babe in arms, proud, tall, erect. She had won.

After Mass I bumped into Tommy Finnucane.

"Any surprises?"

"Didn't every policeman in this part of Galway know the day after the killing that Big John Casey had sworn to get rid of John Joyce? We couldn't prove it and Mr. Bolton wasn't interested in what we knew. We didn't know who was there, and those bastards of Anthony Joyce's crowd had a list. That's all Mr. Bolton needed. I hear that Young John Casey and Pat Lydon enjoyed killing the women and would like to kill some more."

"I imagine they won't do it now."

"They'll wait awhile anyway."

The crowd in church and the larger crowd waiting outside slipped away quietly in the bright sunlight. They were, I thought, beaten, cowed, but not surprised.

I looked for Nora and her baby. And for Josie. They were nowhere to be seen.

"This story will be all over the British Isles by Tuesday morning," I said. "The truth finally about the Maamtrasna murders."

"It's the truth all right, boyo. Or as close to the truth as we will ever get. It won't make any difference, you understand."

I was momentarily startled. Then I realized that he was right. Despite all the evidence, Dublin Castle could never admit its mistakes. The Irish had won again, but as always they had lost.

It's raining now. The wind is rattling the windows of my room. I've had two jars of whiskey. I won't drink any more because it won't do any good. Big John Casey would continue to live in the valley, ostracized perhaps, marked for the rest of his days as a brutal killer, but free.

Myles Joyce was dead.

That was the story.

And Nora?

Dear God in heaven, what am I to do about Nora?!

— 24 —

MY WIFE handed me the sealed envelope.

"Go on open it, will you, Dermot Michael Coyne."

"I will, woman, if you give me a chance, though I have no doubts that you've been absolutely right all along."

YOU'D BETTER NOT.

"Shut up."

The note, on a sheet of white computer paper and in Nuala's neat and precise hand—the handwriting of an accountant—was brief and to the point.

Any idiot would know that Big John Casey was behind the murders. Who else would have had the power in the village to force other men to commit such crimes? Who else would resent a man with a few sheep who dared to steal from his many? Who else would resent the fact that Breige O'Brien had not married him? Maybe the secret society was involved, but politics was only an excuse. Big John Casey had the power to do away with John Joyce and his family and he did just that. He might not have gotten away with it if it hadn't been for the Anthony Joyces and their lies. No one in the family would have dared to inform on him. He didn't want to see Myles Joyce die, though there was no love lost between them. He didn't want to see innocent men go to prison. He was afraid

that Pat Casey and Pat Joyce would inform on him to save their lives, but he was pretty confident that the Brits wouldn't believe them. Still, he must have had some uneasy days until the hangings were over.

Now call your friend An t'Athair Sean O'Laighne and tell him that I was right all along.

Nuala Anne McGrail Coyne.

"So you had the right of it all along," I said, sitting down on our couch. Two white furry critters tried to nibble on my shoes.

"Cut it out, Deirdre."

"That's Dana, Dermot Michael."

Fiona stood at the door of the parlor admiring her progeny.

"I did have the right of it," she said, "but it was evident all along, wasn't it now?"

"Elementary."

She sighed loudly.

"Not that it does us or them any good."

"Except that the truth can be told at last."

"Sure, didn't your man tell it in his articles long ago?"

"It's all forgotten. The record should be made clear and explicit."

"Won't our Ethne do it in her Ph.D.?"

Ah, that was the way the wind was blowing, was it now? Incidentally, like everyone on the island she called the precious doctorate the P Haitch D, the Irish language lacking a soft *h* sound.

"There's something I'm missing, Dermot Michael," she confessed, "as plain as the nose on me face."

"Pretty nose."

She snorted.

"I can't figure out whether it has to do with the past mystery or the present."

"Maybe both?"

She glanced up at me, as if I had said something very intelligent.

"Maybe you have the right of it, Dermot Michael."

"I'll call the priest."

"Tell him that the final installment is under a stack of old church records in a closet in his office and that I'm dying to know how it ends."

"You don't know, Nuala?"

"I don't have a friggin' clue."

The next morning about eleven o'clock Eugene Keenan appeared at our door. There were four Garda cars in front of our house, our own constant protection and three accompanying the Deputy Commissioner.

"Look at all the Garda cars," my wife protested. "What will the neighbors think?"

"That they'll be happy when these crazy Yanks go home!" I said, not doubting the truth of that.

"Jesus and Mary be with this house," Gene said as I opened the door.

Nuala replied in Irish that Jesus and Mary and Patrick should be with all who came to the house.

"Woman," the Deputy Commissioner said wearily, "where's me tea?"

Gene Keenan, a tall, handsome man with twinkling blue eyes, gray-tinged brown hair, and an easy smile, brought out the worst in my wife, just as Jake Lane did. He was a perfect target for her love of banter, something which I was usually spared because I was her "dear sweet husband."

"Well, if them as says they're coming for midmorning tea and expecting warm scones were on time, wouldn't the tea and the scones be ready!"

He glanced at his watch, "eleven o'clock?"

" 'Tis late morning as anyone knows. Midmorning ends at ten-thirty."

"But I smell the fresh scones in the air?"

"Well, if you'd sit down for a moment and stop your complaining, won't we get them for you?"

Nuala departed for the kitchen, and Fiona joined us in the parlor *en famile*. She must have smelled cop because she gave Gene the greeting she reserved for former colleagues.

"Well, isn't it herself and with small ones? Fiona, girl, it's been a long time."

She curled up at his feet, and the pups instantly began feeding.

"She wasn't out in Maamtrasna yesterday, was she?"

"We had Nuala. That was enough."

"And Detective Sergeant Sayers."

"You promoted the woman, did you? Well, 'tis high time, I'd say, and herself a brilliant Garda."

Nuala sailed into the room with Ethne in tow and platters of tea, jam, butter, clotted cream, and scones, dense with raisins. It looked like a good morning for Dermot Michael.

"I've been out there for two and a half hours," Gene Keenan began after Nuala had introduced Ethne, poured the tea, and distributed the scones, an extra one to me. "You can't imagine the dustup this has created. The media are all over the place. Tony Blair and our Taoiseach are screaming. Everyone who might have done it is denying responsibility, and the explosions have destroyed all the obvious evidence. We'll dig out something eventually, but it will take time. Fortunately no one has told them how the warning about the bomb was delivered. The next thing would be the fairie and the leprechauns."

"The telly is saying that the Gardaí think the lads are involved, maybe one of the dissident groups," Nuala observed. Discretely she put another scone on me plate. My plate.

"It seems to have been the kind of car bombs they might use. These days, however, everyone seems to know how to make a car bomb. I don't think it's the lads, but none of us can figure out why someone would blow up MacManus's house, take some shots at you, and then try to kill the whole Howard family."

"Did they want to kill them?" Nuala asked innocently.

"You were out there, Nuala, how could you have any doubts?"

"Whoever planted the bomb didn't know that we'd park behind the Rolls, that the plumber's van would park behind us, and that the Garda would appear with a fourth car. He wasn't counting on four explosions. Nor did he expect that your man would chase poor little Ona out to move the car. He might just as well have figured on exploding the bomb by remote control at some time when no one would get hurt. The car was far enough away from the house that if it were the cause of the only explosion, no one would have been hurt."

The Deputy Commissioner rubbed his unshaven chin. "That's an interesting possibility, Nuala. We've never thought of it. Yet it might have gone off if young Ona opened the door or turned the key."

"Suppose you knew the exact plans of the family for the day and thought that the car would not be touched. You could blow it up at night and scare everyone all the way back to Westminster and not hurt anyone."

"That would point towards that sleepy young Englishman who's Matt Howard's secretary."

"It might."

"He took charge afterwards, I'm told, perhaps to make sure that no one died."

"Or it could have been O'Regan the builder or anyone in the family or one of the servants," I suggested. "Or someone on the outside who had an informant inside."

"We noted," the Commissioner continued, "that the bomb was probably triggered by remote control just before our cars arrived. Someone heard them coming and pushed the button so they wouldn't be able to defuse and examine the bomb."

"Or someone saw them on the road," Nuala observed. "It might have been one of us or it might have been someone up at the top of the mountain where the John Joyce family lived."

"You don't think there's a connection between the killings in 1882 and the present mess, do you?"

"The explosion took place right on top of the old cemetery where the Joyces were buried and many other people from the valley too."

Gene Keenan's frown darkened. Nuala gave him another scone, richly buttered and jellied.

"Are you telling me that the dead might have triggered the explosion?"

"Or someone who thinks that the Brits have been around the valley too long. Or someone who resents that your man's wife has Joyce and Casey in her background and that her branches of the family were on the wrong side."

"My headache is getting worse." The Commissioner sighed. However, he did finish his scone. Our supply was running out.

"What's under the ground on that hill, Commissioner Keenan?"

"Nothing, Nuala Anne, except the bones of the long dead."

"No, I mean what kind of precious metal."

"We've covered that base. There's nothing there."

"Could someone in the government know what's there without your knowing?"

He pondered thoughtfully.

"Maybe, maybe. The bureaucrats are great for keeping secrets from one another."

"Could you find out?"

He nodded slowly. "I think so."

Nuala made a couple of more suggestions about questions for which they might seek answers. Gene Keenan removed a used index card from his inside jacket pocket and jotted notes on it.

"I'm not sure where this is going," he said with yet another huge sigh, "but it will give our people something to do."

"Mind you," Nuala admonished him, "they should be very careful about how they ask the questions. We wouldn't want anyone to know what we're up to, would we now?"

"No, Nuala Anne, we certainly would not."

Nuala presented our offspring, who had been shyly peeking around the door. Nelliecoyne informed the Deputy Commissioner that she had seen him on the telly. He left, shaking his head, as if he had returned to the twentieth century from, let's say, the fifteenth.

The phone rang.

"Jack Lane here, Dermot. . . . You guys OK?"

"Never better."

"What the hell is going on?"

"Me wife will figure that out."

"Just like she figured out where the last segment of the memoir is. I'll drop it off this afternoon. I haven't read it. I figured she should read it first."

In the afternoon, Gene Keenan called.

"Dermot, you can tell that lovely witch she's right. There is a strain of gold in that hill. Not a lot. Not enough for a gold rush, not enough to affect inflation in this country, but enough to bring someone several million pounds. It's been kept a secret because the office in charge doesn't want another Cro Patrick scare."

"I'll tell her."

Which I did.

She nodded in satisfaction.

"Think of it, Dermot, the Joyces and all those other poor souls up there have been sleeping on a bed of gold."

Almost immediately after the phone call, Jack Lane arrived with a thin stack of foolscap.

"I want it tomorrow morning," he said.

"You must come in for tea, An t'Athair O'Laighne."

"And keep you from reading how the story ends? I may not have much sense, but I have more sense than that."

After we had read the story, it was time and long past time to go to bed. Nuala has a ritual every night in which she briskly brushes her long, shiny black hair. Perhaps I should say furiously. Her attire for the ritual varies from hardly anything to a tightly knotted terry cloth robe. I have assumed that this is a signal as to how she views the possibility of lovemaking. That night the robe had three knots instead of two.

However, after our brush with death, I wanted her desperately. Almost uncontrollably. I loved her so much. Nothing ventured, nothing gained. So I took the brush out of her hands, lifted her off the vanity stool, and imperiously pried open the belt of her robe.

"Dermot!" she cried and stiffened in protest.

I discarded the robe and captured both her breasts.

She collapsed against my chest and giggled.

As I wrestled her onto the bed, she sighed. "Wasn't I after wondering when you'd be getting around to it?"

So much for my ability to read the signs.

— 25 —

July 5, 1883

Tim Harrington has asked me to assemble a dossier of the correspondence between Bishop Kane and the Lord Lieutenant. It is a classic example of English arrogance and blindness in the administration of Ireland. I copy the exchange into this journal so in the future I will have it at hand as evidence of the strange mix of blindness and immorality that marks English rule in this country.

After Tom Casey's confession in Letterfrack, the Bishop wrote to Earl Spencer:

> 13 May, 1883.
> To His Excellency, Earl Spencer, Lord Lieutenant of Ireland,
> May it please Your Excellency,
> Having fully and maturely considered the statement publicly made to me on the occasion of my visitation in the parish of Letterfrack on Sunday 12th inst relative to the horrid occurrence that took place at Maamtrasna, I feel it is my duty, in the interests of justice and civil society even for promoting due respect for and confidence in the administration of the law, to lay the whole case before Your Excellency as it came before me.
> On the occasion referred to, a man named Thomas Casey came forward on his own accord and publicly stated that he had been induced under pain of capital punishment to swear away the life of Myles Joyce,

who had been executed in Galway. He declared that Myles Joyce was perfectly innocent, that he (Casey) offered to give information against the guilty parties and was told by the official that unless he swore against Myles Joyce, though innocent, he himself would surely be hanged, that he got thirty minutes for deliberation and then, from terror of death, swore as had been suggested to him.

Being asked why he confessed now and not before, he declared that he was waiting the visitation in his parish when he hoped to receive forgiveness and be restored by the Bishop to the Church. After having made a public confession of his guilt and as evidence of his sincerity, he declared he was ready in the interests of justice to suffer any pain, even death itself if necessary, on account of having been instrumental in taking away the life of an innocent man.

Furthermore, he declared that he was also induced to swear falsely against four men now suffering penal servitude. Taking all the circumstances into account, my own conviction is that this later statement of the wretched man is truthful and sincere and, I may add, that since then has been fully corroborated by another man, named Philbin, one of the leading approvers in the case, and who is, I am informed, prepared to make similar public declaration.

In conclusion, I would ask Your Excellency, in order to allay public feeling so much excited in this neighborhood, to direct a sworn inquiry into the case.

I have the honor to remain, Your Excellency's faithful servant,
John Joseph Kane, Bishop of Galway and Killmacduff

The Castle, Dublin, May 24, 1883.
My Lord Bishop,
I am directed by the Lord Lieutenant to inform Your Grace that your letter of the 13th inst, the receipt of which was acknowledged by His Excellency the following day, has received his most careful consideration.

Before the receipt of Your Grace's letter, attention had been drawn in the House of Commons to the allegation that Thomas Casey, one of the murderers of the Joyce family at Maamstrasna on the 17th

August, 1882, who had been accepted as an informer and had given evidence on the trial, had made a statement to the effect that the evidence he had given on that occasion was false. Immediately thereupon, His Excellency gave instructions that the truth of this statement should be tested in connection with the whole circumstances of the trial and the subsequent history of the witness himself.

It is not usual for His Excellency to enter into details in communicating his decisions on criminal cases, but the present instance is one of such gravity and the statements alleged to have been made attracted so much attention from Your Grace's letter that he was determined to depart from his usual custom and to put the circumstances of the case fully before you.

He has, as Your Grace has requested, inquired fully into the allegations now made by the informers. He forwards to Your Grace a memorandum prepared under his immediate directions and which has his entire approval, setting forth the results of that inquiry. From this memorandum, Your Grace will perceive that there was ample evidence at this trial given by three unimpeached and independent witnesses to convict all the prisoners without the evidence of Thomas Casey or Anthony Philbin and that their recent statements do not shake that testimony that plainly established that Myles Joyce, and the prisoners now undergoing penal servitude, were themselves members of the party who participated in or actually committed the murders of the Joyce family.

With regard to the actual commission of the murders, His Excellency would observe that an idea seems to prevail in the minds of some persons that the guilt of murder is only attached to those who actually fire the shot or strike the blow that causes death. Such an erroneous idea on the part of some of the participators in this horrible tragedy may account for their assertion of the innocence of those members of the party who, although they aided and countenanced the murders by their presence and were, therefore, morally and legally guilty of the crime, may not, with their own hands, have inflicted the wounds that caused the death of their victims.

I now come to the other point in Your Grace's letter. A court of law can only act on the evidence placed before it and, deplorable as it would have been had it been shown that it had in this case been misled by the false swearing of perjured witnesses, the matter becomes far more serious when it is alleged that the course of justice was perverted by the action of officers of the Crown. The statement that Your Grace says Thomas Casey made amounts to this, that he was told by the official that unless he swore against Myles Joyce, though innocent, he himself would surely be hanged, that he got thirty minutes for deliberation and then from terror of death swore as had been suggested to him.

This is so serious a charge, striking at the root of all confidence in the administration of the law, that the Lord Lieutenant has strictly inquired into the matter to see if the allegation has any color or foundation—an allegation that no man should lightly entertain on the unsupported assertion of witnesses who aver themselves to have been perjured.

The communications that took place with Thomas Casey when he volunteered to give evidence and was accepted as an informer, are fully detailed in the memorandum that accompanies this letter. His Excellency has no doubt after the careful examination that has been made of the three officials with whom the communications took place that none of them used any improper means of approaching the prisoners and that the statement above reported by Your Grace by Thomas Casey is absolutely false.

His Excellency feels as strongly as Your Grace, the calamity which would be involved if innocent men were punished for an offense they had not committed, but after the fullest inquiry of which the case admits, he has arrived at a clear conclusion that the verdict and the sentence were right and just.

I have the honor to be, My Lord Bishop,
Your Grace's obedient servant,
R. G. C. Hamilton

The Irish Members of Parliament were infuriated by this exchange both because Spencer himself did not reply to the Bishop but delegated the task to an underling and because the testimony of Thomas Casey was simply dismissed.

They screamed that Spencer had deliberately insulted the Bishop (which he had) and that his memorandum was simply a rehash of a trial that was patently a violation of the elementary rules of justice.

Does Spencer believe the memorandum and the letter? Probably he does, but he is guilty of what the Jesuits at St. Ignatius College would have called "vincible ignorance." His attitude is that English prosecutors simply don't do that sort of thing and those who claim that they do are by definition wrong. There are people in Dublin Castle who knew what happened, as do most of the reporters, even the Protestant reporters. Most of the Catholics in Dublin know the truth too. Spencer could not admit even to himself that such a miscarriage of justice could have occurred because the legitimacy of his role in Ireland would collapse from under him. So I will say in my dispatch summarizing the exchange.

Bishop Kane did not give up easily.

May 25, 1883
May it please Your Excellency,
I have the honor to acknowledge Your Excellency's letter with accompanying memorandum of the 24th inst. Notwithstanding the statements and arguments so ably and so powerfully put forward in the memorandum, I still feel that nothing short of a public inquiry can satisfy a discerning and expectant public. For they feel that the circumstances of the case are very much altered since the trial, and they, therefore, naturally expect that the Government would take advantage of these circumstances to arrive at an exact knowledge of the actual conditions of things.

These circumstances are the declarations of Casey that, in proof of his sincerity after having been repeatedly reminded of his risk and responsibility, he was prepared to undergo any punishment, even death itself if necessary, in atonement for the guilt of having sworn away the life of an honest man, whom he declares to have been altogether absent from the scene of the horrid massacre at Maamtrasna.

The absence of any conceivable adequate motive on the latter occasion while he had obviously the most powerful motive on the former—the saving of his own neck from the halter—deeply impressed all who were present as to the truthful sincerity of his statement. Add to this, apart from the strong universal feeling then, as well as now, prevailing throughout Joyce country respecting Myles Joyce's innocence, the dying declaration of the two other men executed with him as to his innocence as reported in the public press at the time.

It is hardly conceivable how, in the very jaws of death, they would allow themselves to be launched into eternity with a lie on their lips or an equivocation amounting to a lie. There are far fewer than seems to be supposed, who are ignorant of the obvious point of Christian morality that the abettor of and participator in murder are morally just as guilty as the man who strikes the blow or fires the fatal bullet. I assume that this important point was repeatedly and clearly impressed on the witnesses and party accused by the learned counsel on both sides at the trial. In addition, they must have received all necessary instruction and enlightenment on this and cognate subjects from the zealous chaplain of the prison in preparing them for death.

At this moment, the whole case seems involved in mystery arising from the evidence of independent or so-called unimpeached witnesses, respecting whom be it observed, a sifting public inquiry might elicit facts and motives of great importance for the elucidation of truth, and on the other, from the dying declarations referred to.

The exceptional nature of the case, as it now stands, with all its circumstances, would seem to call for exceptional consideration on the part of the Government by instituting a public inquiry.

As regards the official incriminated, towards whom I have no feeling in one way or the other, one could not help thinking that, at the inquiry referred to in the memorandum, he was witness in his own case and it might seem more satisfactory—if not necessary—in order to satisfy reasonable public expectation at a public inquiry where there would be an opportunity afforded of questioning all parties concerned with the prison, if it was fully proved that he had not seen Casey on any other occasions than those referred to in the memorandum.

I have the honor to remain, Your Excellency's faithful servant,

John Joseph Kane, Bishop of Galway and Killmacduff

Dublin Castle, June 23

My Lord Archbishop,

In the temporary absence of Sir Robert Hamilton, I am desired by the Lord Lieutenant to acknowledge the receipt of Your Grace's letter of the 25th of May, which His Excellency has read with attention.

I am directed to inform you that His Excellency is unable to alter his decision that Sir Robert communicated to you in his letter of 24th May and His Excellency must decline to reopen the question.

W. S. B. Kay

Undersecretary

That was that. We tolerate you leaders of popish superstition in Ireland because you are able to restrain your people and thus make our administration of this perverse people somewhat easier. However, we concede courtesy to you only as a matter of convenience. We really don't take you seriously, and we don't believe any "confessions" made in one of your popish religious services. The matter is closed.

Except it wasn't closed and would never be closed. The Catholics of Ireland were convinced that the Crown had bungled badly, hung an innocent man, and sent four innocent men to jail. Even some of the Protestants, including their reporters, were uneasy at the allegations. The Earl Spencer was a monster to the former and a bungler to the latter and so he will be remembered.

"You're a real fire-eater, Edward," Tim Harrington said to me. "It wouldn't take much to send you into the streets."

"I don't think so, Tim. Like you I fight with words, not weapons."

He raised his thick black eyebrows.

"Why is that, Edward?"

"My father fought in our civil war. He went in as an eighteen-year-old Second Lieutenant and came out four years later as a twice wounded Brevet Lieutenant Colonel. He was the only man of his original company to survive. He taught me that war never solves anything."

Tim sighed, as the Irish do, and said, "He's surely right, yet sometimes *you have to fight for your own freedom. If the English don't learn, someday they'll have a mass revolution here that they will not be able to win. It won't be like '98 or '48 or '67. The whole people of Ireland will rise."*

"Is that what you're fighting for in Parliament and what Bishop Kane is fighting for in his letters?"

"We're fighting to tell the truth. We know we'll lose, though we always hope that this time it will be different. We're trying to tell the world how immoral and stupid the English rule here is. What else can we do?"

Indeed, what else can they do?

—26—

Galway Town, August 1, 1883

I came back here from London for unfinished business. I don't believe in dreams. They merely tell us what we have been worrying about. However, Myles Joyce continues to come to me in my dreams. He reminds me gently of my obligation to Nora. What obligation, I ask him? The obligation you accepted in the Green Street Court, he replies with a sad smile. I gave you responsibility for her and you accepted. No one can give his woman to someone else, I plead. His smile grows sadder and then he fades away. I wake up with a start, covered with sweat.

I do not dream of her. The desire I once felt for her, nothing more than shallow youthful lust, is gone. She was so haggard and worn when I saw her last spring it was impossible to want to possess her. Yet, if she does not disturb my dreams, why do I think I recognize her in London whenever I see a pretty girl with long black hair?

This is a fool's venture. Yet I must try. It was not a good summer for crops in Ireland. There will not be, the Irish M.P.s tell me, another famine unless the winter is as cold as last winter. Yet the weak and the old and the very young will be at risk again. My conscience tells me that unless I take Nora and Mary Elizabeth to America when I return the first week in October, they will both die this winter. Perhaps the indefatigable Josie will die too. It is within my power to save them. I don't want this power, but I have it. If Myles of my dreams is correct, I also have the obligation.

Yet, I can succeed only if I can persuade her to come with me, to risk once again the demand of a man in her life. Both Josie and Bishop Kane tell me that she refuses to consider marriage. Perhaps she will not want to resist me. I have no reason to think that, no reason to think that when she sees a horseman in the valley, she may imagine that I have come for her. I will surely have to persuade, perhaps insist. I am willing to do that, though I do not know what the consequences will be for me or for her. One part of me fears failure in this suit. Another fears success.

Tomorrow I will have supper with Bishop Kane and seek his advice.

Galway Town, August 2, 1883

"How will your family react to this strange woman from a savage land when you bring her into their house?"

He refilled my wineglass. Like all good Irishmen we kept our business to the end of the meal.

"We will shortly find a place of our own."

"Still, you will be near your family. Will they dislike her?"

"No, m'lord, not at all. My family is very open and warm. Besides, she has one important qualification."

"And that is?"

"She's a Galway woman!"

He laughed. "Good for them—and the child?"

"Children . . . My mother is impatient to be a grandmother."

"Children?"

"Josie; I cannot separate her from Nora. She needs Nora and Nora needs her."

"What an extraordinary young man you are, Edward Hannigan Fitzpatrick. You are prepared to ride over the Maamtrasna a bachelor and come back with a bride, a daughter, and a niece at the age of . . . How old are you?"

"Twenty-two, m'lord."

"You think you are capable of assuming such obligations?"

"I don't know."

"You love her?"

"I see her every day on the streets of London."

"If she rejects you?"

"I'm not sure I'll accept rejection."

He smiled and sighed. "You are a romantic, Edward Fitzpatrick."

"I will not dispute that, m'lord."

"She will always compare you to Myles, you realize that?"

"I would not blame her for that. Perhaps she will see in me characteristics that she can love."

"It may take her a long time to love. You are prepared to be patient?"

"Certainly."

He shook his head sadly.

"Marriage is not an easy matter, Edward, even when begun under the best circumstances. . . ."

I realized that I was talking myself into a passionate pursuit of Nora Philbin Joyce. Would I really carry her off if she refused me? The thought that I might somehow do just that made me feel bold.

"I will bring them down here. My friends the Corbetts will take care of them for two months while I finish my work in London, so that they can recover their health and strength. I will ask you to preside over a marriage. Then we will go to America."

"You have it all planned out?" he smiled again, not approvingly.

"Yes, m'lord."

"One suggestion, if I may?"

He filled my wineglass again.

"Surely."

"Do not speak to her of love. For all I know she may love you already. She would be wise if she did. Presently, however, she is quite incapable of thinking about love."

"I can understand that."

"She is a canny peasant, Edward. She may be much more than that. Nonetheless, she is a peasant. Such women understand the need for bargaining. Offer her a bargain. If she will come with you, you will save her life and her daughter's. . . . And of course the life of that appealing little ruffian. Such a bargain demands rather little: marriage to a man who will be good to her in return for the life of her child. It will seem an appealing bargain."

I grinned.

"M'lord, I had not thought of such a strategy. Thank you for your wise advice."

I had planned that dinner with the Bishop would make me cautious, careful, prudent. It has, alas, only made me more passionate. Tomorrow I will ride over the mountains to Maamtrasna and seek my destiny.

Galway Town, August 4, 1883

As always Josie waited for me on the road, standing patiently in the bright sunlight. How, I wondered, did she know I was coming?

"Good afternoon, Miss Josephine Philbin," I said, tipping my hat.

"Good afternoon, Mr. Edward Fitzpatrick, sir," she said with a respectful curtsy.

"How are you keeping, Miss Philbin?"

"As well as can be expected, Mr. Fitzpatrick, sir."

I climbed out of the buggy to lead the horse up the last yards to the house.

"And your aunt?"

She sighed.

"She is not well, sir. She has never been well, since her husband died."

"No worse, I hope?"

"A little worse, I think, sir. Sometimes she has the fight left in her, if you take me meaning, like when we forced Tom Casey to admit his crime."

We was it?

"And sometimes not?"

"More often not, sir."

"And your pretty niece?"

"Poorly, sir. She is so pretty, but she is sickly."

"I'm sorry to hear that, Josie."

"Yes, sir . . . Mr. Fitzpatrick, sir?"

"Yes, Josie?"

"Neither will survive the winter, sir. Even if John Casey doesn't have us all killed."

"He's making threats?"

"Threats are being made, sir. He doesn't have as much power as he used to."

"I see," I said, clenching my fists.

"Will you do something, Mr. Fitzpatrick, sir?"

"I will endeavor to do so, Josie."

This time I did not give her any money. I had other plans.

Nora was at her usual post, on the rocker in front of the house, next to the ever-present spinning wheel. She was knitting a thick sweater, for her child perhaps. Mary Elizabeth was in a cradle next to her. Nora was humming the haunting Connemara Lullaby.

"Here's Mr. Fitzpatrick, Aunty."

Nora looked horrible, thin, wasted, old. Had I come too late?

"She always seems to know when you're coming, Mr. Fitzpatrick. I fear that she's fey. In any case, Jesus and Mary be with you."

"Jesus and Mary and Patrick be with you," I replied.

I sat on the tree stump near her chair.

"I'll wet the tea, Aunty."

"Thank you, Josie."

The Irish like to approach matters indirectly. So do we Irish Americans, though not with quite so much circumlocution. My impulse was to offer my bargain immediately. However, I restrained myself and told her about London.

"You did good work there, I'm sure, Mr. Fitzpatrick," she said, perhaps mocking me just a little.

"I wouldn't say that, Nora. I did what I could, what I had to do."

"What you can do, Mr. Fitzpatrick," she said, "is usually very good indeed. You have the Irishman's gift for words."

"Which is not as great as that of the Irishwoman."

She laughed and then her laugh turned into a cough.

I must get her out of here. Today.

Josie arrived with the tea. Nora permitted her to pour it. Mary Elizabeth stirred and whimpered. Nora picked her up and crooned softly to her. The child, very pretty and very pale, went back to sleep.

"I think I'll run to our house for a minute," Josie said and scampered off.

The little brat was probably fey indeed. Or maybe she had guessed.

"I have a bargain to propose to you, Nora," I said heavily. Wrong tone of voice.

"A bargain, Mr. Fitzpatrick?" she looked at her tea.

"Yes . . ." I said, suddenly losing my breath.

"And that bargain is?" She sipped the tea thoughtfully.

"I want you, Nora. With all the power of my soul, I want you for my own."

Not very good. What else could I have said?

"Whatever do you mean?" Her haggard face set in a grim mask.

I had prepared several scenarios on the ride over the mountains. I could not find them anywhere in my head.

"I mean," I said as my face flamed, "that I want your body in my marriage bed."

She flushed too.

"That is improper language, Mr. Fitzpatrick."

I ignored that comment.

"In return for which I will bring you and your daughter with me to America."

"That is an inappropriate offer of a bargain," she said, frowning angrily. "It is, however, interesting."

"I hoped you would find it so."

She lifted the sleeping child into her arms.

"For my own life, I care nothing. In effect, then, you want my body in exchange for granting life to my daughter?"

"And to Josie."

"Josie?" she seemed surprised.

"I will take her to America with us."

"Why ever would you do that?"

"Because you need Josie and Josie needs you. It would be wrong to separate you."

"You're really quite an astonishing man, Mr. Fitzpatrick," she said, examining me carefully with her searching blue eyes. "In exchange for myself, you give new life to the only people in the world that I love."

"That's the bargain I propose," I said awkwardly.

Josie had been the turning point. Perhaps she thought I was crazy, but generously crazy.

"I'm afraid that there's not much left to my body," she said, still searching my face.

"That could easily be corrected."

"When would you propose agreement on this bargain?"

"Now. Immediately."

"Now!" A hand flew to her breast. "You propose to take me up here, at this moment?"

"Certainly not. I propose to take you and your daughter and your niece down to Galway, stopping at Outhergard tonight, where you will live with friends of mine, the Corbetts. They will take care of you until I return from London at the end of September. We will then have a wedding and go to America."

"And your family?"

"You have the one indispensable quality to win their acceptance."

"And that is?" A look of shrewd peasant calculation spread over her face.

"You're a Galway woman."

She blushed again.

"You are a strange man, sir. Very strange."

I was afraid I was beginning to lose her.

"That's what my mother says."

It was an inspired response. She actually grinned at me. "How old is your mother, Mr. Fitzpatrick?"

"Let's see . . . Forty-one I believe."

She was startled. "She must have been, what, seventeen when she married? . . . The same age I was."

"My father was eighteen. His regiment was leaving for our civil war. They admit that they were crazy. They still are to some extent."

She changed the subject.

"And if I should reject your bargain?"

"I will not tolerate rejection."

"Pardon?" Her hand flew once more to her breast. She was suddenly afraid of me. I sensed that this was not a bad development.

"If you don't come willingly now, then I will carry you off."

"Carry me off?"

"I will come to your house some night soon, bundle you up, and drag you to my carriage. Then I will collect Josie and Mary Elizabeth and we'll disappear into the night."

I must have said it with considerable conviction.

"You desire me that much?" she said, not quite able to believe it.

"I want you, and I want to save the lives of the three of you."

"I believe you really would carry me off by force," she said thoughtfully. "That doesn't give me much choice, does it?"

Would I have done so?

I don't know.

Yes, I would have done so.

Then Josie reappeared, at just the right minute. Indeed the dirty-faced mite was fey.

"Josie," Nora called to her. "Mr. Fitzpatrick has a very unusual suggestion. He proposes to take all three of us to America. Do you want to go to America, Josie?"

"Oh, yes, I do!" the child shouted and rushed over to embrace me. "Please! Mr. Fitzpatrick! PLEASE!"

"Very well, then, run down to your house, kiss your ma and your da, tell them that we're going to America, and bring along your things. Tell them that they may have my cow and my house and whatever I leave."

Josie ran down the hill like a filly running for a finish line.

"They love her, Mr. Fitzpatrick. But they have so many. They'll be happy for her."

"We will take good care of her."

"Yes, we will. . . . I'll pack my things. There won't be much. Part of your bargain will involve providing clothes for me and my daughter?"

"Surely."

"May I bring my books?"

"May I help you pack?"

She stood up, shaky now on her feet at the enormity of what she was doing.

"Yes, you may. . . . You are a remarkable man, Mr. Fitzpatrick, quite astonishing."

For the moment that would do as a statement of love.

"I hope you'll always find me so."

"May I bring my red cloak?"

"I would not have it otherwise."

Josie came running back up the hill, her dirty face glowing, a small sack of belongings in her hand.

"Are you REALLY taking me to America, Mr. Fitzpatrick, sir?"

"I really *am*, Josie."

I packed their pathetic little bundles, Nora's wrapped in her prized red cloak, in the buggy. Josie scrambled up quickly, as if she feared I might change my mind. Nora passed Mary Elizabeth to Josie and tried to climb up. She was unable to lift herself.

"I lack the strength to board the buggy, Mr. Fitzpatrick," she said wearily. "You are ill advised to take me with you."

"I'll make that decision," I said, lifting her in my arms. She was dangerously fragile. Our eyes locked and then quickly separated. I placed her in the buggy with great tenderness.

"Thank you, sir," she said. "I am at present a very light burden."

"That will change," I promised.

As we rode down the valley in my buggy, Nora said, "You came up this road a bachelor, Mr. Fitzpatrick. You go down it as a man with a bride, a daughter, and a niece."

It was what His Lordship, the Bishop of Galway, had said.

"I think I'm up to it, Nora."

She considered that.

"I think you are too."

We are in Outhergard now. Nora was uneasy when I showed them into their room.

"I've never been in an inn before, Mr. Fitzpatrick. I'm not sure how to act."

"I'm sure you will figure things out. That thing is called a water closet and that one over there is a bathtub."

"I know what they are, Mr. Fitzpatrick," she said bravely. "I read books."

I escaped from the room, my heart breaking for her. The days ahead would not be easy.

Now in my room I am greatly—and perhaps foolishly—pleased with myself. I have won a wife of my own. She is mine. Or soon will be. Admittedly, the choice was between me and probable death during the winter. But she had given up on life. I had persuaded her to give life another chance.

She does not love me yet. However, I think she does not exclude the possibility of eventually loving me. At least she likes me and even finds me amusing.

There will be many difficulties in the future. I pray to the God who gave me the right words to say today that You will continue to whisper the right words in my ear.

— 27 —

London, September 15, 1883

We lost the motion for a parliamentary investigation of the Maamtrasna affair. Tim had prepared a brilliant case against the trial with enough testimony from Tom Casey and Michael Casey (one of those who had been in jail and confessed to being outside during the crime) and from various people in the valley to destroy the credibility of both the witness and the approvers. Many of the Liberals, with whom the Irish Party is allied, agreed privately with Tim's argument. The Crown had made a mess of the trial. It would be useful if somehow a new trail could be ordered. However, Parliament had no choice but to stand behind Earl Spencer. Otherwise they would seem to have repudiated the legitimacy of the rule in Dublin Castle. The issue for them was not the injustice of the Maamtrasna trial. It was the survival of Britain's right to rule Ireland. Even the Liberals had to support that. Gladstone, the Prime Minister and a staunch supporter of Home Rule in Ireland, would dearly love to find a way out that would placate everyone. Yet, he sees himself bound to stand by Lord Spencer. We all understand that. Even if you want Ireland to have its own parliament again, you cannot turn your back on six centuries of English imperialism.

We had a grand time in the debate, however, because we had nothing to lose. Our arguments were unanswerable and the other side knew it. They had to content themselves with repeating the arguments of the Crown Counsels in the trial. Those arguments were now patently absurd. So we were free to shoot them down like wingless ducks lined up for game hunters. We

made fools out of them. They knew we were making fools out of them. They
had the votes but that was all they had.

A young Liberal M.P. from Manchester remarked to me, early in the
morning after we had shot at them like Lord Nelson had shot at the French
at Trafalgar, "You lads are having a grand time of it, aren't you?"

"I'm an American, sir. I'm not enjoying this at all. If it's a grand time,
it's also a waste of time."

He sighed.

"The sooner we have Home Rule the better. Parliament will be much
duller with all those witty fellows back in Dublin where they belong, but
we'll be able to get some sleep at night. . . . Why are you involved? You're
more than just a reporter, aren't you?"

"I was there," I said simply.

"At Maamtrasna."

"The day after the murders."

"Oh . . . You knew this man Myles Joyce? Good fellow, was he?"

"A royal leader."

"Yes, so I gathered. Another martyr for Ireland, eh?"

"Someday it will all come back to haunt this country, sir."

"I don't doubt it. I don't doubt it at all."

We never had a hope of winning it. We knew we never had a hope of
winning it. Yet we fought like tigers. We had a grand drinking party the final
night as though we had won a great victory. The votes were 219 against our
motion, 48 in favor. An Irish victory!

Sir Randolph Churchill voted with us. There are rumors that he and
Parnell will connive to bring down the Gladstone Government and thus drive
Lord Spencer from Ireland. The Tories, however, will certainly never support
Home Rule. I do not believe that Gladstone will ever win it either. England
is not ready to let Ireland go, not in a halfway measure. Parnell, the leader
of the Irish Party, is a Protestant but as fervent an Irish Nationalist as I
have ever met. Some call him the uncrowned King of Ireland. Perhaps. I
find it hard to like him, however.

So what will happen? If I had to guess, I'd say that within the next half
century, the people of Ireland will have to take their freedom from England.
The Land League tactics have stirred up the ordinary people who merely

want their own land. Some day a real Irish leader, a better educated and perhaps more ruthless version of Myles Joyce, will lead Ireland to its freedom. Violently.

Why do I say that? Because I believe that the English will continue to make the same stupid mistakes they made in the Maamtrasna affair. As the Irish Catholics get more education and make a little more money, the British will make one final mistake that will be the last straw. They do not see the growing power of the Catholics.

They could avoid the total loss of Ireland by granting the meager freedom of Home Rule. Not to do that is the biggest mistake of all.

When it comes to Ireland, the English are dumb.

And blind.

Those will be the themes of the dispatch I will write after a couple of hours sleep.

Then I will return to Galway to claim my bride. My desire for her is unbearable. So too is my fear.

I ask myself whether perhaps it is cruel to fatten her up for the feast as I am doing. Then I tell myself I only want her to be healthy as she prepares for marriage and our trip to America.

Home.

— 28 —

Galway, September 27, 1883

I'm back again at the Great Southern Hotel for the last time, in this trip in any event. We leave Kinsale next week and with a smooth passage should be in the United States by the following week. I sent a cable to my family from London. "Arrive mid-October with Galway princess. Ned." Their reply was immediate. "We knew you would. Mom and Dad."

What if after two months of modern living, my bride-to-be tries to change her mind?

That seems unlikely. Nora is not the kind of woman who backs out of a bargain.

Yet I am afraid. Afraid of losing her and somehow afraid of not losing her. What will the wedding night be like? I have had little experience with women. She was married to one of the most remarkable men in the world. How can I compare to him?

I remember comments in pubs and saloons about women. Complaints about how long it took to get them "in the mood." Astonishment at how patient one had to be with them. And gentle. Someone had said that you never can be too gentle. So I would be patient and gentle and not rush.

I have no idea what that means.

I will walk to the Corbett house across the square tomorrow morning with some considerable trepidation.

Galway Town, September 28, 1883

The Corbetts, knowing that I was visiting this morning, discretely found something to take them out of the house. When their butler showed me into the drawing room, I did not for a moment recognize my bride. She was wearing a light blue dress and a corset, her hair was done up on her head, and she was blooming with vitality.

I must have permitted my mouth to fall open.

She rose, smiled, and extended her hand graciously.

"Have I changed that much, Mr. Fitzpatrick?"

I kissed her hand. She blushed. I was speechless.

"Mr. and Mrs. Corbett have been very kind to us. I never expected to feel healthy again."

"I'm sorry I didn't recognize you. . . ."

"Doubtless you will not recognize Mary Elizabeth either."

She lifted the cooing little child out of her crib and extended her into my arms. Mary Elizabeth was fat, healthy, and happy. She cuddled into my arms and rested her head on my chest.

"Is she not a miracle, Mr. Fitzpatrick?"

"As is her mother."

"Thank you, sir." She blushed, removed the child from my arms, and returned her to her crib. The little girl smiled and giggled.

"Wait till you see Josie. You will never recognize her with her clean face."

"The Corbetts have truly treated you well?"

"Look at me, sir." She sat on the couch next to her daughter's crib. "They have done their best to make me a lady. I have learned about bathtubs and water closets and corsets and good manners and to wear shoes all the time. I have found lots of books to read. As I awaited you, I have been reading this book of Mr. Trollop, whom I find very interesting."

She was uneasy, not sure what kind of impression she was making.

"My mother reads him too. So does my father."

"Do I seem to have been transformed into a lady, sir?

"Nora." I sat down on the couch next to her. "You have never been any less than a lady. No one had to teach you how to be one."

She turned crimson.

"Thank you, Mr. Fitzpatrick."

How many years before I became Edward? And how many more before she would call me Eddie? Or Ned?

I removed the little box from my waistcoat pocket, opened it, and placed the ring on her finger.

"Mr. Fitzpatrick! This is really too much! It is utterly inappropriate! I cannot possibly accept it!"

"You could always give it back to me."

She looked at the ring, looked at me, and then, with a peasant's craftiness, back at the ring.

"Well," she said slowly, "I suppose that now I am wearing it, I should keep it. Really, however, it is too big."

"Nora," I said firmly, "I wouldn't dare make many rules for our marriage. I am, however, going to make one now. Whenever I give you anything, you say, 'Ned, how wonderful! Thank you very much!' No other response will be accepted. Is that clear?"

She looked at me with the penetrating scrutiny that I had become accustomed to during our ride down the mountains.

"Clear enough, Mr. Fitzpatrick," she said with a sheepish grin, "and, I might add, fair enough . . . So this is a wonderful ring! Thank you very much!"

Spontaneously, I leaned over and brushed my lips against hers. Her lips were soft, unprepared, and yielding.

"Oh." She gulped.

I lifted her off the couch, put my arms around her, and kissed her again, firmly but not passionately. She gasped and rested her head against my chest.

"You kiss very effectively, sir." She sighed.

"Thank you, ma'am," I said and kissed her for a third time, this with some hint of the passion that was now raging within me. She trembled but did not pull away until I released her.

She steadied herself, holding on to my arm for support.

"You take my breath away, sir."

"So do you," I said.

She laughed, the first real laugh I had ever heard from her, a laugh with church bells and surf and the song of mountain birds.

"Shall we go find Josie?" she gasped.

"Indeed. I warn you, however, that I propose to steal kisses from you whenever possible."

"I expect you will, sir."

We encountered Josie waiting outside the door of the drawing room, doubtless knowing that we were about to enter the corridor.

"Mr. Fitzpatrick!" She hugged me. "Is my face pretty now that it doesn't have any dirt on it?"

"Your face has always been very pretty, Josie, dirt or no dirt."

"Do I smell nice with this perfume?"

She danced around me joyously.

"Do you like my dress?"

"You are dazzling, Miss Josephine!"

"Are you really going to take me to America?"

"Really!"

She bounded back down the corridor to the play room of the Corbett daughters.

"She didn't notice your ring," I protested.

"Yes, she did, Mr. Fitzpatrick. Josie notices everything. She thought it discrete to leave us alone."

"So I could kiss you again?"

I did indeed kiss her again, more passionately than the previous time. This time she responded in kind.

I also caressed her, violating ever so slightly her modesty.

"That was truly inappropriate, Mr. Fitzpatrick," she said, embarrassed and distraught.

"It wasn't," I insisted.

"Then neither is this!"

Thereupon she kissed me with furious passion. It was my turn to gasp.

This was not, I thought as I returned to the hotel in a cloud of delight, part of the bargain.

She might not want to love again. But she was a young woman with a

*young woman's passions (about which I know nothing except that they exist).
Perhaps she found me an attractive young man. The "perhaps" is, as she
would say, inappropriate.*

*With the ordeal of the wedding day ahead I find that notion quite con-
soling.*

Kinsale, October 3, 1883

We sail tomorrow morning. My wife is sleeping in our stateroom. Josie
is next door to us with Mary Elizabeth since she insists with total determi-
nation that we need to be left to ourselves. Josie enjoys having an uncle
again.

"Why do you call Mr. Fitzpatrick 'Ned,' Aunt Nora?"

"Because"—my wife blushes—"that is his name."

My wife blushes often and becomingly. She blames my lack of respect
for her modesty.

"Uncle Ned!" the lovely, well-scrubbed urchin shouts joyfully and em-
braces me.

I glance at Nora's exquisite face, as I rest my pen. She seems peaceful
and content with her fate. Yet the three of us will watch the disappearing
towers of the Kinsale church tomorrow morning with very different thoughts.
I will reflect on the last incredible fifteen months of my life and yet be glad
that I'm going home with my prize. For Nora and Josie it will be a farewell
to their homeland, which they may never see again. For Nora it will be a
physical departure from all that remains of the great man who was once her
husband. She talked about him only once in the last several days. It will be
a long time before she speaks of him again, I think. Yet, she will never forget
that the little that is left of him lies in the quicklime under the Galway jail.

At our wedding dinner, she was radiant and gracious. I have learned
that she is a bit of an actress and can play many different rolls. She avoided
my eyes during the dinner. Possibly I avoided hers. After the Corbetts and
the Bishop and Marty and Marie Dempsey had left us and Josie carried
Mary Elizabeth to our suite in the Great Southern, my new wife said to me,
"Would you mind terribly, Mr. Fitzpatrick, if we walked over to the salmon
weir and said a couple of decades of the rosary?"

"On the contrary, I think it is a very good idea."

So, under a gray and gloomy sky, we strolled over to the salmon weir and turned towards the prison. We said precisely two decades of the rosary, a leave-taking for both of us. Then we walked in silence back to the Great Southern, both of us preoccupied with our own fears.

At the entrance of the hotel, she murmured, "I am frightened, Mr. Fitzpatrick."

"Of me?"

She nodded.

"I will never hurt you, Nora. I will always respect and cherish you."

"I know that," she said softly.

"Then what do you fear?"

"Your passion and your strength."

"Will it help any if I tell you that I am afraid of you too?"

She laughed, "And what do you fear in me?"

"Your passion and your strength."

"Oh," she said quietly.

In the room, I helped her out of her dress and corset, just as if we were an experienced married couple who had made love many times. She suggested that we kneel and finish the rosary. I agreed again, relieved that we had postponed the moment of truth. On her knees next to me she shivered through the final decade of the rosary.

So, for that matter, did I.

Then she was very generous with herself. She deftly directed my efforts. I was very patient and gentle and tried not to rush. We both experienced great joy.

Then, suddenly and without warning, we seemed to be snatched up in an overpowering love that for a few moments made our human passion tiny and united us with all the joy in the universe.

Afterwards, we laid next to each other in bed, our bare shoulders touching.

"Was I satisfactory, Mr. Fitzpatrick?"

"Superb, Mrs. Fitzpatrick."

"You are quite good with a woman, sir. You take away all our secrets."

"I'm glad you are pleased," I said tentatively.

"Very pleased, sir."

I wasn't good with women and I didn't take away any secrets as far as I could remember. But I was a young husband with a beautiful wife and her words were the kind of approval for which I hungered.

Then she sighed and continued.

"You deceived me that day in the valley when you threatened to carry me away."

"Oh?"

"You did not speak of love."

"I was afraid if I did I would lose you."

"You surely would have. . . . Now I feel that I am bound by my bargain to permit you to love with all the skill and the passion you possess."

I did not like the way the conversation was turning.

"That troubles you?"

"Only that I must tell you that I will never love you in return."

What does a new husband say to that?

He doesn't say a thing because his wife sobs wildly and mutters terrible things in Irish.

Instead of talking, I put my arms around her and let her sob.

Finally she stopped. She did not try to escape from my embrace.

"I am sorry, Mr. Fitzpatrick. My behavior was thoroughly inappropriate. I did not mean to say that."

I drew her closer. Both of us were too exhausted to have bothered to put on our nightshirts. She was soaking with perspiration.

"I must say some things to you, sir, perhaps to make amends for ruining this sacred night for you."

"I don't think it's ruined."

"The first thing I must say is that I have known all along where Josie found the money that kept us alive. I am deeply grateful for that gift."

I said nothing.

"Second thing," she went on, "is that I also read the article you wrote about me in the Chicago Daily News. My brother sent it to me. It made me blush. It makes me blush at this very moment. I can't believe that I was the person you described. Nonetheless, I was vain enough to be pleased for a moment and then the horror of what was happening recaptured me. Since

Mary Elizabeth was born I reread it often when I was ready to give up and die. That woman, I told myself, would never give up."

"And didn't."

"She came very close. . . . The third thing is very difficult for me to discuss, but I must on this night while we lie in each other's arms."

"Naked in each other's arms."

She laughed.

"I have noticed that. . . . Did you ever talk to Myles about me?"

"No. I never spoke to him about anything."

"I thought not. Yet he told me the last time I saw him the day before he died that you would come for me to take me away and I should go with you. He described you as that nice-looking young American journalist with the blond hair."

"He did!"

So I told her of Myles's smile of approbation and invitation in the Green Street Court.

"How very like him!" She sighed. "It was the sort of man he was."

I remained silent.

"Then that day up in the valley when you finally came as Myles had promised, in my stubborn pride and despair, I almost refused you. I would have if you hadn't been clever enough to mention Josie. While I was preparing to reject your offer, I knew that up in heaven Myles was greatly displeased with me."

"He is pleased now?"

"Oh, yes. Naturally."

I searched for something to say.

"Would you really have carried me off?"

"I would certainly have carried you off before John Casey had a chance to kill you as he killed the John Joyce family."

"Yes, I think you would have. You are such a romantic, thank God."

"Tell me mother that when you meet her."

"You can depend on it, I will. . . . There is one other thing I must say and then I am yours to do whatever you want."

"And that is?"

"Oh, Neddie, my dearest, I love you so much! I will always love you!"

Neddie is it, I thought to myself, as the wedding night continued. I think I have won the woman.

Even though I am still an unseasoned young man with little knowledge of the world and practically no knowledge of women, I am at least a little more mature than I was a year ago.

Or even yesterday.

—29—

"I'M NOT sure whether those behind these crimes ever wanted to kill anyone," Nuala began her presentation in the dingy conference room of the Clifden police barracks. "They wanted to scare certain people. To scare them, they tried to scare others. They were greedy, but their greed, unlike that of others, did not extend as far as murder. It might be easier for them if they admit their plots now. While the Gardaí don't yet have the detailed evidence that would justify the public prosecutors in bringing charges, they will eventually collect that evidence. Since their plan has backfired and will never work, they would be wise to admit it and accept lesser charges than attempted murder while they still can, especially since while they came close to murdering many of us, I don't think they intended to do so."

No one would have guessed that this poised, professional-sounding woman had suffered from depression. Or that indeed she was from the West of Ireland. Now she was the sophisticated Trinity College graduate, almost a West Brit. Almost, God help us all, a Yank.

She glanced around the room—Colm MacManus, Seamus Redmond, Sean O'Cuiv, Margot Quinn, Matt and Daphne Howard, Simon Tailor, Tomas O'Regan. None of them moved. Declan McGinn and Deputy Commissioner Keenan watched impassively. Other Gardaí stood around the room. One sat at a writing table taking notes. Detective Sergeant Peig Sayers, blond and attractive despite her dark suit and pinned-up hair, stood at the door next to a recording machine.

She kept her eyes on the ground so that she didn't have to look at Simon Tailor.

"No volunteers?" Nuala glanced around. "Very well. When the time comes for a trial your lawyers will doubtless work for a plea bargain. That will become more difficult as we tell more of the story. The first critical point is that there is gold under the Ballynahinch manor house. Not a lot of gold, mind you, but enough for a couple of million pounds of profit. The relevant ministry has kept this fact a secret, even from the Garda, lest there be demonstrations and protests at the prospect of tearing down the hill and the old cemetery. However, some few people knew about it and others suspected it. If you, for reason of your position in society began to suspect, what better time to find out for sure than when the manor house was being restored?"

Nuala looked around the room again. Still no volunteers.

"It seemed interesting that the cemetery would be covered up with park land. Despite what we were told at our lunch with the Howards, the cemetery was clearly evident as such. I have here a picture which shows it only ten years ago. I don't imagine the quiet people who remain in the hills much liked the thought of it being desecrated, but they assumed that His Lordship was up to the same tricks as his ancestors and were no more eager to get into a battle with him than were their ancestors a century and a half ago. By covering the cemetery the builders also covered the strain of gold, which, if you can imagine it, was a bed on which the dead of Maamtrasna had rested for centuries. If those who had discovered it might have told others about their discovery, prospectors searching for the cemetery of the Church on the Hill, as it was called, would never have found it. Moreover, those who wanted the gold knew that when the day came that they could claim it, they would have to move very quickly, perhaps under the pretext of excavating to recover the cemetery. Whether preservationists would have let them get away with it is another matter. I think they would not have. That suggests to me that this scheme, so dramatic in its manifestations, was ill conceived from the beginning and badly executed in its actuality. Any comments?"

There were none.

Nuala sighed, the first West of Ireland trait in her discourse.

"Why then did they hire someone to blow up the T.D.'s house and someone else to shoot at a water-skier whose name they did not know? Obviously they wanted to scare someone. But the T.D. was not likely to leave his district, the owners of Renvyle House are not likely to sell, and Dermot and I will be going back to America shortly. Who then was the target? Obviously they were building up to frightening off Lord Ballynahinch. Or to give the illusion that he had been frightened off. Might he have done it himself? He is obviously a very rich man and a few million pounds more or less should not matter to him. But money always matters to people. Moreover, he has incurred many extra expenses from his public service for Mr. Blair's administration. If he discovered gold on his land, he might find it useful to desert the house because of the threats to himself and his family and return permanently to England. Then his people could move in and quickly strip away the gold before anyone could stop them."

Sweat was pouring down Matt Howard's face. He didn't seem very genial anymore. His wife was holding his hand. Simon Tailor looked dour.

"Anyone want to say anything?" Nuala asked.

Not a sound.

"Very well. You may think you can bluff it out, but I assure you that you are wrong."

Obviously this was an informal hearing. Those who might be involved could easily demand to call in their solicitors. To do so, however, would be to admit their guilt.

"A professional car bomber, of whom there are all too many on this island still, could easily have planted the bomb the night before in the Rolls. The Gardaí already have leads as to the name of the bomber. It was known that no one would use the car the next day. An absent conspirator, probably up on the mountain where the John Joyces lived, could wait for the proper moment and detonate the explosive device by a radio signal. One imagines the horror the conspirators experienced when we parked our car behind the Rolls and then the plumbers, poor men, parked their car behind ours. Still, not to worry.

No one would be driving the Rolls that day. Even if someone would drive it, perhaps the ignition would not set off the bomb. I am told, however, that sometimes the starter mechanism will ignite a car bomb that is designed to be controlled remotely. Whether our friends knew this or not remains to be seen. Nonetheless, they surely must have been frightened when they saw Ona Howard rush from the house towards the Rolls. Not only might she die, everyone in the house could well die from what would now likely be an explosion of three cars, two of them vans. Fortunately, in the event, Ona did not enter the car. Someone up on the mountain watching the subsequent events must have watched with astonishment. Perhaps he did not know that there might be a danger that the bomb would explode when Ona turned the key in the ignition. Perhaps he did not know what three—or as it turned out—four explosions would do to the people in the house, especially as shattered window glass rained on them. Surely he was astonished by the hasty evacuation engineered so ably by Mr. Tailor. He didn't know what was happening. He did see the then Constable now Sergeant Sayers peer under the car. He knew then that the Gardaí knew of the bomb. He wondered desperately what to do. He was not, I repeat, a cruel man, only venal and stupid. He did not want to do physical harm to anyone. He could not understand perhaps the reason for the retreat of those present in the house to a mound that marked the edge of the cemetery. He had no desire and no reason as it first seemed to him to detonate the bomb—and probably no idea of what it could do. But the Garda bomb squad was on its way. They would disarm the bomb and, as he knew well, easily discover who had made it. Desperate with fear, he hesitated. Then when he saw the blue cars and vans rushing up the valley, he made his decision. He pushed the button that activated the countdown mechanism in the bomb and took a hasty departure.

"Does anyone wish to comment?"

The bells of the Anglican parish church of Clifden rang the twelve chimes of noon.

Sherlock McGrail glanced around the room. No one said anything, no one moved.

"Very well, I will now loosen your tongues. The Garda have learned from some of those who worked on the restoration of the house that assayists dug holes in the ground of the old cemetery during its construction. . . ."

"It was all his idea." Tomas O'Regan leaped to his feet and waved his hands at Colm MacManus. "He had heard rumors in the Dáil about gold out here. He persuaded me to investigate when we were restoring the manor. He was right, there was gold; not a lot perhaps, but enough. He said we ought to cover the cemetery as a precaution because those few who knew about the gold all said it was under a cemetery. He said he would take care of the rest. I didn't even know there was a bomb under the car or that he was up on the mountain waiting for the family to leave in the other car. I came for lunch only because Matt insisted. I had no part in his crazy scheme of bombs and shootings. I didn't think Matt would back off. I didn't do anything!"

We all turned towards the T.D.

He jumped from his chair and ran from the room.

"Off to see his solicitor," Declan McGinn murmured. "Do you want to make a statement to us, Mr. O'Regan? If you do, I hereby advise you of your right to a solicitor and tell you that anything you have said so far cannot be admitted as evidence."

"Yes," O'Regan said truculently, "I'll make a statement. No need for a solicitor. I am one . . ."

His face crimson with rage, Matt Howard jumped towards O'Regan.

"You fucking bastard! I trusted you and helped your career and you tried to kill my wife and daughter!"

I intercepted him. He struggled for a bit and then relaxed in my grip.

"Linebacker, I suppose?"

"A long time ago."

"Dear, wonderful Dermot." Daphne sighed.

"Who was the spy?" Matt demanded. "It couldn't have been Simon. He could never keep the schedule straight and probably didn't know it."

Simon blushed and smiled ruefully.

"I guess there are advantages in being absentminded."

"We know who she was," Declan cut in. "We talked to her earlier. Her family was beholden to Colm. She didn't know what he was up to."

"I'm sure the Gardaí don't need me to tell them that the T.D. was conspiring with the Russians to ship the gold out of the country, maybe by Aeroflot or maybe by one of their submarines. He's a gombeen man but not a very smart one."

"He'll spend time in jail for one or the other of his crimes," Commissioner Keenan assured us. "He'll wiggle and evade, but at the end of the day we'll get him."

"Dermot and I knew all long that O'Regan wasn't telling the truth because he lied about the cemetery. Father O'Laighne had shown us a picture of it taken not ten years ago."

Dermot didn't know that at all, at all. Nuala, however, did not want me to feel like Doctor Watson.

THAT'S ALL RIGHT, YOU ARE HER WATSON.

"I know THAT."

"I knew that there were hints in the Maamtrasna murders about the crimes in the valley and vicinity today. But I didn't understand what the hints were. Then I realized that John Casey was a man of political power in the valley, a man willing and able to corrupt others and to persuade them to risk their lives for him. Myles Joyce was a man everyone respected, but he lacked wealth and more importantly a propensity to corruption. As Lord Action said of the Vatican, power corrupts and absolute power corrupts absolutely. John Casey's power was not absolute by the standards of the outside world, but it was by the standards of the valley.

"Who had that kind of power down here today? The T.D. was a man of limited powers on the world stage, but in this corner of the West of Ireland he had collected a lot of obligations. In Dublin he had enough power to track down the rumors about the gold beneath Diamond Hill that even the Garda had not heard. So I began to ask myself whether this comic little man might be corrupted not so much by the power that he actually had but by the power he thought he had.

"Then I wondered why he would pay someone to blow up his own house. The answer was obvious. No one would suspect him for the more serious plans he had devised. The plans would not have worked, you say. Lord Ballynahinch is not the kind of man who runs away. Nor sells his property at a loss. I believe that to be the case. Then I realized that the only danger to me when I was skiing was that the shooter might make a mistake. The only danger to anyone in this story was that a mistake might have been made in the plot. Everyone in the manor house might have died by mistake just as Myles Joyce died by mistake. It is time and past time to protect both Renvyle and the valley from more of Colm MacManus's mistakes."

The participants in our seminar drifted away. Tomas O'Regan was led by two Gardaí to another room, where he would make his statement. The Howards shook hands vigorously. Peig whispered something in Simon's ear. He blushed and nodded his head.

Finally only Gene Keenan and my wife and I remained in the room.

"We would have figured all of that out eventually, Nuala Anne," he said with a grin.

She grinned back. "Even without my telling you about the gold?"

"Fair play to you! . . . You and your family must return to Ireland often—only give me advance warning if you don't mind."

—30—

"YOU HAVE to admit," Jack Lane said as he ordered our dinner for us, "that the young woman had courage to go off to America with that very young man."

We were in the restaurant of the new Station House in Clifden, a town twelve miles south of Renvyle and so beautiful that one half suspected it was created for color videotapes. Jack was taking us to supper to celebrate our multiple victories, past and present. It was a lovely spring evening with the smell of flowers in the air and the sun persisting in its refusal to set as it would have in Chicago at this time of the year.

We had turned from the MacManus story to that of Ned and Nora. The T.D. was fighting every inch of the way. However, the Public Prosecutor had him boxed in. He would probably plea bargain. No charges could be brought against Tomas O'Regan because it was impossible to prove how much he knew about MacManus's schemes. He certainly did not know about MacManus on the mountain with the remote control or he would have found an excuse not to come to that fateful lunch.

"Sure, I wouldn't know about that, An t'Athair Sean O'Laighne," my wife said in an antagonistic mood. "Hadn't himself picked out poor Neddie for her? And wasn't he a grand, brave, romantic fella? Would not I meself have gone off to America with a fella like him? What did she have to lose?"

"And, in his own way, dependable too," I agreed. "You should excuse the expression, but he was a man of honor."

"Come to think of it," Nuala added with a crafty smile, "didn't I go off to America with the same kind of fella?"

"After him to be more precise," I corrected her. "But I appreciate the comparison."

"A matter of minor details." She snapped her fingers. "Sure weren't you at the airport waiting for me? And wasn't he a big lug just like you?"

"And wouldn't she run the show in America, just like certain other people I know?"

"Despite your banter," Jack Lane insisted, "I think she was very brave."

"Oh, wasn't she terrible brave altogether and herself having to choose for life when she was afraid to. Trusting poor dear Ned was no problem, at all, at all. Trusting herself and God, that was another matter."

"I wonder what happened to them in Chicago," Jack Lane said as the white wine appeared. "I suppose that we'll never know."

"As a matter of fact, we do know quite a bit," I said, reaching into my jacket pocket and producing a sheaf of documents.

It was not too often during my adventures with Nuala Anne that I had a chance to take center stage. I relished those rare opportunities.

"Hasn't me brilliant husband sent an e-mail to his riverence back in Chicago to find out the rest of the story?" Nuala Anne said, driving me off center stage. I had not, needless to record, told her I was putting George the Priest into play, much less showed her the results.

"Well, then," I said, "it won't be necessary to go into the details."

I put the dossier back into me pocket. My pocket.

"Och, sure, Dermot Michael, I have no idea at all, at all what's in them communications, if you take me meaning."

She might or might not know what was in them. However, I would still be permitted to recapture center stage for the moment.

"You two are crazy," Jack Lane said, looking suspiciously at the fish course—poached Galway salmon, of course.

"Anyway," I said, "I quote from George the Priest: 'If you had paid any attention to Chicago Catholic history, little bro, you would know that Edward H. "Ned" Fitzpatrick was one of the most famous Chicago journalists at the end of the last century and the beginning of this one. He made his name initially by incisive and brilliant reports for the old *Daily News* about the Land League war in Ireland. He married a fearsome Irish woman he met there and they returned to Chicago and settled in my parish on North Park, so I have the records of the baptisms of three of their four children and the Confirmations of all four. The oldest, who must have been born in Ireland, entered the Daughter of Charity and would later work at Marillac House on the west side until the time of her death in the late 1950s. The three younger ones married at our little church and migrated eventually to Austin and lived on West End Avenue, where the great old homes of that neighborhood were. A couple of their grandchildren, Ned's great grandchildren, went to St. Luke's with us and live in River Forest now. Ned and his wife celebrated their fiftieth wedding anniversary, according to our parish jubilee book, in 1932 and died respectively in 1936 and 1938. Perhaps they knew our grandparents.

" 'They were active in Chicago civic life, both religious and secular. I attach a picture of them from the same jubilee book at a parish function with Archbishop Feehan in 1901. Quite distinguished looking couple, are they not? If I didn't know better, I'd think herself was your virtuous wife.' "

"Let me see!" The aforementioned virtuous wife pulled the picture from my hand. "Oh, glory be, would you look at them awful clothes!"

Jack Lane peered over her shoulder.

"And at the face . . ." Jack Lane caught his breath. "The same to-hell-with-all-of-you look!"

"And the same pride on the face of her poor dear husband!" Nuala made the sign of the cross and wept. "Sure, when they let me into heaven won't the both of us have to wear name tags!"

She continued to weep, tears, I think, of joy.

"So her gamble on life and love worked?" Jack Lane asked.

"What about Josie?" Nuala Anne demanded.

"George the Priest says there's a record of a marriage between one Mary Josephine Philbin and a man named James O'Leary. It was a tragic union. They both moved to the South Side."

"And?" Jack asked.

"And what?"

"What was tragic?"

"Why, moving to the South Side!"

"That's like a Galway woman, poor dear thing, marrying a Kerryman."

"God forgive them both," Jack murmured.

"My brother has a lot more stuff," I said. "I'll make copies for everyone, especially for Ethne, since someone has decided that she's doing her dissertation at Loyola on the subject. . . . Two other interesting notes. They were both involved in the first World Parliament of Religion at the World's Columbian Exposition, which must have been ten years after they came from Europe. And, minor note, herself must have been quite a singer because, according to George, for forty years she was in charge of everything musical that happened in Immaculate Conception Parish on North Park."

Nuala blessed herself again and wept some more.

"And Myles Joyce's daughter became a holy nun who took care of the poor and the orphans! I'm sure he's pleased about that."

"Isn't it strange how real they all are to us?" Jack Lane tasted the Rhone red wine that was offered for the lamb course and nodded his approval.

"And aren't they around us even now, laughing at our curiosity," Nuala Anne said, yielding to more tears, doubtless satisfying.

"You really think they're around, Nuala Anne?" Jack Lane asked, glancing around the dining room, as if he expected to see Nora and Josie and Ned.

"Ah, sure, An t'Athair O'Laighne, isn't that what the Communion of Saints means? And didn't we know that even before St. Patrick came?"

"Do you sense their presence, or do you just believe it?" the priest asked.

Nuala frowned as if she did not really comprehend the question, which maybe she didn't.

"Sure, what's the difference, An t'Athair O'Laighne?"

My wife's theology is a blend of modern skepticism and ancient Celtic devotion. God, one should excuse the expression, help anyone who tried to expose any inconsistencies. Moreover if she thought those on the other side of the Communion of Saints were lurking near us in love, I would be the last one to suggest that she was wrong. She knew too much to be wrong on such a matter.

Did she experience the lurking presence of Nora and Ned in our modern dining room at the Station House?

I would not have bet against it.

"Have you found out anything about the other characters in the story, Jack Lane?" I asked as I finished off my share of the rack of lamb and looked around for more food.

"I talked to an old fella who still has some sheep on those hills, named Sean Casey as might not surprise you. Lord Ballynahinch owns most of the land these days, but he lets the remnants of the old families run their sheep on the land, a not unprofitable business these days, courtesy of the EU. Young Brigid Joyce, Pat Joyce's wife, went back to her parents' home, fought with them, and then migrated to America and was forgotten. When the survivors were finally freed from prison they came back to the valley. Big John Casey continued to live like he was a big man, but he was never very happy again. Most of the people in the valley simply ignored him. He and his son fought constantly, apparently about the killings. The son eventually left home and no one knows what happened to him. Anthony Joyce, the false informer, lost all the money the English gave him, as did the men who were with him. He was badly injured in some kind of dynamite blast, the results of which he carried with him till he died at the age of eighty. Life in the valley continued as it had before. No one forgot what happened, but no one did anything more about it. The next generation forgave if it didn't completely forget and the descendants lived in peace until they slowly abandoned the valley."

"That's the way it should be in Ireland, of course," my wife said briskly.

"And what did he say about Myles Joyce?"

"He wasn't sure what happened to his wife and daughter, but there was a story, he told me, that she had married an American and they went off to America. Some said they came back later for a visit, but he wasn't sure about that."

"Did you tell him?"

The priest shook his head, "Ah, no. You don't want to mix historical fact with legend, do you now?"

"Did he think Myles was a hero?"

"One of the greatest men in the history of the West of Ireland, he said. Sometimes he still runs through the streets of Galway. And you can hear his cries for justice from the quicklime under Michael Brown's ugly gray Cathedral, which was built where the jail used to be."

"That's silly superstition." Nuala waved her hand dismissively. "He does no such thing. He knows that justice was finally done and that his wife had a happy life, even if she had to die too, like all of us."

That settled that.

"Did you have any doubt, Nuala," Jack asked as he refilled our claret glasses, "about what Nora would do?"

Me wife hesitated.

"Well, not to say doubts exactly, if you take me meaning. Still she was free, wasn't she now? She could act like a terrible eejit, couldn't she have, and chosen to refuse life? Women do that, you know. So do men. Sometimes it's what your man said about Waterloo, a close run thing."

"And the turning point was Ned's kindness to Josie?"

"Och, I'm sure it was, poor dear man."

We chatted about other things, including our return to Chicago and to Grand Beach for the summer, where I would finish my new novel and Nuala would continue to work on her paintings.

The manager of the hotel approached our table anxiously.

"Was everything all right, Jack?" he asked the priest.

"Grand altogether."

"Ms. McGrail, Mr. McGrail?"

"Brilliant!" Nuala answered for both of us with a wicked wink.

"We wouldn't want to impose on you," he continued, rubbing his hands nervously, "but we're so glad you have honored us with this visit, and we wondered if you'd ever consider singing a song for us? Just one?"

My wife usually refused such requests with a blunt statement that she had retired from singing. This time, however, she looked at me timidly.

"Do you think it would be all right Dermot if I did?"

My stomach tightened. It was the high tide and the turn.

" 'Tis your call, Nuala Anne."

"It always is, isn't it now. . . . Well, Mr. Farley I might just sing one."

I almost warned her not to strain her voice.

The manager produced a guitar. A reverent silence descended upon the dining room.

It was all a carefully staged event. Nuala had persuaded Jack to help her stage it. I felt an enormous weight lift off my shoulders.

"My favorite song, these days," she said, taking on her entertainer persona as easily as she would slip into her bra, "is a Yank song that has to be Irish in spirit because it comes from a part of America where many Irish settled and sang Irish music. It is a blend of Irish sadness and hope. The singer laments the loss of the river of her childhood but will never lose her love for it, even though she has found a new and mighty river where she is now."

Amazingly this old American folk song had become Nuala's most successful recording, her first platinum single. Its very popularity was somehow involved in her decision to stop singing. "I never want to hear that ugly melody again," she had cried. "Damn Anonymous for writing it."

As a critic had written, "In this song, Ms. McGrail has achieved a mature blend of her two heritages, the melancholy of Ireland and the expansive hope of America. No one has ever sung 'Shenandoah' with deeper feeling. Perhaps no one ever will."

As soon as she began singing it that night in Clifden, I knew that she had been practicing secretly, probably while out running with Fiona. Her voice had never been in better form or under better control. Tears sprung to my eyes. My Nuala Anne had come home again.

Away, you rolling river,
Oh, Shenandoah, I long to hear you,
Away, I'm bound away,
'Cross the wide Missouri,
Shenandoah, I love your daughter,
Away, you rolling river,
I'll take her 'cross the rolling water,
Away, I'm bound away,
'Cross the wide Missouri.
Shenandoah, I long to hear you,
Away, you rolling river,
Oh, Shenandoah, I long to hear you,
Away, I'm bound away,
'Cross the wide Missouri.

As she sang she watched me anxiously, wondering about my re-action. She saw the tears in my eyes, smiled, and sang the song again.

Then we ducked our heads under the low bridges as we went from Albany to Buffalo, fifteen miles a day on the Erie Canal, and beat the drums slowly and played the fife lowly as we walked the Streets of Laredo and celebrated simple gifts and danced with the boatmen on the Oh-Hi-Oh.

Everyone in the room was weeping as my wife brought the sad beauty of American folk music home to Ireland where it had started.

"Sure, won't I be keeping you here all night now? Well, I must sing one more song, which is for me anyway a kind of theme song, though it's not about a Galway woman at all, at all, but about a tragic young woman in Dublin's fair city who will be remembered whenever any Irish person sings about her."

So naturally she sang about Mollie Malone who still pushes her wheelbarrow through streets broad and narrow.

Weren't the tears flowing like the River Liffey when she finished?

"Sure," she went on, "isn't that special to me because I sang it on the night I fell in love with a man? And isn't the ending a sad one too. For him. Didn't he marry me!

So she sang it again with all her heart. For me, just the way she had done that first foggy night in O'Neill's pub down the street from Trinity College.

That night in bed I accused her of practicing on her morning runs with the wolfhound.

"Sure, didn't I have to cheer the thing up and herself pregnant."

I didn't comment.

"And I wanted to be sure, Dermot, before I tried it again. Before I chose for life, if you take my meaning."

I wrapped my arms around her.

"I knew you would eventually."

"Haven't I been a terrible eejit altogether? Singing is in my blood. I love it. I have to learn not to obsess about it. Maybe I'll have to take time off every couple of years, but I'll always come back to it."

"I knew you would," I said, though I had never been sure.

"Besides if I had been blown up in that house and had to face Himself, wouldn't He have said to me, 'Nuala Anne, aren't you a friggin' eejit and meself creating you to sing.' "

"I don't think God would have used that kind of language."

"God," she said in that tone of voice that means that the further discussion of the issue is closed, "can use any language he wants."

"More than likely, He would have said, 'Nuala Anne, would I be after minding you taking some time off and meself loving you with all me heart?' "

She pondered that.

"You have the right of it, Dermot Michael, just like you always do."

"You owe me one, Nuala Anne McGrail."

"Don't I owe you a whole life, just like Nora owed poor Ned?"

Then, like Ned with Nora, I sensed that I was somehow captured by an all-embracing love that was more powerful and more determined even than the love between me and me wife. My wife.

And, like Ned, I felt that, unseasoned male that I was, I had grown up a little.

— AUTHOR'S NOTE —

The story of the Maamtrasna murders is a fictionalized account of actual events. Both "fictionalized" and "actual" are important words. The events in the story actually happened in the West of Ireland in 1882. A family of five were brutally murdered and a sixth member barely survived. Informers, for their own purposes, lied about who the killers were. Five of the ten men arrested were not involved in the crime in any way. Nonetheless, in as corrupt a violation of justice as one can imagine, one of these men died and four served long jail sentences. Dublin Castle, the seat of English misrule in Ireland, covered up its mistakes. An attempt by Irish Nationalist Members of Parliament to reopen the case failed, as it was doomed to. The innocent man who was executed, Myles Joyce, is one of the great Irish folk heroes of the nineteenth century. One reflects, as does the narrator of my story, that the trial was not unlike that of blacks in the South at that time or Native Americans in the West. Nor are such travesties of justice, especially the immunizing of witnesses, absent from the tactics of American prosecutors today. Father Jarlath Waldron's wonderful book about the incident (*Maamtrasna: The Murders and the Mystery*. 1992. Dublin: Edmund Burke) provides a detailed historical account of the Maamtrasna story. When I picked up a copy of the book in Kenny's Bookstore in Galway, I realized that the story would make a wonderful novel.

History and historical fiction are necessarily not the same thing. The purpose of history is to narrate events as accurately as one can. The purpose of historical fiction is to enable a reader through the perspective of the characters in the story to feel that she or he is present at the events. Such a goal obviously requires some modification of the events. Thus the fictional characters in this novel are Edward H. Fitzpatrick, Nora Joyce, Thomas Finnucane, Martin Dempsey, and Josephine "Josie" Philbin. Moreover because of the constraints* of the Nuala Anne series, I have moved the story from the region west of Lough Mask in the current County Mayo (though it was in Galway at the time) to the County Galway of the present and from the Archdiocese of Tuam to the Diocese of Galway. Because of this change I have had to reconstruct somewhat the geography of the story. Bishop John Kane is also fictional. The exchange between him and the Earl Spencer was in fact between Archbishop MacEvilly of Tuam and Spencer (an ancestor of the late Princess Diana). For narrative purposes I have compressed the time of events in the years after the execution.

I have also tried to simplify the problem of the names of the people involved. The area in the region is quite properly called Joyce Country. Many families share the same name. The victims, the informers, and some of the killers were all Joyces.

Thus the reader of this novel can believe that the main historical events actually happened. The reader must also realize that many of the historical details have been changed to fit the needs of novel writing. For precision of detail the reader must turn to Father Waldron's book.

I share Father Waldron's fury at this story of corruption and injustice. However, out of respect for his work, I have taken only one sentence from his book. On page 108 he writes, "The next man called into the dock was destined to become a folk hero whose name would never die."

Amen to that.

I'm also grateful to my colleague and friend Micheal McGreil S. J.

---

*The three major constraints, from which many minor ones flow, are that Nuala Anne and her trusty spearcarrier, Dermot Michael, must solve a mystery from the present, a mystery from the past, and surmount a new crisis in their love.

(whom Nuala Anne claims as a cousin!) for his input on Maamtrasna and for the story of the 1982 cross that he attempted to place at the Joyce house.

In the story I follow Father Waldron's custom of using the English version of the names. However John Joyce and John Casey were surely know as Sean Joyce and Sean Casey in their own times and Myles Joyce's Irish name was surely Molua.

Grand Beach, Chicago,
Autumn 1999